I0687379

Hiding From The Blind

Hiding From
The Blind

Brad Barham

Bridgeview Press
Philadelphia

ISBN-13: 978-1-7322784-0-0
BBN-10:1732278407
Bridgeview Press
920 South Street, Suite 8
Philadelphia, PA 1914

Chapter 1

Philadelphia, Pennsylvania 1998

"Damn it!" John shouted as he slammed his fist into the wall, sending shards of sheetrock flew across the room. "I can't take this shit anymore!" He rubbed his aching knuckles. "I wasn't flirting with that guy—"

"Then what the hell would you call— John, your hand is bleeding. Let me—"

"Get away. That guy and I were discussing actors in *Magic Mike*. Nothing more." Clenching his teeth and glaring at Don, John said, "Your jealousy is killing me—us." He walked to the door then looked back at his lover. "We need some apart time. Time for *you* to work on your attitude. I love you, but I can't take your shit anymore. I'm outta here!"

Don and John, both age thirty-three and prison guards, had met in the employees' gym at the state prison. Their hard, gym-worked bodies caused an immediate and reciprocated lust-ful attraction for the other. After dating four months, they rented an apartment and lived together, but mutual interests and emotional harmony were in short supply.

After nearly recovering from the emotional breakup with John, Don grew horny. A night at the tubs seemed like a good place to break his three-month "dry" period.

Don parked in the shadows then walked along a narrow street in a northern Philadelphia suburb. Yellow sodium vapor streetlights cast a dark shadow of his strong physique on the broken sidewalk. *Hope the place is filled with hot numbers.*

At 69 Wonder Street, Don pushed open the red door of The Vapors bathhouse and entered its cramped lobby. The space strained to contain a chair and a dust-covered fake Ficus tree bathed in pink light. A four-foot-square opening in one wall half-hid a young clerk. His muscular-swimmers build almost burst through his lavender t-shirt. *Now, there's a hunk I could eat,* Don thought as he scanned the clerk's name tag. "Jeb, do you have any rooms available?"

Tossing his long blond hair from his face, Jeb said, "Hi, big guy." Jeb eyed Don from cap to leather flip flops. "Don't think I've seen you before. So, what'll it be . . . the Saturday special?" He stared at Don's chest. "It's obvious you work out,
but I hope you aren't here to use the gym because it has been converted to guest rooms."

"Don't worry. I'm here for a work over—not a work *out*. Maybe you can help." *God I hope so!*

Jeb extended his hand and stared into Don's eyes. "My real name is Jebadiah. My shift is over at midnight. Maybe I could meet you upstairs and make *sure* you have a good time."

Don sized up Jeb while shaking his hand. "Why not?" *Now we're talking!* "I'll save something–just for you."

Jeb smiled, handed Don a towel, a room key, and then winked. "I know where your room is. I'll find you— help you relax—take a load off your mind."

"Maybe I'll save one." *You bet I will.* Don turned to leave but stopped. "What's with all the graffiti in the neighborhood? It's horrible. I don't remember seeing it the last time I was here."

"It's the damn gangs. They're staking out territory.

Four months later, the chief of police called Don into his office. "Have a seat, Don."

"Thanks, sir." *Wonder why does he want to see me?*

The chief pushed his chair back and said, "The superintendent wants to start a Save the Youth Project. I'm assigning you to his task force. Community leaders believe the northern neighborhoods' graffiti is a symptom of a problem—a solvable problem—the kind of shit that often leads to shootings and stabbings. Local civic leaders don't want that. All it takes is for one gang to paint over another gang's paint job and boom! There's a fight—sometimes deadly. We have to stop the shit before there's open warfare."

So? What am I supposed to do?

"With your experience working with those young hoodlums at the state prison, you're just the man to head the new project. Congratulations. You're in charge. By the way, you get
a raise."

For a moment, Don's head whirled, then he realized his mouth gaped. "Thanks, Chief . . . I guess. I'll do my best.*"* *Can't say this excites me.*

The chief shook Don's hand. "You'll work from the thirty fifth district with a team of three officers. Don't disappoint me.

Needing input about how to reduce juvenile crime in North Philadelphia, Don and his team met with civic leaders, ministers, priests, Boys and Girls Club officials, the Scouts, and school officials.

The advisors agreed. "Idle time. That's the problem. The kids need something to do—a job, but their lack of education is against them. We need to create jobs for them."

After considering the input, Don set up a meeting with gang graffiti artists. "Want a job?" he asked the fifteen artists gathered to hear his proposition.

One man asked, "You paying and how much?"

"You guys like to paint, and I want you to paint—just in a different way. I need artists to paint murals like those in center city." Don noted a few smiling faces in the group. "Several paint stores have contributed paint and brushes. You guys do a good job, and I'll pay you and get you lots of public recognition."

7

Several guys laughed at the offer.

Twelve artists from two gangs agreed to pain and start two murals.

A highway underpass had been designated the project site. Its retaining walls were covered with perverse slogans. The sidewalks were littered with trash, mattresses, broken shopping carts, discarded tires, urine, and shit, all of which the gangs cleaned up. Because the underpass divided the chosen gangs'
territory, each group would paint a one-hundred-foot long wall in the other's area.

Don frequented the worksites noting the murals' progress, lack of trash, and the artistry of one hot-looking painter, Alvaro, of the Eagles gang. He had become the Eagles informal leader.

"Hey, Alvaro! Guys!" Don shouted, scanning the mural. "I like what I'm seeing." *Especially you, Alvaro!* "Keep it up."

Alvaro's artistry had attracted Don's attention, but so did Alvaro's blondish hair, which towered above his Latino peers and contrasted with his olive complexion. He had a lean, muscular build, sparkling blue-green eyes, and a permanent boyish smile. Don lusted for Alvaro and wanted to know more about him.

"Alvaro, you look eighteen or nineteen, but how old are you?"

"You're a lousy guesser. I'm twenty-five. Maybe my 50% Swedish, 25% Italian, and 25% Mexican heritage tricked you."

Gosh damn it kid, ya got a hell of a bod.

While Don saw beauty in Alvaro's physique, he knew the kid needed his strength for self-defense, but he hoped Alvaro used his bod for more than street fights.

Despite Alvaro's life on the streets, he had a disarming and gentle personality, and could, when needed, speak "the king's English." His fellow gang members referred to him as "Judge" because of his arbitration skills.

When arriving or leaving the worksite, Don often slapped Alvaro on the back then let his hand linger there before it slid onto Alvaro's butt. *Now that's a real ass— something I can appreciate. So far, he doesn't seem to mind my hand. Does he like it or does he allow it just because I'm boss?*

One day, while visiting the site, Don mentioned something to Alvaro about his own interest in weight lifting. "I once had a physique as good as yours—maybe better."

"You worked out?" Alvaro asked, staring at Don's chest and arms.

"Yep. Used to bench pressed 350 pounds for three reps—sometimes four."

"No way."

"Way." Don smiled. "Did chest flies with fifty-pound dumbbells."

Alvaro smiled. "You do look kinda big for a cop. Most of them lift nothin' heavier than a donut."

"Ouch!" Don shook his head. "That's not nice."

"Well?"

"How often do you and the other guys workout?"

"Hell, we workout almost every day—have to."

"Understand you guys have a gym in the hood?"

"Yep. In an abandoned building. Place is secret. Don't want nobody stealin' our stuff."

"How'd you get your *stuff*?"

Alvaro smiled and stared at the sky. Flashing his pearly-white teeth, he said, "We stole it."

"All of it?"

"Nope. Just most of it. Some, we made."

"Whatta you do about workouts in the winter?"

"We build a fire . . . in an oil drum. Keeps us warm. Place gets a little smoky, but we stay warm."

9

"I'd like to workout with you sometime. Get to know the guys on their own turf. *Maybe see some nice bodies.* Would they mind?"

"Don't know. I'll ask 'em."

"Great."

Don had used the police gym on an irregular basis. He also had a lifetime membership in a commercial gym, which he had shared with his former partner, but their breakup left Don with little interest in working out until now.

Alvaro climbed the scaffolding to return to his painting.

Don noted Alvaro had almost finished painting a tree. "That tree is looking pretty good but paint some leaves on it will ya?"

"Sure." Alvaro painted a two-foot-long leaf outline over a tree limb then shouted, "Is that big enough?"

"Smart guy, eh," Don chuckled. "Looks like the one Adam wore. Tell the guys I like what I see—except for your fig leaf."

Following the conversation about workouts, Don had a rekindling of interest in weightlifting. He visited the police gym on a regular basis and soon noted the fit of his uniform had become snug. *Gotta keep this up. Keep my chest growing if I'm gonna attract mister right.*

Finishing a workout, he admired the reflection of his Improving physique a gym mirror. "Hmm." *Not bald like a lot of cops.* He moved closer to the mirror and stared at his face. *That Vapors' clerk said my eyes were beautiful . . . been told I'm good looking . . . nice smile, cute dimples, fine cleft chin.* Don turned, scanned his torso, and then fondled his crotch. *Cock and balls ain't bad. Got compliments on 'em at the tubs. What's not to love here?* Don stared at his pecs. *Who wouldn't want to suck on these babies?* He chuckled as he bounced one pec and then the other.

The murals were finished without incident. On the unveiling day, underpass traffic had been detoured, and the street taken over by the press, a TV crew, the mayor, city council members, community leaders, and project contributors.

Beaming with pride, gang members stood in front of multiple Dollar Store sheets used to cover their murals. After several speeches, each gang leader revealed their painting. The crowd's applause delighted the artists. They shared back slaps and hugs then both groups shook hands in the middle of the street.

Don smiled. *The chief is going to be happy with this.*

Each gang received a plaque of recognition and a check for fifteen hundred dollars.

After the dignitaries left, Don addressed the two gangs. "Men. The press and TV crews will visit this site from time-to-time. If any gang member defaces the other group's mural, offenders will cease to get publicity and won't be invited to participate in future projects, and that means *no more money.* Also, the guilty will be prosecuted for defacing public property."

The next day, Don, Alvaro, and his gang met for a beer and to view their pictures on the front page of the *Philadelphia Inquirer*.

Three days later, Don received an unexpected call from his ex-lover, John. He said, "I see you and your thugs are making headlines with your gang murals."

"You referring to the newspaper article?"

"Yeah, saw you and those hoods smiling like Ali Baba's thieves."

"Well, I'm hoping they'll give up stealing and fighting. So far, there hasn't been any defacing of the murals, and trash has ceased to accumulate at the site. That's what I call a success."

"Yeah, but I couldn't help notice the guy standing beside you in that photo. He looks Latin, and man is he *hot*."

"His name's Alvaro, and he's Latino."

John chuckled. "Which part is Latino?"

"Hope I get a chance to find out, but I'm not sure if he's

11

straight, gay, or maybe plays around."

"Don't let his baby looks fool you. I've known a few straight-acting Latinos who turned out to be devils in bed."

"I've suggested we workout sometime. I'm hoping to see him naked while showering, but so far, he hasn't accepted my invitation."

"Well, don't give up, Don. Stay healthy and keep me posted. Oh yeah. Don't try to own him. You know how jealous you can get and how that affects your relationships."

Damn, don't you ever quit. "Bye, John."

The second mural would be painted at a major suburban intersection where gang warfare had been a problem. Don needed an experienced manager to oversee the project and wanted Alvaro to take the job. It would give Don another opportunity to feel out Alvaro.

Since Don did not have Alvaro's phone number, he had to physically search for him.

Driving for half an hour through rundown gang territory, Don spotted Alvaro. He and a group of tough looking guys played soccer in a vacant lot. Don pulled to the curb, blew his horn, and then got out of the car. He waved and yelled to Alvaro. *Damn, the kid is looking good. Maybe he'll take that sweaty shirt off.*

Alvaro kicked the ball to one of his bros then walked to Don's car. "Officer Don. What are you doin' here?" The men did a complicated set of gang shoulder bumps.

"Looking for you." Don said, staring into Alvaro's questioning blue-green eyes. "How would you like to be my project manager for another mural?"

"Another one?"

"Yep," Don said, nodding. "The city got a grant so you and the painters will be well paid. As my project manager, you'll receive twice the pay of the others. The site is a four-story building, meaning it'll take a lot of paint time as well as scaffold-building time. Are ya interested?"

"Hell yes." Alvaro slapped Don's shoulder. "When do

12

we start?"

"Two weeks. Give me your cell number. I'll call when we're ready."

"Okay, but whatta ya doin' till then?" Alvaro asked.

"I'm setting up a national conference on gang control. You guys are my example."

Four weeks later, Don stopped at the intersection to check on the new mural. This one had multiple images of people doing various industrial activities.

"Officer Don," Alvaro called as he jumped down from the third rung of the scaffolding ladder. "How ya doin'?"

Don slapped Alvaro on the back then let his hand slide to Alvaro's butt. Alvaro didn't seem to mind. *Damn! That ass is hard as ever, and he doesn't seem to mind my hand. Is he really straight?* How's the painting going?" Any problems?"

"Nah," Alvaro said. "Sometimes a painter or two don't show up, but otherwise we're doing great. Sometimes, traffic backs up with rubberneckers, but we don't mind if they're women." Alvaro smiled. "One girl, in a hot convertible, 'took our picture' if ya know what I mean."

Don chuckled, "Careful. Those things bite." *Did he say that to let me know he's straight?*

Don yelled to the crew, "I'll be back at five o'clock to pay you guys."

Several painters, who heard him over the roar of traffic, cheered.

Don slapped Alvaro's back and said, "I've arranged for Aston's Check Services to cash the guys' checks—for free. Let let them know that taxes had to be deducted."

"Shit. They ain't gonna like that."

"Can't help it, but hey, some money is better than no money."

"I guess," Alvaro said, frowning. He smiled and eyed Don. "You been working out or just growing?

Is this gratuitous flattery, or is he really digging me?

13

"First of all, call me Don. Okay?"

"Okay . . . *Don*."

Interesting, Don thought. *He's observant.* "Yep, I've been working out. Our little talk about lifting got me started again."

"Well, don't get *too* big."

"Yeah, like that's gonna happen quick! Well, gotta go."

Don returned to the worksite at 5:00 p.m. and called the painters to gather. When called, each man yelled his name and took an envelope. Some kissed it. Others waved it like a flag.

Knuckles kissed his check then yelled, "What's it gonna be bro's—booze or broads?"

Junk Boy yelled, "Why choose. We got money. Buy both."

"Guys!" Don yelled. "Don't get carried away. I don't wanna have to lock you up for disorderly conduct or procuring."

Alvaro received his check last. "Thanks for the opportunity ta work on the mural, Don. Several weeks ago, I said I'd ask the bros about your workin' out with us. Well, you're in."

Don slapped Alvaro on the shoulder. "I'd like that. Give me a chance to get to know you guys." *And you in particular, young man.*

Alvaro chuckled. "We're like those union guys, we work half days on Saturdays. Meet us here at noon, and we'll go for a workout."

Chapter 2

Don exited his 1999 Mitsubishi then leaned against the right front fender while waiting for the artists to gather their supplies. "Hello guys!" he yelled. "Alvaro. Let's talk."

Alvaro scrambled down the scaffolding, passing two slower moving men.

God, that ass is looking good, Don thought.

Alvaro skipped every other rung until he reached the ground where he wiped his hands on a rag.

"How'd it go today?" Don asked, shaking Alvaro's hand longer than necessary. *Wish I had his cock in my hand.*

Alvaro smiled. "We got lots of encouragement from passersby today. It's a great way to meet girls. Two asked me out for drinks after work on Monday."

"Careful of the women, kid," Don said, scanning the mural. "They'll have you married before ya know what hit you." *Hope this girl shit is just talk . . . or . . . is he testing me?*

"Were you ever married?"

"Nope," Don said, frowning. "Just lived in sin." He backed up a few paces, covertly scanned Alvaro's backside, then said, "The mural is coming along well."

"Thanks. The guys are happy with it. How 'bout you?"

"I couldn't be happier, and the community likes it."

"Great. Are ya ready for that workout?"

"You bet. Got my stuff in the trunk."

"You didn't bring fancy threads did ya?"

"Just regular gym clothes. Why?"

"We don't have a fancy gym. No lockers, no showers, no air conditioning. We work out in our street clothes."

Shit! No naked guys in the shower. "Hadn't thought about that."

"Never mind, you'll manage."

"Would you and some of the guys like a ride. There's room."

"Sure. I'll get 'em."

15

Don, Alvaro, and four bros crammed themselves in Don's car for the ride to the gang's ghetto. On the way, they passed burn-ed out cars, dilapidated buildings, and shabbily-dressed men sprawled on sidewalks. Some used doorways for shelter from the hot noon sun.

What a shitty neighborhood, Don thought. "Is that guy dead?" Don asked, pointing to man slumped against a building.

"Could be," Alvaro said. "Could be . . . drunk . . . drugs or dead."

"Could be all three," Fingers chuckled in the back seat.

Don parked in a trash-strewn lot next to a boarded-up brick building. *What in the hell am I getting myself into?* Gang graffiti marked its walls as a place controlled by Alvaro's gang, the Eagles.

"This is home sweet home," Alvaro said, pointing toward a derelict building. "I suggest leaving your billfold in the trunk. You can change inside but be ready to hightail it out of here in case there's a raid. If that happens, you might be leaving your clothes, and you wouldn't want to leave your billfold in yer pants."

"I didn't know the boys in blue still raided the area."

"Not the police," Alvaro said. "Other gangs."

"I thought you guys had buried the hatchet."

"Can't count on it," Alvaro said as his bros laughed and exited the car.

Don placed his billfold in the trunk, got his workout clothes, and then locked the car. *This is crazy.* "Will my chariot be safe here?"

"Maybe," Alvaro said, "it looks like a dealer's ride."

"Shit. That means someone could break in looking for drugs."

"Maybe."

Alvaro and a bro ran ahead then disappeared down an outdoor stairwell.

16

Don caught up and watched the men tug at a rusted basement door that resisted being opened while producing a high-pitched squeak.

"That's part of our alarm system," Alvaro said. "We don't oil it. If it squeaks, we know someone's comin'."

That could also make it difficult to get out in a hurry, Don thought.

Stepping over discarded food containers, beer bottles, used syringes, needles, and a decomposing rat, the group walked across the dark, dank basement floor dotted with water puddles. The smell of mildew and putrefaction filled the air of the God-forsaken space. A shaft of dusty light streamed through a broken window pane, illuminating the far corner.

"This way," Alvaro said, heading for a dilapidated wooden stairway. He glanced back at Don. "This leads to the club house but don't lean on the handrail. It's not safe."

Neither is that ass, but what have I gotten myself into?

On the third-floor landing, Alvaro tugged at another rusty door. It squeaked its resistance to being opened.

Alvaro yelled, "Ten, forty, twenty, thirty."

"What's that about?" Don asked.

"Just letting the bros inside know we're coming."

Stepping into a large open space, Alvaro said, "This space once held hundreds of looms. The only thing left is the oil-stained wooden floors and bare-brick walls."

The room reeked of marijuana smoke and kerosene—the former fueled gang members; the latter fueled lanterns for lighting and heat during the winter.

The first room contained a lone basketball hoop. One man picked up a basketball, dribbled it, and then shot a basket. The other guys walked toward the makeshift gym next door.

Several pieces of dilapidated furniture were scattered around the gym. A couple of stained mattresses leaned against one wall, waiting for God knows what. The workout space felt crowded with twelve men waiting to use one bench press.

Some of the gang members stared at Don. Not

17

everyone had met him.

Don's stomach did a flip flop. *Alvaro invited me. I'm sure I'll be safe.*

"Bros," Alvaro said, "Officer Don is my boss. He's gonna workout with us so watch your language." Alvaro Smiled. "He's never heard curse words so cool it."

There were a few chuckles and a round of hellos as Don attempted complicated handshakes and shoulder bumps.

"Guys," Don said, "thanks for letting me join in."

"Use our *changing* room if you'd like," Alvaro said, pointing toward a doorway. "There's nails for hangin' things. We promise we won't peek while you're changing—unless ya want."

What the hell did he mean by that?

Don changed into a white t-shirt and shorts then returned to see several men waiting to do bench presses.

Alvaro took his turn on the bench press and asked, "Don, spot me, will ya?"

Don walked to the head of the bench and prepared to spot Alvaro. "When you're ready," Don said.

Staring sideways, Alvaro chuckled. "You oughta wear something under yer shorts otherwise I won't be able to lift."

"What are you talking about?"

"I can see right up yer stuff," Alvaro said, pointing up the leg of Don's shorts.

"Thought you might need inspiration." *That's the second time he's joked about sexual things. What is he thinking?*

Alvaro winked. "Yeah, but not that kind . . . not here." *Where then?*

Several guys did various upper body exercises while Don waited his turn to do bench presses. *There are some hot, hard bodies here.* "Don't know about you guys, but this heat is killing me." Don wiped his brow. "How do you work out when summer comes?"

"You get used to it," Alvaro said. "I told you, we might have to run, so we stay dressed." Alvaro tugged at Don's shorts. "We can't afford 'spensive threads."

"Not less we steal 'em," Carlos chuckled.

Alvaro's undershirt dripped with sweat as he struggled with his last three bench presses.

Ready to assist, Don stood at the head of the bench. A large bead of sweat fell from his chin onto Alvaro's throat.

"Hey, man!" Alvaro yelled, wiping the offending drop. "Take yer sweat someplace else."

"Sorry," Don said, stepping to the side. He removed his sweat-soaked t-shirt then used it to wipe his face.

"Show off," Alvaro said. "We know ya got big tits."

"Glad you have good eyesight," Don said, bouncing his pecs. *Wanna know what else I got?*

Alvaro finished his reps, sat up, and stared into Don's hairy abdomen. "Nice six-pack. Okay, you're next. Want me to take some weight off the bar?"

"No way. I can lift far more than you—ya little runt."

Don added forty pounds to the bar then did ten reps. He stood, wiped his face with his t-shirt, then flexed his pecs. Two guys, waiting their turn for the bench, whistled. Don bowed, offered a middle finger gesture of gratitude and laughed. *Isn't anyone else going to take something off?*

"Okay," Don said to a waiting man. "The bench is yours. I know Alvaro can't spot the weight you're going to lift, so I'd be happy to stand in for him."

Alvaro elbowed his way to the head of the bench then glanced at Don. "I could spot this amount of weight with one hand and never put a bro in danger."

Carlos laid down on the bench and said, "Use both hands, Judge. No showin' off!"

"Alvaro ain't got the balls to spot that," Don said.

"Hell, I got the balls," Alvaro said boisterously. "Wanna see 'em? I've already seen how little yours are. Mine are man sized."

19

"You wanna compare balls?" Don asked and tugged at the leg of his shorts. *God, I hope you do.*

"Hell, you'd lose," Alvaro said, gripping the barbell with both hands. "You'd wind up looking bad, and I wouldn't want that to happen ta my guest."

"How kind of you," Don chuckled. "Now, let's get back to lifting."

Several bros completed their workout and tried to cool off by fanning themselves, but boarded-up windows and a lack of air circulation added to the misery and stench of the sweat-humidity filled room.

"Since we're finished," Don said, "let's go to the car and turn on the air conditioning?"

"Thought you'd never ask," Alvaro said, wiping sweat.

Following Alvaro and three bros, Don threw his wet t-shirt over his shoulder, gathered his street clothes then headed for his car.

Alvaro's wet t-shirt clung to his torso, revealing his thick chest and six-pack. He often pulled at the sweat-soaked shirt in an attempt to cool off.

"Quit pulling at yer damn shirt," Don yelled. "Take it off. You'll cool faster." *And you'd make me happier.*

"You just wanna see my hard bod."

"Hell, I've seen little boy's bodies before."

Alvaro pulled his t-shirt over his head as he neared the car. "Shit! You ain't seen one like this."

Don glimpsed Alvaro's square, hairless pecs reflected in a car window. *Nice!* Don opened all the car doors, started the engine, and then turned on the AC. He and the bros stood outside, waiting for the car to cool enough, so they could sit on its leather seats. Minutes later, the men stuffed their sweating bodies into the car. Alvaro rode shotgun.

Don headed for a bar to buy the guys a round of beer. He noticed Alvaro glancing at his pecs and sweat-curled chest hair more than once.

20

Frightening Don, Alvaro thrust his hand, karate-chop style, into Don's cleavage. "Hey, bros, check this out. Look how deep Don's tits are."

The bros were quiet as Don grasped Alvaro's hand and flattened it over his sweaty nipple. "Wanna play with it?" *Yeah. Make my nipples happy.*

"Don't you wish?"

You bet I do.

"Hey, Alvaro, stop blocking the air," Butch yelled as everyone tried to place himself in the flow of cool air wafting from dashboard vents. "We're trying to cool off back here."

"Too bad we can't workout in here," Alvaro said.

"Yeah," Max said, "we could put a bench press back here if we took out this seat."

"No thanks," Don said.

"You're right," Alvaro said. "We'd need a van. Maybe we should *borrow* one."

Don shook his head and glanced at Alvaro. "Better not. Has everyone cooled off?"

"Getting there," Knuckles said.

Days later, Don needed to check on the mural's progress. He parked his unmarked police car at the site, tooted his horn, and exited the vehicle. He waved to the artists working on the outline of two human heads at the top of the mural.

Alvaro waved back then scrambled down the scaffolding to greet his boss.

Never get enough of that ass. "How's it going?" Don asked.

"Smooth as gloss enamel," Alvaro said, moving his flattened hand left and right.

"It's looking good," Don said. "That face at the top is quite life-like."

"Yeah. We're kinda likin' it."

"After my workout with you the other day, I wondered if you'd like to join me for a workout at my gym."

21

Alvaro shook his head. "Uh, I wouldn't fit in. Got no fancy gym clothes."

"I'll loan you some."

"You mean a *real* gym with store bought stuff, matched dumbbells, chrome things, mirrors, lockers, showers, bright lights, women, and air conditioning?"

"That and more."

"Hell, Why not? Beats my place!"

"All right. Pick you up tomorrow—five o'clock." *I'll finally, get to see you naked.*

Chapter 3

Alvaro wore a yellow polo shirt and tight yellow shorts, sporting sharp creases. He waved as Don pulled to the curb.

Damn, kid, you are looking hot today.

Don stretched to open the passenger door. "Hop in man. How ya hanging?"

"Great," Alvaro said, getting into the car. "I took off early. Went home, showered, and changed." Alvaro pulled down his sun visor and primped in its mirror. "I Wanna look *gooood* at yer fancy gym." He pushed the sun visor up and pulled down his shirt tail. "Gotta please the ladies."

Ignoring the comment, Don pulled into traffic and asked, "What's the street talk about our project?"

"Everybody likes it. An old lady asked us to paint her house, and a preacher wants us ta paint Jesus on a wall of his church."

"Sounds like you guys could branch out if you wanted." Don rested his hand on Alvaro's bare thigh. *Hmm. He doesn't seem to mind. I'm going to let it stay.* "You know, the Picassos of Philadelphia."

"Might do it. What kinda money we talking about?"

"Good money. There're lots of opportunities. Just put your minds to it—give up all this gang shit."

"Don't ya tell nobody, but we hid gang stuff in the murals. Gotta look hard, but it's there—disguised."

"No way!"

"Yep. I'll show you sometime."

Don made his way along one of Philadelphia's alley streets then parked beside a large brick building near the Delaware River. He replaced his hand on Alvaro's thigh. *He still hasn't reacted.* "In the 1700s, this used to be a tobacco warehouse. Its large interior space was destined to become this great gym. Let's go in."

"I hope it looks better inside than outside," Alvaro said. "It needs a mural."

23

"Maybe the owner will hire you guys."

Don presented his membership card at the service desk and nodded toward Alvaro. "He's my guest. I'm paying his fee."

Pulling out his billfold, Alvaro said, "Thanks, but I pay my own way."

"No way. I invited you so sign in."

Don collected his change while Alvaro signed the guest book.

The men headed for the locker room. Alvaro often stopped to stare at the amenities of the upscale club. Just inside the locker room, he asked, "Are those lockers real wood?"

"Yep, and don't scratch them." *The kid seems impressed.*

After rummaging through his gym bag, Don pulled out a set of white gym clothes and handed them to Alvaro. "Here are the threads I promised."

Alvaro examined the shirt and shorts. His teeth gleamed in the frame of his smiling, tanned face. "I hope ya washed 'em?"

"Maybe."

Turning his back, Alvaro undressed.

God, don't tell me he's shy.

The guys donned their gym clothes then headed for the circuit-training area where two rows of twenty exercise machines stood side-by-side.

"Here," Don said, "you use each machine for ten reps then move to the next without resting. If we do everything right, we should be finished in an hour."

"An hour? Why rush?"

"Good question," Don said. "I'm in no hurry, but this area is for guys who are. If you want more time, we need to move to another area."

"There's more than one gym in this place?"

"Yep, and one just for women."

24

"Wow. Let's check that out."

"No can do, good buddy." *There he goes again with that woman shit.*

"Can't we just peek?"

"The door has no window, so you can't see in. Sorry."

Looking disappointed, Alvaro said, "Okay . . ."

In the regular gym, Alvaro's jaw sagged as he scanned countless pieces of exercise equipment and about twenty men intent on becoming Mister America.

"Are these floors real wood?" Alvaro asked, looking at his image in the reflective, polished floor.

"Yep. 300 years old." Don pointed at the exercise equipment. "There are over 150 pieces of equipment here. They're separated by body part. Where do you wanna start?"

"I like free weights," Alvaro said, walking toward the rear of the room.

"Fine. That's where we'll start. There's an empty bench press."

After ninety minutes of working out, Don said, "You look tired. Had enough?"

Alvaro wiped sweat from his brow and sighed. "Yeah. I don't know when I worked this hard."

"Whatta ya say we shower?"

"Fine. I need a cold one."

"After showering, we could spend some time in the Jacuzzi if you'd like."

"Never been in one."

"Never?" Don asked.

"Never. But it sounds good."

The guys showered in opposite showers.

I love looking at that ass, Don thought, *but why does he always turn his back?*

Don left the shower, dried his feet, then wrapped a towel low around his waist. *Let the kid see my six-pack.*

"On the shelf to your left are swim shorts," Don said, pointing to a rack near the door marked Jacuzzi. "Pick your

25

size. We need to wear them in the Jacuzzi."

"Any women there?"

"Nope. Just guys."

"Then why wear shorts?"

"We respect member's modesty. No nudity." *Is he wanting to be naked?*

After Alvaro selected a swimsuit. Don watched his butt cheeks contract as he pulled on the trunks. Each lifted leg provided a glimpse of his low hanging balls.

Damn, I hope his cock matches those nuts.

"I don't mind being naked," Alvaro said, looking over his shoulder. "Do you?"

Don stared into space. "Nope."

"Then join the bros Tuesday nights at the "Y." Just guys. No swim suits—plus it's free."

The men headed for the Jacuzzi.

"Do guys swim naked there?" Don asked, holding the door open for Alvaro.

"Naked-as-Jaybirds," Alvaro said, smiling.

"I didn't know any "Y" had nude swimming anymore."

"Wanna go some time?"

"Would you be there?" Don asked.

"Yeah."

"You'd swim naked?"

"Hell yes. Every Tuesday. Join us. I'd get to see what ya got."

Don's heart quickened. *Then why are you so shy here?* "I'm game, and I'd see what *you* got." *Damn! Now we're getting someplace.*

Alvaro grabbed his crotch. "Maybe I'll show you sometime."

Don hurried into the white-tiled Jacuzzi room, smelling of pine oil and chlorine. He rushed into the water to hide his growing erection while saying, "Alvaro, set the wall timer for maximum."

Having done so, Alvaro entered the bubbling water then sat down opposite Don.

Staring at Alvaro, Don slumped back against the tub.

Their toes touched. Moments later, Don felt Alvaro's foot walk halfway up his leg. Don smiled and thought, *Atta boy.*

Alvaro's foot then moved farther up Don's leg.

"I bet I know where that foot is going," Don said.

"Bet you don't."

"Then I'm going to cover my cock and balls."

"You took your cock out?" Alvaro asked, eyes wide with shock.

"I thought your foot wanted to touch it." *Hope it still does.*

"Talk about ego," Alvaro said. "What makes ya think that?"

"Cause you're afraid to touch it with your hand," Don said. "If you wanna touch it just ask."

"You'd have trouble finding the tiny thing let alone having someone touching it."

Don stood and pulled at the leg of his swimsuit as if to let his cock fall out. At that moment, two elderly hairy men entered the room. Don sat down.

"How's the water?" one man asked.

"Great," Don said.

The new arrivals took seats in the tub and then dropped their heads backwards onto the tub's rim and closed their eyes.

Beneath the bubbling surface, Don re-exposed his package.

Alvaro smiled, pointed toward his crotch then gestured with his forefinger and thumb that his cock had a diameter of three inches. Feigning a morning's wakeup arm stretch, he moved his index fingers toward each other to indicate his cock had grown to ten inches.

Don smiled then mouthed, 'You wish.' *God, I'd love to see it.*

Alvaro stifled a chuckle as he moved his index fingers

27

apart, indicating his cock had grown to twelve inches.

Don shrugged and mouthed, 'Who cares?' *Now we're getting somewhere.*

The Jacuzzi timer emitted a loud buzz and its pumps shut off.

Don didn't dare get out of the tub to reset the timer—not with a hard-on. "Sir," he said to one of the hairy men. "You're closest. Would you please reset the timer?"

"Will do," the stranger said. "No fun sitting in still water."

After a few minutes, Don asked Alvaro, "Had enough?"

"Whenever."

"Let's go." Don turned to the men in the tub and said, "Enjoy."

Naked, Don and Alvaro, never facing each other, threw their wet swim suits into a designated receptacle in the shower room.

Don asked, "Still hiding it?"

"Ya wanna see it?"

"No. I know you're ashamed of it." *Hope you're not.*

"Ashamed?" Alvaro said. "Hell. I'm proud of it."

"Then . . ." Don watched Alvaro's butt and waited to see if he would show his crotch. *Now, he's getting shy.*

"Then what?" Alvaro asked, looking over his shoulder. He placed his hands over his crotch and faced Don. "Are ya ready?"

"That's up to you," Don said, holding his towel over his crotch as he faced Alvaro.

Alvaro moved his hands aside. A snake and two apples fell into view. He cradled his cock in his palms then extended them toward Don.

Oh my God! "Not bad," Don said, turning his back to dry off. *God! What a handful, but I'm going to play disinterested.* Don wrapped his towel around his waist then headed toward the lockers.

"What are you hiding?" Alvaro asked.

"Nothing. But I don't show mine to just anybody. Most guys pay to see it. I charge even more to touch it or suck it."

I think I have a penny."

"Maybe later . . . when I'm broke."

Don dressed, while looking over his shoulder. Alvaro had a twinge of anger written on his face.

"What's with this shy shit? You playin' with me?"

"No, but I don't go around showing off my cock. It needs lots of tender loving care. Got any?"

"Only one way to find out."

"I'll give you a chance," Don said, "Tuesday, at the YMCA.'"

"Who says I'll be there?"

"You'll be there—I know it." *God knows I will.*

Alvaro muttered, "We'll see."

Silence hung like steam in the locker room as the guys dressed then left the building.

The ride to Alvaro's ghetto location incited little conversation. Don's car had too little cubic footage for the unspoken tension.

Alvaro exited the car. "Thanks for the workout. See ya at the wall."

The remainder of the weekend, Don wondered if Alvaro thought he had been played as a fool. Would he use the gym scenario as a reason to quit?

Monday afternoon, Don drove to the mural site. He blew his horn, exited the car, and waved to Alvaro. As project manager, Alvaro had to talk to his boss.

Don watched Alvaro make his way down several scaffolding platforms. *Is he moving slowly because he doesn't want to see me?*

Alvaro approached Don who extended his hand. Alvaro shook it, using a weak grip.

To be heard over traffic noise, Don yelled, "How's it

going?"

"What?" Alvaro asked, cupping his ear.

Don moved closer. "How are things going?"

"Okay," Alvaro said. "We ran outta paint this morning. Had to search all over to get the right color, but we did." He gestured toward the mural. "Whata ya think?"

"Looking good. The guys are doing a great job."

"Glad ya like it."

"I have good news. Remember, you said my gym needed a mural? Well, I spoke to the owner. He's going to commission one. He's already selected a designer. Drawings should be ready by the time you guys finish here. Oh, yeah. I got everyone a raise."

"Great," Alvaro said then smiled. "We can use the money."

Alvaro yelled to the artists, "Guys, we got another project."

Those able to hear the news stopped painting, yelled their approval, and then clapped.

"It couldn't have come at a better time," Don said. "The city is running out of money. Can't get them to cough up enough shekels to pay for another mural." *And I don't wanna give up watching you work.*

Alvaro smiled. "Keep trying, boss. We need the work."

"Don't worry, I will. By the way, you guys going skinny dipping tomorrow?"

"Why ya asking? Wanna marvel at my stuff again, or are ya looking for sympathy?"

"A little of both," Don chuckled, slapping Alvaro on the back. "I shouldn't have denied you certain . . . pleasures. Gotta make it up to you."

"Yeah, we're goin', but the pool ain't heated. The cold will make yer thing even smaller."

"Then pull on it—stretch it to its full length."

"Maybe one of the bros will help," Alvaro said then

smiled. "I don't bother with small stuff."

"Nah! Mine needs hands like yours—hands accustomed to big things." *I'll let you have a go at it.*

"Don't worry," Alvaro said. "Some of these bros can compete with the best."

"We'll see. Meet you Tuesday at seven."

Don phoned the "Y" to inquire about pool hours.

"Pool's open from 10:00 a.m. until 6:00 p.m. for the general public," the clerk said. "At 6:00 p.m., the pool is open to men only—natural swimming.

Don arrived at the 1920s era YMCA before his painters. He wanted to see each of his artists' "stuff" as they entered the pool area.

Humidity and the reek of chlorine crowded the air in the natatorium. The wet white wall tiles were reminiscent of the décor in New York City subway stations.

Don swam for half an hour, waiting for the artists' arrival. He wondered how much longer he could tolerate the cold water. *Is it this cold so guys won't get erections?*

The room soon filled with the echoes of jocular voices of nude men. When Alvaro entered the pool area, his jaw dropped on seeing Don swimming in the far end of the pool. The kid dived in and swam toward his boss.

Damn! Don said to himself, *He dived in too quickly. I wanted to see more crotch.*

Don waved and called to several painters who trailed in, waving back.

"Didn't think you'd show up," Alvaro said, shaking water from his hair.

"And I wondered if you'd show."

"Had to," Alvaro said. "Wanted to check you out, and from what I see through the waves, it's tiny."

"Blame it on cold water. Ya gotta pull on it to see its normal eleven inches?"

"I'm afraid I'd have to pull so hard it would break off."

31

Don winked. "It won't break off, but it might cum off."

"You think I care?"

I hope so. "I can read you better than you think, kid. I know you wanna see it up close, but I also know you wanna play with it."

"You wish!" Alvaro said and swam away.

Don followed Alvaro's untanned ass and contracting butt muscles as they propelled him toward his bros playing polo in the deep end. *God, what an ass? I'd follow that any-where.*

"How you doing, guys?" Don asked, swimming to the edge of the activity.

"Okay," the guys said, throwing the ball from man-to-man.

"Want in?" Max asked.

"Sure, I'll play backfield." Don swam toward the middle of the pool. He would have a better view of crotches and asses if he played back.

The guys kept the ball moving. Lots of above-the-water action allowed Don to note the guys were as well hung as Alvaro had said. On a few occasions, Alvaro leaped from the water revealing his hairless, muscular body and all his manhood cloaked in a patch of curly, black pubic hair.

I'm surprised the kid is so long in eighty-degree water.

Within an hour, the pool filled with naked men. A lifeguard ordered the game of polo stopped for safety reasons. From then on, the bro's swam and splashed each other. Don treaded water and spoke with several artists. He gathered information about the mural and tried to discover which of the men might be swingers.

Pool hours over, the artists headed for the showers.

Don kept several bros between him and Alvaro to keep Alvaro guessing about his cock size as long as possible.

As Alvaro and his friends dressed, Don said, "Good night, guys. Thanks for the game. Good night, Alvaro. See you at the mural." *We've got to do this more often.*

Several days passed while Don worked on plans for the youth conference he would host in three weeks. With plans completed, he decided to visit the mural site.

When he arrived, he tooted the horn of his long, silver Lexus and watched Alvaro, wearing tight shorts, make his way to the ground. *What an ass. Can't wait to fuck it.*

"How's it goin', boss?" Alvaro asked, eyeing Don's car. "Nice ride!"

"Thanks. Got some good news. Got a grant for another mural. Everything should be ready when you finish the gym site."

"Always glad to have money coming in." Alvaro said, eyeing the Lexus.

"I have my own good news. I won a small lottery jackpot. I used some of the money to buy a Jacuzzi for the apartment and, as you can see, a Lexus."

"I didn't think the city fathers would give a cop a fancy ride like that, but I can't believe you got a Jacuzzi."

"Yep. I have a roof terrace where the Jacuzzi fits right in. I installed a reed-fence for privacy. I call it my Garden of Eden. Like to see it sometime?"

"Do we wear fig leaves?"

"Hell no," Don exclaimed.

Don't tell me yer gonna be naked."

"Hope that won't embarrass you?"

"Me? Whatta I have to be afraid of?"

Don thought, *Me?* "Possible 'snake' bite," Don said. "Gardens have snakes."

"Shit, small ones don't bite."

"Mine is a water snake, and it grows . . . right before your eyes. Excite it and it gets big and dangerous." *It might even shoot you.*

"Then I'll stay out of the water," Alvaro chuckled.

"I'm sure you'll be safe, but like doctors making anti-venom to treat snake bites, ya have to keep it milked. It rarely

33

bites, but if it did, it wouldn't kill you—if it's been milked of its—"

"So you milk it?" Alvaro asked, grinning.

"It's best when it's milked by a snake lover. Milking it could save a life."

"Now, that's information I'll add to my store of medical facts. Maybe I should bring a snakebite kit."

"Maybe," Don said. "How about I pick you up after work?"

"I'm supposed to eat with a friend tonight."

"We could have Margaritas in the Jacuzzi if you can change your plans, and then I'll cook. You do like pasta, no?"

"I love pasta, Margaritas, and Jacuzzis. Let me see if I can get a rain check from my friend."

"Okay. Pick you up at five o'clock."

Chapter 4

Don parked his Lexus below the new mural where Alvaro waited, pacing the sidewalk like a novice hooker. He wore a tight, baby blue t-shirt and clingy white shorts that revealed his sex and religion.

Alvaro waved. "Hey, boss!"

"How ya hanging, kid?" Don asked as Alvaro entered the car and checked out its interior.

"Nice," Alvaro said. "I like the smell of a new car." He ran his fingers over the leather then looked at Don. "You always ask how I'm hanging. Is that all you think about?"

How'd you guess? "Sorry," Don said, sounding apologetic. "It's an old California saying. Has to do with surfing—nothing to do with your little cock and big balls."

Don looked over his left shoulder before pulling into traffic.

"Big balls! How do you know I got big balls?"

"I've seen your 'apples.'"

"You're funny. I bet you got *cherries*. They probably match your twig."

"I got cherries alright but too big for you to pick," Don quipped.

"Oh, I could pick 'em, but I'd just be spitting seeds."

"Not into seed are you?"

"Seed? What are you talkin' about? Oh, I get it." Alvaro said and winked.

"*Seed*. Not bad stuff."

"I hate seed spitters," Don said, "but 'apple eaters' are welcome in my Eden."

"Some things are for biting. Some chewed. Some sucked. Some spit out."

Don chuckled, "Glad you know the difference."

"Mind if I change the station?" Alvaro asked, reaching for the radio. Without waiting for an answer, he tuned in a salsa station then squirmed like a hooker doing a lap dance.

35

"Like to dance do you?"

"You bet. Every chance I get. Ladies love my moves." Alvaro grinned. "They like holding my butt when we dance. Gotta admit I got a nice butt."

God, do you? "I hadn't noticed," Don said, trying hard not to laugh.

"Admit it. You like it," Alvaro said, slapping Don's thigh. "I caught you staring at it—many times."

"That's wasn't admiration my friend—just pity for having such a fat one."

"Ha! Bet you won't be able to keep your hands off it."

"You think I wanna play with your ass?" *Please say yes.*

"You know you do," Alvaro said, aligning his body parallel to Don's.

"Then, why accept my invitation?"

"Curiosity."

"About what?"

"I wanna to see how tiny *it* is."

"Hell, you could have asked me to take it out while we were parked at the mural. You don't have to go to my place for that." Don used both hands to gesture about his cock size while weaving through rush hour traffic.

Alvaro's face went ashen. "Watch your driving. I don't wanna die in a wreck."

"Just ask." Don continued, ignoring Alvaro's request to slow down. "Want me to pull over and show it to you—then take you back to the project? That would cure your curiosity and give you time to eat with your friend."

"You promised me a Margarita, Jacuzzi time, and pasta. You can't back out now. Besides, it's probably too small to get outta your fly. I gotta make sure it's as small as I know it is. No excuses like your zipper is in the way or ya can't get it out 'cause you're sitting."

Traffic came to a stop. Don craned his neck to evaluate the situation. "Looks like an accident ahead. I'll use the

36

shoulder and get off at that exit."

"Isn't it illegal to drive on the shoulder?"

"Not if you're a policeman." Don pulled onto the shoulder and drove toward the exit. "Got any girlfriends?"

"Several."

"Ya like fucking girls?"

"You bet," Alvaro said, "and some of 'em give great head."

"Which do you prefer, a good fuck or a good blow job?"

"All depends on what the girl is like."

"What do you mean?"

"If she's got nice tits, I'll fuck her. I like ta suck tits when I screw. If she ain't got 'grapefruits' or bigger then I want a blow job."

"Ever have a guy blow you?"

"Hell, a mouth's a mouth. As long as the person is good at it, I don't give a damn whose is doing it."

"Ever get fucked?"

"Who wants to know?" Alvaro asked, looking out the passenger window.

"Ever give a blow job?"

"Who cares?"

Don smiled as he and Alvaro made eye contact.

"Well, we'll have to see how talented you are," Don said. *God, I hope you're good.*

"I'm not concerned about *my* talent. It's yours I'm worried about."

"Ha. Ha. We're almost there." Don pointed ahead. "We'll see who has talent."

"With my talent, I'd win one of those reality shows. That is if they'd allow live sex on TV."

Don parked next his condo building and slapped Alvaro's hairless thigh. "Come in and bring that fat ass."

"You live here?" Alvaro asked as he stared up at the Italianate mansion turned condominium.

37

"Yep, me and all those fancy statues."

Don led the way up the stairs to his second-floor apartment. "Anyone ever tell you your fat ass jiggles?" Alvaro asked, slapping Don's butt cheeks.

Keep that up. "That's not jiggling. It's just beckoning you to admire it." *And other things I hope.*

Don opened the apartment door then turned to see Alvaro's angelic face starring up at him from two steps below. Don kissed him on the lips—a lingering kiss that caused Alvaro to kiss back with equal passion. Each man's tongue explored the other's devouring mouth.

Alvaro grabbed Don's crotch.

Now, we're getting somewhere, Don thought, feeling his cock harden in Alvaro's grip.

Still kissing, Alvaro moved up two steps.

Breathless, Don pulled away. "Wow. Thanks, but there's time for that later." He stepped inside his apartment. "Come in. Have a seat. I'll get the Jacuzzi started. The heater is on a timer, but I need to add some antifoam stuff—get it mixed in."

Don walk through the bedroom to the terrace where he removed the Jacuzzi cover. After adding some chemicals to the water, he turned on the circulators.

"It'll be ready in five minutes," Don said, walking past Alvaro in the living room and heading for the kitchen. "I'll mix some Margaritas while the tub does its magic."

Followed by Alvaro, Don entered the kitchen where he got tequila, glasses, and a bottle of Margarita mix from a cabinet.

"Nice kitchen," Alvaro said, running his fingers over a granite counter top.

"Glad someone noticed. Damn stuff added a lot to the cost of this place." Don eyed the amount of tequila he had poured in Alvaro's glass. "How strong a drink are you allow-ed?"

"Pffff. I'm part Mexican. Remember? I like lots of

tequila."

"How's this?" Don poured more tequila.

"A little more. Remember, I'm Mexican."

Don obliged, poured his own drink, and then added ice to both. *Is he wanting to get drunk? Does need to in order to have sex?*

Don picked up a two-quart, plastic pitcher. "I'll fill this with Margaritas for the terrace. Don't want us tracking water inside to get the next round." Don stirred the liquids then pointed toward the bedroom and the terrace beyond. "While I finish mixing drinks, take yours and get in the tub. There's a towel on the bed. You can leave your clothes there. I'll be right out."

Alvaro gave Don a short, hard kiss, a quick grope, and then went to the bedroom. He stripped, walked to the terrace, and then eased into the bubbling water as Don watched.

There's that ass again.

"This feels good," Alvaro yelled, over the roar of the motor.

"Glad you like it!" Minutes later, Don, wearing a towel tied at his waist, walked onto the terrace. "How's the water?"

"Love it," Alvaro said, turning his face and palms to the sky. "It's nice to be outside."

"How's your drink?" Don asked, holding out the Margarita-filled pitcher. "Wanna top it up?"

Alvaro downed the last mouthful of his elixir. "Excellent. Fill 'er up."

"Move over, I'm coming in."

Don stepped into the tub opposite Alvaro, placed his drink on the ledge of the tub, and then turned his back. He removed his towel then lowered himself into the water.

"You're ashamed of it aren't you?" Alvaro asked.

"Ashamed? No. Protective? Yes. I want to protect you from fainting when they see how big it is."

"Bullshit," Alvaro said, slapping the water.

"Why don't you move over here . . . get a handful? Find out for yourself." *Please do.*

39

"I don't travel fer *nothin'*," Alvaro said, with a sneer of jocular sarcasm.

"What do I have to do? Slap you in the face with it?"

"I'll bet once it's in your hand there's nothing left for slapping."

Don crawled across the tub then crouched before Alvaro. Without warning, he stood, shaking his crotch and water in Alvaro's face.

Alvaro's eyes grew to the size of plates as his mouth gaped, and he gasped. "That's the—"

Don cock-slapped Alvaro's face.

Startled, Alvaro grabbed Don's cock with both hands. "I've never seen such a cock."

Don freed his cock then slapped Alvaro's face several times. Alvaro tried to catch it in his mouth, but Don prevented its capture. Seconds later, Don pulled Alvaro's face against his crotch. "Want to swallow it—to the root?"

"I can't, but I want it in my mouth," Alvaro mumbled, his face squished against Don's crotch.

"Then say please and swallow."

Before Alvaro could speak, Don thrust his cock down the kid's throat. He tried to gag, but the engorged cock prevented it. Alvaro's face turned red and then a dusky grey as fear and a lack of oxygen filled his eyes with fright. He could not breathe.

Don withdrew his cock, leaving Alvaro gagging, coughing, and gasping.

"I've never had anything like that," Alvaro said between coughs.

"Not as small as you thought—is it? If I didn't think it would kill you, I'd put it back—deep down your insides."

Alvaro, still wearing a look of disbelief, starred into Don's eyes then gripped Don's balls as they dangled just above the frothy surface.

Don wiped a rivulet of water from his hairy abdomen and felt his cock throb in sync with his heartbeat. "If you can't swallow it, let's use that dainty ass?"

"I couldn't—"

"What?" Don rolled his eyes and stared at the sky. "Your ass is out of bounds, and you can't swallow it."

"Time will tell," Alvaro said shrugging and sipping his drink.

Maybe he has to be drunk to fuck? Better back off until he's downed a few.

Don sat down in the water and stared at Alvaro. "Man, I'm sorry about the way I just acted. It's just that you got me so fucking worked up, I kinda lost it. Slide over here? Let me show you some hospitality."

Alvaro took a swig of his drink, stared at Don a second, and then slid along the bench to the other side of the Jacuzzi. He leaned back against the tub, placed his arms on its ledge, and spread his legs. He lifted his crotch above the surface then let it sink.

"May I?" Don asked, reaching for Alvaro's crotch.

"Help yourself."

Don grasped Alvaro's cock. It grew until it poked its head, snorkel-like, above the surface.

"Nice," Don said. "Didn't know Latinos got circumcised."

"I had nothing to do with it." Alvaro took a sip of his Margarita then grabbed Don's half-submerged cock. "I've never seen such a 'twig.'"

"Why don't you shake the 'bough'?"

Alvaro obliged.

"Ya got good hands, kid."

Don spread his legs, rested his head on the tub's ledge, and then closed his eyes. He stroked Alvaro's cock in sync with the kid's hand action. Eyes closed, the guys became lost in their fantasies.

Minutes later, Don placed his hand over Alvaro's and said, "Slow down. I'm close. Don't want to lose it. Not now."

After another minute of Alvaro's hand action, Don

41

said, "Better stop. I'm close."

"Stop everything?"

"Just for now. You can finish later. How about you?"

"I can hold on for a long time, but I can also cum two or three times if I get the right action."

"Oh, to be twenty again."

"Hmmm. How old are you?" Alvaro asked.

"Thirty-eight."

"Sweet" Alvaro said, grinning. "Never made it with an old guy before."

Don sat up and stared at Alvaro. "Who the fuck you calling old?"

"You're a lot older than me."

"Not that much."

"Whatever," Alvaro said as he closed his eyes and squirmed his head against the tub's edge. "Keep stroking."

"You wanna get off?"

"Up to you. You wanna get me off?"

"No," Don answered. "We'll do it together—later."

Alvaro moved to the opposite side of the tub where he put his drink on the tub's ledge. Seconds later, he raised his drink in a toast and gulped the remaining liquid.

"That's beautiful," Don said.

"What is?"

"You," Don answered. "Nice tanned bod, big cock, and great balls. Oh, yeah, nice white ass framed by a tanned back and legs."

"Speakin' of balls, stand up. I wanna see yours."

Don took a sip of his drink then stood. His cock throbbed over his dangling bull balls.

Alvaro grabbed them. "Ya got good hands, kid."

"Not only do you have a huge cock, you got the biggest, lowest-hanging balls I've ever seen. Must be the hot water."

"Glad you like 'em even if you damned them with faint praise."

42

"I didn't say I liked 'em. I just dig 'em." Alvaro squeezed Don's nuts. "How do you like 'em played with?"

"Treat 'em however you like. I don't mind if they are gripped, pulled, squeezed, slapped, shaved, sucked, weighted down, oiled, or shocked as long as you play with my cock."

"Good. I think your balls and me will get along fine. I like all that stuff—except shocking."

"Well, let's see how you entertain 'em," Don said, squeezing his nuts toward the end of his stretched sack.

Alvaro slid around the tub's bench until the men's thighs touched. Don grasped Alvaro's nuts and squeezed them.

The kid spread his legs and gave Don the same care.

"More pressure," Alvaro said. "I'll let ya know if it's too much."

"Yeah, give mine a good squeeze too." *Damn, that feels good.*

Alvaro tightened his grip until Don began to squirm. "Ease up a little. Good. Keep the pressure right there, kid. Right there . . . Damn, that feels sooo good."

"How 'bout pulling on mine?" Alvaro said. "Yeah. Pull 'em . . . That's it."

Alvaro squeezed Don's nuts while he stroked his own throbbing cock and moaned.

"Thought you didn't want to cum," Alvaro whispered.

"I don't, but it feels so good."

"Yeah, know what ya mean." Alvaro stroked his own cock as the men became lost in their fantasies.

Don stopped jerking off and dropped Alvaro's balls. "Better cool it."

"Ah!" Alvaro frowned. "I looked forward to seeing how big a load you had."

"I only have one, but it's a big one. Been saving it—just for you. Sit down and have some Margarita while I cool off."

"Just 'cause you're close doesn't mean I don't enjoy attention," Alvaro said.

43

"What the hell," Don said, gripping Alvaro's cock. "Sit close. I'll play with your snake but leave mine alone." *What a handful.*

Alvaro's ass rose off the bench in response to Don's pleasuring the kid's cock.

Don stared at Alvaro's half-submerged pecs then tongued the nipples. Alvaro moaned his delight and raised his head. For a moment, the men stared at each other then kissed with the passion of oversexed teenagers. Open mouths tried to consume the other. Seconds later, lips parted as each man "came up" for air.

"Better cool it," Don said, standing. "Getting too close."

Alvaro slumped onto the bench and stared at Don's crotch. His dangling balls were too enticing to ignore. He grabbed Don's butt and pulled him forward. After several attempts, Alvaro stuffed the balls in his mouth. Don's cock throbbed against his forehead. Alvaro pulled it away then stroked it while he squeezed his lips around Don's nuts and tugged them away from their roots.

Don moaned, arch backwards, and tweak his own nipples. "That feels sooo good. Keep it up, kid."

Alvaro quickened his strokes. Don moved his hands from his nipples to his belly. Alvaro must have seen that as a sign Don neared climax, so he stopped stroking.

"Glad you stopped," Don mumbled. "I couldn't hold out much longer."

Letting Don's nuts fall from his mouth, Alvaro said, "Yeah. Thought you'd lose it, man."

"We don't want that do we? Let's take a break."

Don sat down beside Alvaro and stroked him.

"You like my snake don't you?" Alvaro asked.

And how! "Some snakes are likeable, and yours enjoys petting."

Alvaro chuckled, "Yeah, but it also likes to hide."

"Oh it does, does it?"

"Yeah. In deep holes."

"Well, stand up," Don said, standing and staring at the kid's snake. Don drew it close to his mouth then swallowed it. Alvaro gasped as Don initiated several strong swallowing motions. The muscular waves of throat contractions caressed Alvaro's engorged cock to the point of causing his knees to buckle. Don stabilized them by grabbing Alvaro's butt and pulling it forward—as if trying to swallow Alvaro's lower body.

"*Por dio,*" Alvaro murmured and grasped Don's head.

Don pulled his head from Alvaro's crotch. As the cockhead neared his lips, Don teased it then let it fall from his mouth.

Alvaro exhaled. "Never felt that swallowing thing before. That's a hell of a sensation."

"Glad to hear that. Got to keep the customer happy." Don dropped his head back and sighed. "We keep talking about taking a break, but we haven't. I need a rest, a real rest."

Alvaro moved to the opposite side of the tub and sat down. Both guys leaned back and sipped their Margaritas. Don looked into Alvaro's eyes while his foot walked up the kid's leg. It soon reached his long, loose sack where Don worked his toes under Alvaro's nuts. *Nice!*

"Wiggle 'em," Alvaro said.

Don wiggled his toes, jostling Alvaro's balls. "Feels good." Alvaro took a sip of his Margarita then spread his legs.

Don slid down and moved his other foot onto Alvaro's nuts and held the low hangers between his feet. To the kid's delight, the feet tugged the balls downward. Alvaro smiled and emitted a prolonged moaned.

"Since you liked that, let's try this," Don said moving the soles of his feet onto Alvaro's cock where they rolled it. "Ever fuck feet?"

Alvaro raised his head. "Once—with two guys. Each used a foot to stroke me. I shot all over their feet, but they kept doing it. My load and their stroking made me so sensitive I had

45

to beg 'em to stop."

"Want me to get you off with my feet?"

"Later. For now, just stroke it."

Don's feet stroked and rolled Alvaro's cock.

"Love it," Alvaro said, "especially on the head." With each rolling foot stroke, Alvaro moaned. "Better stop or I'll fill this tub."

"Hmm. I don't want to plug the plumbing, so I'll stop."

Don sat up and took a swig of his drink then asked, "Hungry?"

"I could eat . . . something other than cock."

"Well, let's start supper. Cock comes later. Make sure you dry off. Don't track water on the carpet."

After drying, the guys went to the bedroom. Alvaro reached for his clothes.

"Oh no you don't," Don said. "I like watching your ass, the snake, and those apples."

"You staying naked?"

"Of course. Might wanna stuff my sausage some-where. Wouldn't want clothes to slow me down."

"Naked is fine with me. I can slap your nuts when I want."

"You said you like nut action. Ever wear a ball-stretcher or weights?"

"Not store bought. Me and a couple of the guys once played with a belt around our nuts. We found some old gears in our building and hung them from the belt holes. Felt good."

"So you guys played around, eh?"

"We were drunk."

"How many times?"

"Three, maybe four . . . but only once with weight."

"Wanna try a real ball-stretcher?"

Alvaro shrugged. "I'm game."

Don took a stretcher and some weights from a dresser drawer. He sat down on the bed and held the stretcher toward Alvaro. "Let me put it on you."

46

Alvaro stretched his balls so Don could place the opened, two-inch-wide, leather strap behind them. Pushing aside scrotal skin, he forced shut the chrome snaps on the front of the strap. Alvaro lifted the stretcher to see his captured balls bulging below its end.

"That ring at the bottom is for weights," Don said. "How much can you handle?"

"Damned if I know." Alvaro pointed to a lead weight laying on the dresser. "Use that one. I'll let ya know if I like it."

Don hung a one-pound weight on the ring. "How's that?"

"Feels good," Alvaro said, looking in the dresser's mirror to watch the weight swing between his thighs.

"Want more weight?"

"Maybe a small one?"

"There. How's that?" Don asked, adding a quarter-pound weight.

"Let's leave it at that."

"Okay. Let's start the pasta."

Alvaro started to follow Don to the kitchen but stopped to say, "The weights feels weird when I walk."

"Too much weight?" Don asked.

"Na. It's the swinging. Feels strange."

"Spread your legs," Don said, waddling a few steps to demonstrate.

Alvaro took a few steps, legs spread. "That's better."

Don chuckled and gave Alvaro's weight a nudge, causing it to swing farther back between his thighs.

Alvaro smiled.

"Would you cut the lettuce?" Don asked.

"You trust me with a knife?"

"Only on lettuce."

Don glanced at Alvaro's semi-erect cock and thought, *Oh to be twenty again.*

Culinary tasks completed, Don asked, "Let's eat on the terrace."

"Sounds good."

Sitting at the terrace table, Alvaro said, "The weights felt better when they were hanging."

"Then push your seat straps apart and drop your balls through."

"You think of everything." Alvaro pushed his weighted balls through a space between the plastic straps.

"Happy to help. Sometimes I wear weights out here and let 'em hang like that."

Don toe-nudged Alvaro's weights.

Alvaro leaned back and sucked air. "Feels good, but how much weight do you wear?"

"Twice what you're wearing. Maybe I should hang some. No reason for you to have all the fun."

"Yeah," Alvaro said eyes widening. "I'd like ta see weights swingin' from a cop's nuts."

Don left the terrace for a few minutes then returned, wearing a stretcher and two weights.

"Sick!" Alvaro said. "I didn't know balls could stretch that low. Looks good."

Happy to entertain the younger generation. Don bent his knees and humped his hips causing his weights to swing back and forth.

Alvaro grasped Don's nuts to assess the weight. "Can't believe your wearin' two pounds."

Don sat down in his chair then opened a space for his nuts. "Didn't mean to distract you from your supper."

"Seeing your stretched nuts is worth eating cold pasta."

"Want it microwaved?"

"Would you mind?"

"No," Don said, taking Alvaro's plate.

Minutes later, Don returned with the warmed pasta.

After finishing dinner, Don and Alvaro took the tableware to the dishwasher.

Don bent over to retrieve a dropped fork. As he righted himself, his face brushed Alvaro's cock. In a flash, he swallowed it and released Alvaro's ball stretcher, so he could tug on the liberated nuts. He repeated his famous swallowing action, came up for air, then returned to swallowing Alvaro's snake. In seconds, Don sensed Alvaro's approaching climax. He swallowed hard, took a breath, then swallowed again.

Alvaro's body stiffened, writhing and squirming like a dog locked in coitus. He moaned and pulled Don's head hard against his crotch as he climaxed. Don felt a flood of heat in his throat and continued to swallow. Seconds later, Don withdrew his head, freeing the convulsing cock then embraced the spent Alvaro.

"Let's go back to the tub," Don whispered. "You can rest there."

The men relaxed in the Jacuzzi and discussed Alvaro's past. His family life had been troubled. He fled home at age fourteen, lived on the streets, became involved with alcohol, drugs, petty robbery, and earned a few bucks selling his body and dealing drugs. Dealing brought him in contact with his gang. They provided stability, security, and acceptance.

The revelations provided insight into Don's growing emotional attraction for Alvaro. *We were both denied emotional support. Maybe I see me in him. Are my feelings for him really a substitute for loving myself? God! I don't want to think about it.*

Don topped off their drinks. As he sat down in the Jacuzzi, Alvaro reached for Don's nuts. He winked. "Ready to play again?"

"Nah, just fondling the apples. They feel good in this hot water."

"Don't forget the limb they hang from." *Hope you shake it a bit.*

"Guess I owe you a windstorm, eh? To pay for supper."

"You owe me nothing." *Is he reverting to his street life thinking he owes me sexual favors?*

"Your pleasure is my pleasure," Alvaro said, lifting

49

Don's hips to the surface. He gripped Don's nuts and pulled him closer, took his cock in his mouth, tongued its head, then swallowed it. Half-way down, Don pulled Alvaro's head deep over his aching crotch. Alvaro gagged.

Don looked down at Alvaro's angelic face then withdrew his cock. "Dry off. Let's go to the bedroom." *I'd like to bury my cock someplace else.*

Don threw back the comforter then pulled Alvaro onto the bed. "Lie face down."

"I can't take that," Alvaro said, staring over his shoulder as Don straddled him.

"Relax. I'll teach you."

Don rolled a condom on his cock then fingered Alvaro's ass. Alvaro lifted his hips. Don squeezed KY on his fingers and resumed ass playing. After minutes of manipulation, Don managed to get four fingertips inside. Don stretched the kid then sat over his white butt, rubbing his cock over the waiting ass. Alvaro drew his butt cheeks apart. Don accepted the invitation. He moved deeper and deeper, pausing to feel Alvaro's relaxation. Alvaro moaned and wiggled his hips, begging for more action. Don soon reached the depth of Alvaro's pleasure. Don paused a moment then fucked the wanton ass. *Damn. That feels good.*

Alvaro sucked air. "Oh . . . Mmm . . ."

Don took care not to be too vigorous. He wanted Alvaro to enjoy the experience and accept future fucks. After a few of Don's slow, deep thrusts, Alvaro synchronized his hip action with Don's thrusts then quickened his movements to match Don's pace. In minutes, Alvaro must have sensed Don was nearing an incredible climax and increased his contribution of friction-pleasure.

Don grasped Alvaro's hips, pulled the fast-moving butt closer to his crotch, and then thrust faster. Don stiffened then yelled loud enough to frighten animals while thrusting to the depth of Alvaro's expectation. Sweating, Don shuddered and collapsed on Alvaro's back, panting like he had had a heart attack.

"You okay?" Alvaro asked, concern coloring his voice.

Don caught his breath. "Never felt better!" *Never.* Having regained his strength, he rolled over and stared at the ceiling. "And you said you couldn't take me."

"Didn't think I could, but . . . that finger stuff helped."

Don embraced Alvaro. "Our sex is wonderful, but just being with you makes my day."

"The feeling is mutual." Alvaro kissed Don's encircling arm. "Let's shower. I'll soap your back."

Chapter 5

A handsome, well-built young man wearing a blue pin-striped suit and red tie walked two hundred feet ahead of Don. The man paused to light a cigarette then leaned on the sign warning visitors to stay back from the edge of the cliff. The man took a few steps closer to the edge and peered below.

How strange to see someone dressed so smartly way out here, Don thought.

Suddenly, the cliff edge sheared, and the man fell from sight. Don rushed to the precipice and stared below. Four feet below the edge, the man dangled in the air, gripping a rock with one hand.

Don dropped to the ground and stretched out on a slab of sunbaked granite, its heat almost burning his abdomen. With one hand, he grabbed a nearby bush and extended the other hand toward the man's pleading hand. "Grab my arm!" Don yelled.

Each man managed to grab the other's forearm.

Swinging his body, the man struggled to get his feet against the cliff wall but failed.

Don felt the man's grip slipping. *I can't let him fall.*

The man's begging eyes stared into Don's eyes. Don knew his face mirrored the man's abject horror.

Don's grip weakened, slipping on the man's hair-less arm.

"Hang on!" Don yelled. "Let go of the rock. Grab my arm with both hands!"

Against all willing, Don's grip slipped more. His hand ached with fatigue. He could not maintain his grip.

Quarter-inch by quarter-inch, the stranger's hand slid farther down Don's forearm. The friction caused Don searing pain. Thin strips of skin peeled from his forearm to his wrist. *I don't dare let go of the bush to grab him with both hands.* "God help us."

The last inch of Don's fingertips lost contact with the

man's arm. The man's eyelids and lips retracted as his mouth gaped open—too filled with fear to utter a sound.

"No! No!" Don yelled, watching in horror as the man plummeted toward the floor of the ravine. Only the faint sound of his fluttering coat and tie reached Don.

Don went limp, closed his eyes, and sobbed, "No! No!"

Don awoke with a start. He lay belly down on the heating pad used at bedtime to ease his backache. His right arm, caught between two spindles of the headboard, held him hostage. His right hand gripped a wad of bedding. "God, what a dream!"

Sitting on the edge of the bed, Don recalled hearing that dream objects were symbols of life experiences. *Was that man Alvaro? Why should I fear losing him. Is he mine to lose? Is my subconscious telling me I fear not holding onto him? Letting him get away?*

After a planning session about another youth conference, Don drove to the four-story mural nearing completion.

He parked two hundred feet away and watched the artists. Alvaro wore only shorts. His torso glistened with sweat under the noontime sun. His white shorts, caught in a grand wedgie, framed his bubble-butt. "God damn, he's beautiful." Don continued watching for a few minutes then drove closer. He parked, tooted his horn, and then exited the car, waving to the painters.

Alvaro waved then climbed down the scaffolding.

Don stood below, his heart racing as he admired Alvaro's butt. *I could watch that ass all day. Didn't think I'd ever feel like this again.*

"How's it hanging?" Don asked when Alvaro reached the last rung.

Alvaro grinned. "You know how it's hanging." He left the ladder and extended his hand into a lingering handshake.

"Have time for lunch?" Don asked.

"You're the boss. If you say I have time, I have time."

"Tell the guys we have some business to take care of. We'll be back in an hour."

"You don't mind sweaty-me sitting on Lexus leather?"

"You can't hurt good leather. Get in."

Don rested his hand on Alvaro's warm thigh as they rode toward a local workman's hangout where no one dressed fancy, but the restaurant did require shirts. Since Alvaro didn't wear one—much to Don's delight—they ate alone outside, shaded by an umbrella. Don's chosen table shielded the guys from the view of diners inside.

The day's heat and hot hamburgers were countered with cold beers, rubbed against sweating brows.

"Let's hope a cop doesn't see you sucking beer," Alvaro said.

"Don't worry. That won't happen here."

To cool off, Don loosened his tie, opened three shirt buttons, and then rolled up his sleeves.

The men ate and exchanged lingering glances. They permitted their hands to touch, while passing ketchup back and forth. Don let his knee rest against Alvaro's bare leg. They exchanged pressure on the other's knee, accompanied by smiles of gratitude.

When the meal ended, Alvaro asked, "What kind of business required this break?"

"None." Don grinned. "I just wanted to have lunch with the most beautiful man in Philadelphia."

"I love the thought, but don't you care that I have work to supervise. Hadn't I better get back."

"I'd like to stay for a while," Don said, forcing a frown and gripping Alvaro's leg, "but I know we can't."

"Don't worry. There'll be other opportunities."

"I hope so," Don said, "but first, I have something for you."

"Me?"

55

"Yes, you." Don put his hand in his pocket and then withdrew a fist. "Hold out your hand."

Looking perplexed, Alvaro complied.

"Close your eyes," Don said and placed something on Alvaro's palm. "Okay. Open your eyes."

Alvaro stared at his hand. "Oh, my God." He held up a gold bracelet. "I don't know what to say."

"Thanks would be fine." *Glad he liked it.*

"Thank you." Alvaro stared into Don's eyes. "It's beautiful. Thank you."

"Hold out your wrist and I'll latch it on . . . there. How's that?"

Alvaro turned his arm. Sunlight flashed from the bracelet's faceted surfaces. "What's the occasion?"

"You. You're the occasion. It's an expression of my interest."

Don stroked Alvaro's bare thigh as he sped through several intersections.

"You shouldn't be runnin' red lights," Alvaro said as if he feared for his life.

"It's okay. I'm on police business."

At the worksite, Don parked at the curb. Looking up at the mural, he said, "Looks like you should be finished in another day."

"Yep, we promised delivery by tomorrow, and we'll do it."

"That's good." Don squeezed Alvaro's thigh. "We'll be able to do the formal presentation at the end of the week. That means more publicity and work for you guys."

"Great. We're tired of this one."

"Changing the subject, what're you doing for supper?"

Alvaro chuckled. "Fuckin' you I guess."

Using his whole hand, Don tapped Alvaro's face. "Not interested in my cooking?"

"Can't we eat *and* fuck?"

"I'll guarantee supper," Don said. "Nothing more."

"Fine. Pick me up at 12th and Forbes. The guys won't see us there."

"Deal." Don squeezed Alvaro's thigh. "Are they starting to ask or joke about us?"

"No, and I don't want 'em too."

"Then you had better take that bracelet off."

Boarded shops and dilapidated apartment buildings glowed in the setting sun as if they were on fire. This part of Alvaro's neighborhood seemed as livable as hell, but there he stood on the designated corner, sexy as ever. Dressed in pressed, tight baby-blue shorts and shirt, the colors complimented his tan.

Don smiled as he pulled to the curb. *Now, that's a sight.*

Alvaro entered the car. He sat, back against the door, with his left knee on the seat. "This car sticks out like an abscess on a butt."

Don placed his hand on Alvaro's thigh and let it rest there. "Don't blame me. You picked the spot."

Alvaro tuned in his favorite radio station, turned up the volume, and then squirmed like the seat burned his ass.

"Calm down," Don said, patting Alvaro's thigh.

"Can't help it. I dig this music. Don't forget, I'm part Latino."

At Don's building, the men climbed the stairs to the apartment with Don leading the way.

"You staring at my ass again?" Don asked.

"Just wondering how it can shake so much."

"I shake it for you, my friend." Don opened the door. "I made Margaritas before I left to pick you up. They're waiting for ice. Thought I'd make Fettuccini Alfredo tonight."

"Sounds good, but aren't we getting naked for some tub time?"

"Asking like a man, eh? You know if we're naked, you might get fucked."

Alvaro chuckled. "Not me."

"We'll see. You get naked, and I'll get the tub and Margaritas ready but first . . ." Don stared into Alvaro's blue-green eyes then their lips met. Tongues explored the depth of the other's oral lust as erections grew. Don pulled away. "Whew. I think we're both about to explode. Better cool it for a minute."

Don added chemicals to the Jacuzzi as Alvaro stripped.

Don returned to the bedroom. *Wow!* "Looking good," he said, fondling Alvaro's balls.

"Oh no you don't," Alvaro said, pushing Don's hand away. "Not unless I get a kiss and a handful of you."

"Okay." Don kissed Alvaro. Their bodies melded as their French kiss time vied for a Guinness record.

Don feigned outrage that he had to strip, but he did.

Alvaro grabbed Don's balls and squeezed them. Don returned the favor and pulled Alvaro close. Staring into Alvaro's angelic face, Don kissed his soft lips. Alvaro kissed back, hard. Don welcomed the warmth of Alvaro's body pressed against his. Their cocks pulsed against the other's abdomen. Don dropped to his knees, mouthed Alvaro's man-hood, and swallowed several times.

"Thought we were going to get in some tub time," Alvaro said.

"Let's," Don mumbled, emptying his mouth.

Don got ice from the freezer then the guys headed for the Jacuzzi.

The men settled into the bubbling water and relaxed. After a moment, Alvaro's foot walked up Don's shin, knee, and then his thigh, stopping when his toes rested behind Don's nuts. Alvaro wiggled his toes, jostling the balls.

That's a start. "Is that all you're going to do?" Don asked.

58

For a moment, Alvaro sat motionless then moved his foot deeper into Don's crotch until his big toe reached Don's hole.

Don moved his hips forward and smiled. "Never been toe fucked."

Alvaro pushed his toe inside. Don spread his legs, welcoming the intrusion. Alvaro wiggled his toe. "Ya like that don't ya?"

"Not bad," Don said. *But don't stop.* "Glad you cut your nails." Don raised his butt as a tingly pleasure spread throughout his body.

Alvaro withdrew his toe then crawled between Don's legs. First, he tugged Don's balls, then one, two, and three fingers found their way inside Don. He rolled over and raised his butt. Alvaro rubbed his cock across Don's begging ass then slid inside as Don rested his head on the tub's ledge and moan-ed. Alvaro thrust with increasing vigor. He grabbed Don's hips and pulled his butt closer to the root of his cock. Alvaro with-drew and re-inserted his cock several times, teasing the waiting hole before reentering.

Don moved his tightened butt back and forth, attempt-ting to capture Alvaro's cock, but he resisted the friction and fucked with growing vigor.

"Hang on," Alvaro said.

Don's butt hungered for Alvaro's load. He worked his ass to increase the pleasure of Alvaro's approaching climax. "Come on, kid."

Don stroked his own cock to the edge of exploding. As Alvaro's pace accelerated, so did Don's hand. A split second later, both guys unloaded. Alvaro collapsed on Don's back and panted. Don continued to work his ass, sending Alvaro to a place of intolerable pleasure.

"Stop!" Alvaro said. "I'm too sensitive."

"Can't take it?" Don chuckled.

Alvaro uncoupled then stood. "That's one hot ass."

Don smiled. "Thanks. *Can't wait until the next time.*

Ready for a shower?"

"Yeah."

"You go first. I need to add chemicals to the water."

Minutes later, Alvaro left the shower. Don handed him a towel, saying, "Someone taught you well, kid."

"I learned a few things, living on the street," Alvaro said, drying his back.

Don flicked his towel on Alvaro's ass, pulled his wet body close, and then gave him a long hard kiss.

Don ducked under the water and yelled, "We'll have to do that fucking thing again."

Frowning, Alvaro said, "I'm not fucking that hairy ass again. I like smooth butts."

"For action like that, I'll shave it. On second thought, you shave it."

"We'll see."

Don and Alvaro saw more and more of each other. One reason being Don negotiated more mural commissions for the painters, but the two men also enjoyed the other's company. They were bonding.

Alvaro rented an apartment outside the hood where his fellow painters preferred to live.

"I like being independent," Alvaro said, when asked to move in with Don. "Having my own place lets me live like regular people. Besides, if I lived with you, the guys might think I was kept—for sex."

"Hell," Don said, "they probably think that anyway."

"Nah. They know I've had sex with men—and liked it. Hell, most of them have had guy sex, but they know I don't need yours or any guy's money, and I like that."

"Yeah, but it's difficult going to bed each night without you, but I understand where you're coming from."

Alvaro gave Don a kiss. "Someday it'll all work out. You'll see, but you have to know I have feelings for you."

"Me too," Don said. *I wonder if he knows how much?*

Two weeks later, Alvaro helped Don celebrate his

60

birthday with a home cooked dinner in Alvaro's apartment. For desert, he presented Don with a birthday cake. Its decoration read, 'Happy Birthday, Don. Love, Alvaro.'

"You have no idea how happy you've made me," Don said, choking up. "I love you too."

"And I love you too. You also get a birthday kiss." Alvaro gave him a hard, breathtaking kiss.

Don pulled at Alvaro's shirt tail while he tugged at Don's zipper. Soon, the guys were naked, attempting all the positions of the Kama Sutra. In a matter of minutes, they had spent their sexual energy through thunderous climaxes then lay sweating, panting, and staring at the ceiling.

"Didn't know people could become human pretzels," Alvaro chuckled.

"Well, now you know, but from now on, please don't wear clothes when you invite me here."

Don gave Alvaro another kiss.

"Don't I undress fast enough?" Alvaro asked.

"Impossible, but why deny me the beauty hidden under all that permanent-press shit? No, naked is better. All the time."

"How about you?" Alvaro asked squeezing Don's balls. "Will you be naked when I visit?"

"Have you forgot. I pick *you* up. You want me driving naked?"

"Just leave the pants off. Wear a long-tailed shirt. You could drape a towel over your lap if you're beside a tall truck."

"Don't you ever stop talking?" Don asked then gave Alvaro a kiss.

The men rolled onto their sides. Motionless, they stared into the other's eyes.

"Penny for your thoughts," Alvaro said.

Don kissed him. "Cock, balls, butt, lips, chest, cock, balls, butt, lips, nipples—"

"Me too."

"It's late," Don said, looking at the clock. I need to

be up early tomorrow, and you too, but you knew that."

Alvaro turned out the light and snuggled against Don's back.

God, *I love feeling him next to me,* Don though. *I Didn't think I'd ever feel like this. Hope he feels the same way.*

At 6:00 a.m., Alvaro's phone rang.

"Don't answer that," Don mumbled, nibbling on Alvaro's nipple.

Alvaro went to the dining room to get his cell phone from his shorts. "Hello," he said, returning to the bedroom. He seemed to focus on the caller's voice as he sat down beside Don.

Don heard a spirited voice jabbering in Spanish at the other end of the call. "What's up?" he asked as Alvaro slammed his phone on the bed.

"Some son-of-a-bitch threw paint all over our new mural—it's ruined! I gotta get down there."

"I'll drive you," Don said, reaching for his underwear. "Have the police been notified?"

"Yeah. They're there."

Don raced his Lexus to the mural, his portable emergency light flashing on the roof.

Two police cars, lights flashing, were parked at the scene. Screeching to a halt, Don parked beside the patrol cars.

Alvaro exited the car and ran to his friends milling about, talking, and pointing at the mural.

Don raced behind him and flashed his badge to one of the policemen. "Who discovered this shit, and who called it in?"

"About twenty minutes ago," a patrolman said, "a call came from a pay phone. The caller identified himself as One Better."

Don joined Alvaro at the foot of the mural and inspected three eight-foot-square areas splashed with white paint. *Damn the son-of-a-bitch who did this!* "Paint's still fresh," Don said, touching the sticky paint.

An empty paint can lay in a pool of paint on the sidewalk.

"It's ruined!" Alvaro said, his voice filled with rage.

"Get this paint can to the lab," Don shouted to an officer. "See if they can lift any prints."

Morning traffic had stalled, due to rubber-necking drivers. "Keep moving," a policeman yelled and waved for drivers to move on.

Alvaro paced the sidewalk surveying the mural. "Who the fuck did this?" He shook his head as he looked at the white paint on the sidewalk and mural. "Don, look! Someone left their signature here—at the lower edge of the mural. See it? It's small, but it's the Hood's symbol. Son-of-a-bitch! They probably did it with their finger."

"Just because that's a Hood symbol doesn't mean they did it. Another gang could have drawn that."

"No. The Hoods did this," Alvaro said, slapping the air. "I know they did. Word on the street is they're upset about all the Eagles' painting, money, and publicity. They're fuckin' jealous! They ain't top of the hood no more."

"You know where they hang out. Right?" Don asked. "Tell that inspector. He'll get to the bottom of this shit."

"Don't worry," Alvaro said, shaking his fist. "Us Eagles will get those guys. We'll get 'em!"

Don grabbed Alvaro's arm and stared him in the eye. "Listen to me. *NO* fighting. You've been clean for a long time.Let the police handle this."

"Don't worry 'bout us." Alvaro shrugged. "We'll be okay."

Don gripped Alvaro's shoulder and squeezed it. "Promise me you won't fight."

"I promise."

Three days later, Don grappled for his cell phone as it rang on the far side of the bedside table. He rubbed his eyes

63

and looked at the clock— 4:45 a.m. "Who the fuck's calling at this hour?" He asked as he answered the phone.

"Detective Johns?" the caller asked.

"Yes. Who's this?"

"I'm Officer Wilson from central. We responded to a bloody altercation between the Hoods and the Eagles gangs. I know you worked with gangs and thought you'd want to know."

"Thanks, but you said *bloody*? What happened?"

"The hooligans had guns and knives. One guy was shot dead. Several were stabbed. Four were hospitalized."

"Which gangs?" Don asked, forcing himself awake.

"The Eagles and Hoods."

"Eagles?" Don gasped, "Who's in the hospital?"

"All I have are first names. There's a Juan and a Carlos from the Hoods; a Roberto and Alvaro from the Eagles."

"Oh God," Don muttered. "Which hospital got the Eagles?"

"Temple."

"Thanks."

Don zipped his pants and buttoned his shirt as he left his apartment. He sped toward Temple's emergency department like an Indy 500 racer headed for the finish line.

He screeched to a stop beside the ER entrance then dashed from his car.

A security guard yelled, "Hey, you can't park here. Move it!"

Don flashed his badge and sprinted into the emergency department. He pushed several people aside at the receptionist's desk while waving his badge.

"Hey, wait yer turn," an angry man yelled.

"Later, sir," Don said. "EMTs just brought in some wounded gang members," Don said to a clerk. "One is Alvaro. Where is he?"

The disgruntled looking receptionist pushed her glasses

higher up her nose, rifled some papers, and then scanned her monitor. "He's in surgery."

"For what?"

Dragging her finger down the screen, she said, "Stab wounds to the chest. That's all I know."

Don slumped against the clerk's privacy partition. "Oh god," he murmured.

"Are you okay?" the receptionist asked.

Aching deep inside, Don nodded then moped to a lobby chair. "Shit!" *Why did he get involved in a fight? I begged him. . . he promised.*

Minutes later, Don regained his composure and re-approached the receptionists. "Who's the surgeon—for Alvaro?"

The receptionist scanned her monitor then flashed a false-looking smile. "Doctor Richardson. He's the on-call surgeon."

"I know him. When is he expected out of surgery?"

"I have no idea."

"Keep checking, please." Don pointed toward the waiting area. "I'll be in there. Call me as soon as you know anything—anything at all."

Don took a chair in the far corner of the waiting area. From that location, he could watch for Doctor Richardson if he passed. Don cradled his head in his hands, wept, and then mumbled a prayed, *Please, God, don't let him die. Get him through this.* Don wiped tears with the back of his hand. *Please, God, don't let him die.*

The receptionist gave Don a box of tissues. "Take these. Are you related to Alvaro?"

"Thanks," Don said, taking some tissues. "He's a friend . . . He worked for me."

"I'm sorry . . . I'm sure he'll be alright. He has the best doctors."

"I hope so." Don looked at the floor and blew his nose as the receptionist returned to her desk.

Don forced himself to his feet then paced the waiting area. Twenty minutes later, he took a corner seat, leaned his head against the wall, and then fell asleep.

"What?" Don said, shaking his head.

A nurse shook his shoulder. "Officer, Alvaro is in recovery. He's doing well. You can see him in about three hours. Why don't you go home? Get some sleep . . . come back at ten thirty."

"Guess I should. Here's my card. Please get it to the recovery room nurses. They are to call me if anything, and I mean anything, changes."

Don stared through a window in the door of the intensive care unit. He watched a wall clock, mounted behind the nurses' station, move from 10:29 to 10:30. He pushed a button to the right of the door and waited.

Moments later, a female nurse walked to the door and peered out. Don held his badge to the window. She opened the door allowing a gush of cold air to escape, carrying the smell of alcohol and disinfectant past his nose. *God, I hate the smell of hospitals.* A cacophony of beeps and whirring sounds assaulted his ears as he stepped into the bright space.

"How may I help you, Officer?"

"I'm here to see Alvaro, the man with stab wounds."

"Please. Come with me."

Don's heart stopped when the nurse pushed aside the grey curtain beside Alvaro's bed.

"He's a little groggy," the nurse said, "but he knows where he is. He can't speak due to the endotracheal—I mean throat tube."

"Oh, God." Shock rifled Don's psyche as he came face-to-face with Alvaro's condition. Everywhere Don looked there were tubes and beeping machines. A plastic bag of blood-tinged liquid hung below the bed. A large, blood-stained dressing covered Alvaro's chest from which a blood-filled tube drained into a bedside bottle. His rib cage rose and fell in sync with the clicking sounds of a machine attached to the tube protruding from his mouth.

Pointing to the respirator, the nurse said, "His lung was punctured. That machine helps him breathe. His arms are restrained so he can't pull at the tubes." The nurse turned to leave. "Stay as long as you want."

Don shook his head as a tear rolled down his quivering cheek. He stared at Alvaro's bruised face. *Damn it! Why didn't you listen to me?* The one tear became a torrent of despair. He moved to the side of the bed and gripped Alvaro's hand—cold and pale blue, it resembled death. He rubbed the hand between his in an attempt to warm it.

"I asked you not to fight," Don whispered, anger coloring his voice. "You promised you wouldn't fight. Now look at you—what have you done? Damn it, don't you listen to anybody?"

Don sobbed as he sat down in a chair and held Alvaro's cold hand.

Alvaro stirred. He half-opened his eyes, glanced at Don, and then closed them. Don squeezed Alvaro's hand. He weakly returned the grip.

Don bent over the bed and whispered in Alvaro's ear. "Doc says you're doing fine. You'll live to fight another day, but you had goddamn better not—ever."

Eyes closed, Alvaro managed a small smile around his breathing tube.

Praying Alvaro would be safe, Don kissed him on the forehead. "I'll be back. Now rest."

During the next week, he spent hours at Alvaro's bedside.

Weaned from his respirator, Alvaro's breathing tube had been removed. This allowed him to be transferred to a private room overlooking the city. He and Don spoke of many things but spent most of their time talking about sexual things they would do to each other after discharge.

One day before Alvaro's discharged date, Don arrived at the hospital feeling anxious and worried.

"What's up, Boss?" Alvaro asked, wincing and pushing himself up in bed. "You don't look good."

"Not good," Don said, giving Alvaro a kiss then walking to the window and staring into space.

"What is it? What's wrong?"

Don shook his head. "District Attorney says he's going to prosecute you, Roberto, and all the other gang guys—for manslaughter, maybe murder. He's determined to press charges without a grand jury."

"What?" Alvaro exclaimed then moaned, clutching his chest wound. "No way!"

Don frowned. "I spoke to him, about you, but . . . his mind is made up. Let's face it—somebody was killed. The gun hasn't been found yet, but when it is, somebody is going to be charged with murder."

"What does this mean—for me?" Alvaro asked, his face white with worry.

"You were part of a gang that killed a man. If you are found guilty, you could get twenty to life."

"Shit! What am I gonna do?"

"Right now, I don't know. Guessing you don't have money for an attorney, I contacted the judge. He'll appoint a public defender."

"Thanks. And you're right. I don't have money for a lawyer!"

"Well, sit tight. I'm working on this."

The next day, a uniformed policeman knocked on Alvaro's door. "You Alvaro?"

"Yeah."

"You've been charged in the death of a Hoods' gang member. You're under arrest."

Before Alvaro could respond, the policeman handcuffed him to his bed rail.

Shocked and breathless, Alvaro tugged at the cuff. "No, this can't be happening."

From that moment on, a uniformed policeman stood guard outside Alvaro's door.

Later that day, Don arrived to find Alvaro handcuffed to a chair watching television. Don closed the door then gave Alvaro a hug and a kiss.

"Not so tight," Alvaro grunted. "Hugging hurts my chest."

"Sorry, but I've got *good* news," Don said. "You'll be discharged tomorrow," A tear formed in Don's eye. He wiped it and cleared his throat. "You'll be transferred to the local precinct station where you'll wait trial."

"Trial!" Alvaro said. "You gotta stop this. I didn't kill nobody. For God's sake do something, Don. Take care of me!"

Hearing Alvaro's plea, Don ached to his core. "I'm doing all I can, kid, believe me. I got a public defender assigned to your case. He'll be visiting day after tomorrow but don't worry."

Don sat down on the bed and held Alvaro's hand. "I'm working on something. I'll be allowed to transfer you so try and relax. You'll need something to wear after discharge. Since I have your apartment key, is it okay if I get you some clothes?"

"Yeah . . . Whatever."

"Okay. See you tomorrow."

A tear running down his cheek, Alvaro said, "I've heard about young guys in prison. I won't survive there. Don't let them do this to me."

"I'm trying," Don said.

Don kissed Alvaro on the forehead then the lips. Don turned to leave, their fingertips the last points of contact.

Alvaro watched Don walk toward the elevator. He appeared to carry unbearable sorrow, leaving Alvaro to confront his troubles alone.

Chapter 6

On the way to his office, Don stopped by the hospital to deliver Alvaro's clothes.

Six hours later, Don returned and dismissed Alvaro's guard. He gave Alvaro a lingering kiss.

Cuffed to his chair, Alvaro had been dressed except for a shirt. Don admired the chest he loved so much then noted how well Alvaro's surgical scar had healed.

Alvaro pulled at his slacks. "Thanks for bringing these." He smiled then said, "A hot orderly helped me get dressed. He liked helping with my underwear. I think he has a foot fetish from the way he handled my socks and feet. I dug the way he unzipped . . . uh zipped my fly—slowly."

Don chuckled. "Can't trust you can I?"

Alvaro tugged at his chrome bracelet. "The orderly couldn't get my shirt on 'cause of these."

"Let me help." Don said, opening Alvaro's cuffs then nibbling his uninjured pec. "Now, get your shirt on."

Buttoning his shirt, Alvaro said, "You don't know how much I've missed that tongue and your hugs."

"Then stand still and I'll give you one."

After a long hug and a kiss, Alvaro finished buttoning his shirt then extended his wrists. "I know you can't take me without the cuffs."

"Sorry." Don frowned then placed the cuffs around the wrists he had often held, while making love. "Glad you know the rules. I brought this sweater to cover your *jewelry*. Don't want everybody staring at them."

Don led Alvaro to the nurse's station where he signed release papers just as an orderly arrived with a wheelchair.

"I'll handle that," Don said, commandeering the wheelchair then adjusting its footrests.

Alvaro sat down in the chair and looked up at Don. "Is the orderly sharing his salary with you for doing his job?"

"Consider it an act of Christian charity."

Don adjusted the sweater over Alvaro's cuffs then pushed the wheelchair to a bank of elevators. He pushed the down button then rapped his fingers on the chair handle. After a few minutes, an elevator arrived.

"Thank God it's empty," Don said as the door closed. "I have a plan, and you need to listen carefully before some-one else gets in. Do exactly as I say. Understand?"

Wrinkling his brow, Alvaro looked up and said, "What are you talking about?"

"I don't want you going to trial. There's no doubt you'd have to build time just because you accompanied the guy who shot the Hoods' guy—you're an accomplice. I don't want you going to prison for that. I couldn't take it."

"Hell, me either. I don't want prison, but what can you—no, what the hell can *we* do?"

"We've got to get you out of the country."

Disbelief flooded Alvaro's face. "Outta the country?"

"Yes, damn it! Out of the country."

"Shit, where do I go, and what the fuck do I do for a job—money!"

"Quiet down," Don ordered and slapped the side of Alvaro's head. Pressing a hand on each of Alvaro's shoulders, Don said, "Remember, we're in a hospital. Now listen. I bought you a plane ticket to San Diego."

"Shit!" Alvaro waved his cuffed hands in the air. "San Diego is *not* outta the country."

Don put his hand over Alvaro's mouth. "Listen to me. When you get there, go to the bus station and take a bus to Mexico. When you get to the border, walk across. I've faked a passport for you. You then get lost in Tijuana. Mexico isn't likely to extradite you if you're caught."

Alvaro shook his head. "What the hell am I gonna do in Mexico?"

"Lay low. That's what. Remember, I told you a while back that I'd won some money? Well, I saved some.

72

We can live quite well on what's left."

"What?" Alvaro asked wide eyed. "You're comin' to Mexico?"

With a lump in his throat, Don said, "Do you think I'd just let you walk out of my life?"

"Hell, man. I didn't know you cared *that* much."

"Well, I do." A broad smile crept across Don's face. "Have for a long time."

"I had trouble admitting it to myself—loving you I mean, but I didn't know ya loved me."

"Well, I do," Don said, shaking the wheelchair to make his point.

Alvaro looked up and puckered his lips. Don kissed him.

"Okay, but what do we do now?" Alvaro asked, trying to gesture.

After a slight jolt, the elevator door opened at the lobby. People stepped aside then glared at Alvaro's exposed handcuffs.

"This is embarrassing," Alvaro said, trying to rearrange the sweater.

Don adjusted the sweater. "Sorry, Kid."

"What are we gonna do now?"

"Tell you at the car."

Don pushed Alvaro's wheelchair outside then parked It beside the door.

"Okay. Let's get out of here," Don said, helping Alvaro to his feet.

With Alvaro still handcuffed, the men wove a diagonal path between cars and crossed the hospital parking lot. Don had parked his unmarked car at the far end of the lot. A break in its chain-link fence would accommodate Don's plan for Alvaro's escape. Three orange traffic cones sat in front of the breach to deter people and cars from going through the

73

opening.

At the car, Alvaro asked why Don had not driven his Lexus.

"Sold it this morning," Don said then smiled. "We won't be needing it anymore."

"What?"

"No use leaving it here to who knows what."

Don looked around to make sure they were not watched then ripped off the right outside pocket of his blazer.

Surprised, Alvaro asked, "What are you doing?"

"Never mind. Let's get those cuffs off."

"What?" Alvaro asked, leaning against an adjacent car as Don removed the cuffs.

Don dropped the cuffs on the ground. "In the glovebox is a ticket and some cash." He pointed to the rent in the fence. "Drive this car through there then go to the Northway Church parking lot. Leave the car there. Take a bus to the rail station then take the airport train. You have just enough time to make the flight. When you get to Mexico, buy a cellphone and call me at the number I've written on your ticket folder."

"I can't believe this," Alvaro said, eyes wide. Can't they trace calls?"

"Yeah, but you'll be calling a phone that belonged to a convict. I sneaked it out of evidence lockup. Nobody's gonna trace it, because they won't know it's being used. Plus, it's decommissioned. I borrowed a SIM card and bought some prepaid time for it. It's safe—for now."

Alvaro shook his hands. "Okay. The cuffs are off—now what?"

"I want you to hit me on the top of my head—hard enough to create a bruise, and then I'll lie down and pretend to be unconscious until someone finds me."

"Damn, man. I don't like hitting ya—not on the head."

"Just do it, damn it. Do it! Then get the hell outta here!"

Don braced himself for the blow. Alvaro raised his joined fists and brought them down on Don's head. He winced.

"Damn! I didn't say hard." He then arranged himself on the ground as if he had fallen—arms and legs askew.

"Sorry," Alvaro said, kneeling beside Don. "You okay?"

"Yeah. Now get out of here."

Alvaro moved the traffic cones, drove through the fence opening, and then headed for the church.

Don had lain on the hot asphalt for what seemed to him a week, when a parking patron walked by and saw Don lying on the ground. He knelt beside Don and shook his shoulder. "Sir! Are you okay?"

Don remained still.

The stranger shook Don's shoulder harder. "Are you alright?"

Don pretended to awaken from a stupor. "What?" Don asked. "Where am I?"

"You're in Temple's parking lot. Are you okay?"

Don pushed himself semi-upright, leaned against a car, and then touched his scalp. "Ouch! What time is it?"

The man looked at his watch. "Three thirty."

"God. I've been here a long time." *Alvaro should be in the air by now.*

"I'll go for help—from the hospital."

Don rubbed his temples. "Yeah. Please." He wanted hospital documentation of his bruise to document his story of Alvaro's attack and escape.

Don sat on the ground while the stranger went for help.

Ten minutes later, a nurse and two orderlies, pushing a gurney with a wobbling wheel, rushed to Don's aid.

The nurse stooped and asked, "Does anything hurt?"

"My head," Don muttered. "Damn prisoner slammed my head against my door frame. He must have taken the cuff keys from my coat pocket. It's ripped off." Don glanced about. "The son-of-a-bitch has taken my patrol car too."

"You're a police office?" the nurse asked.

75

"Yeah, youth division." Don held his head and moaned.

"We'll call your station, but, first, we need to get you seen by a doctor."

The nurse placed a plastic brace around Don's neck. The orderlies lifted him onto the gurney then pushed it to the ER.

Don's nostrils were assaulted with the smell of alcohol and antiseptics as his gurney passed the triage area then entered an examination bay.

A short, dark haired doctor entered the bay and introduced himself as Doctor Lance. He asked a few questions about Don's injury and symptoms then recorded the information. The doctor examined Don's scalp, noting the size of the bruise. Don winced, when the doctor touched it. He made more notes then said, "We'd better x-ray your skull—rule out a fracture." He looked up from writing. "Need anything for your headache, and are you allergic to any medications?"

"Yes to the headache; no for allergies."

"Nurse," Doctor Lance called, "give this officer an Oxycodone before going to radiology."

Nurse Keene leaned into Don's space. "Are you allergic to any medications?"

"No. Nothing."

Moments later the nurse returned. "Take these. They may make you a little sleepy, but they'll ease your headache."

"Good. I haven't been sleeping much."

"Hold out your right arm please. I need to put this ID band on your wrist before you go to radiology."

Don returned to the ER and waited for his X-ray results. He continued to complain of a headache, wanting everyone to believe he had had a concussion.

Without warning, Don's police captain entered the curtained cubicle.

"Captain. What are you doing here?"

The captain looked concerned. "A nurse called to

report you had been injured. How are you?"

"Got a bitch of a headache, and my scalp is sore as hell."

"What happened?"

"Talk about gratitude. That Alvaro kid slammed my head against the car. Knocked me out. Looks like he found my cuff and car keys—stole my car."

"I'll put out an APB. We already have him in our system because of past arrests. Don't worry, we'll catch him and get our car back."

"Yeah, I love that car."

"Don't worry about the car. Nurse says you'll probably be sent home in an hour or so. Take a few days off—a week if you need it."

"Thanks, Captain."

"No problem. Call if you need anything. Stay well."

The captain pulled the curtain closed then left.

Don looked at his watch. *The kid's plane should be about ready to land.*

Doctor Lance entered. "Officer, I have good news. No fractures. We'll monitor your vital signs for a while. If all goes well, we'll let you go, but you should not drive for a few days. Let your concussion clear. If your headache persists for more than two days, or if you develop any worsening symptoms, contact your doctor right away." Doctor Lance extended his hand. "Here's a prescription for pain pills. You might need them."

The men shook hands. "Thanks, doc."

"Good luck Officer. Hope you get your car back."

Nurse Keene checked Don's blood pressure, pulse, and shined a light in his eyes, to check his pupils' reaction, every hour.

After two hours, she said, "Everything is stable. You're ready for discharge." Looking at his record, she asked, "Do you have a primary care physician to whom we can send your records?"

"Doctor Orlando on 12th Street, and would you please call central station for me? Tell whoever answers that I need a ride?"

"Certainly."

Minutes later, a uniformed policeman entered Don's cubicle. "Office Johns? I'm Jim Morris. I'm your ride. Ready to go?"

"You bet. Thanks for coming."

"No problem. I was cruising nearby."

Don signed discharge papers and sat down in a wheelchair ready to be pushed outside by an orderly.

Don feigned pain as he got inside the patrol car parked at the exit. He did not speak during the drive home but rested his head in his hands. *Hopefully, he's on a bus for Tijuana by now.*

Don finished a third beer and paced from room-to-room in his apartment, waiting for Alvaro's call. The slightest hint of a phone ring sent Don running for his "borrowed" cell. "Calm down," he mumbled over and over. "Stay calm." He looked at his watch. "He should be over the border by now."

Ninety minutes later, Don's borrowed cellphone rang. "Thank God!" He grabbed the phone. "Alvaro?"

"Yeah, boss. I'm in Tijuana. Had to wait in a hell-of-a-long line to cross the border. I got a quick search but no problems. Think they were looking for weapons. I crossed with a group of guys from Penn State. Tried to blend in."

"Glad you're safe. There's an APB out for you so stay clear of tourist spots. I don't want some American Joe seeing your picture on CNN and then see you sitting across from him in some popular watering hole and call border patrol or the FBI—worse yet CNN."

"Thought you said Mexico doesn't extradite."

"The Mexican government is cool, but that's not to say some bounty hunter might not try to get you state side for a reward."

"Shit. Hadn't thought of that. When are you coming down?"

"I'll be there tomorrow. I'll fly to San Diego and cross the border like you did. Now, find an out of the way hotel and call me when you have an address."

Don waited while his boarding pass, with a fake name, came off his home printer. Knowing his colleagues would search his apartment when they realized he had skipped town, he cleared his hard drive and then removed it and the printer's cartridge for ditching later.

He packed personal items then got the remaining $977,190.00 lottery winnings from under his mattress. "This should last a while," he said, fanning a stack of large denomination bills.

Don walked several blocks east of his apartment, stomped on the hard drive and printer cartridge then scattered the pieces in some bushes.

He hailed a taxi. "Airport," he said, pulling his ball cap low over his eyes. He said nothing as the driver made his way to Philadelphia's International Airport. *God, I hope this goes as planned. Can't afford to get caught.*

"Which airline?" the driver asked.

Don intended to fly United but said, "Air France."

He lied, in case police ever questioned taxi drivers about which departure area Don had requested. After making his way through security with a passport "borrowed" from Evidence Lock Up, he went to the food court and ordered lunch.

As someone prepared to page a passenger over the PA system, the pager must have dropped the microphone. A sharp thud echoed throughout the airport. Nerves on edge, Don jumped like a field and track contestant jumping hurtles. His elbow almost knocked a diner's drink from his hand.

"Sorry," Don said and took a deep breath. *Calm down, Don. Calm down.*

Don sat in aisle seat 12 C, reading. He often had to adjust his magazine because some unapologetic passenger struck his arm with luggage.

A well-dressed Latino stopped beside Don. "Excuse me, *señor*. I have seat A—by the window."

"No problem," Don said, letting the stranger push by.

Flight 418 took off with an empty seat between Don and the Latino. After a while, Don closed his magazine and asked the stranger if he wished to read it.

"Thanks," the strangers said, rubbing his sparse mustache.

Don passed the magazine, reclined his seatback, closed his eyes, then slouched. Mentally exhausted, he fell asleep.

Sensing something physical had happened, Don shook his head as he awoke. "What?"

The Latino shook Don's shoulder. "The captain turned on seatbelt sign. There is turbulence ahead. I see your belt not fastened."

"Thanks," Don said and buckled his belt. After a few moments of waiting for turbulence that failed to materialize, Don looked at the stranger. "You live in San Diego?"

"No," the man said, "just passing through. I live in Mexico. My aunt and a cousin are picking me up in San Diego."

"Small world," Don said, "I'm going to Mexico—Tijuana."

"That's where I'm going," the stranger said then smiled. "I live there. You on vacation?"

"Yeah. Vacation."

"Been to Mexico before?"

"Once—to Cancun—for a week."

"You'll find Tijuana different than Cancun," the man said. "It is *no* resort."

"That's kinda why I'm going there. I want something different."

"That it is. I'd be happy to show you around, if you'd

like."

"That's very nice of you."

The conversation paused for a moment. The stranger asked, "Would you like a ride to Tijuana? My Aunt Maria is meeting me."

"Uhhhh . . . that's a mighty kind offer. Uhhhh . . . What's your name?"

"Raoul," the stranger said, extending his hand.

Don shook Raoul's hand. "Nice to meet you, Raoul. I'm Don."

"Nice meet you, *Señor* Don. Where you from?"

"Lived in a few places," Don said. "Last was Chicago. I've been in Philadelphia visiting a friend."

"I visited a friend too," Raoul said, lowering his voice. "But he's in jail for being illegal."

The men passed time by discussing Tijuana, and Don's learning some useful Spanish phrases.

Outside the arrivals area, Raoul walked toward a woman Don knew had to be Raoul's aunt. She flashed a broad smile and a gold, front tooth. Dark skinned, she stood five feet tall and had long, straight black hair. Her red, tent-like dress, covered with white printed flowers failed to hide her pumpkin proportions.

She waved her hand over her head and called out, "Raoul." The two of them hugged then exchanged cheek kisses.

"Jose is driving around," Aunt Maria said. "He didn't want to pay to park, so we wait for him at stop for bus."

"Aunt Maria, this is Don," Raoul said. "We met on the plane. He's going to Tijuana."

"You're coming with us?" Maria asked, shaking Don's hand then holding it captive between her meaty, rough hands. She stared into his eyes. "What you worry about?" she asked. "What you run from?"

Don felt stunned. *Why is she asking that?*

"Don, I forgot to tell you Maria's a *bruja*—a witch,"

Raoul said. "Don't worry, she's a good witch. She can see things—the future. She's usually right."

"I'm always right," Maria said, looking at Don with squinted eyes.

"*Señor* Don, you be careful."

Seconds later, a 1960 well-cared-for canary-yellow Cadillac stopped and blew its horn.

"That is my cousin," Raoul said.

"Wow," Don said. "Haven't seen one of these cars in God knows how long. It's beautiful."

Raoul and Don placed their bags in the trunk then sat on the back-seat. Maria needed all the unused space on the front seat for herself.

Other drivers blew their horns at Jose for blocking traffic by stopping in the no pickup zone. Jose ignored the horns as Raoul introduced Don to the driver.

"Nice ride, Jose," Don said. "You've taken very good care of this car."

"Have to," Jose said. "Can't afford another one. Sorry, air conditioning isn't working, but I drive fast. We'll get lots of air—God's air conditioning. But hey man, I got a shaking sound system. Want to hear it—"

"No!" Maria said. "My ears still ring from the racket you played on the way here."

"Don and me met on the plane," Raoul informed Jose. "He's going to Tijuana on vacation. Thought we'd give him a ride."

"Sure," Jose said then laughed. "A dry-back."

"Dry-back? What's that?" Don asked.

"You know 'wet-back?'" Jose asked. "Well, a 'dry-back' is a wet-back who slips back to Mexico over land."

Maria slapped Jose on the arm. "Shame. That's not nice."

Small talk flowed like tequila between the Mexicans who conversed in Spanish.

"Sorry, *Señor* Don," Raoul said, "we talk about a

cousin who is getting married Sabado—sorry, Saturday."

"Poor guy," Don chuckled.

The day's heat waned, and cooler air flowed through the windows.

"What happens at the border?" Don asked.

"Sometimes nothing," Jose said, "sometimes everybody gets searched. Hope you no carrying guns or marijuana."

"Not this trip," Don said then smiled.

"Good, because the border's just ahead, and traffic is already backed up—bad."

The twelve southbound lanes of border-crossing traffic crept along. As the sun set, drivers turned on their headlights. Jose's rearview mirror reflected a car's high beams in Don's eyes. He squirmed and twiddled his fingers. *God, I hope I don't get searched.* He didn't want to declare his cash or have the guards find it and confiscate it.

"You okay, *Señor* Don?" Jose asked, apparently seeing worry on Don's face reflected in the rearview mirror.

"Yeah. Just tired. It's been a long day."

After ninety minutes of waiting, Jose's car reached an immigration officer's booth. The officer's name badge read Gonzales.

The officer looked at the Mexican license plate on the Cadillac. "Everyone a Mexican citizen?"

"*Si*," Jose replied, "except for *Señor* Don—he's an Americano."

Officer Gonzales stared at Don. "Where're you from?"

"Philadelphia," Don said.

"Got identification?"

"Driver's license?" *Better not show the passport.*

"Pass it over, sir."

Don handed his license to the officer. He stared at it then Don. "When was this photo taken?"

"Same day I got the license, Officer. I don't remember the exact date, but it's on there."

"What's the purpose of your visit?"

"Vacationing. Two weeks."

"Got any alcohol, cigarettes, or plants?"

"No, Officer. Nothing."

Officer Gonzales stepped out of his booth. He carried a long-handled mirror that he slid on the ground, inspecting the car's undercarriage. Finished, he placed the mirror in his booth and yelled, "Driver, open your trunk, please."

Jose pulled the trunk release.

Out of the rear window, Don had a partial view of the officer looking around the trunk's interior. The officer removed the luggage then lifted the covering of the trunk's floor. Don held his breath. *Oh God, don't open my luggage.* Thud-like sounds suggested the officer had banged on the spare tire and trunk walls then closed the trunk.

"He's searching for drugs," Jose whispered.

The officer walked to Jose's window. "The rest of you have ID?"

The Mexicans handed over their identification cards.

The officer compared photos to each traveler then returned all the cards. "Move on. Have a nice trip. Don, enjoy your vacation."

"Thanks, I will." *Thank God, he didn't search me or my bag. What if he found my cash? Don't want to think about that.*

The car entered Mexico, passing street vendors selling fruit, bottled water, car insurance, cigarettes, and cheap tequila. Farther on, the pace of traffic and level of city noise increased.

Don's phone rang. "Who the hell's that?" Don opened his cell phone and said, "Hello . . . Okay. See you soon." Don tapped Jose on the shoulder. "Are you going near the center of Tijuana?"

"Kinda," Jose said. "Where you want to go, *señor*?"

"Hotel Castello, at Parque Garcia."

"I know this park," Jose said. "I take you there."

"Thanks, I'd appreciate it." Don sniffed the air. "What is that smell?"

84

"Good, no?" Jose chuckled. "That's perfume from dump."

Jose made his way through congested traffic then slowed at the east corner of Parque Garcia. Colorful flowering plants flooded the area with a symphony of fragrances. Pulling to the curb, Jose pointed across the park. "There is hotel—in middle of block."

"Jose, may I give you some American dollars for my ride?"

"No, *gracious, señor*. Bringing you to our city is my honor."

"*Señor* Don, if you're staying long, I'd be happy to show you around," Raoul said. "There are many things to see and do other than drink Margaritas. Handing Don a piece of paper, he said, "Call this number, if I can help."

"Thanks. Might take ya up on that." Don handed Raoul a paper. "For now, take these phone numbers. One is mine and the other belongs to my local friend. Let's stay in touch."

"We will," Jose and Raoul said.

"Be *very* careful," Aunt Maria said.

Jose pulled the trunk release, so Don could get his bag.

"Thanks for the lift," Don said, closing the trunk then waving goodbye as Jose pulled into traffic.

Don looked across the park and mumbled, "Well, old guy. This is the start of the rest of your life. Embrace it."

Don dodged an army of vendors, hawking alleged Panama straw hats and Cuban cigars as he crossed the park, heading for Alvaro's hotel.

|

Chapter 7

Don entered the cool, dark hotel lobby. Heavy wooden furniture and exposed broad ceiling beams defined the colonial themed décor. He walked past the desk clerk like a registered guest then climbed the squeaky wooden stairs to the second floor. He made his way down a long corridor to room 207, took a deep breath, and then knocked on the door. *Hurry up kid.*

"Who is it?"

"Don."

The door opened two inches, and Alvaro peeked over the chain guard. "Don!" Alvaro unchained the door.

Don stepped inside and bear-hugged his briefs-wearing lover with such vigor Alvaro had difficulty breathing. The men then kissed with the passion of lovers separated for weeks.

"Were you undressing for me or are you just hot?" Don asked.

Alvaro wiped his brow. "Both, but mostly 'cause of the heat."

Don placed his bag on a chair. "Yeah. It's hot in here."

"The AC is out. Somebody's supposed to fix it, but so far they haven't." Alvaro stopped hand-fanning himself. "Man, am I glad to see you! I've missed you something awful."

Heart racing, Don hugged Alvaro. "I've missed you too. How've you been?"

"Okay but a little frightened. My picture's been on CNN."

"You had to expect that. They'll probably run it for another day or so, and then you'll be old news. No doubt, mine will be on in a day or so, and then I'll be old hat."

Don looked around the room outfitted with cheap furniture and bad examples of amateur Mexican painters. "Got anything to drink?"

"Tequila. Want a Margarita?"

"Hell yes! Stir 'em up while I get undressed?" Don stared at

Alvaro. "What's with those undies? Take 'em off."

Alvaro grinned, stepped out of his underwear, and then mixed Margaritas.

Don undressed and hung his clothes on the last two plastic coat hangers in the door-less closet. He crept up behind Alvaro and hugged his waist.

"My god, you're hard," Alvaro said, grinding his ass against Don's crotch.

"I've missed that ass," Don said, "but I also missed your crotch." He gripped Alvaro's cock and kissed his neck. "You're hard too."

"Of course," Alvaro said. "Just waiting to play hide-the-sausage."

Tightening his grip on Alvaro's waist, Don said, "Careful. You're in no position to talk about hiding anything."

Alvaro turned and held up a sweating glass. "Take your drink, before the ice melts."

Don dropped to his knees and swallowed Alvaro's cock.

"Guess you aren't interested in drinking," Alvaro said, closing his eyes and dropping his head backward.

Taking a breath, Don said, "Careful with the drinks. Don't spill 'em."

Don swallowed Alvaro's cock and stimulated it with his special swallowing technique. Sensing Alvaro's growing urge to climax, Don stood, hugged, and then kissed him.

"Didn't want you cuming with drinks in your hand," Don said. "Don't much care for Margaritas down my back."

Alvaro placed the drinks on the dresser then fell to his knees like a supplicant paying homage to Priapus. His tongue worked its magic on Don's cock head, the shaft, and then his balls, which Alvaro sucked, one-by-one, into his mouth.

Don moaned. "Grip them with your lips and pull."

Alvaro tugged at the captured balls and stroked Don's cock.

"God, I've missed that. Keep it up, kid."

Alvaro continued stroking Don's cock while moving his other hand to Don's butt and fingered his ass.

"Not now," Don said. "I want your cock—but later. Just keep stroking me."

An unexpected knock on the door startled the guys. Without warning, the door opened and in walked a tall, light-skinned Latino, late twenties, carrying a wooden toolbox.

"Oh! *Perdon!*" The man said, blushing and staring at Don's erection. "I no know people in room."

"That's okay," Don said. "I hope you're here to fix the AC?"

"*Si, señor*, for the AC. Sorry!"

Don looked at Alvaro and shrugged. "No need to worry now. He's already seen us."

Alvaro blushed, pulled on his underwear, and then glanced at the ceiling. "Whatever."

Don noted the name Jorge embroidered over the front pocket of the repairman's jumpsuit, unbuttoned to the waist. *He's showing a lot of muscular cleavage for a Mexican.*

Naked, Don sat down on the bed and pointed to the window. "That's the AC, Jorge. It's broken." *God, I'd like to fix you.*

Jorge pushed the sun-faded drapes from in front of the rusted control panel, removed its cover, and then probed inside. In minutes, he sweated as he looked at the slow-moving ceiling fan.

"It doesn't do much," Alvaro said, "There's something wrong with its controller."

Jorge went to a wall switch then turned a knob, but the fan remained on low speed. Using his sleeve to wipe sweat from his brow, he said, "Sorry for fan."

He returned to the AC then probed its guts. "*Hace mucho calor*. Sorry. I speak in Spanish. I mean to say it very hot here."

"Yeah, we know, Don said. "That's why your here.

You can drop the top of your jumpsuit if you want to cool off." *Please. I'd like a better view.*

"*Permiso?*" Jorge asked.

"*Si,*" Don said. "Permission granted."

Alvaro glared at Don and mouthed, 'What are you doing?'

Don mouthed back, 'He could be fun.'

Jorge wiped his forehead then pulled his arms from his jumpsuit, letting its upper-half hang from his waist. The jumpsuit had hidden softball-sized biceps and a muscular, hairless chest where sweat traversed beefy pecs.

God! Don thought. *What a chest.*

Jorge sat cross legged on the floor and probed the guts of the AC. After a few minutes, he held up several multicolored wires. "*La problema.*"

Don moved closer to inspect the wires. His crotch met Jorge's head. Jorge pulled several wires into view so Don, sporting a semi-hard cock, could see the offending strands.

Jorge looked up, past Don's cock, then into his eyes. Jorge smiled then said, "See?"

"I see," Don said, staring at Jorge's glistening chest. "It is okay, no?"

"*Si, Señor. Muy* okay!"

Jorge grabbed Don's cock. Don grasped Jorge's head, pulled it to his crotch, and held it there. Jorge managed to pull his head back a bit then serviced Don's growing erection. Jorge's attention continued until Don withdrew his cock and slapped it against Jorge's face. He seemed to welcome the sting of the cock on his cheeks. He opened his mouth in an effort to capture the weapon but had to wait until Don decided to grant the repairman's wish then thrust his cock down Jorge's throat.

Not wanting to be left out of the action, Alvaro shed his shorts, rubbed his cock over Don's butt cheeks, and then teased his hole. Alvaro reached for KY and anointed the waiting ass. Taking some time, he pushed his way inside. Don

90

tensed for a second then returned to enjoying Jorge's talented mouth. Alvaro reached around Don's waist and grasped Jorge's head, pulling it and Don's butt closer to his thrusting hips.

Jorge managed to push his zipper farther down, freeing his cock, which he stroked in sync with his attention to Don's cock. Jorge's tempo increased as he sensed Don's impending climax.

Alvaro shot his load.

Seconds later, Don climaxed as did Jorge.

Don moaned and then yelled, "Oh . . . Godddddd !"

Despite a mouthful of hard flesh, Jorge moaned a l oud, "Ahh."

The three men remained united for a moment. Jorge swallowed hard then stood. His jumpsuit fell to his ankles. He pulled it up, pausing midway as his zipper reached the level of his balls. He let everything hang outside like a spent trophy, while he reinserted his arms in the sleeves.

Uncoupled, Alvaro clung to Don's back and forced his knees locked as he recovered. "I'm goin' to shower."

"Fine," Don said, placing his hands on his knees and staring at Jorge's exposed crotch. "I'll be in right after you."

"Sorry for the mess, *señor*," Jorge said, searching in his toolbox. He pulled out a rag, wiped his load from the floor, and then stuffed his cock and balls inside his jumpsuit. He zipped the suit to chest level and smiled.

Exhausted, Don slumped onto the bed.

Jorge returned to the AC, and after a few seconds, it hummed. "Now you have room *frio, señor*."

"Thanks," Don said. "Too bad it didn't work during sex. I'm drowning in sweat."

"Me also, *señor*.

"You're welcome to shower," Don said, pointing to the bathroom

"Thanks. I would like that."

Alvaro exited the bathroom, drying his back as

Jorge removed his sandals and jumpsuit. He wore no underwear.

"Jorge, wait a minute," Don said. "Turn around."

With a look of puzzlement, Jorge faced Don.

Don scanned Jorge's body. "Damn, man. For a Mexican, you've got quite a set of nuts and a hell of a cock. Nice bod too."

Jorge smiled. "Thank you, *señor*. I am glad you like me."

Alvaro grasped Jorge's nuts and bounced them in his hand. "Those suckers are big. Heavy too."

Don took the repairman's cock in his hand, squeezed it, then fondled his balls. "Glad I met them. Maybe we'll meet again."

"*Si*," Jorge said then smiled.

"What say we shower, Jorge?" Don said, "You can do my back. Okay?"

Jorge blushed. "*Si, señor*. I wash it."

Don adjusted the shower water flow then held a bar of soap toward Jorge, but it slipped from his hand. Jorge smiled a shy, toothy smile then bent over to retrieve it. As he did, he backed his ass onto Don's crotch.

"Wish I could, good buddy, but I can't. Not now, maybe later."

"*Si*, later."

The guys lathered up with lots of suds and played with the other's cock and balls.

"Time to dry off," Don said, stepping from the shower. *Now, that's what I call a service man.*

Each man dried off then walked into the bedroom where Alvaro sprawled naked, on the bed.

"Jorge," Alvaro chuckled, "thanks for fixing the AC— and Don,"

"Yeah, Jorge," Don said, "thanks for fixing me."
And again later I hope.

Jorge dressed under the lustful gaze of his hosts then gathered his toolbox. "Bye."

"See you later," Don said, closing the door.

After a simple dinner in a *cocina economica*, Alvaro and Don returned to the hotel, stripped, lay on the bed and enjoyed the repaired air conditioner.

"What's bothering you?' Don asked.

"You surprised and hurt me a little when you said you wanted to have sex with Jorge."

"Hell, I didn't think you'd mind a threesome. In fact, I thought you'd like it."

"Technically speaking, *I* didn't have a threesome. You did."

"What are you talking about?"

"You were 'lucky Pierre,' not me."

"Are you saying you want to be in the middle next time?"

"No. It's just that I thought *I* was special—not just somebody for a threesome."

Don sat up, stared at Alvaro, and then gripped his arm. "You are special. *Very* special. If you don't like threesomes, we won't have any."

"Good, because I don't like sharing you."

"Okay. Enough said."

The two kissed, assumed the "spoon" position, and then fell asleep.

Don's cell phone rang, awakening both men.

"I'm not answering that," Don said. "You and I are the only ones who know that phone is operative. Somebody knows it's missing and they're trying to track its location, but . . . on the other hand who would know its new number? Hmmm."

"Does that mean your police friends are on to you?"

"Maybe. Turn on the TV—CNN."

Don and Alvaro stared at the TV as the day's news rolled by. Minutes later, Don's picture appeared on the screen. An announcer said, "This policeman is suspected in abetting the escape of a gang member implicated in the murder of a

Philadelphia gang member. The victim allegedly vandalized one of Philadelphia's outdoor murals painted by the escaped gang member. If you see this man, contact local police. He may be armed and dangerous."

"Well, it happened," Don said. "I'm now a suspect. That phone call might have been my old security chief. He's in charge of evidence protection. I don't know how, but he might be checking on his missing phone. Hope they haven't missed the passport I took." Don turned off the TV. "We gotta be very careful for a few days."

"Whatta ya mean?" Alvaro asked, pouring Margaritas.

"First, I need a new cell phone. A prepaid one like yours—a local one. That way there's no way of identifying me. Shit! I gave Raoul the number of my stolen phone. I hope that wasn't him calling, but I can't risk calling him. When I get the new phone, I'll call and give him my local number, but for the time being, we need to do room service. Three meals a day."

"How long?" Alvaro asked, handing Don his drink.

"Three days . . . at least three."

Alvaro extended his arms by his side, corpse like. "We'll be found dead from all the sex we'll have for those three days."

Four days had passed since CNN broadcasted Don's photo. He and Alvaro were suffering from cabin fever.

Finishing his morning coffee, Don flipped through a local newspaper. "Oh my god! Jesus Gonzales, that famous Mexican soccer player, is will play the Dominican Republic team in Mexico City in two days. We have to go."

"Great!" Alvaro said, rubbing Don's thigh. "I love soccer—especially the player's legs—chunky one. That's one of the reasons I like you—chunky legs." Alvaro sipped his coffee then said, "Gonzales is supposed to be gay. Man, what I wouldn't give to have his legs wrapped around me."

"I thought you were an ass man. Besides, no more threesomes. Remember?"

94

"But can't I have a twosome?" Alvaro chuckled. "By the way, I like legs *and* ass, but I can't fuck a leg."

Don phoned AeroMexico for flight reservations to Mexico City. "Glad I brought this gay guide," he said, tossing the book to Alvaro. "Search it while I'm on the phone. Find a gay hotel or B&B."

After searching the guide, Alvaro said, "There are lots of places."

"Find one in, or close, to the gay area. There's a map on the back cover."

As Don finished jotting down flight information, Alvaro said, "I found a hotel." He showed Don the hotel ad and photos.

"Looks like a nice place," Don said, phoning the hotel. After he secured reservations, he asked the clerk, "Do you know anyone who could get me two tickets for the big soccer match?"

The receptionists replied in an effeminate voice, "*Si, Seño.,* Jesus Gonzales is my cousin."

"Your cousin?"

"*Si.* My cousin. He'll get tickets for you—I think. He has one for me; I'll ask for more."

"I'll pay well," Don said. "Please see what you can do."

Don felt apprehensive about going through airport security, so he and Alvaro wore sunglasses and baseball caps, hoping the fashion items would prevent their being identified. Don's heart pounded as the security guard glanced at his stolen passport. Alvaro held out his passport, but the guard ignored it and waved him through.

From Mexico City's airport, the guys took a cab to the gay hotel. They were surprised to see the lobby filled with female mannequins dressed in outlandish drag.

A young, thin effeminate receptionist eyed Alvaro and

Don from head to sandal. His blond hair had black roots in need of bleach. He wore a frilly white blouse, a tight grey skirt, and a name tag reading Juan.

Don signed the guest book, using the name on his stolen passport. "Into drag?" he asked, noting Juan wore red sequenced high heels.

"You like my shoes?" Juan asked. "My group does two shows a week."

"Maybe we'll get to see one."

"I get you front row seat, baby. Let me know when you want to go."

"Any word about our soccer tickets?"

"I asked my cousin. I should hear from him soon. I'll call you when I do."

"Is your cousin gay?" Alvaro asked, flashing a wishful smile.

"*Si.* Everyone knows."

"So I've heard, but I wanted to know for sure."

"Accep' my word—he's gay, and you are his type," Juan said and winked.

"I'm keeping my eye on you," Don said, shaking his finger at Alvaro. "Let's go to the room and unpack."

An hour later, Juan called. "*Señor* Don. I have you two tickets. I'll meet my cousin before the game. Would you like join me?"

"And meet Jesus Gonzales?" Don asked as his gut turned with anticipation.

"*Si, señor*. Meet Jesus."

"You bet." *I can't imagine this is happening to me.*

"No, *señor*. We don't gamble."

Don chuckled. "No. I meant we want to meet Jesus. We'll see you tomorrow. Will you be wearing heels?"

"I'd like to, but Jesus kill me if I wear heels to dressing room."

Chapter 8

Don, Alvaro, and Juan met in the shabby-chic lobby be-fore leaving for the arena.

"You're not wearing heels." Don said, eyeing Juan's shoes.

"No but look." Juan unbuttoned his shirt to reveal a black peekaboo-lace bra.

Don laughed. "That's one way of making a point even if it's hidden."

"I don't know what you mean, but you like it, no?" Juan asked.

"It's cool. No, you're cool," Alvaro said, "and I like your perfume. It smells like Jasmine."

"You like it, no?"

"Uh . . . yes . . ." *No, I don't!*

"Thank you."

After donning his large-frame sunglasses, Don and Alvaro lowered their red ball cap over their face as Juan hailed a cab.

At the Azteca Arena gate marked *JUGADOROS*, Juan pursed his lips, blew a kiss to a security guard, and then waved his special tickets. The guard frowned. He opened the gate then directed the men to the Mexican team's dressing room.

Traversing the basement corridors of the arena, Don heard the capacity crowd shouting its praises for the Mexican team. Their roar would have shamed a fighter jet's engine.

At the dressing room door, Juan flashed his tickets to a guard then entered a room filled with boisterous banter.

Never thought I'd be in a place like this, Don thought.

"Where is Jesus Gonzales?" Juan asked a guard inside the door.

"Down the hall, turn left," the guard said, giggling as he stared at Juan, swishing away in tight Capri pants.

Don followed Juan as he made his way through a dressing room filled with raucous laughter, the smell of rubbing alcohol and Absorbine Jr.

Juan found his cousin among the players, most wearing nothing more than underwear or towels. He introduced Don and Alvaro as friends staying in his hotel.

"Welcome to Mexico," Jesus said, pulling his satin shorts over his bulging jockstrap then reaching for a shirt. His hard, well-worked torso muscles rippled as he tugged at the jersey.

For the few seconds that the shirt covered Jesus' head, Don admired the jock's rock-hard body. *What a specimen*.

"You're taller than I expected," Alvaro said, eyeing Jesus' frame.

"For a Latino-looking guy, you're kinda tall yourself," Jesus said, smoothing his long, black hair and staring into Alvaro's eyes.

"Most of me is European," Alvaro said then smiled. "Only the big part is Latino."

Jesus smiled then sat down on a bench to pull on his socks. "Hope it's the important part."

"Well, I'm all American," Don said.

"Glad you guys could come." Jesus slapped Alvaro on the back. "Mexico needs tourists' dollars."

Don watched Jesus' hand slid down Alvaro's back Then stop on his butt. Alvaro tensed his glutes and smiled. Jesus smiled then slapped the butt.

"Shit," Don murmured. "The kid liked that too much."

"Sorry guys, but I gotta go," Jesus said, looking first at Alvaro and then his gay cousin. "Want to meet after the game? Have a beer or two?"

"Bueno," Juan said, glancing at each guest. "You guys want to come?"

"You bet and thanks for inviting us," Don said. "See you after your win."

"Yeah! Me too," Alvaro said, flashing a pearly smile. "Good luck!"

"Yeah. Good luck," Don said, slapping Jesus on the

shoulder. "Win for Mexico."

Several members of the press were finishing postgame interviews with the towel-clad goal-winning Jesus and the goalkeeper. With his back against a wall, Don waited for the press to leave and watched several naked players mill about.

Jesus finished his interview then spied his guests. He walked to Alvaro, retied his towel, and looked him in the eye. "My last goal was for you."

This guy really piles it on, Don thought. "Great header."

Alvaro blushed. "Exciting. Fastest game I've ever seen. You must have a headache from heading so many balls."

"Head's fine." Jesus looked at Don. "Did you like the game?"

"I did, and I enjoyed your playing." *God. Did I say that. I'm not falling for his shit?*

"Glad you liked it. Glad we won—it means extra pesos in my pocket." Jesus slapped Alvaro on the back. "Some of the guys are going for a beer and maybe a few Margaritas. Want to tag along?"

"We'd love to come," Don said. *Gotta keep an eye on Alvaro.*

Alvaro smiled. "Of course."

"Meet me at Juanita's," Jesus said to Juan. "You know the place. Sorry, but I have to go. Team members must leave the arena on the team bus. It's a security thing. See you guys at Juanita's."

A large space, Juanita's Bar had a homey feel. The décor consisted of red, white, and green everything. Sports banners, photos of Mexican soccer players, and matadors were every-where. Strings of dried red chili peppers covered the walls.

Don had just been served a Margarita when Jesus and several of his teammates entered to a standing ovation. Many patrons scampered for autographs and photographs. Almost ignoring their fans, the players relented, and Jesus, wearing tight, crotch-revealing pants, made his way to Don's table.

"Hello guys. Alvaro," Jesus said. "Glad you could make it."

Juan whispered to Don, "My cousin dresses like a matador. See his crotch."

"Looks good to me," Don said. "I'm into balls—especially soccer players' balls."

"Alvaro, what are you drinking?" Jesus asked.

"Margaritas," Alvaro said, holding up his glass. "We ordered one for you."

"*Muchas gracias*. I love them."

Don pulled out a chair for the soccer hero. "Have a seat, Jesus."

"Thanks," Jesus said, taking a seat beside Alvaro. "Mind if I sit here?"

"Okay," Don said under his breath. *This guy has targeted Alvaro for conquest. Worse yet, Alvaro seems star-struck.*

"Uh, yeah. The seat is yours," Alvaro said, nodding. "Please."

Jesus leaned back in his chair. "Man, am I tired." He placed his outstretched right arm over the back of Alvaro's chair.

I can't believe he is so brazen, Don thought, *and Alvaro doesn't think I mind.*

Jesus let his legs spread. His right thigh fell against Alvaro's left leg. He pressed his leg against Jesus who returned the action.

Gut churning, Don glared at Alvaro then asked Jesus, "How long will you be in town?" *Hope you're leaving soon!*

Jesus slapped Juan on the back and said, "A few days to visit my cousin. Juan hasn't said how long he can put me up, but I hope to be there for three . . . maybe four days."

"That's great," Alvaro said.

Conversations were focused on soccer, but most were

100

Ping-ponged between Jesus and Alvaro.

Don wondered if Alvaro knew why Jesus had flattered him.

Condensation from Jesus' glass dripped on Alvaro's trousers. Jesus grabbed his napkin and blotted the damp spot. Alvaro tensed his thigh muscles and raised his thigh against Jesus' hand.

I saw that, Don said to himself.

"Thanks," Alvaro said then smiled.

Don nudged Alvaro as if to say 'stop.'

After several Margaritas, and feeling no pain, Don decided Alvaro and he should leave. "Guys. It's time for us to leave."

Jesus slapped his cousin on the back. "I have to get some things from my hotel, but I'll be at yours in an hour."

Don whispered to Alvaro, "Remember, no three-somes."

Back at his hotel, Don closed the door to his room then yelled at Alvaro. "What the hell's going on with Jesus? I thought we agreed—no threesomes."

"Calm down. I had a little fun, nothing more."

"You expect me to believe *nothing* happened between you and that . . . that man? You rubbed his leg, and he rubbed your ass, and all the time you smiled."

"I can't help it if he finds my ass attractive. You do and I don't get angry at you."

"That's different. I love you. I want to be with you— not some other guy—just you! Why do you think I left America, and why am I bank rolling our stay here?"

"Is that it, Don? You think you bought me?"

Alvaro stiffened his arms to his sides and wadded his fists. "You think you own me?"

"I probably could, if I wanted to, but I don't. I'm shar-ing my life, my exile, and my money with you, because I care for you—I love you, damn it."

"Well, you're acting awfully jealous for a man in love."

Don grabbed Alvaro's arm. "Don't roll your eyes at me, smarty pants."

Alvaro sighed. "I'm sorry but give me some space for God's sake. You've been around—a lot. I'm young, still learning, but you're teaching me to be jealous, and I don't like that."

Don puffed his cheeks and exhaled a long, slow sigh. "I'm gonna take a walk, before I say something I'll regret."

Exasperated, Alvaro stripped, jumped onto the bed, and then watched a recording of the game he had just seen at the arena. He focused on Jesus' legs. *He's hot.*

Alvaro's phone rang. "Hello," he said, expecting to hear Don.

"Alvaro?" This is Jesus. Just checked in. Wondered what you were up to."

"Nothin much, why?"

"Mind if I drop by?"

"Uh, I don't know. Don isn't here."

"Just for a minute?"

"Okay. You know my room number since you called it. Come up or down from where ever you are."

Alvaro pulled on his underwear then continued to watch the recorded game while he waited.

Hearing a knock on the door, Alvaro asked, "Whose there?"

"Jesus."

Alvaro opened the door, TV remote in hand.

"Nice to see you," Jesus said, scanning Alvaro's body. "Where's Don?"

"He's somewhere cooling off." Alvaro pushed the remote's pause button. "We had an argument."

"So . . . why are you in your underwear?" Jesus asked, placing his palms on Alvaro's chest then letting them slide to

102

his abdomen. "From what I can see, you should never wear clothes."

"You're not shy are you?"

Alvaro pushed Jesus' hands away and folded his arms across his chest.

"Being shy gets one nowhere," Jesus said then smiled. "I see you're watching a tape of today's game."

"Yeah. Get ta see things from a different angle than at the stadium. Replays are great."

"Why pause on the frame of me kicking a scoring ball?"

"Simple. I let you in and pushed pause." Alvaro shifted his weight and cleared his throat. "Okay . . . I admire your legs. You got some powerful legs, man. No wonder you're such a great kicker."

"Into legs are you? I'd be happy to let you see them—up close."

Jesus started to roll up a too-tight pant leg. "This isn't going to work. Better take them off." In a flash, Jesus stepped out of his loafers and removed his pants.

Alvaro held his breath when he saw Jesus wore no underwear. *Never thought I'd be this close to something that big.*

Jesus placed his pants over a chair. The bottom edge of his polo shirt just covered his crotch. He flexed his left leg muscles for Alvaro's inspection then pointed to some peculiar characteristics of the left leg then his right leg.

Alvaro could not take his eyes off Jesus' cock as he showed off his legs. "Those legs are hot, but man, you're one hung dude."

"So I've heard." Jesus lifted his shirt to reveal the family jewels in toto. "Had them all my life. We're inseparable."

Alvaro reached for the low hanging nuts. "I've never seen such nuts."

Jesus spread his legs for Alvaro's better appreciation

103

of his balls. "You like nuts, eh? Have at 'em. They like attention."

Alvaro manipulated the hairy globes as Jesus' cock stiffened. Alvaro released them then pulled Jesus' polo shirt over his head. Naked, Jesus teased Alvaro by flexing his hairless pecs. Alvaro ran his hands over the smooth, beckoning chest and six-pack. Jesus extended his right foot to the waistband of Alvaro's underwear. There, his talented toes maneuvered their way behind the elastic band then pushed the briefs to the floor.

Alvaro offered no resistance. He stepped out of his underwear then kicked them onto a chair. *Now what?*

Jesus pulled Alvaro close, allowing the kid's right hand access to his balls while Alvaro's left hand stroked Jesus' cock. Jesus moaned then stroked Alvaro's cock.

Alvaro tongued Jesus' nipples and cleavage.

Jesus grabbed Alvaro's butt, and pulled him against his own hard body. "Nice ass," Jesus whispered.

"Thanks, but it's not as hard as yours."

"Yours is just the way I like 'em—not too hard, not too soft. Let's have a look."

Jesus turned Alvaro's butt into view then patted it. "Nice. Real . . . nice."

Alvaro flexed both butt cheeks then flexed each solo. *Hope you fuck it.*

"Nice," Jesus mumbled and squeezed each cheek. "Now that's talent."

Jesus pulled Alvaro's butt against his crotch. The jock's gyrating hips, cock, and pubic hair ground against the young butt. Jesus stroked Alvaro's cock. With his left hand, he tweaked Alvaro's left nipple. Moments later, he rubbed his cockhead against Alvaro's hole then found its way inside.

Alvaro pulled away. "We shouldn't. Not here. Not now."

Jesus whispered in Alvaro's ear. "You know you want it, and you want it now. I know you do. Got a rubber?"

104

"Uhh . . . yeah, but we shouldn't."

"Get the rubber. I'll let you put it on me."

"God, I want to, but Don could come back any minute."

Jesus backed away. Sounding put off, he said, "Well, I might as well get dressed and get out of your way."

"You can't just . . . I want you to fuck me, but . . . okay. But we have to be fast."

Alvaro searched his travel bag for a condom. He returned wearing a smile, and a more erect cock. He tore foil from the condom and said, "It's lubricated." *You gotta fuck me!*

Jesus held his tool, so the rubber could be rolled onto the rock-hard cock then pulled Alvaro to the bed. "Bend over," he said, pushing on Alvaro's shoulders.

Alvaro thrust his butt in the air. *Can't believe I'm gonna get fucked by this guy.*

Jesus teased the kid's hole then made his way into Alvaro's expectations. The to-and-fro action began at a slow pace then sped up. Jesus slapped the begging butt, producing moans of pleasure from the gaping mouth of a young man lost in ecstasy.

After two minutes, Alvaro sensed Jesus was on the verge of exploding and tightened his ass.

Jesus' panting morphed into moans as his sweat fell on Alvaro's back. The jock sped toward a climax and with a self-muffled yell, released his load to Alvaro's rejoicing as he jerked off.

Suddenly, the door opened. "What the hell?" Don yelled. "Son-of-a-bitch! I turn my back for a minute and you're two-timing me with that damn ball player! Damn you, Alvaro!"

Jesus decoupled then stood at the side of the bed, staring at Don. "Wish I knew you were coming back."

"I bet you do, you son-of-a-bitch. I oughta kill you," Don yelled. "No, I oughta kill both of you. Alvaro, you're a damn betrayer!"

"For god's sake, Don. Calm down. We're just having

105

sex. This is *not* some secret love affair. It's sex—just sex."

"You think you can love me and have sex with other people—this damn ball player? Think it won't affect our relationship? Then you're crazy!" Don stared at Alvaro with a glare short of a death ray. "Kid, you're on your own. I'm out of here."

"You're the crazy one," Alvaro said. "Sit down and listen for a minute."

"There's nothing to talk about. Your ass said it all."

Alvaro sat down on the edge of the bed, dropped his head in his hands and cried as Don gathered his belongings then threw them into his suitcase.

Jesus removed his condom, sat down beside Alvaro, and hugged him. "Mind if I shower."

Don threw the last of his things in his bag. Glancing around the room, he saw an unopened condom. He picked it up, stared at it, and then threw it at Alvaro. "Take it, you son-of-a-bitch. You can use it after I'm gone."

Don fled the room, slamming the door.

"Now what am I goin' to do?" Alvaro asked between sobs.

"Don't worry," Jesus said, returning to Alvaro's side. "We'll think of something."

Alvaro continued to cry. He jabbed a pillow and yell-ed, "Why am I such a damn fool? Why do I do this shit?"

"Don't be so hard on yourself," Jesus said, squeezing Alvaro's hand.

"In my own stupid way, I love Don. I've gotta find him and apologize."

"He's too upset to listen. Let's shower then have a drink. I'll help you plan a strategy."

Alvaro showered, dressed, and then picked up his phone.

He had an unsettling thought. "Don won't stay in Mexico City. He'll go back to Tijuana. I'd better call him."

"You think so?"

"Yeah." Alvaro took out his phone, searched for Don's number then realized he had a problem.

Jesus stared at Alvaro. "You look awful. What's wrong?"

"Don and I have the same kind of cell phone. He took mine and left his. Shit! My phone has numbers that I don't have anywhere else."

"That's not a bad thing," Jesus said. "You now have a legitimate excuse to call him—to get your phone back. Go ahead, call him. I mean call *your* phone."

"Maybe I should let him cool off a day or so. He'll soon realize he has my phone. Maybe *he'll* call me."

Like a rat fleeing fire, Don raged along the hotel's hallway. His suitcase often swung against the wall as he muttered, "Son-of-a-bitching kid. Who does he think he is? Irreplaceable?" *Thinks he can trash my affection like that? Why the hell did I get involved with him?* Don ran his hand over his head then struck a wall. "Fuck him!"

At the front desk, Don paid his bill.

"Any forwarding address?" Juan inquired.

"How the hell do I know!"

"Will *Señor* Alvaro continue his stay with us?"

"Fuck. Ask him."

Don stormed out of the hotel, just avoiding being struck by several cars as he crossed the street. He walked to a nearby park and sat down on a rickety bench. Lost in thought, he stared at traffic.

An elderly street vendor approached him. "Cuban cigars, *señor*?"

"Get the fuck away from me!"

The old man muttered something in Spanish and left.

What am I going to do. Explore other parts of the gay area? Check into another hotel . . . go to another city . . . leave Mexico? I need a drink.

He hailed a taxi. "Take me to the other side of Zona

107

Rosa."

The driver let Don out at an attractive outdoor bar. He pushed his way between three-foot-high planters laden with red and white roses then took a seat in the shade of a green and white striped awning.

Moments later, a young, pallid waiter arrived. Shaking long black hair from his face, he took Don's order. Don watched the waiter's bubble butt, framed by tight beige slacks, disappear into the building's dark interior. *Shit. That ass reminds me of Alvaro's.*

When the waiter returned, Don asked, "*Habla Ingles*?"

"*Si, Señor*. Uhhhh, I mean, yes."

"I need a hotel—a gay one. Can you recommend one?"

"*Si*. The Angel Hotel. It's just off the square on a quiet street. Rates are fair, has a pool, a full breakfast is included, and it's clothing optional. My friend used to work there." The waiter smiled. "The scenery can be very nice—if you know what I mean."

"Thanks. I'll take a look."

Don finished his drink then ordered another and then another. When he first sat down, he had sat in shade, but the sun had moved, and he found himself sitting in the sun, drunk, and sweating.

"*Señor*, the waiter said, "Should I call a taxi to take you to the Angel?"

Don burst into tears. "I don't know what to do. I just found my lover cheating on me—getting fucked by that damn soccer player."

The waiter patted Don's shoulder. "I am so sorry. I know how you feel. I've been there."

Looking into the waiter's face, Don said, "Thanks for your understanding, uh . . ."

"Rico. Name's Rico."

"Thanks Rico."

"Was the soccer player a professional?"

108

"Yes, damn it—Jesus Gonzales!"

"Oh, him. Everyone knows about him. He has a way of hooking up with young guys. He likes them fit, trim, and under twenty. He's said to have a huge cock he likes to poke up young butts."

"That's how I caught them—fucking."

"Sorry," Rico said, revealing a long, sad face. "It hurts to be betrayed. You won't want to hear this, but the hurt *will* go away—with time."

"I want it to go away now," Don said. "Get me another Margarita."

"Maybe you shouldn't?"

"Hell! Bring me a *double* and use the good stuff—*reposado*."

Rico left then returned with a weaker looking drink than requested.

While Don nursed his drink, the bar filled with young men for happy hour. Happy hour meant two-for-one drinks.

An attractive, young Mexican man took a seat next to Don's table.

The man smiled, revealing gleaming white teeth. He made eye contact with Don who wiped tears to better appreciate the stranger's European shaped face, green eyes, and Roman nose. Don mentally undressed him of his tight, bulging pants and form-fitting shirt. *Wow! Wow! Wow!*

"*Habla Ingles*?" Don asked.

"*Si, señor*. Are you okay?"

"Just got something in my eye," Don muttered. "You dress like a matador. Are you?"

"What?" the stranger asked.

"Are you a matador?" Don asked, rubbing his eyes.

"Are you sure you're okay?"

"Just got something in my eye. You!"

"I don't usually cause men to cry."

"Sorry. I didn't mean to imply you caused me to cry. What's your name?"

"Pepe."

"Pepe, I'm Don."

The men shook hands, but Don didn't want to let go. "Where're you from?" he asked.

"Tijuana. I'm here on vacation."

"Tijuana—nice city," Don said. "Been there."

"Funny," Pepe said, frowning. "I never heard anyone refer to Tijuana as *nice*."

"It's okay. Served my purpose. I'll probably be going back in a few days."

"What brings you to Mexico City?" Pepe asked, pushing his chair into the shrinking shade.

Don stared at the sky for a moment. "Just vacationing. Looking for mister right."

"A man like you shouldn't have trouble finding him.

You're good looking, got a nice body, nice smile . . . everything you need."

"You're very kind." *Glad someone finds me desirable.*

"Just truthful."

"May I buy you a drink, Pepe?"

Pepe winked. "Sure. Make it a Cosmopolitan—after all—I am."

"Ah! I like a *straight,* forward man." Don said, twisting his lips like he had bitten into a lemon. "Pardon my choice of the word *straight*—hope to god you aren't."

"Me? No. I'm into men—men your age."

"What a coincidence," Don said, slurring his speech. "I'm into men your age . . . and drinking Margaritas."

Pepe chuckled. "You don't know my age."

"Your old enough." Don waved to the waiter. "Rico, bring this gentleman a Cosmopolitan, *por favor*."

Don took a swig of his Margarita.

"How many of those have you had?" Pepe asked.

"Not enough."

"I'd guess you've had a few."

110

Don smiled and winked. "Yeah . . . A few."

"There's no reason to squint," Pepe said. "Move to my table and get out of the sun."

"That's kind of you."

Don grabbed his drink then moved to Pepe's table.

Pepe's drink arrived. He took a sip and stared at Don's chest. "How often do you work out?"

"Not enough. And you?"

"Everyday. My hotel has a nice gym. You'll have to workout with me."

"Where are you staying?" Don asked.

"The Mission Hotel. And you?"

"Nowhere. At least not yet. Been thinking of checking into The Angel. Do ya know it?"

"Sure do. Spent a night there last week. It's very nice, but they don't have a gym."

"Yeah, but they're clothing optional."

"I know. I took advantage of that."

"Hmmm. Think the hotel would be a fit me?"

"Absolutely. Its manager and guests would love to see you strolling naked around the pool. You would be good for business. I'd even stop by for a peek."

"You would, would you?" Don asked, speech slurred. "Come with me to check in. We can enjoy the pool together— get to know each other."

"Enticing," Pepe said, "but the sun's low, and we wouldn't get much of a tan."

"I thought you were interested in seeing me naked—not getting a tan."

"Interesting perception," Pepe said raising his glass to Don's in a toast.

"Maybe I'm wrong, but I thought *you* were interested in getting naked too."

Pepe appeared to think for a moment. "Why don't we stop all this guessing, and let's both get naked in your room." Pepe sipped the last of his drink. "We could visit the pool

111

later—get a moon tan."

"I like logical men," Don slurred.

"Let's get a taxi."

"Let me get the check," Don said. "You get a taxi."

The men sat close to each other in the rear of the beat up, vintage VW Beetle taxi. Each pushed his thigh against the other's. Don moved his leg up and down Pepe's leg. The young Tijuanan smiled and pulled his pant leg to his knee. Don smiled, hiked his pant leg and rubbed his bare leg against Pepe's calf while muffling a chuckle.

God, Pepe has a muscular leg and what a bulge.

The driver monitored the erratic traffic with the intensity of a surgeon as he maneuvered through the city's narrow streets. "I drive slow because many accidents happen in this part of city. Hope you no in hurry."

"Take your time," Pepe said, taking advantage of the driver's interest in traffic to grope Don.

"It's very interested," Don said then smiled.

"Who does he hang out with?"

"Two *big*, *long*-time friends."

Pepe smiled. "I hope they're swingers."

"The biggest—heaviest."

Pepe feigned jerking Don off through his pants.

"Keep that up and he'll come out to play," Don said, spreading his legs in the confined space.

Leaning over the front seat, Pepe asked the driver, "*Que tan lejos queda* to The Angel?"

The driver took a moment to translate Pepe's mix of Spanish and English.

While Pepe leaned against the front seat, waiting for an answer, Don tweaked Pepe's nipple.

"OOOOhhhh. Do you have more than one hand?" Pepe asked.

"One will have to do for now."

"What?" the driver asked.

112

Pepe repeated his question about distance to the hotel.

"Fifteen minutes," the driver said.

"That gives me time to rough up your 'friend,'" Don said, rubbing Pepe's pants-restrained cockhead head with slow, circular motions.

Pepe smiled. "I can imagine how that would feel if you were using your tongue."

Chapter 9

From the back seat of the parked taxi, Don looked up at the faded-blue "bubble" awning bearing the name Angel Hotel. "Guess we're here," he said.

Don paid the fare and the men exited the cab.

"Mind if I carry that?" Pepe asked, reaching for Don's luggage. "I don't want to go in without something to hide my hard-on."

"Shit!" Don said. "Show it off. That's something to be proud of."

"Please," Pepe pleaded. "You go first."

"Okay, you carry the bag but don't poke a hole in it."

"Welcome to the Angel," the Aztec-looking clerk said, extending his hand toward Don. "I'm Carlos. Do you have reservations?"

"Not about you."

"What?"

"Never mind," Don said. "Gotta room?"

"For you, *si*. A wonderful garden room."

"Have a lot of guests this time of year?" Don asked, surveying the lobby's Art Deco décor of silver and black.

"There are two other guests," Carlos said, eyeing his new guests' bodies. "We're glad to have you staying with us, *señor*. Do you want twin beds or a queen?"

"Do we look like twins?" Don asked with a tinge of sarcasm in his voice.

"Don't mind him," Pepe said. "He had too many Margaritas. Queen size would be fine."

"Your room is just off the pool," Carlos said. "I hope you take advantage of *all* our options. You will have a direct view of the pool *and* our guests from your opened door. Please, feel free to meet and greet."

Carlos rang the desk bell, and an attractive, well-built young man entered the room. "May I take your bag?" he asked.

"It's a small bag." Don smiled. "I'll carry it, but you

115

may carry my friend."

"I'll get myself to the room, thank you," Pepe said and adjusted his crotch-hiding bag.

The bellboy led the way to the room. Inside, he smiled at Don. "Want me to undress your friend?"

"No, thanks," Pepe said.

Don tipped the bellboy. He left and closed the door.

Don opened the door and yelled, "Bring us two large Margaritas—big ones." He stared at Pepe. "Well don't just stand there—undress. Or do I call the bellboy to help you?"

"You go first."

Don sat down on the bed to remove his shoes and socks.

Standing, Pepe used one foot and then the other to hold hold his shoe steady, while he pulled each foot from its loafer. He stood on the toe of one sock then the other, pulling each foot free.

Don stood then unbuttoned one shirt button. Pepe matched Don's action, button-by-button, until both shirts were totally unbuttoned. Don pulled his shirt from his trousers.

Anticipating Don's immediate shirt removal, Pepe let his shirt fall to the floor, but Don left his shirt hanging on his shoulders. He smiled and scanned Pepe's smooth, muscular chest. Don's shirt remained on his shoulders while he unbuckled his belt and pulled it from his trousers.

Pepe frowned. "I don't have a belt."

"No belt," Don said. "Then you can't beat my butt."

"I'm sure you'll loan me *your* belt."

Pepe unzipped his pants as did Don. Don unbuttoned his trousers' top button then nudged his pants downward. Pepe started to do the same, but his pants fell to the floor.

Seeing Pepe wore no underwear, Don smiled. *God, what a handful.*

As Pepe stepped out of his trousers, Don wondered how Pepe kept his package in his pants?

Naked, Pepe displayed his manhood at full attention.

116

His cock bounced in sync with his heartbeat. Cold air from the AC caressed Pepe's crotch, causing his balls to retract.

"Let me stretch those back to full length," Don said grasping Pepe's nuts.

Don pulled his cock and balls over the top of his briefs. "Look. They want to play."

"Do they always hide behind cotton?"

"Not always," Don said. "Why don't you invite them out?"

Pepe pushed Don's underwear to the floor then stooped and stared into his crotch before swallowing Don's begging cock. "Hmm," Pepe moaned. Don started to pull away but relented, letting his cock be captured by Pepe's throat.

Don's steel-hard cock throbbed as it neared climax. He thrust with vigor, anticipating a soul shaking climax. "Oh God!" he yelled. His knees began to buckle, but Pepe pulled them against his chest and held them with the determination of a steel rigger joining a skyscraper's beam.

Pepe released Don's spent cock, dropped his head backward and exhaled. "You okay?" Pepe asked, staring into Don's eyes.

"I will be . . . in a moment."

Standing, Pepe pulled Don close, gripped his butt, and then pushed a finger inside.

Don smiled then slurred, "Why not?" He stretched out, face down, on the bed.

Pepe took a lubricated condom from his pants, rolled it on, and then straddled Don's hips. Using his cockhead, Pepe teased Don's ass as he squirmed his butt's acceptance of the anticipated penetration.

"Look in the side pocket of my bag," Don said. "I have condoms."

"I'm using one."

Pepe probed deeper. After a few thrusts, he found Don's pleasure spot and concentrated on maximizing his pleasure. Don tightened and moved his ass in sync with the escalating tempo

117

of Pepe's thrusting. Pepe soon climaxed. Don squeezed the erupting cock and held it with a death grip as Pepe collapsed on Don's sweaty back.

"What a ride," Pepe said.

"Yeah. Nice fuck!"

Both men lay still for a moment then Don, squeezing and rocking his hips, stimulated Pepe's cock.

"Sorry," Pepe said. "It's dead—for now."

"I can wait."

"Shower time," Pepe said. "Where is it?"

"Behind you."

The men showered and then rested, naked and spread eagle on the bed where Pepe played with Don's balls.

"What say we take a dip?" Pepe asked.

"Why not? Skinny dipping or suits?"

"Naked, I don't have, nor do we need, trunks. Besides, I want to watch your nuts."

"Only if I can jiggle yours," Don said.

Don opened the door and looked to the left and then right. "No one's here."

"Ahhh, the sun's gone," Pepe said, sounding disappointed as he stepped outside. He took Don's hand. "Let's go. The pool is ours."

Naked, Don walked past some low shrubs then stepped onto the pool's coping, still hot from the day's baking sun. He knew Pepe watched his nuts as they dropped beneath his butt as he stooped to cup a handful of water then let it fall through his fingers. "Feels good," Don said.

"I bet they do—nuts that is—feel good."

"Do what?" Don asked.

"Your nuts. I bet they feel good."

"Well, find out underwater."

Don dived into the pool while Pepe sat down on its edge, his feet dangling in the water. Don swam toward him, pushed his legs apart, and grabbed his slack nuts. Pepe inched his butt to the edge of the coping then let his nuts hang over it.

Don swallowed and tongued them as he stroked the attached cock.

"You can play with my nuts," Pepe said, "but my cock is dead for a while."

"That's okay, I like playing with it."

Moments later, Don swam away then motioned for Pepe to join him. Pepe dived in then treaded water as the men exchanged small talk and gropes.

From the shadows at the far end of the pool, a voice called, "Mind if I share the pool?"

Don looked into the shadows and saw a tall, well-built *gringo* sporting thick pecs and a wide and deep six-pack. Suntan lines defined his pale hips. Over his shoulder hung a long towel hiding his crotch.

Late twenties, Don thought. "Come on in. The water's great."

"Yeah!" Pepe said, "plenty of room."

The newcomer walked to the middle edge of the pool then removed his towel, revealing a long cock draped over large balls.

Pepe whispered to Don, "Oh my god. That's one nice, shaved crotch."

"Yeah. Quite a sight."

"What?" the stranger asked.

"Quite a night," Don said.

"Yeah." The stranger walked down the pool's steps.

Don watched the man's cock and balls swing with each descending step. His noteworthy crotch disappeared under the surface as its owner frog stroked his way toward Don.

"I'm Harry," the stranger said. "That is between body shaves, I'm hairy."

Almost on impulse, Pepe rubbed his hand over Harry's smooth chest.

Wish I'd known," Pepe said. "I'd have shaved it for you."

"Yeah? That might have been fun. Next time, I'll give

119

you a call—save me the work."

Sensing Harry's playful intent, Don moved closer to him and grabbed his crotch.

"This *is* a playful crowd," Harry said, his cock growing hard in Don's hand. "Even underwater, that feels good."

Harry grabbed Don's cock. He made it bounce in Harry's hand.

Pepe tweaked Harry's nipples. Harry returned the favor.

Several times, the men's hands changed exploratory positions on the other's body.

"Now this is why one stays at a gay hotel," Pepe said, rubbing Harry's butt.

"Would you guys mind if my partner joined us?" Harry asked.

Don smiled then looked at Pepe. "We wouldn't mind, would we?

"Not at all," Pepe said.

"Great, I'll get him. His name is Gregg."

Don watched Harry's muscular butt as it propelled him up the pool steps then toward a room at the far end of the pool. Minutes later, Harry and Gregg, naked, walked to the pool.

Don scanned Gregg's broad, hairy pecs and washboard abdomen. He too had a floppy cock and swinging balls.

"How're you doing, guys?" Gregg asked.

Harry dived into the pool followed by Gregg. Harry surfaced, shook water from his face, and introduced Gregg. "Don has a nice cock and great nuts."

"May I?" Gregg asked, grabbing Don's crotch.

Caught unawares, Don said, "Sure. They don't mind." *Nor do I.*

In a flash, each man had an underwater handful of someone else's crotch, butt, or nipples.

Pepe seemed attracted to Gregg's curly chest hair. He permitted Pepe to curl it and rub his pecs—sometimes tweak-

120

ing a nipple.

"Like chest hair?" Gregg asked, tugging Pepe's cock.

"That and your hairy abs." Pepe rubbed his hand over the valleys separating Gregg's mountainous six-pack muscles.

Don thought, *Pepe's a fickle butterfly. I thought he was into me but look at him.*

Gregg pulled Pepe against his hairy body then rubbed himself against Pepe's smooth torso.

"Your body hair is softer than I expected," Pepe said.

"I use conditioner, when the hair isn't shaved off."

"Both you guys shave your bods?" Pepe asked.

"Yeah, from time to time," Gregg said. "Just shaved him a couple of hours ago." Gregg squinted at Pepe. "You seem awfully interested in shaving."

"Sometimes, I shave my crotch," Pepe said, "but I dig shaving hairy guys—"

"Watch out Gregg," Harry said. "You might wind up *totally* naked tonight."

"If Pepe wants to shave me, why not?" Gregg said, pulling at some chest hair. Might be fun."

Don rubbed Harry's butt. "You must have just shaved your butt. It feels very smooth."

"Yep, so I can better enjoy pubic hair being rubbed against it."

Picking up on the indirect invitation, Don rubbed his crotch against Harry's butt.

"Nice," Harry said. "Keep it up."

Don reached around Harry's waist and stroked his cock. His other hand explored Harry's ass.

"I'd love it deep inside," Harry said, squeezing his butt cheeks against Don's exploring finger.

"I bet it gives a great ride," Don said, pushing a finger inside. "Why don't we go to my room? Let me check out the ride."

"Okay," Harry said. "Got rubbers?"

"You betcha."

121

"Pepe, see you in a while," Harry said. "You and Gregg have fun.

Gregg and Pepe treaded water, watching the two men leave the pool, Don's crotch planted against Harry's butt.

"That Don has a nice ass," Gregg said. "It's muscular. Must be hard."

"Yeah and he knows how to use it," Pepe said.

"I bet you're no slacker." Gregg rubbed Pepe's butt as he swam away. "Where're you going?" Gregg asked.

Pepe looked back and smiled. At the edge of the pool, he placed his folded arms on the coping then cradled his head.

Gregg swam up behind him.

"Never had any complaints," Pepe said, pushing his butt against Gregg's crotch.

"I could better care for that in bed," Gregg said. "Why don't we go to my room?"

The guys left the pool with Pepe pulling Gregg's balls like a steam engine coaxing a train uphill.

As the men entered the room, they exchanged a French kiss while Gregg tugged at Pepe's butt cheeks.

Pepe spied a can of shaving cream and a razor on the bedside table. "Is that what Harry used to shave himself?"

"That's what *I* used to shave Harry."

Pepe looked Gregg in the eye and flashed a sheepish grin. "Is it time for your shave."

Gregg smiled then looked into Pepe's eyes. "You wanna rub that cream all over my bod and crotch, don't you?" Gregg mimicked shaving his chest. "Pull that razor slowly across my pecs. Shave around my cock and asshole? Get me really, really naked?"

"How'd you guess?" Pepe asked, his rock-hard cock losing a pearl of pre-cum.

Gregg picked up the razor and removed the old blade. "We need a fresh one."

Pepe shook the can of shaving cream as his host returned from the bathroom with blades and towels.

Gregg dropped the towels on the bed and jumped onto its middle. He spread his legs, fluffed his balls and adjusted his cock. "You've done this before?"

Pepe grinned then said, "I have a master's degree in shaving." He shook the can then lavished shaving cream across Gregg's pecs, lingering to play with each nipple. Gregg smiled his approval and folded his hands behind his head. Pepe spread cream over the hairy abdomen and crotch then tweaked his own nipple while he stroked Gregg's cock. Gregg snapped a new blade onto the razor's handle. "Start with my crotch."

"Why there?" Pepe asked, still stroking Gregg.

"Tell you in a minute."

Pepe lathered Gregg's cock then worked the cream into the sac. With careful strokes, he shaved around the base of Gregg's rod then wiped debris from the razor. Every few seconds, the half-shaved cock received a hand stroke.

As Gregg lost pubic hair, Pepe fingered the shaved skin. "Can't leave any stubble."

After removing a few hairs from Gregg's cock shaft, Pepe turned his attention to Gregg's balls. Pepe stretched the scrotal skin. "I want a nice flat surface for shaving," he said. "No nicks."

Gregg glanced at Pepe's handiwork. "I like the way you pull nuts. Keep it up."

Pepe shaved the front of the sack then started on the backside.

"Don't shave too far toward my ass," Gregg said. "Shaving there will be easier when I turn over for you to shave my butt."

Pepe ran his fingers over Gregg's pubic area and balls. "Good. No stubble." He towel-dried everything then said, "Check it out."

Gregg felt his pubic area and smiled. "Feels good." He scanned the area. "Looks good but shave all the pubes."

Pepe complied then asked, "How's that?"

"Great," Gregg said, handing Pepe a condom he had taken from under his pillow. "Roll it on me."

A puzzled look crossed Pepe's face as he rolled on the condom.

"Want a ride?" Gregg asked.

"With all this cream on your belly and chest?" *This is strange.*

"Yeah. Go ahead. I'll show you why."

"Okay." Pepe guided Gregg inside.

Pepe rode the steed and tweaked Gregg's lathered nipples.

After a minute, Gregg said, "Finish shaving my front."

"While we're fucking?"

"Yeah. Love feeling the razor getting my chest naked while I fuck. Makes my cock harder, and I fuck better."

Pepe sprayed more cream on Gregg's chest then stopped his ride long enough to spread the lather.

"Don't stop riding," Gregg said. "Shave me while we fuck."

"This is a first. I've never done both at the same time."

Pepe continued his ride while he shaved and felt for stubble. "There. It's done."

Gregg wiped the remaining cream from his chest then quickened his thrusting.

In near sync, Pepe stroked himself. While he neared climax, he tweaked Gregg's nipple.

Gregg emitted a loud moan. His body tensed as his pelvis reached for the ceiling, bucking Pepe skyward.

Pepe continued jerking off while Gregg's bare chest waited for its reward.

"Do it man," Gregg pleaded. "Drop that load on my pecs—my shaved chest,"

Pepe obliged, spewing a hot load across Gregg's pecs then shuddered as he gave up the last of his gift.

Gregg yelled a long "Ahhhhh," climaxed, and then shook as if having a seizure.

Pepe spread his load over Gregg's chest and abdomen then leaned forward, settling onto Gregg's chest.

"God, that load was hot," Gregg said, scanning his chest. "It felt so hot, I thought I had blisters. I loved it."

Pepe cleaned Gregg's chest, rolled off the captured cock then rested. "What a ride."

"Glad to be of service." Gregg said, sounding exhausted. "It's company policy to satisfy guests. We want you to *cum* again."

"I'd love to. What are business hours? Later, today I hope."

"Okay, but let's get a shower then see if the guys are at the pool."

Don and Harry swam as Gregg and Pepe entered the pool area. Gregg smiled and jumped in beside Harry.

"You're looking very naked," Don said, rubbing Gregg's glistening chest and abdomen.

"Couldn't resist Pepe's offer of a free shave," Gregg said.

"I hear he's good with a razor?" Don said, sitting down on the pool's edge, legs dangling in the water.

Harry swam to Don and grabbed his balls. Looking at Gregg,

Harry said, "Can't get enough of Don's nuts. They remind me of yours."

"Maybe I should check 'em out," Gregg said then swam to Don, stroked his cock, and fondled his balls.

Don extended his arms behind him, leaned backwards, and spread his legs. "That feels good, but it'll take a while until I can work up another load to show my appreciation."

Pepe tweaked Don's nipples while the other guys entertained Don's crotch as he moaned and surrendered to their pleasures.

"Why didn't this happen *before* I shot my load, Don said. "You guys don't play fair."

125

"I don't need a load to enjoy your nuts," Harry said, rubbing and tugging Don's balls.

Don leaned farther back on his elbows. Moments later, he lay on the coping, feet in the pool, moaning with ecstasy. *Have at it, guys.*

"Even half-hard, your cock fits nicely in my hand," Gregg said. "No need for you to unload—yet."

"Hey guys," Pepe said, "Let him regain his strength, and then we'll attack him."

"I like the sound of that," Don said, flapping his feet and splashing his admirers. "Please do." *I'll never tire of this kind of attention.*

The guys allowed Don to rest while they swam around dunking and splashing each other.

Later, Don dived in and swam toward Harry. "How long you and Gregg been together?"

"Five years. And you and Pepe?"

Don chuckled. "Five hours."

Harry grinned. "I thought you'd been together for years."

"No wonder they're not fighting," Gregg said to Harry then smiled.

Pepe looked at the garden clock. "Hey guys, it's time to hump Don."

"Yeah," Don said, "it's time you raped me. Let's go to my room."

Don threw some condoms on the bed then stretched out on his right side in the middle of the mattress. He patted it, beckoning his guests to join him. Stretching out behind Don, Gregg rubbed his crotch against Don's butt. Don handed Gregg a condom, which he donned then fingered Don's ass. After a moment of play, Gregg maneuvered his cock inside then worked Don's eager ass.

Harry watched for a moment then crawled onto the end of the bed. Lying on his left side, head to toe with Don, he swallowed Don's cock. Don moaned as Harry's talented mouth

126

performed its magic.

"Pull my balls, while you suck me," Don said to Harry.

Harry tugged Don's nuts toward the foot of the bed.

"More," Don said then moaned. "Yeah. That's it."

Pepe got on the bed then French kissed Don as Don stroked Pepe's cock. Seconds later, Pepe changed position so he and Don could do a titty sixty-nine. Pepe jerked off while he and Don sucked and nibbled each other's tits.

Surrendering Don's cock, Harry asked Pepe to swing around a bit. "I wanna play with your cock while you guys suck tits."

The tangled group of four men seemed lost in their fantasies.

Neither intended to synchronize climaxes, but it seemed that might happen.

Gregg could not hold off. He pounded Don's ass with growing intensity as everyone's level of sexual tension reached a crescendo. Gregg yelled, "I'm gonna cum."

Don worked his ass against Gregg's crotch, while concentrating on keeping his cock in Harry's mouth.

Pepe suddenly stood and shot his load on Gregg's half-exposed chest as Gregg fucked Don.

Harry's throat worked Don's cock until it exploded. Harry then stood and shot his load on Gregg's chest, while Gregg climaxed inside Don. The room echoed with sequential sighs, sounding like a broken calliope.

After Don had given his all, he and the others found a place on the bed to catch their breath.

Pepe looked at the bedside clock. "Guys, I have to go."

"I think we all need a rest," Gregg said.

"Yeah," Don said. "I have lots of towels. Everyone can shower here if you want."

Pepe showered, dressed, and then wrote on hotel stationary as he said, "Don, here's my hotel and cell number. Call me if you want to start all over."

Gregg and Harry used their own towels to wipe off.

"It is getting late," Gregg said, gesturing toward Don. "We'll see you later.

Within seconds, Don's room emptied. He felt lonely.

He showered and returned to bed where he fell asleep, thinking of Alvaro.

Chapter 10

Conversations in Spanish woke Don. He squinted at the bedside clock. "Damn, 7:00 a.m. Why do maids have to be so cheery?" He rubbed his forehead. *God, what a headache.* He forced his head from the pillow and sat up, scanning the room for his travel bag.

He held his head, so it would not explode, and searched his bag for aspirin. He took two and returned to bed, reawakening at 11:00 a.m., his headache much relieved. *Well, what do I do today?*

Don dressed and went to the breakfast room. A waiter brought him coffee and an English language newspaper. He scanned the photo on the front page. "Shit. It's Jesus." The picture showed him shaking hands with the director of an orphanage. Jesus had been signing soccer balls for its residents. Behind him stood Alvaro—smiling. "Damn him!" Don exclaimed, slamming the paper on the table. Several diners stared in his direction. "Sorry," he said.

Don searched his cellphone for Alvaro's number then realized he had Alvaro's phone. He assumed Alvaro had his. "Shit!" *What am I going to do now? I don't remember my number, and he has erased all calls.* Don scrolled through the phone's address screen and found a number for Raoul. *I'll call and ask if he has my number.*

Raoul's phone rang several times. "Speak," Raoul said.

"Raoul, this is Don—from the plane. How are you?"

"*Señor* Don, nice to hear from you. How you are?"

"I'm in Mexico City and need your help."

"Anything for my *amigo*."

"Do you have the number for my cell phone? My friend and I got separated and somehow, we have each other's phone. I can't remember my number, so I can't call him."

"What a surprise. I am in Mexico City. I'm with Aunt Maria. We came to visit our cousin—in hospital. *Momento*. Let me look for your number."

"My friend's name is Alvaro."

"*Si*. Alvaro. Hold a minute. Here it is. *Su numero* is 999-227-6940."

"Thank God you had it. How long are you in town?"

"Several days. Want to meet?"

"Why not? I'm staying at The Angel Hotel near the Zona Rosa. It's a very nice place. Want to meet here for drinks this afternoon?"

"Is three o'clock okay?"

"Sure. I'll be waiting for you."

Don gave his address then closed his phone. He stared at it for a few moments thinking, *Should I call Alvaro . . . What the hell—why not?*

Anxious, Don answered his ringing phone.

"Hello . . ." Alvaro said.

"Alvaro, it's Don. How are you?"

"Not so well. I was almost afraid to answer."

"What's wrong?" Don asked. "Are you sick?"

"No. Not sick, sick. Just missing you."

"I'm missing you too. I dreamed about you last night. I'm calling to say I'm sorry for the way I acted."

"And I'm sorry for what I did."

"What say we bury the hatchet . . . see if we can work things out?"

"Do you mean that?"

"I do. I'm staying at The Angel Hotel, in the Zona Rosa. Meet me here for lunch and bring my phone."

"I'd love to. See you at twelve noon?"

"Okay. I'll be waiting," Don said, feeling a tingle of anticipation.

"Thanks," Alvaro said, his voice morphing into joy.

So Don could see Alvaro when he arrived, Don waited in the hotel lobby, pacing as time passed. Twelve noon came and went, and Alvaro was nowhere to be seen. *Where the hell is he?*

130

At two o'clock, Don abandoned his vigil and went to the dining room to have lunch. *Should I call? Maybe something bad has happened.*

With a menu in one hand and a phone in the other, Don listened as his distant phone rang and rang. *Shit. He's not answering.*

At three o'clock, Don returned to the lobby and waited for Raoul.

"How nice to see you," Don said, standing and extending his hand to Raoul. "I didn't know your aunt would be coming. Nice to see you again, *señora*."

"*Señor* Don, nice visit you," Raoul said.

"How's your cousin?" Don asked, furrowing his forehead with concern.

"He very sick. I think he dying."

"Sorry to hear that," Don said, looking into Raoul's eyes and gripping his arm. "How are you?"

"*Bien*, thank you. Just tired of sitting around the hospital doing nothing. I watched a soccer match, but other than that not much."

"Yeah, great game," Don said. "I saw it. Met a relative of Jesus Gonzales who invited Alvaro and me to meet Jesus and see the game—as Jesus' guest."

"*Señor*, you very lucky. You met Mexico's greatest soccer player. Tickets impossible. I paid as you say in America, prices without hair."

"Scalped," Don chuckled. "Let's have a drink in the garden. It's a pleasant place to relax."

"This some place fancy," Maria said then smiled. "I bet we have good Margarita here."

"They make the best, and you can have all you want."

Don enjoyed his guests, drinks, and the tranquility of the well-tended garden with its flowering Birds of Paradise, bougainvillea, mamey and banana trees. Every few minutes, he sneaked a peek at his watch, wondering what had happened to Alvaro.

131

As the grandfather clock in the hotel lobby struck four, Don heard someone call his name.

"Alvaro, is that you?" Don asked.

Alvaro stepped into the doorway leading to the garden.

Don rushed to him. They embraced for a minute. "I was beginning to think you weren't coming," Don said, struggling to hold back tears of joy. "Oh, how I've missed you."

"I almost didn't come," Alvaro replied. "I was too ashamed."

"Bull shit! I'm so happy to see you I could yell, but I won't." Don slapped Alvaro on the shoulder so hard he almost knocked Alvaro into the garden. "Raoul and his Aunt Maria, from Tijuana, are here. Remember, they gave me a ride from San Diego?"

"Hello everyone," Alvaro said, walking toward Don's guests then shaking Raoul's hand.

"*Señora* Maria, how are you?"

Maria shook Alvaro's hand and held it. She stared into his eyes then closed hers and exhaled.

"What is it?" Raoul asked. "What have you seen?"

"What is he talking about?" Alvaro asked, staring at Maria, then Raoul and then Don.

"Maria is a witch," Don said, "a good witch. She sees things—future things."

"What did you see?" Don asked.

"I see trouble." Maria narrowed her gaze as she looked at Alvaro. "Much trouble. You must leave this place, this city. There is danger."

"Why should I be in danger? I have no enemies in Mexico."

"I see *mucho* trouble. You must leave México."

"Thank you. I'll think about it, but for now, I want a Margarita."

Ninety minutes of pleasantries passed as the group chatted, enjoyed the garden, and drank.

Looking at the wall clock, Raoul said, "*Señor* Don, I

am sorry, but we must go back to hospital."

"I understand," Don said, standing to bid his guests farewell.

"Keep in touch," Raoul said as he and Maria left.

Don and Alvaro sat down, staring at each other.

"What's all that danger stuff?" Alvaro asked. "It's spooky."

"I hope it isn't about police looking for us," Don said. "By the way, I saw your picture in a local English newspaper. Think it's wise to be photographed for a newspaper—a popular one?"

"Who knows? But yeah, that was me. Jesus thought I'd like tagging along for his orphanage visit. Met a lot of nice kids."

"What's going on with you guys?" Don asked.

"Nothing. Not since you know when."

"Then relax. You look like you're strung tight enough to snap."

"Sorry. I'm a little nervous."

"I know how to relax you," Don said. "Let's order another Margarita and go to my room. I'll rub your back."

Alvaro bit his lip, smiled, and then nodded. "Sounds good."

Minutes later, the waiter placed two Margaritas on the table. Each man took a sip.

"Come," Don said, taking Alvaro's hand, "Let's go. Bring your drink."

Don led Alvaro into the room, embraced him, and then gave him a kiss. Don unbuttoned Alvaro's shirt. He returned the favor and tugged at Don's shirttail. Soon, both men were naked. They continued kissing as each fondled the other's growing erection.

"God I've missed you," Don said, hugging Alvaro.

"I don't know what I would have done if I had been unable to call you." Don pushed away. "Don't forget. We need to exchange phones."

133

They kissed then Don said, "I've been crazy thinking about you." Don stared into Alvaro's eyes. "I love you so much."

"I couldn't get you out of my thoughts."

"I have to admit, I'd gotten used to wakening up with you beside me," Don said.

"Me too. Especially with that 'woodie' of yours."

Don led Alvaro to the bed where the kid jumped onto its middle.

He lay on his back, placed his hands behind his head, and smiled.

Don grinned. "Want your cock sucked, do you?"

Alvaro broke into a broad grin. "Why should I deny you my pleasure?"

Don crawled between Alvaro's legs and kissed his cock. His tongue moved over its head and then onto the globes that awaited its arrival. He took the balls in his mouth and jostled them before tugging them with his lips. He stroked Alvaro. Seconds later, Alvaro squirmed and lifted his hips off the bed.

"Slow down, tiger," Alvaro said.

"Okay—for now."

Alvaro assumed a sixty-nine position. "Now, we can both play."

He tongued Don's cock and tugged his balls. Alvaro had trouble swallowing Don's large cock, but he persisted.

Don's tongue stimulated Alvaro's cock shaft then he swallowed the cock. Don's throat muscles gripped the thrusting cock, causing Alvaro to moan. He wrapped his muscular legs around Don's head and pulled it closer to the root of his cock, providing Alvaro with maximum pleasure.

When Alvaro climaxed, Don grabbed his head-encircling legs and held them, while stimulating Alvaro's cock.

Alvaro gasped, surrendered Don's cock, and yelled his tormented pleasure.

"Damn it!" Don yelled. "Don't stop."

Alvaro resumed sucking Don's throbber. Don's body stiffened. He held his breath, and with a near convulsion, he grabbed his belly, emitted a room-filling moan, and climaxed.

For a fleeting moment, the room grew quiet. The spent men went quiet, while stroking the other's thigh, catching their breath, and regaining their strength.

The next morning, Don awoke first. He looked at Alvaro. *I'm so glad you're back.* He lifted the sheet, scanned Alvaro's body, smiled. and then left to take a shower. He turned the water to a low flow to prevent waking Alvaro then stepped inside.

"I'm next," Alvaro said, peeking around the shower curtain.

"God. You scared me. Come in. It's big enough for two."

Preceded by his woodie, Alvaro entered and stood under the water. He started to lather up but stopped to embrace Don. He grasped Alvaro's cock and manipulated it to full length then pulled Alvaro forward for a lingering kiss.

"Nice to see *both* of you are alive," Don said.

"Yours seems to be waking up too," Alvaro said and slapped Don's balls.

Don smiled. "You have an hour to quit that."

They kissed while stroking the other's cock. Within seconds, each man climaxed. They hugged each other as their knees threatened to buckle.

"God! What a way to start the day," Don said.

Alvaro chuckled. "Can't say you're not awake now!"

Don rinsed off then left the shower while Alvaro lathered up.

On the desk, Alvaro's phone buzzed, indicating a voice mail waited.

Should I? Don thought. He sat down in the desk chair, opened the phone, and listened to the message. "Alvaro, this is Jesus. What happened to you last night? I waited over an hour.

Call me."

Don mumbled, "And he said nothing was going on with Jesus. Liar."

Don erased the message and placed the phone on the desk, just as Alvaro entered the room, drying his back.

"You're looking mighty sexy this morning," Don said.

"You're not looking too bad either, especially those nuts. I guess a hot shower agreed with 'em."

Don leaned back in the chair and fluffed his crotch. "Glad you like them. They thank you for last night." He picked up his underwear. "Ready for a breakfast of *real* food?"

The dining room buzzed with Spanish conversations from the all-male crowd.

Don and Alvaro took seats at the only available table. A waiter waved, acknowledging their arrival, then raised his hand to his lips silently asking if Don wanted coffee. He and Alvaro nodded.

Moments later, their coffee arrived. Don ordered an American breakfast then glanced into the lobby where he watched a swishy delivery man place booklets in a rack for free gay publications.

"Who the hell is that swishy queen," Don asked.

Alvaro chuckled. "Guess it's the delivery queen for the *Gay Bar Guide*. I'll get one. Let's see what's happening this week."

Alvaro selected several gay publications then returned to the table.

Just as he sat down, breakfast arrived. "Ugg. These eggs have a very strong smell of cilantro, " Alvaro said, placing his papers on an empty chair.

Don took a bite of his eggs. "This cook puts cilantro on everything." He pushed the eggs to the edge of the plate then took a bite of toast. "So much for an American breakfast."

The guys ate and discussed what they might do. After looking through several tourists' guides, they decided to visit the Floating Gardens of Xochimilco's. Don wanted to ride on one of its floral-decorated boats.

Don ordered a third cup of coffee, while Alvaro returned to the room to brush his teeth. Don thumbed through several pages of a gay guide. On its back, he perused several pictures of scantily-clad men photographed at various bars and dance clubs in the Zona Rosa. He saw a large picture of Alvaro, sans shirt, kissing Jesus Gonzales, also sans shirt—at a local watering hole known for its backroom.

"Shit!" Don said, backhanding the photograph.

Looking shocked, the waiter said, "Sir! There are guests here."

Don stormed out of the restaurant, heading for his room. He opened the door and saw Alvaro talking on his cellphone.

"Gotta go," Alvaro said, closing his phone.

"I see you found *your* phone," Don snarled. "Talking to that damn Jesus, were you?"

"Yeah. He called me."

"Give me the damn phone," Don yelled.

Moving too fast for Alvaro to grip his phone, Don snatched it then scanned the incoming calls screen.

Don felt his face warm as anger grew in his gut. There's *no* call from Jesus, you lying son-of-a-bitch!"

He scanned the call history and saw Alvaro had called Jesus a minute before he arrived. "You lied to me, you son-of-a-bitch! *You* called Jesus!" Don threw the phone on the bed then waved the local gay guide in Alvaro's face. "Look what I found. Look, damn it. Look!" Don flashed the photo of Alvaro and Jesus kissing in the notorious bar.

"I can explain that," Alvaro yelled. "We were dancing. That's all—just dancing."

"Half-naked guys kissing in a gay bar known for backroom sex and you call that nothing!"

Alvaro glared at Don. "Whatta you want from me? Why the hell are you so damn jealous?"

"I love you, or at least I loved you," Don said, shaking

137

his head. "Why the fuck do you think I'm in this god-forsaken country? Think I wanna be here? Hell no! I'm here because I love you. I risked going to prison for you, and this is how you repay me!" Don struck the desk. "You have put both of *us* in danger. Maybe by the staff of this hotel, or maybe some dumb visiting jock, one who's here to fuck and suck then picks up one of these damn magazines and remembers seeing your mug on CNN—a wanted man." Don leaned over Alvaro and intensified his stare just short of shooting flames. "How stupid can you be?"

Alvaro stood transfixed—too frightened to move.

Don threw the magazine on the bed and sat down on the desk chair. He dropped his head in his hands and stared at the floor. "I can't go on like this." He shook his head and stared at Alvaro. "I can't do this anymore! You need to decide between him or me. Ya can't have both. What's it gonna be?"

"Don. You know I want to be with you. We have great sex. I'm happy with you."

"How the hell do I know you're not just saying that . . . for my money—my money. Is that it? You want—no—need me for my money."

Alvaro threw his hands in the air. "You know you mean more to me than, money. Yeah, it's true. I don't have any money, but I don't want you just for your money."

"We'll see," Don muttered, staring at the floor. "If I see or hear you've been with him again, I'll—"

"You'll what?" Alvaro asked, eyes flashing with rage.

"You'll see," Don muttered. "You'll see. Damn it, I'm going for a swim."

Don stripped as he stormed out, slamming the door.

Alvaro slumped on the bed then heard a loud splash. He opened his phone and stared at the dial. "Shit! I'm calling him."

Chapter 11

"Jesus. I'm sorry I had to hang up," Alvaro said. "Don has been on a rampage."

"Sorry to hear that. You still want to get together tonight?"

"I'd like to, but not sure I can—or should, but I need a change of scenery—have some fun."

"I'll be at the Rock around midnight. They have a great DJ. Stop by if you can. Later, there's a pool party at a friend's house—lots of good looking, naked guys. Hell, all kinds of naked men. You'd have fun. Who knows, you could be the hit of the party.

"Sounds hot but it depends on what's going on with Don. I'll try, but I can't promise."

"Okay but keep in touch."

"Okay. Bye." Alvaro closed his phone and looked toward the pool. *Maybe I should try to calm him down.*

Don swam in circles as Alvaro strolled naked along the coping.

Two naked, dark-skinned men, with gym-worked bodies, lounged nearby. They looked at each other and then at Alvaro. "*Buenos tardes, señor*," they said in unison.

"Afternoon," Alvaro said then sat down on the edge of the pool, near the strangers, and stared at Don.

"Young man, you obviously spend a lot of time in the gym," one of the men said.

"Uh huh."

Don glanced at Alvaro as he slid into the water then swam toward him. Don remained in the middle of the pool.

"Don't come near me," Don said.

"Please, let me explain wh—"

"No need to explain. I know where your allegiance is."

"No, you don't. You just think you do."

"Shit," Don said, slapping the water. "Your actions speak volumes. Now, leave me alone."

"Before I got here yesterday, Jesus and I had discussed going to a house party. When I decided to come here, I had to let him know I wouldn't be joining him. That's why I called him. Nothing more."

"You expect me to believe you after catching you in a bold face lie?"

"Alright. You win!" Alvaro stopped treading water. "So, I lied, but I lied to save me, *you*—us—from your misunderstanding of my actions. You weren't ready to hear or appreciate the truth."

Don sank, resurfaced, and spat water. "You know I love you, but . . . what do you want from me?"

Alvaro skimmed his hand over the water. "I obviously want to be with you, or I would've been gone by now."

"I'd like to believe you, but I think you're here because you need money! Even if you say you don't need *my* money, you seem to need him and *his* money more than you need or want me."

"Shit!" Alvaro slapped the water. "Yes, I need money. Who doesn't? But don't worry about me. I can get money. . . lots of ways. See those guys behind me. I bet they'd pay me for sex. Truth be known, I could make a lot of money selling my body. I've done it before, and I can do it again—to very hot guys. I can't count the times I've been propositioned since I've been in Mexico."

Don slapped the water. "Don't say that. It's disgusting. You know I don't like you being with other guys."

"Well, quit acting like a jealous brat! If you drive me away, I'll have no choice but to do whatever it takes. I have ta eat."

"Don't raise your voice," Don whispered. "People are listening. Have you no idea how your actions hurt me?"

"I'm sorry if I've hurt you. I promise to be more attentive but cut me some slack for God's sake. You gotta give me some space."

"Space for what?" Don put his hand over Alvaro's

mouth. "Don't answer. I don't want your attention. I want your love." Don moved away and slapped the water. "Can you say *I love you*, or is that too much to ask?"

"Don, you earn love. You don't take it. You can't force it or buy it. It's given."

"That's a two-way street, kid . . . Can we agree to work on it?"

"I promise I'll try, but you have to do your part, Don. Now, let's get dressed and go to those floating gardens."

"Okay, but you leave first. I want to watch your butt.

Don and Alvaro spent the afternoon in the floating gardens. They shared a *trajinera* boat lathered with multiple bright colors. The boat's billboard style boarding area bore a plethora of wilted "silk" flowers.

Floating along ancient Aztec canals, the men drank Margaritas and enjoyed a mariachi band playing in a boat that had stopped beside the men's boat to ask for money.

The grassy banks of the canal hosted numerous groups of children who braved the polluted water to swim alongside tourist boats to sell trinkets made in China.

The men's cloud of personal distrust seemed to have lifted. Don often laughed over various whimsical sights along the way.

After a long ride, the men stopped to visit an open-front canal bar. Rustic wooden furniture along with red and white checkerboard tablecloths provided some semblance of decoration. Glossy red enamel paint covered its walls and ceiling. The space reeked of cilantro.

"Oh no. Not cilantro," Alvaro said.

Scanning the room, Don said, "Looks like these Mexicans might be Chinese. Let's sit under a ceiling fan. It's hot in here."

The guys ordered Margaritas. After three rounds, Don had mellowed. He had his feet propped on the chair next to him.

Alvaro felt he could mention Jesus and his invitation

141

to a house party. "How would you like to meet some local gay men—nice people—at a pool party."

"Why would I want ta do that?"

"Who knows how long we'll be in Mexico?" Alvaro asked, shrugging. "We should get to know some locals. We need friends."

"Why should I meet these 'party' people?" *Bet Jesus will be there.*

"Lots of reasons. First, they're fun. They're edu-cated; they speak English; they're professionals, socially connected, wealthy, and nice. You'll like them. Besides, I'd like to see in-side one of those big, expensive houses."

Don picked a lime slice from his drink. "How did *you* meet these people? Not as a trick, I hope."

"God, no!" Alvaro sighed. "Now, don't get angry, but I met them through Jesus."

Don gritted his teeth. "Of course, you did." Don raised his voice. "I thought we weren't going to mention *him* again."

"Don, don't get me wrong, but why can't you see him as an acquaintance—someone who can open doors for us?"

"Kid . . . I know you guys have some kind of romantic relationship. God only knows what, but it looks sexual to me, and I don't like using people—not the way you do it."

"Okay, okay. We had sex, but there's *no* love between us. We had sex—just sex. And you? Have you had sex with anyone since you stormed out?"

"What I've done doesn't matter. It's what *you've* done that's important. You're responsible for all this angst. I could lose you, and I don't want to." Don looked into his drink and then into Alvaro's eyes. "Do you have any idea what love is? Real love?" *I doubt it.*

Alvaro looked at Don. "Forget about losing me, you won't, but please, let's go to the party. There'll be great music. We can dance, meet some nice people, make future business connections, and enjoy free booze. You know you can't say no to free booze. If you'd like, you call Jesus . . . get directions."

Don waved to the waiter for another round. "I don't want to talk to him. And I don't want you talking to him."

Alvaro, dialed Jesus' number, and then handed his phone to Don. Don held it away from his ear so Alvaro could also hear the conversation.

"Alvaro?" Jesus answered.

"No. This is Don. I understand that Alvaro and I have been invited to a party."

"Yes. You're both invited."

Don motioned for a waiter to loan him a pen. "What is the address?"

"It's 514 *Calle* 193 between 102 and 103." Party starts at nine o'clock. I know you'll have a good time. We've had our problems, but I'm glad you're man enough to put them aside. Maybe we'll have time to talk, get to know each other."

"We'll see. Bye." Don closed the phone and handed it to Alvaro.

"You know Mexican parties never start on time," Don said. "There's no reason to get there early."

"Well then, let's have dinner here and then take a taxi. That should put us there at about eleven o'clock . . . when the festivities start."

Before the aged, backfiring VW taxi neared its suburban destination, the guys heard salsa music. It flooded the country side. Bright party's lights illuminated the neighborhood, almost crowding the full moon from the sky.

The driver took his fare and said, "Enjoy the fiesta."

"Sounds like we're at the right house," Alvaro said. "Look at the size of this place. It's a mansion."

"That it is," Don said, raising his voice, "but I don't know how much of that music I can take. Why does it always have to be so damn loud?"

"Cause its Mexico."

The guys walked to the gate of the walled villa.

"Look up, Alvaro said. "See how the stars sparkles.

143

Ya can't see them downtown with all its smog."

"Smell that Jasmine," Don said. "Reminds me of my aunt's house back in Pennsylvania . . . Bucks County. It's a homey smell."

A security guard looking like Mister America stood at the gate holding a clip board. He wore a grey uniform two sizes too small for his muscular frame.

Don whispered to Alvaro, "That's the guy who should be naked."

"*Su nombre, favor*?" the guard asked.

"Don and Alvaro," Alvaro said.

"*Gringos,* eh?" The guard flipped through several pages on his clipboard. "*Perdon. Su nombre* is no on list."

"I'm glad you speak English," Alvaro said. "We're friends of Jesus Gonzales. Is he here?"

"*Si, Señor,* but I must ask the host about your admission. Wait here."

The guard's thighs were so large they caused his pants legs to rub creating a sshh, sshh sound as he walked.

Minutes later, the guard returned with Jesus. "Hey guys. Sorry I didn't get your names on the list. Do come in."

Mister America opened the gate, permitting Alvaro and Don to enter. Jesus embraced Alvaro then tried to embrace Don, but he extended his hand, blocking Jesus' embrace.

Jesus shook Don's hand. "Glad you could join us. Come on back. I'll introduce you to Doctor Juan."

Jesus and his guests pushed their way through a crush of men ranging in age from twenty to fifty. They packed the inner courtyard, which surrounded an Olympic sized pool. The crowd could be divided into two groups: drinkers or dancers. Most of the guests were shirtless; a few wore swim suits. Two large black speaker boxes sitting on the roof of a nearby building belted ear-splitting salsa music.

Jesus located Doctor Juan and introduced Alvaro and Don. The doctor, wearing a stuffed Speedo, sized up Alvaro and shook his hand.

144

Don thought, *Juan is surprisingly well built for an older Mexican. I wonder if Alvaro will find him attractive.*

Juan shook Don's hand. "Welcome to my home." Doctor Juan pointed toward a small building. "The bar is inside. Feel free to visit it often. Most of my guests speak English so introduce yourself. Have a good time."

"Thanks," Don said. "What's the occasion, Juan?"

"Uhhh . . . its Friday."

"Thanks," Alvaro said. "Sorry we're late. We were so busy we forgot to bring swim suits."

Doctor Juan smiled then said, "Don't worry. You'll be okay without one. All of these guys will soon be naked." Juan winked. "Might have more fun because you don't have suits. Now get a drink and enjoy yourself."

Doctor Juan left to greet other arriving guests.

"I didn't like the sound of his laugh about skinny dipping," Don said, holding open the screen door to the bar house for Alvaro to enter. "I hadn't bargained on this being *that* kind of party."

"Señor, what is your drink preference," the black tie attired, bare chested bartender asked. His swim suit so small it faked its job of covering his bulging package.

"Margaritas, *dos*," Don said. "By the way, your English is very good. Quite proper."

"Thank you, *amigo*."

"Careful!" Alvaro chided Don for being too friendly. "Enjoy your drink and let's see how many guys speak English."

Drinks in hand, Don pushed his way through the crowd to an out-of-the-way spot where he and Alvaro leaned against a wall to watch some dancers. For a minute, Don observed one particular shirtless dancer, wearing tight blue shorts. *Nice!*

Don nudged Alvaro and nodded right. "Look at the build on that older guy."

"Nice pecs," Alvaro said. "Butt isn't bad either. Too bad he isn't naked, but I couldn't help but notice that blond boy in the tight yellow swim shorts at the end of the pool. I think he has

145

a cucumber and a couple of potatoes in his shorts."

Don took a sip of his drink. "Yeah, hard to ignore those groceries." *I could feast on that.*

A baby faced, shirtless man with a thin muscular build, approached the men. "You are Americanos?"

"Yep. How'd you guess," Don said, surveying the man's hairless body. "This is Alvaro and I'm Don."

"I'm Pedro. Would you like to dance, *Señor* Don?"

"Uh . . . maybe later."

"Be kind, Don," Alvaro said. "Think of international relations. Pedro likes older men. Dance with him."

"Thank you, Pedro," Don said, "but I'm not a dancer."

"Alvaro will hold your drink. Won't you, Alvaro?" Pedro asked, taking Don by the hand. "Come. Let's dance."

"Go dance, Don," Alvaro said. "I'll hold your drink."

"Okay, Pedro. Let's give it a try."

With arms flying in all directions, most of the dancers appeared to be involved in a free-for-all fight. With his awkwardness and flailing arms, Don blended in.

Alvaro laughed at Don's studied attempt to be cool.

Shirtless, Jesus approached Alvaro. "Nice to see you again, but I thought you and Don were past history."

"There's still something between us," Alvaro said. "I don't know how strong it is or how long it will last, but we're together."

"In any case, I'm glad you came." Jesus grinned. "Want to dance?"

"Thanks, but I'm babysitting Don's drink until he gets back from dancing with that baby-faced guy."

"Don will like him," Jesus said. "His name is Pedro. His bubble butt likes to be fucked by an older man. He could be your competition."

"We'll see," Alvaro said. "Don will be safe if he's dancing. Besides, I can keep an eye on him from here. Wait until he comes back for his drink then we'll dance."

146

Jesus pointed to Alvaro's right. "You could put those drinks on that table. No one will bother them."

"That wouldn't be smart. I'll dance with ya when he gets back."

Jesus moved to Alvaro's side and put his arm around the kid's waist.

"Please, don't do that—not in front of Don."

Jesus' hand slide down Alvaro's back until it rested on his butt. Jesus smiled and gripped it.

"Don't do that, Jesus."

"Relax. Don can't see my hand."

Alvaro shook his head. "Please, take your hand away. You're asking for trouble."

"Okay, okay. But I want at it later—hear."

Jesus walked away but looked back several times.

Alvaro watched Don and Pedro gyrating within an area of one square meter. *They're having way more fun than me.*

A young man with a tight build, wearing a skimpy red swimsuit, approached Alvaro. The man wore a broad smile and flashed his electric-green eyes.

"*Méxicano o Americano?*" the man asked.

"American."

"Welcome to México. My name is Ponce."

"Are you a friend of the host or Jesus?"

"Both."

Ponce glanced at the two Margaritas held by Alvaro and said, "You must be very thirsty."

"Oh no." Alvaro shook his head. "These aren't mine. Well, one is. The other belongs to a friend. He's dancing . . . over there."

"Why don't you put the drinks on that table, and I'll teach you to salsa."

"I can't move fast enough to salsa," Alvaro said then thought, *What the fuck. Why not?* "But I'm willing to try."

Alvaro tabled the drinks then he and Ponce found a dance space beside Don and Pedro. Don and Alvaro made intro-

147

ductions to each other's dance partner.

After dancing for a minute, Pedro asked Alvaro, "Want to share a joint?"

Pedro pulled a reefer from the waistband of his swimsuit then held it toward Don and Ponce.

Ponce grinned. "Yeah."

Alvaro looked at Don. "Wanna share?"

Frowning, Don said, "No thanks."

"Don't be a party pooper," Alvaro said. "Try it. You'll like it."

Pedro pulled a cigarette lighter from his waistband then lit the joint. He and Don walked to where his and Alvaro's drink waited. Seconds later, Alvaro and Ponce followed them.

Alvaro took a hit then passed the joint to Don. He looked at it as if he didn't know what to do with it.

"Try it," Alvaro said, a trail of smoke cloaking his words.

"I prefer Margaritas," Don said. "Smoke as much as you want, but I'm having another drink."

Over an hour, Don consumed several Margaritas.

Alvaro drank and smoked.

Pedro and Ponce giggled and ate everything in sight. They soon became a little frisky—not only with each other but everyone within arm's reach. Several times, they groped Don and Alvaro.

Carrying a megaphone, Doctor Juan walked among his guests and announced, "Five minutes. In five minute, the lights go off. Be careful but have a good time."

Don's vision dark-adapted enough for him to see eighty percent of the guests were naked. Many swam or splashed about in the pool while others engaged in a grope fest. Ponce laughed and tugged at Pedro's pants, as he pulled at Ponce's swimsuit.

Jesus, naked except for one sock, approached Don.

Alvaro asked Jesus, "Had a little to drink have you?"

"Just a little," Jesus said, speech slurred. "Aren't you

148

guys going swimming?"

"I'd like to," Alvaro replied, "but Don won't let me."

"Don, Don, Don," Jesus said. "Why don't you, me, and Alvaro get wet?"

"Nah," Don said. "With that big cock of yours, Alvaro and I wouldn't get any gropes."

"So that's how it is," Jesus said, groping Don and Alvaro. "There, you've been groped. Now, we can get wet."

"Don, please," Alvaro said. "Let's enjoy the pool."

"Okay," Don said and waved his hands in the air. "But behave yourself. Jesus, keep your hands off Alvaro."

Alvaro undressed faster than most people blink, but Don undressed with the speed of a glacier, removing everything but his briefs.

"Take those off," Alvaro said. "No one wears underwear."

"Yeah," Jesus said, pulling at Don's briefs. "Take 'em off. Show off that thing."

Don pushed Jesus' hands aside. "Thanks. I'll do it myself."

Alvaro smiled and pushed Don's briefs to the ground while looking him in the eye. "Step out, Don." Don raised his feet. "Now, doesn't that feel better? Freer?" Alvaro bounced Don's nuts in his hand. "Let's get 'em wet."

Alvaro grabbed Don's crotch then pulled him along the coping to the deep end of the pool. Alvaro jumped in, pulling Don behind him. Both men sank to the bottom then resurfaced among an army of naked swimmers.

"I don't know why, but the water seems cold," Alvaro said.

Don embraced Alvaro. "I'll keep you warm. That's what lovers do."

"And I think you're pretty wonderful too."

"Then say it."

"Say what?" Alvaro asked.

"Say you love me."

"Oh, Don. You're drunk. You know how I feel about you."

"Then say you love me."

"Okay. I love you."

"No, say it like you mean it."

"I do," Alvaro said, feeling perturbed.

"You're lying. You don't love me."

"Don, you're drunk. We should leave before something bad happens."

"I don't want to leave. I'm having fun."

"Hey *gringo*," a square shouldered stranger, with big biceps said, tapping Don's left shoulder.

"Who are you?" Don asked, with slurred speech.

"I'm a *gringo* admirer," the man said.

"I meant what's your name?"

"I'm Ricky. Want to play with my balls?"

Shocked by the directness of the question, Don asked, "What did you say?"

"I hear *gringos* like to play with big balls, and mine love to be played with, or I could play with yours if you'd like." Ricky fondled Don's and then Alvaro's balls.

Alvaro pushed the hand from his crotch, but Don allowed Ricky to continue fondling him.

"Don. What are you doing?" Alvaro asked. *I've got to get him out of here.*

"I'm letting Ricky play with my balls. They like it. You can play too, if you want."

"You want your nuts played with, I'll do it," Alvaro said, through clinched teeth. "Ricky, let go of Don's balls. Those are my property."

"But he doesn't mind," Ricky said, smiling, "and I don't mind sharing them."

A wave, just short of a tsunami, happened behind Alvaro. He wiped water from his eyes and noted Jesus had cannon-balled the pool. He swam alongside Alvaro and groped him.

150

"Alvaro, my friend," Jesus said. "Seems Don is busy being groped, so I hoped we could play."

A stranger approached Alvaro from behind then rubbed his crotch against Alvaro's butt.

"Stop that!" Alvaro yelled, pushing the stranger away.

"Yeah. Stop that," Don said.

""I'm Ricky. I though you guys were having a groupie."

"Well we're not!" Alvaro said.

"I've been watching your butt," Ricky said, "and I want to fuck it."

"Damn!" Alvaro said. "Don, let's get out of here."

Don turned to Alvaro, "Say hello to *Ricky*. He has a *big* dick that would feel good up your ass."

Ricky groped Alvaro.

Gut churning with anger, Alvaro pushed the man's hand away then grabbed Don's arm. "Let's get outta here."

Don grabbed Ricky's crotch and said, "Alvaro, my boy. If *you* don't wanna get fucked, maybe Ricky would fuck me."

Alvaro stared Don in the eyes. "You're drunk. We need to get outta here."

"Not now. I wanna get fucked!"

"Be that way! Maybe Jesus and I'll do our thing."

"Okay, okay, but Ricky is going to fuck me, aren't you Ricky?"

"*Si señor*, I fuck you good."

Unsure of what to do, Alvaro grabbed Jesus by the arm and pulled him to the shallow end of the pool. As they kissed, Alvaro glanced sideways to see how Don would react, but Ricky had moved behind Don. Don's facial expression changed. Alvaro knew Don had just been mounted.

Grabbing Jesus' cock, Alvaro indicated he wanted to be fucked. Jesus obliged. After a few seconds into his tryst, another guest attempted to mount Jesus. He turned to the interloper and said, "Wait until I'm finished with Alvaro."

Despite his intoxication, Jesus managed to climax.

151

Exhausted, Alvaro forced himself from the pool and sat on the coping. In disbelief, he watched Jesus beckon the stranger who had propositioned him minutes ago.

"Hey," Jesus yelled to the man, "you can fuck me now."

The drunken stranger and another guest stumbled though the shallow water toward Jesus. The first man, weight 240 pounds, mounted Jesus. The weight caused Jesus to sink, almost drowning him. Jesus managed to surface. With the coupled man in tow, he edged his way toward Alvaro's position. The man on Jesus' back never missed a thrust. Jesus pushed Alvaro's legs apart then swallowed his cock.

Don became enraged when he saw Jesus' head in Alvaro's crotch. Forcing his way through a sea of bodies, Don headed toward Alvaro. Ricky, struggled to remain coupled with Don as he clung to Don's neck and wrapped his legs around Don's hips.

Don yanked Jesus' head from Alvaro's crotch, while shouting, "God damn son-of-a-bitch. I told you to leave him alone."

Ricky yelled to Jesus, "Hey, can't you see we're fucking?"

"We're getting out of here," Don yelled, pulling on Alvaro's leg.

"Get away, Don. You're drunk," Alvaro said, prying at Don's hand. "I'm not going anywhere. You think it's okay for Ricky to fuck you, but it's not okay for me to have fun with Jesus. I'm staying. You do whatever ya want but do it without me."

Doctor Juan arrived. "Why the fuck is going on here, gringos? The neighbors are going to complain"

"Sorry about the ruckus," Alvaro said, "but Don's a little drunk."

"You two are louder than the music," Juan said. "If you don't quiet down, you'll have to leave."

"I'd like to stay, but Don wants to leave and take me with him. I don't wanna go."

152

"You're welcome to stay," Juan said, helping Alvaro from the pool, "but I think I should call a taxi for you, Don."

"Please do," Alvaro said. "I'll get him dressed. Ask that big guard to help me get him in the cab?"

"I heard that," Don slurred.

"Hope you'll be staying after he's gone?" Juan said, placing his hand on Alvaro's shoulder.

"Why not? The party is just gettin' started."

Doctor Juan smiled and slapped Alvaro on the butt. "Good. I'm looking forward to getting to know you."

"What?" Don asked.

"We're leaving," Alvaro said.

Alvaro helped Don up the pool's steps then helped him dress.

After dressing him, Alvaro told Don the two of them were leaving. Alvaro needed the help of two guests to get Don to the gate. The muscular guard stuffed him into the back of the waiting taxi where he fell asleep.

This guard is a hunk, Alvaro thought as he admired the guard's boulder sized biceps. *Love to see him naked.*

Alvaro gave the driver some money and instructed him to take Don to the Angel Hotel.

As the taxi disappeared into the night, Alvaro sighed and walked toward the compound. *Glad that's over with.* Alvaro eyed the guard. "Care to join me for a drink?"

The guard smiled but said nothing.

Alvaro entered the bar and found a different bartender. "Margarita, favor."

The bartender smiled and placed a Margarita in Alvaro's left hand. Each man's fingers lingered against the other's.

"My name Hugo," the bartender said through a welcoming smile.

"I'm Alvaro." *And you are fucking hot.*

"Why are you only guest wearing shorts?"

Alvaro winked. "I want to leave something to your

153

imagination."

"Sorry. I no have imagination. You no want me make bad guess do you?"

"What if I told you I'm not wearing underwear? Would that help?"

"That is a start, but my imagination still fuzzy."

Alvaro chuckled, "Then your imagination is pretty good 'cause there's something fuzzy under my shorts."

Alvaro felt someone grip his shoulders, from the rear.

"Give me these shorts," Jesus said. "Join me in the pool."

"Sorry but Hugo wants my shorts."

"*Si,*" Hugo said, "but I help naked Jesus undress you."

"I don't mind if Hugo watches," Jesus said and slapped Alvaro on the butt, "Are you stripping or not?"

Putting down his drink, Alvaro winked at Jesus. "Why don't you do it?"

"Okay." Jesus unbuttoned Alvaro's shorts then fished inside for his cock. Having found it, he pulled the growing cock into view.

Alvaro stepped out of his only piece of clothing. "How is that?"

Hugo clapped in appreciation and handed Alvaro his Margarita.

Doctor Juan walked by smiling. "You guys okay?"

"We're fine," Jesus said. "Want to feel?"

Juan grabbed Jesus' cock then Alvaro's.

Alvaro reached for Doctor Juan's nuts, smiled and said, "They're as big as Don's."

"Glad you like them," Juan said. "Why don't we go inside? The three of us could make a daisy-chain. You could play with my balls while we're circled up."

"Let's go," Jesus said.

"Why *nut*?" Alvaro chuckled.

Warm and stuffy, Juan's bedroom bore a hint of mildew.

154

A king-size bed dominated the space, which overlooked the swimming pool.

Alvaro assessed Juan's muscular backside as he started a mini-split air conditioner. Alvaro knew Juan had big nuts, but now he had an erection to match, and Alvaro wanted it—where ever Juan wanted to put it.

Juan threw back the flowery bedcovers and crawled to the center of the bed. Alvaro followed then surrendered his cock to Juan's warm mouth. *Wow! What talent!* Alvaro had never experienced the tongue action demonstrated by Juan.

"Wait for me." Jesus said, dragging his balls over the men as he got into position then sucked Juan's cock.

Juan interrupted the activities. "Let's circle up."

Heads to crotches, the men arranged themselves in a circle and pleasured the other. Alvaro's wish had been granted. He had Juan's fat cock in his mouth.

As pairs of hands roamed from body part to body part of the nearest man, it seemed each man focused on getting the other off. After minutes of intense hand and oral action, each man reached his objective. A sudden increase in the volume of salsa music almost drowned out the explosive moans of Alvaro's climax. Spent, he stretched out on the bed as if dead.

"I don't know about you guys, but I need a rest," Alvaro said. "Is your invitation to spend the night still open, Juan?"

"You and Jesus are most welcome to stay."

"Will you sleep with me?" Jesus asked Alvaro.

"Only if you promise to fuck me in the morning."

Chapter 12

Don awoke with a pounding headache. *Why do I punish myself like this?* He looked around the hotel room to orient himself. "How did I get back here?"

The clock radio read 1:47 p.m. "Shit. The day's half gone."

He searched the bathroom for aspirin. Closing the medicine chest, he thought he heard something. *Is my head exploding or is someone knocking?*

The door to Don's room creaked opened and someone said, "Afternoon, Tiger. It's me, Alvaro. Is that just a morning woodie, or are you ready to fuck?"

"Shit! I hadn't notice you weren't in bed." Don rubbed his throbbing head. "Where've you been?"

"Probably where you've been—passed out. I spent the night at Juan's."

"Now, I remember," Don said, holding his head. "You and Jesus were fucking, sucking, or something. Why did you treat me like that?"

"Now, that's calling the kettle black. Ricky and you weren't singing Sunday school songs. I wanted us to leave together, but you told me to fuck off—so I did."

Don backed to the desk chair and sat down. "I don't remember that, but shit, I was drunk."

"I'll say!" Alvaro moved farther into the room. "Want some coffee?"

"Sure. Why not?"

"Then I'll get some. Be back in a minute."

In a daze and naked, Don walked onto the patio and sat down at a poolside table.

Minutes later, Alvaro returned with coffee. He chuckled on seeing Don's nuts hanging over the edge of his chair. "Don't tell me you're trolling at this hour?"

"Funny?"

Alvaro sat down, appearing lost in thought.

Don drank his coffee then moaned and rubbed his head. Peering from beneath droopy eyelids, he stared at Alvaro. "I've gotta quit drinking. It's going to kill me."

"Morning guys," someone said, from behind.

Naked, Harry and Gregg walked in front of the guys. They carried towels and tall glasses filled with what looked like Mimosas.

"May we join you?" Harry asked.

"Sure. Pull up a seat—but do it quietly," Alvaro said. "Don's not feeling too well. He had too much to drink last night."

"Where did you guys go?" Gregg asked, tucking his towel between the rungs of his chair. "We missed you."

"Some rich doctor's pool party," Don said. "A friend of Jesus Gonzales . . . the soccer player."

"You guys know Jesus Gonzales?" Harry asked, eyes filled with expectation.

"Yeah. He fucks Alvaro," Don blurted. "Daily."

"He's one hot dude," Harry said. "He could fuck me any time. Think you could have him fuck Gregg and me? Or just me—at least introduce us?"

Gregg said, "Harry means could *you* arrange for Jesus to fuck *him.*"

Pointing at Harry, Alvaro said, "Got it. We can try, but knowing Jesus, I'm sure he'd like to fuck you. I once heard him say something about liking to fuck shaved butts."

"Shit, I'll shave it fresh," Harry said, "or maybe I could find Pepe and have him do it."

Alvaro stared at Gregg's chest for a second. "Your chest hair is growing back. It'll be ready for a shave in a few days."

"I'll let you know when it's ready," Gregg said, slapping Alvaro on the thigh.

"Well, I came for a swim," Harry said, placing his towel on the table then walking down the pool steps.

"Yeah," Gregg said, "it's time to cool off."

"Why not," Alvaro said, heading for Don's room. "Gotta undress."

"You guys go ahead," Don said. "My head can't take moving around."

Naked, Alvaro returned and joined Gregg and Harry in the shallow end of the pool. The three swam around discussing local gay bars. Alvaro often rubbed his butt against Gregg's pubic stubble.

"That stubble feels so . . . good," Alvaro said, smiling.

"Alvaro . . . Is sex the only thing you think about?" Harry asked.

"Absolutely not. Sometimes I think about sex."

"Glad to hear that," a voice resounded from the side entrance to the pool area.

"Oh, God!" Don said, raising his throbbing head. "It's Jesus."

"Hello everyone," Jesus said, walking to the pool's edge. "Just passing through the neighborhood and thought I'd stop by—say hello—see how Alvaro and Don are doing?"

"Alvaro's fine," Don said, "but I'm dying."

"The wake begins in an hour," Alvaro said.

"I know what you mean," Jesus said, staring at Alvaro. "I drank too much. I didn't hear you leave this morning."

"Didn't wanna wake anyone," Alvaro said, "but meet my friends. This is Gregg and his partner, Harry."

"Glad to meet you," Harry and Gregg said, waving wet hands.

"Why don't you join us, Jesus" Gregg said, splashing water. "It's very refreshing."

"Yeah," Alvaro added, "get naked and join us." Alvaro pointed to Don's open door. "You can leave your clothes in there."

"Hell. I'm not shy. I can undress out here."

Gregg held his breath as Jesus did a playful striptease.

Don held his breath as he waited for the jock's renowned tool to fall into view.

159

Jesus stepped out of his briefs, paused to let his admirers take in his crotch-bounty, and then sauntered down the pool steps. He smiled as his crotch disappeared beneath the waves.

"What's it like being around all those naked players in the locker room?" Gregg asked.

"Nothing unusual," Jesus said. "Just what you'd expect. There's some teasing, towel whips, laughs, jokes—nothing more. I'm sorry to disappoint you, but there's no sex."

Harry chuckled, "Well then, I'm not going to play soccer."

Not wanting to be left out of the fun, Don walked to the pool steps and eased himself into the water. When it reached his crotch, he paused. "Make room for my crotch."

"Feeling better?" Alvaro asked.

"My aspirin hasn't fully worked yet." Don gripped his head. "I think I'm pushing things a bit. Head is killing me. I should lie down . . . take more aspirin."

"What time do you wanna get up?" Alvaro asked.

"Maybe five."

Harry whispered to Gregg, "There's nothing's as sexy as a naked soccer player."

"I'll flip you to see who gets to fuck him first," Gregg said.

Alvaro said, "I heard that."

"Given we're in the water, would you accept rock, scissors, paper instead of a coin toss?" Harry asked Gregg.

"Done," Gregg said, starting with rock.

"Shit. Your rock wins over paper," Harry said.

Gregg swam toward Jesus and inquired about the party he and Alvaro had attended.

"We had a wonderful time," Jesus said. "Lots of good looking, naked guys—like you and Harry. Too bad you were not there."

"Flattery will get you everywhere," Gregg said, grasping Jesus hand and rubbing it over his shaved butt.

"Smooth," Jesus said. "Tighten it."

Gregg flexed his glutes.

Jesus rubbed each butt cheek. "Now, that's a fucking ass."

"How'd ya know?" Gregg chuckled. "It's a bad ass. It oughta be fucked. Want to invite Alvaro and Harry?"

"Why not? I love orgies."

Gregg said, "Harry. Alvaro. Want a matinee?"

"Love matinees," Alvaro said. "How about you, Harry?"

"Not in the mood—yet."

"Well, we'll see you in a while," Gregg said, pulling Jesus and Alvaro toward the steps.

Harry swam around for a while then lounged in the sun and read a gay novel. By the time he finished his forth Mimosa, shadows engulfed the patio. Hearing someone cough, he looked up from his book to see Don, naked, leaving his room.

"How's the dead?" Harry asked.

"Feeling better," Don said, scanning the space. "Where is everyone?"

"They're in our room fucking Jesus, or each other, or something."

"Knowing Alvaro, he's the one getting fucked," Don said, rubbing his eyes. "I can't trust him anymore!"

"Though you guys had an open relationship."

"Alvaro wants one, but I've seen too many couples breakup over sex outside their relationship—present company excluded. I love him, but I admit I'm jealous. Can't help it."

"I used to be jealous about Gregg, but after five years we've worked out our fears. We fuck around, but we're still together."

"Yeah, but you guys are working. Earning your own money. Alvaro doesn't. Makes me wonder if he's here just for financial security. Don't get me wrong. We have great sex, but I don't like him fucking around. I'm not sure he always uses

161

protection. That concerns me."

"I understand, but you can't own him, and God knows you can't buy love."

Harry heard unfamiliar distant male voices. They grew louder, as they neared the pool area. Restless, Harry waited to see who would arrive.

Two muscular men, wearing tight t-shirts, shorts, and carrying backpacks, entered the area and walked toward Gregg. The tallest one had short brown hair and a baby face. The other stood six feet tall, had blond hair and a square jaw. Both oozed sexiness.

Eyeing the naked men sitting poolside, the new arrivals said, "Hey guys. Nice to see this place is clothing optional."

Don waved to the guys and pointed to Harry. "Harry is a sexy looking naked man isn't he?"

"Looks like Harry works out," one stranger said.

Harry flexed a bicep. "Glad you like. Where you guys from?"

"I'm Richard and this is James, my lover," the taller man said. "We're from Cincinnati. And you guys?"

Don stood, sucked in his gut, and extended his hand. "I'm Don, from Philadelphia."

Harry extended his hand. "Hi. I'm Harry. We're about To order drinks. May we order some for you?"

"What are you drinking?" Richard asked.

"Mimosas," Harry replied.

"Haven't had one in years," Richard said. "Order two. We're going to shower then we'll join you."

"Make sure you're naked," Don yelled as the new arrivals walked away. "Clothes aren't optional."

Harry rang the waiter bell. Minutes later, drinks were ordered then delivered.

Naked, Richard and James returned wearing towels over their shoulders. Both men wore chrome ball stretchers. They puffed up their chests and sucked in their guts.

I can't believe the size of those weights, Harry whis-

162

pered to Don, "and they have the squarest pecs I've ever seen."

"Yeah, their builds are a cross between a swimmer, a wrestler, and a powerlifter," Harry whispered, "and they trim their pubes, but I can't get over the heft of those ball stretchers. These are my kind of men."

Richard and James walked to the pool's edge, tossed their towels onto chairs near Harry's table then dived in, making nothing more than a ripple on the water's surface.

"I hope they don't drown with all that weight," Harry said.

Richard and James surfaced and spat water.

"You guys aren't professional divers are you?" Don yelled.

The newcomers swam toward Don. "We used to dive for a college team; went to the Olympics, but we didn't win. A year ago, we switched to weight training."

"It shows," Harry said as he scanned Richard's butt floating above the water. "How much do those ball-stretchers weigh?

"These weigh a pound," Richard said

"What do you mean, *these*?"

"We have two pounders," James said, "but we don't wear them often—just during sex."

Don pointed to Richard, "Bet James' weight feels good slapping your butt while it's getting fucked?"

"Is that a question or a statement of personal interest?" Richard asked, grinning.

"Maybe," Don said and sat upright.

"These are your drinks," Harry said, pointing to the newcomer's mimosas.

Richard and James exited the pool and walked to Don's table, stopping to get their towels on the way.

Harry thought, *That Richard has my kind of crotch.* Harry whispered to Don, "Look at the cock on James."

"Yeah," Don said, watching both guy's weights.

The swimmers sat down at Harry's table. Their weights

163

clanged against the wrought-iron chairs as the men hoisted their drinks in a toast.

"Here's to a wonderful vacation and new friends," James said.

"May we have lots of sun, fun, and sex," Harry added.

James eyed Harry and asked, "You shave your body for swimming or sex?"

Harry laughed. "For speed fucking."

"I like that little pubic 'moustache' over your cock," Richard said, admiring the artful trimming of Harry's pubes.

"I like a little hair down there," Harry said. "Who wants a crotch looking like a hairless ten-year-old kid?"

"How's the party scene in Mexico?" Richard asked, staring at Harry's cock.

"Ask Don," Harry said. "He's the party guy."

"What kind of parties?" James asked, picking up his drink.

Don smiled then said, "Last night, we partied in one of those mansions in the suburbs. Lots of Margaritas, food, Coronas, marijuana, a pool, and naked men."

"Sounds hot," Richard said. "How'd you get invited?"

"Through a soccer player we know."

"Minor or major one?" James asked.

"Jesus Gonzales," Harry said. "*The* Jesus Gonzales as in World Cup soccer player. Harry pointed toward his room. "As a matter of fact, Don's partner and mine are fucking with him right now."

"Damn!" Richard said, staring at the closed door.

"Heard about him," James said. "Like to meet him sometime. He has killer legs . . . the kind you want wrapped around your head while sucking their owner's cock."

"Wait till you see his cock," Harry said, "and his ass. Its muscles have muscles."

"Speaking of legs," James said, "Don, you have some serious legs. Ever play soccer?"

Don extended his right leg and flexed his quadriceps

164

then his calf muscles. As he did so, he fluffed his balls. "Never played soccer—just worked the legs a lot."

Richard stared at Don's crotch. "I can't believe you were sitting on those balls. They're huge. Largest I've ever seen."

"Sometimes they get in the way," Don said, fluffing them as he spoke.

"When are those guys are coming out?" James asked, nodding toward Harry's room.

"They've been in there long enough to fuck an army," Harry said. "Gregg should be out soon—to get a Margarita."

"Richard and I haven't had lunch," James said. "I'd like to get something to eat, but I don't want to miss meeting Jesus."

"James, how long will you guys be in Mexico?" Harry asked,

"Four or five days. Why?"

"Well, Jesus is interested in Alvaro. Since Alvaro and Don are here indefinitely, I'm sure you'll see and meet Mister Soccer before you leave."

"Richard, I'm starved," James said. "What say we go eat? My belly can wait for Jesus."

"Okay," James said. "Guys, we'll see you later."

"There's a great little cantina to the right—two blocks down," Don said. "The food is homemade, authentic stuff."

"Thanks. We'll check it out," Richard said as he and James picked up their towels then headed toward their room.

Those guys are incredible," Don said, holding his index fingers about twelve inches apart while smiling. *Hope I get one of those in my mouth.*

"I bet Richard is friendlier when he's hard," Harry muttered through a smile while holding his index fingers fifteen inches apart.

"And I bet you'll find out just how friendly," Don said. *Hope I'm first.*

Harry and Don finished their drink then ordered another

165

round. While they waited, Gregg, still naked, returned.

"Where's Alvaro and Jesus?" Don asked, looking up at Gregg while shading his eyes.

"They're still making babies," Gregg said. "I couldn't keep up with them."

"I'm of a notion to go in there and break 'em up," Don said, a tinge of anger coloring his voice. *Why does Alvaro do this to me?*

"Then you better hurry," Gregg said. "I think they're getting ready to leave for a party,"

"Don, could you get us invited?" Harry asked.

"Shit, all you have to do is wait for Richard and James to return," Don said, swilling his drink. "With those guys, we could party right here."

"Who the fuck is Richard and James?" Gregg asked, furrowing his brow.

"Just two, tall, good-looking, well-built dudes with big cocks and ball weights," Don said, smirking. "They checked in while you were making babies. I think one of them wants to shave Harry."

"The newbies are ex-Olympic divers," Harry said, putting down his drink. "They have the kind of bodies you'd like, Gregg. They're into weightlifting, and I don't mean just ball weights."

"Well," Gregg said, scanning the area. "Where are these Adonises?"

"They went to get something to eat," Don said then gulped his drink. "Don't worry they'll be back. They're eager to meet Jesus. Speaking of Mister Soccer, I'm going in Harry's room. See what's going on."

Shaking his head, Harry said, "I don't think I'd do that, Don."

Don walked toward Harry's room, just as Alvaro and Jesus stepped outside. They walked toward the pool, hand-in-hand.

"It's about time," Don said, pulling their hands apart.

166

"Quit acting like you own me," Alvaro said, pulling his hand free of Don's grip.

"Relax, Don. I'm returning him safe and sound," Jesus said, flashing a smirky smile.

"Guys! No fighting," Harry said, staring at Don. "I want to enjoy my Mimosa in peace."

"Fuck you, Harry. Drink all you want, but this discussion is between Alvaro and me—nobody else—so cool it. Since we're new acquaintances, you and Gregg need to know that Alvaro is a bit of a whore." Don interrupted his tirade to take a swig of his Margarita. "And Jesus is his whoremaster."

"Shut your hole," Alvaro yelled.

"Yeah, shut your hole," Jesus said. "Show Alvaro some respect. Do you know why he enjoys my company? I show him respect—that's why. You ought to try it sometime."

"If you think respect is fucking him every chance you get then kiss my ass, Jesus."

"I'd kiss your ass, but your head is so spread over your butt there's no room for a kiss."

"You need to cool it, Don," Alvaro said. "Have a drink. Take a nap. Jesus and I are going to a party."

"Oh no you're not," Don yelled, grabbing Alvaro's arm.

"Jesus, you can't leave now," Harry said. "There are two Olympic swimmers who are dying to meet you. I think you'd be interested. They should be back soon."

"Always glad to meet a fan—especially swimmers," Jesus said, grinning. "I like swimmers' long, lanky . . . *cocks*." Jesus chuckled and wagged a finger at Harry. "You thought I'd say bodies didn't you?"

"Is that why you like Alvaro so much?" Don asked, sneering.

"No, Don," Jesus said, contempt almost smothering his words. "I like him for his arse. At least I know how to fuck it."

"Guys, I thought we were going to be gentlemen," Harry said. "No fighting!"

"Let's get out of here," Alvaro said to Jesus. "I wanna

167

go to that party."

"Relax. We'll can go later. There are swimmers to meet."

"I don't want to wait," Alvaro said. "I wanna be around fun people. I can't take any more of this bickering shit. I'm getting my clothes."

Alvaro stormed off toward Don's room.

Inside his room, Don grabbed Alvaro's arm, pulled him against his chest, and then stared him in the eye. "You're not going anywhere, kid. You're staying here where I can keep an eye on you."

"You're not my keeper," Alvaro said, tugging at Don's grip. "I'll go anywhere I want. I don't need your permission."

"You son-of-a-bitch!" Don yelled, slapping Alvaro. *Oh God, what have I done?*

Caught unawares, Alvaro grabbed his stinging red face and stared at Don in disbelief. A tear rolled down Alvaro's cheek. "That's it!" he yelled. "I'm out of here."

Alvaro gathered his clothes then rushed from the room—bare feet slapping the concrete deck. Approaching Harry and Gregg, he asked, "May I shower and dress in your room?"

"Sure," Gregg said. "What's going on?"

"Are you okay?" Jesus asked.

"I'm outta here!" Alvaro yelled and turned toward Jesus. "What's the address for that party? I wanna go ahead."

Jesus followed Alvaro into Gregg's room. "What happened?" Jesus asked.

"That son-of-a-bitch slapped me." Alvaro reached behind the shower curtain to adjust the water. "I need some away time."

"Okay, here's the address," Jesus said, writing on hotel stationary. "I'll join you in a little while. Tell Ricardo, he's the host, that I sent you, and I'll be by later. Sorry you and Don aren't getting along."

Don sat down on his bed, sulking in the dark room. He hung his head in his hands and murmured, "What the hell came over me?" He struck his fist against his palm. "Why did I hit him?" Don stared at the door. "That little shit! Does he think he can just run over me?" Don paced, wept, and murmured, "What the hell am I doing?"

Glimpsing Jesus' pants hanging in the closet, Don became enraged. "Fuck the son-of-a-bitch!" He yanked the clothing from their hangers then hurled them onto the walkway. The shirt and underwear landed on nearby bushes. "Get this shit out of my life!"

Don slumped to the floor and stared at the tiles. He spotted Jesus' shoes and socks peeking from under the bed. He stuffed the socks in the shoes then hurled them out the door. "Don't forget these!" he yelled then stretched out on the bed, face down—sobbing.

"Shit!" Jesus said. "That son-of-a-bitch has thrown my clothes out."

"Don's out of control," Harry said, shaking his head. He's one jealous son-of-a-bitch."

Jesus waited to see if Don would throw anything else. After a minute of quietude, Jesus collected his clothing then took them to a chair at Gregg's table.

Returning from lunch, James introduced himself then said, "Quite a game you played the other day."

"Were you in the arena?" Jesus asked, sizing up newcomers James and Richard.

"No. Damn it. Had to watch it on TV, but I'd like to see you play sometime—in the flesh."

Jesus chuckled. "Me to. I need the money."

"Can we order you guys a drink?" Gregg asked.

"Sure," Richard said, "but first we want to get out of these clothes, so we can swim. It's a hot one today."

James and Richard went to their room while Gregg

169

called for a round of Margaritas.

Minutes later, Richard and James returned carrying towels and wearing nothing but ball weights. The newbies stopped at the table where their drinks waited. They took a swig then dived into the pool.

"I see what you mean about swimmer's bods," Harry said,

"I hope they don't drown with all that weight."

"Yeah, and a couple of nice asses too—real muscle butts," Jesus said.

"Are we going to divide and conquer or work together?" Gregg whispered to Jesus.

Smiling, Jesus said, "You know I'm a team player."

Chapter 13

Richard and James exited the pool, wiping water from their face.

As James dried off, his cock flopped in Jesus' face. "Ah, a Prince Albert," Jesus said, staring at James' cockhead.

"May I see?" Gregg asked, lifting James' cock to examine the jewelry. "Nice." *But a cock sucker could break a tooth on that thing.*

"Glad you approve," James said.

"Gregg, leave the guys alone," Harry said, while staring at the Olympians' crotches. He patted the chair beside him and looked at the new arrivals. "Have a seat. I hear you're from Cincinnati."

"That's where we live now," Richard said, "but we were born in Indianapolis. That's where we trained for the Olympics, but that was years before we moved to Cincinnati."

Harry nudged Jesus. "This heat is getting to me. What say we take a dip?"

"I agree," Jesus called to the other men. "Hey guys, we're going in. Join us."

"Absolutely," James said, while he and Richard walked to the edge of the pool.

"Everybody, jump in on three," Harry said. "One . . . two . . . three!"

The five men created a splash and wave that almost emptied the pool.

"Jesus, you have killer legs," James said, rubbing the soccer player's thigh.

Jesus floated on his back. "How's that?" he asked, holding his leg above the water.

James eyed the muscular leg. "Looks good." He stared at Jesus' crotch. *That cock is getting hard.* "You work those legs a lot?"

Up righting himself, Jesus said, "Some. But I've always had big legs."

Gripping Jesus' thigh, James said, "Tighten."

Jesus smiled and flexed his thigh. "How's that?"

"Nice," James said and slid his hand to Jesus' crotch. *What a handful. Can't wait to eat it.*

Jesus smiled. "So is your hand. Nice that is."

As James fondled Jesus' crotch, Richard moved behind Jesus and gripped his butt with both hands. Jesus pulled James' crotch against his cock while staring into James' eyes as if to say, 'okay.'

"I'd invite you to my room, but I don't have one," Jesus said and winked.

"Our room is available," Richard said.

"Ours is closer," Gregg said.

Jesus squeezed James' butt. "Let's all go to Gregg's room."

Richard removed his ball stretcher as Gregg jumped on his bed—spread eagle up.

Sitting on Gregg's chest, Richard dropped his balls over Gregg's face. He then fondled Richard's cock. One by one, his balls were sucked into Gregg's mouth then tongued. Richard raised his hips, stretching his captive balls, while fucking Gregg's fist. With locked lips, Gregg stretched the balls farther. Richard moaned his approval. Seconds later, Gregg and Richard took a sixty-nine position. Gregg tightened his lip-lock around Richard's nuts, stretching them farther, while he stroked the Olympian's cock.

Jesus grabbed Gregg's butt cheeks and squeezed them. Out of appreciation, Gregg squirmed his tightened glutes.

Watching the action from the side of the bed, James rubbed Jesus' butt. Jesus released Gregg's butt, fell to his knees, tongued James' Prince Albert, and then sucked his cock.

After seconds of oral pleasure, Jesus pushed James into an all-fours position on the bed then straddled his butt. He cock-teased the waiting ass and soon had it begging to be violated. Jesus took a lubricated condom from the bedside stand, rolled it on then slid his cock inside. James flattened himself on the bed, expecting the fuck of his life. "Give it to me, man."

Harry stood on the bed, one foot on each side of James' neck. Facing Jesus, Harry offered his cock to the agile soccer player fucking James. Jesus grinned, mouthed the cock, and sucked it as he rammed James' butt. James managed to get his hand under his own crotch and stroked himself.

The room filled with moans and intermittent utterances of ecstasy as sexual tensions grew.

Jesus sensed James neared a climax and quickened his thrusting, managing to climax just as James' hand-job produced a load. On climaxing, Jesus jerked backward causing Harry's cock to fall from his mouth, spreading Harry's load on James' back.

"Wow," James said. "Thanks."

Gregg stroked Richard to climax and let the load fall on his own chest. A moment later, Richard got Gregg off then fell on the bed, exhausted.

"Wow!" Jesus said, "Someday, I'd like to be fucked with a Prince Albert."

"Happy to oblige," James said, "Maybe tomorrow?"

Looking at bedding scattered about the floor, Harry said, "We need to clean up this mess."

"No need," Gregg chuckled. "The maids are going to burn it."

After a short rest, the guys showered then everyone went to the pool.

"Think I'll hook up with Alvaro at the party," Jesus said, standing as the other men sat down at their regular tables.

Slapping Jesus on the butt, Harry asked, "Think you could get us invited?"

"Yeah, we'd like some local color," James said. "Meeting local men would be great."

"I don't know guys," Jesus said, preening in front of a reflective window. "My friend's house is small, so he limits crowd size, but . . . I'll call you if I can swing it."

"What's the location?" James asked.

"Get some paper and I'll write the address," Jesus said, continuing to preen.

Moments later, James returned with a writing pad and a pen.

Placing the pad on a table, Jesus said, "Here's the address. Hope we can get together. I'll call if I can get you guys invited. Sorry, but I have to go now. Oh, give me your phone number."

James and Richard had just finished their umpteenth Margarita and relaxed at what had become their poolside table. Afternoon had become evening, and the street noise around the Angel Hotel faded. The heavy scent of jasmine filled the humid evening air. The buzz of jovial conversation emanated from the hotel's bar, filled with local gay men. Many of them peeked into the pool area to see who might be naked.

Gregg and Harry supposedly napped in their room, perhaps in anticipation of partying all night with Jesus and his friends.

The door to Don's room squeak open. "He's up," James whispered to Richard.

Walking zombie-like toward James and Richard, Don rubbed his eyes and asked, "Where is everybody?"

"We're drunk, but we're here," James said. "Harry and Gregg are sleeping. They'll be joining Jesus and Alvaro at some party later on. We're hoping to go if there's space."

"Alvaro and Jesus are still fucking?" Don asked, holding his head as if trying to prevent it from exploding. "I need a drink. Where's that damn bell?"

"Sit," James said, patting a chair then ringing the waiter bell. "I need one too."

Cringing, Don said, "Please, don't ring that again. My head can't take it."

Richard raised his head from the table and muttered, "Me too."

Minutes later, a waiter arrived, carrying a tray of

174

Margaritas. Behind him came Harry and Gregg, naked.

"Don't you guys ever dress?" James asked.

Richard looked at the blushing waiter and asked, "Do you ever undress?"

"On special occasions," the waiter said, placing the last drink on the table.

"This is a special occasion," Richard said. What's taking you so long?"

"Shit!" Harry said, staring at Gregg. "We forgot to dress."

Shrugging, Gregg said, "No need unless Jesus calls."

"I hear you guys are going to a fuck party," Don said, his eyes half open. "God, my head hurts."

"Who knows?" Harry said. "It might be a suck party."

"Fuck. Suck. That's all Alvaro wants to do anymore," Don muttered. "He'd have sex with a mouse, a knot hole—anything—but me."

"Oh, Don. Get real," Gregg said. "You're always giving the kid a hard time. Slack off, go with the flow, and see what happens. Being jealous doesn't help."

"I can't help it." Don said. "By the way, what time is it? . . . Tell me it's the same day."

Harry looked at the wall clock. "It's eleven."

"Damn! Guys, I gotta get something to eat," Don said. "I'll see you in a bit."

"Then you'd better get dressed," Gregg said.

Don sat alone in the El Toro, a restaurant one block from his hotel. Listening to "*corazon*" songs about lovers and broken hearts, he became depressed. For a moment, He picked at his favorite meal then pushed his plate back. He waved to the waiter. "Check, *por favor*."

After examining the check, Don rifled through his billfold, withdrew a peso note like it weighed a ton and placed it on the table.

He shuffled toward the hotel. *Should I stop in the bar*

175

or see if the guys are at the pool? If they're there, we'll have a drink. God, should I have another drink?

Don walked past the dimly-lighted garden to the pool area where Richard and James drank Margaritas.

"Mind if a dressed man joins you naked guys for a drink?" Don asked, trying to generate a laugh.

"Nope," James said, "but why don't you get naked."

"Can't," Don said. "Might get you guys too excited and you'd rape me."

James chuckled then said, "You can't be raped. You're too willing, and we're too drunk."

"James, I think it's time for bed," Richard said. "You ready?"

"Go ahead," James said and picked up his half-empty glass. "I'll be in when I finish this."

Richard drank the last of the water from his melted ice, grabbed his towel, and then staggered toward his room.

While Don stared at Richard, James said, "Been with that man for five years, and I still like looking at his butt."

"You both have nice asses," Don said. "So does my Alvaro."

James downed the last of his drink then said, "Don, he is not yours. Love him but know you can't own him."

"I know. I know."

"Well, my drink's finished." James pushed back from the table. "I'm going to bed. See ya tomorrow."

James removed his towel from the table, revealing the writing pad left by Jesus.

"What's this?" Don asked, fingering the paper.

"The party address," James said. "Jesus left it in case we were invited. Since he didn't call, guess we're not invited. Well . . . goodnight, Don."

"Nite," Don said and picked up the pad. He looked at the address. *Shit! I'll invite myself.*

Don looked beyond the hood of the taxi to the pine trees lining the rural road. He soon reached the address written on the paper and exited the cab. He guessed the nearest house to the party address had to be half-mile away. As the taxi left, Don thought, *God, I hope this is the right place. Getting a taxi here could be hell.*

He walked to the ornate iron gate of the walled estate and peered inside. Far to the right, he saw a caretaker sized house and beyond that a large, well-cared for hacienda style home. Pulsing party music and fragrant jasmine vied to fill the night as bass notes shook the villa's walls. Don looked at his watch. *One thirty-five. Party's just getting started.*

He pulled a weathered rope connected to a bell hanging inside the gate. A cooling evening breeze blew past as he waited for someone to come to the gate, but no one responded to the rung bell. *I doubt the feeble sound of this shitty bell reached the house.*

Don stepped back and looked at the house number. *Right place.* "Shit! I'll let myself in." He reached through the gate and lifted the latch. The gate swung open. "Hello!" he yelled. "Anyone here?"

No one replied.

A path of white stepping stones led toward the caretaker's house from which salsa music roared. The full moon made it easy to follow the path, which Don treaded as if one of the stepping stones might crack under his feet. *Bet there's not this much moonlight in el centro. The damn smog ruins everything there.* He took a deep breath. *Ahh. The air smells better here.*

Step-by-step, he crept toward the whitewashed cottage. The trip could have taken thirty seconds, but he stretched it to minutes for fear of what or whom he might encounter.

Taking the last step to the gate of the caretaker's courtyard, he took a deep breath and pushed open an ornate iron gate. Inside, a group of about twenty-five, bare-chested young men laughed and drank. Several were naked. Several more wore only underwear.

Few men took notice of Don's arrival. However, one man looked at him, smiled, and then approached him. "*Señor, gringo. Amigo de* David?"

"*Si!*" Don responded, "A good friend."

"*David esta en la casita,*" the stranger said and pointed to a small building painted a bright blue.

"*Gracias.* I'll find him."

Don wondered if David hosted the party.

While he might know the host's name, he had no idea about his appearance. *Hell, I'm not here to meet the host. I'm here to find Alvaro.*

Don pushed his way through an undulating sea of sweaty-chested, dancing guys who blocked the entrance to the blue building housing the bar. A sign over the doorway read "*Casita de Amor.*" Below the verbiage, he read the translation, "House of Love."

Several guests stepped aside, almost acknowledging Don's clothed presence. He walked through the building's front room then entered the kitchen—painted Blessed-Mother-Blue.

Blocking the rear screen door stood a temporary bar constructed of beer crates and an old door. Behind the bar, a young, naked bartender dispensed beers. His hands were busy serving beers and fighting off guests who wanted to grope his ample crotch, rub his bubble butt, or tweak his inviting nipples.

Don spotted Alvaro's backside just outside the screen door. He spoke to a man hidden in the shadows. Neither wore a shirt. *At least he's not naked or fucking somebody.*

Don decided to play it cool, get a beer, roam around, and find out to whom Alvaro spoke.

He elbowed his way to the bar then winked at the bartender. "*Corona, por favor.*"

"I know you are gringo with accent like that," the bartender said then smiled.

"It shows?"

The bartender smiled and winked. "*Sí.*"

"But not as much as you show," Don said, staring at the young man's crotch.

"I'm paid to be naked. The *anfitrión*—sorry—I mean the host, he believes more guests come for party if bartender is naked."

"I'm glad he feels that way." Don smiled. "I approve of his choice and your decision to bartend."

"Thank you, *Señor*. Sorry. But no can talk now. I must serve. You come back later, no?"

"I understand. Maybe I can hire you to bartend a party for me sometime."

"Sure. I give you beeeeg discount."

"Deal. By the way, who trimmed your crotch into that interesting heart shape?"

"The host did. He doesn't like much hair there."

"That didn't bother you?"

"*No mucho.* I traded hair for *pesos*. It grows back." The bartender smiled then turned to another guest.

Don lingered for a moment, admiring the bartender's muscular back, butt, and ample crotch then walked out the front door.

He leaned against a courtyard wall and observed the crowd. Minutes later, he saw Harry and Gregg, naked, exit a clump of bushes. Each had an arm around the shoulders of a laughing, naked young Mexican.

Don mumbled, "Bet they've been up to no good." He watched them for a second. *Ut oh. They're coming this way. Don't want them to see me.*

Don retreated to the shadows where he continued to survey the crowd, watch a few guys get groped and chuckled about a drunken man who kept trying to pull down a younger guest's underwear. *From the bulge in that kid's underwear, I know why he guy wants the kid's "drawers" off.*

Don peered behind a low bush and saw a skinny guy,

179

pants at his ankles, getting a blow job. Don inched along the wall until he had a better view of the action. *By the way his butt is contracting, he's about to shoot. Good for him. Hell, even my dick is getting hard.*

After the upright guy shot his load, he pulled his kneeling friend to his feet, hugged, and then kissed him.

"How sweet!" Don muttered, a tinge of sarcasm in his voice. *They're in love. I'd better see what Alvaro is up to.*

Don drained his bottle and headed to the bar for another beer.

"*Mas?*" the bartender asked.

"*Sí,*" Don said, "a beer and a look. What's your name?"

"Tito."

"Tito, I'm Don," Don said, shaking the wet hand Tito had used to fish a beer from ice water.

"Sorry for cold hand. Nice meet you, *Señor* Don. You want a *Corona*, no?"

"*Corona, sí.* I could rub your hand until it warms up, if you'd like."

Tito smiled and patted the back of Don's hand. "You are a good man."

Don looked past Tito to Alvaro who continued to talk to a man in the shadows. As Don watched, Alvaro glanced his way. A look of surprise crossed Alvaro's face. His mouth gaped as he moved from view.

Don wondered if Alvaro would come around the building to greet him. He exited the front door and turned left, expecting to see Alvaro. Much to Don's surprise, Alvaro was nowhere to be seen. Don looked along the path that ran toward the hacienda, and then in back of the *casita*. *Where the fuck?*

Alvaro had disappeared.

"What the hell? Where the fuck did he go?" Don asked. *I'll wait here . . . see who's coming and going. If he moves, I'll see him.*

Perturbed, Don leaned against the *casita,* switched his bottle from hand to hand, drank some beer, and surveyed an

180

area of a hundred eighty degrees, hoping to see Alvaro.

Don quickly finished his beer and wanted another.

After talking to Tito for a few minutes, Don left the *casita* with a Corona. Rounding the corner of the building to retake his survey spot, he saw a crude wooden ladder being lowered from the *casita's* roof.

"Shit." *He's been hiding on the roof.*

Don crept to nearby shadows and waited for Alvaro to leave his roost.

Scraping sounds continued as the ladder descended over the edge of the *casita* roof.

Someone must have decided to change music CDs because the night suddenly became quiet. Replacing the din of dance music were the squeaks of Alvaro's leather sandals as he climbed down the ladder. Trying to discern Alvaro's whispers, Don cupped his ears to listen.

"Coast's clear," Alvaro said, looking skyward.

Jesus stuck his head over the edge of the roof.

"Good! I don't want a run-in with Don."

Salsa music suddenly blasted the guests as Jesus reached the ground and began to lower the ladder.

Bastards. "Look who's here," Don said, stepping forward to confront the men.

Looking shocked, Alvaro and Jesus stared at Don as they let the ladder slam against the wall.

"Don, remember where you are," Alvaro said. "We are guests here. Please don't make a scene."

"Scene? I'm not here to make a scene. I'm here to take you home—away from that corrupter behind you."

Jesus pulled Alvaro behind him and said, "When he wants to go, I'll take him, but he's not ready to leave."

"Don, please . . . ," Alvaro pleaded, "leave me alone!"

"You can't be happy with that . . . ballplayer," Don sniped. "He'll soon be a has-been, and you'll be left with just having been fucked. Don't you see he's using you? All he wants is your ass!"

"Hell, he can have it! He treats it well—better than you."

Before Don could blink, Alvaro kissed Jesus then glared at Don. "He even kisses better."

Alvaro's defiance left Don feeling angry, hurt, and at a loss for words. Alvaro must have sensed Don's volcanic anger would explode, so he backed away. For a split second, Don stared at Alvaro. *Damn you, you son-of-a-bitch!*

"Come," Jesus said, taking Alvaro's hand and turning away.

"Oh no you don't," Don yelled. "He's not going anywhere with a soccer bastard! If I can't have him, you can't either."

Don lunged faster than Jesus could avoid Don's death-delivering hands. They engulfed Jesus' throat. Despite Jesus prying at the strangling fingers, Don's grip tightened, and he roared like a mad man. Jesus' face turned grey-blue and filled with unfathomable fear. The veins on the white of his eyes became engorged—ready to burst. "Die, you bastard!"

Alvaro jumped on Don's back, pulling and prying at his death grip, but Don's strangling hands could not be loosened.

Don growled like a lion protecting a fresh kill.

Panicky, Alvaro yelled, "Let him go, you son-of-a-bitch!" With clinched fists, Alvaro beat Don's face and yelled, "Help! Help!"

Two men entered the fray, yelling, "Stop! *Alto!* Stop!"

One of the newcomers joined Alvaro in prying at Don's hands while the other pulled on Don's torso. Neither of the men could disengage Don's death grip.

"Die, you son-of-a-bitch! Die!"

As Don yelled, he threw Jesus around like an alligator dispatching its prey.

The man pulling on Don's torso released his arm lock then slapped Don's face. Don stopped growling and glared at the stranger as if he wanted to kill him. Don released one hand and reached for the slapper, but another man tackled Don, knocking him to the ground. Falling, he released his grip on Jesus' throat.

Alvaro and the three strangers pounced on Don. Despite having his arms and legs pinned, Don flailed and writhed. Realizing he could not escape, he went limp and bawled.

Pushing through the onlookers, the naked, fiftyish-looking host, David, stormed onto the scene. "*Que pasa*?" he yelled. Looking down at Jesus, he asked, "What's going on?"

Rapid exchanges of Spanish descriptives were offered by Jesus and several men. David pulled Alvaro and the other guests off the pinned, weeping assailant.

Looking relieved, Jesus slumped against the *casita,* clutching his throat. He made the sign of the cross and looked heavenward, moonlight revealing bruises forming on his neck.

In English, the host addressed Don, "I don't know you, *gringo*? How the hell did you get in?"

"I'm Don. I know Jesus."

Jesus stood erect. "This *bastard* crashed the party!"

Harry and Gregg pushed their way through the crowd and stared in horror at Jesus.

"Jesus, are you okay?" Gregg asked.

Jesus nodded.

Harry shook his head. "Jesus . . . I'm sorry. We left your note with this address on the poolside table. That's how Don got here."

"Jesus," David asked, "did you bring these two gringos?"

"Yes and no." Jesus pointed to Harry and Gregg. "I invited them, but they came ahead of me. I gave them the address."

David shook his head. "If it didn't take a long time for the police to arrive, I'd call them. Have them take all *gringos* to jail." David shook his fist at Don. "I want you *gringos* out. *Now*! Get dressed. Get out. I'll call a taxi."

David pushed his way to the front of the casita yelling,

"*Música*. Start *la música!*"

The crowd dispersed to resume drinking and dancing as Jesus and Alvaro headed toward the far end of the property. Jesus, clutching his neck, limped. He had injured his right leg in the scuffle.

Don leaned against the *casita* then slid down its wall until he sat on the ground. There he waited with Harry and Gregg, under the watchful eye of David.

"What the fuck came over you?" Harry asked, giving Don a disgusted look.

"Who knows?" Don muttered staring at the ground.

"Let me help you up," Gregg said, extending his hand to Don. "What caused this ruckus?"

Don shook his head. "I just . . . lost it. Alvaro and Jesus were rubbing my nose in their shitty disrespect, and I lost it."

"Don," Harry said, "you can't go around trying to kill people just because they disrespect you."

"You guys don't understand," Don said, clinching his fists. "I love Alvaro. Damn it! I love him!"

"Better learn to love from afar," Harry said. "If you don't, you know where you're going to wind up? Jail—a *Mexican* jail—that's where.

"Yeah," Gregg said, "a *Mexican* jail. Ouch!"

"A taxi should be here soon," David said, glaring at Don.

"Gregg and I gotta get dressed," Harry said, "so we're ready to leave when it arrives. You better go with us, Don."

Gregg and Harry left to get their clothes, while David, glaring, stood over Don.

Don hung his head and sobbed. "What have I done?"

Minutes later, Harry and Gregg returned. "Come on," Harry said, gripping Don's shoulder. "Stop the crying."

"Yeah, buck up," Gregg said.

A young man approached the *gringos*. "Your taxi is here."

"Thanks," David said, watching Gregg and Harry

184

coax Don toward the front gate and the waiting cab.

Harry sat in the front seat as Gregg pushed Don onto the rear seat and then sat beside him and said, "Hotel Angel, Zona Rosa, driver."

Chapter 14

The taxi pulled to the curb in front of the Angel Hotel. "Don, we're home," Harry said.

Don sat up and stared at the ripped back of the driver's seat.

Harry paid the driver as Gregg exited the rear compartment.

"Come on, Don," Gregg pleaded. "Get out. The driver needs to pick up another fare."

"I don't wanna go in there," Don mumbled. "Not this hotel. Not that room."

"Come on," Harry said, stooping to look Don in the eye. "We can sit in the garden and talk."

"We can get a Margarita," Gregg chuckled. "Maybe two."

"Yeah," Harry said, "let's have a drink, sit, and talk."

Don slid across the seat toward the open door. Shaking, he placed his feet on the pavement then stood beside the curb. He slammed the door then faced the cab, resting his hands on its roof. "How did things get so fucked up?"

Abruptly, the cab lurched away, causing Don's arms to fall to his side. "What the fuck?" The cab's squealing right rear tire just missed his toes.

Harry went ahead to get their room keys.

Gregg took Don's hand and pulled him toward the hotel steps. Don mopped into the lobby where Gregg said, "Could we get three Margaritas?"

"*Si señor*," the clerk said. "Bar is closed, but I'll make them for you."

"Thanks. Three. Make 'em strong."

The men walked through the garden where the temperature seemed ten degrees cooler than on the street. The full-moon fought the city's muddy smog to illuminate jasmine and red hibiscus blossoms that graced the edges of the garden. In-ground floodlights highlighted the Spanish colonial stone architecture that had once been an interior wall of a private home, now part of the hotel's garden wall.

Harry and Gregg headed for their usual poolside table, hidden in the shadows.

"Sit down, Don," Harry said, scraping a chair over the concrete as he pulled it away from the table.

Gregg, sprawled in his chair, emitted a loud "whew," then kicked off his shoes.

Don stared skyward. "Everything here is so different than in the country, isn't it?"

"What's different?" Gregg asked.

"The sky," Don muttered. "In the country, you can see the stars. Here, the sky is muddy. Can't see a damn thing. It's like there's no heaven."

"That's a cloud," Harry said. "In a minute, it'll pass then the moon will shine through—maybe."

"You were lucky tonight," Gregg said, patting Don's arm. "You know you almost killed Jesus. Thank God, you didn't."

"Yeah," Harry said, cocking his head to one side. "Thank God, David didn't call the police. You could have been in all kinds of trouble—deep shit. What the hell came over you?"

"Hell, I don't know," Don said, squirming in his chair. "I saw red, and . . . I lost it."

"I've never seen such rage," Gregg said, holding up Two clenched fists. "Such determination and strength. Those guys couldn't pull you off."

"*Caballeros*," the desk clerk said, placing a tray on the table, "Your drinks. Who gets the bill?"

"Charge 'em to our room," Harry said. "and add a twenty-peso tip."

"*Gracias*," the clerk said then walked away, throwing his tray in the air like an Italian twirling pizza dough.

For a moment, only the kitten-like purr of the pool's pump intruded on the tranquility.

Don picked up his glass, licked the salt from its rim, then gulped the Margarita.

Gregg and Harry sipped their drinks.

The desk clerk returned to hand Harry a piece of paper.

"What's this?" Harry asked, unfolding then silently reading its contents.

> Guys,
>
> I'm in the lobby. Can I sleep on your sofa tonight? My things are in Don's room, and I don't want to get them now, maybe tomorrow, but I need a place to sleep a couple of hours. If it's ok, write yes on this paper and give it to the clerk. He'll return it to me. Please! Don't let Don know I'm here.
>
> Thanks.
>
> Alvaro.

Harry scribbled something on the paper then handed it to the clerk.

"What's that about?" Gregg asked.

"Just something about the tip I added to the bill," Harry said. "Well guys . . . It's late. I need to get to bed." He stood then gripped Harry's shoulder. "Let's get some shuteye. Bring your drink."

"Yeah, I should get some sleep," Don said, pushing himself from his chair. "See ya tomorrow. Thanks for your help tonight."

Quietude returned to the pool.

Alvaro peeked into the area to make sure Don had left the pool. Seeing no one, he crept to Gregg's and Harry's room then tapped on their door.

Harry inched the door open to confirm that Alvaro had

189

knocked. "Come in. Surprised you're here."

"Me too." Alvaro ran his fingers through his hair. "Jesus got drunk and wanted to fuck everyone at the party. I'd had enough, but he didn't want to leave, so I left. I had money for the taxi but not enough for a room, so here I am. Thanks for taking me in."

"For God's sake, please don't tell Don," Gregg said. "Who knows how he'd react."

"The desk clerk has seen me around so much he assumed I'm a co-guest in Don's room and gave me a key—no questions asked. Tomorrow, I'll let myself in *our* room, get my things, then I'm outta here."

"Where will you go?" Harry asked.

"Jesus invited me to move in, so I'm moving in."

"What are you going to do for money?" Gregg asked.

"I'll get a job—off the books of course." Alvaro smiled. "If I have to, I'll pimp myself. My bod is a hell-of-a-lot better than the rent boys I've seen here. If things get bad, I'll start painting again."

"I didn't know you were a painter," Gregg said.

"Yep!" Alvaro said, feeling some pride. "Did some big stuff—murals—on the sides of buildings."

"Where?" Harry asked.

"Philadelphia," Alvaro said, his voice rising.

"I know those murals," Harry said. "Saw them when I visited Philadelphia eight years ago. I bought a picture book about them.

Must be a lot more since then."

"Some are mine," Alvaro said, first feeling proud then uneasy about his admission. "I know you guys want your beauty sleep. What say we get some shuteye?"

"Don't get offended," Gregg said, "but Harry and I sleep naked."

"Hell, I've seen your everything," Alvaro said, removing his shirt. "I sleep naked too."

#

Alvaro awoke to the aroma of fresh coffee brewed by Gregg.

"I ordered breakfast for you," Gregg said. "It should be here soon. Didn't want you running into Don in the dining room."

"Thanks. I don't wanna see him."

Moments later, someone knocked on the door. "Room service."

Harry opened the door to accept the breakfast tray. He handed it to Alvaro and said, "Enjoy. Gregg and I will eat in the dining room."

Alvaro hugged his hosts on their way out the door. "Thanks guys." He turned on the television and ate his burrito. After listening to local salsa bands, he turned to ESPN. An announcer reported Jesus Gonzales would conduct a soccer camp for orphans at the Stadium Azteca later that day. Alvaro thought, *Shit. He'll be so hung over he'll barely be able to stand much less kick a ball with orphans.*

Alvaro switched to CNN news and listened for anything having to do with him or Don. After watching for an hour and hearing no mention of their names, he relaxed. *Guess we're old news.*

A boisterous crowd filled the hotel's deco-style dining room. Many nearby, gay shop owners met there for pastries and Coca Colas, before opening their shops.

Gregg and Harry spotted an empty table in the back of the dining room and headed for it. Before sitting down, Harry opened a nearby window, took a deep breath, then coughed. "This air will kill us."

A waiter handed menus to the men and asked, "Coffee anyone?"

"Two. Black. Thank you," Harry said.

"*Si señor.*" the waiter said then left.

"Know what you're going to have?" Harry asked.

"I'm tired of burritos. Think I'll have pancakes."

Minutes later, the men's breakfasts were ordered, served, and then finished, in short order.

"Ut oh," Harry said. "Don't look now, but Don just walked in, and he's coming this way."

"Morning, guys," Don said, sporting a happy face.

"My, you're in a good mood," Harry said, watching Don wince as he lowered himself onto a chair.

Don moaned then said, "I became so worked up last night I had to take a sleeping pill, but at least I had a good night's sleep. Best since I don't know when." Don accepted a menu from the waiter. "Man, am I hungry."

"Sure you're not cock hungry?" Gregg quipped then smiled.

"That too," Don said. "Did you guys get a look at that Tito—the bartender at the party?"

"Couldn't help it," Gregg said. "Naked-as-a-jaybird with a worm fit for an eagle. Had a great bod too."

Harry said, "I marveled at how he tolerated the gropes and hazing by the guests."

Don smiled then said, "He told me David paid him well to work naked," Don said. "Offered to give me a discount, if I hired him to bartend a party. The thought of having him as a naked bartender makes me want to rent a house just to throw a party."

"Wouldn't it be cheaper to *rent* him and forget the party?" Gregg asked.

Don's stirring spoon kept striking the inside of his cup as he asked, "What makes you think I'd have to pay to get him naked? I'm in pretty good shape, and I know how to fuck." Don puckered his lips. "Shit, I have a blue ribbon in cock sucking."

"He must be all of eighteen or nineteen," Harry said. "Think he digs older men?"

"Who you calling old, *amigo*?" Don asked, slapping Harry on the back.

"You're in your late thirties, right?" Gregg asked.

192

"And you guys think a nineteen-year-old wouldn't enjoy sex with a thirtyish young man?

Don't forget I attracted Alvaro, and he's twenty."

"Speaking of Alvaro," Harry said, putting his cup down. "What's happening with you guys?"

Don sighed then sat motionless. He appeared to stare at the cathedral bell tower sticking above the red-tile rooftops across the street. He cleared his throat and shook his head as if coming out of a trance. "He'll be back. I don't know when, but he'll be back."

"You're certain?" Gregg asked.

"I'm sure . . . I love him, and I know he wants me. He'll be back. It's just a matter of time."

"What if he doesn't . . . come back?" Gregg asked, putting down his cup.

"Don't you worry. I'm not. He'll be back. I just have to wait—give him time."

"Well," Harry said, wiping a crumb from his lip, "we gotta be going."

Gregg signed the check. "We've got some sightseeing to do."

"Have a great day," Don said, waving. "I'm going to Teotihuacan.

I've always wanted to climb those pyramids—especially the Temple of the Sun."

Alvaro searched for his phone and found it between Gregg's sofa cushions. He dialed Jesus.

In a tormented sounding voice, Jesus said, "*Buenoos diiiiaaas*."

"Jesus, it's me, Alvaro."

Jesus' voice perked up. "Where the hell are you?"

"I spent the night at the Angel."

"Don't tell me you spent the night with that bastard Don."

"Hell no. I slept on Gregg's and Harry's sofa. They're

193

having breakfast right now."

"Why are you calling at this hour?"

"I saw on ESPN that you're gonna do a camp at Azteca today."

"Oh shit! I forgot about that! Thanks for reminding me."

"Can I join you? I Promise I'll stay out of the way."

"Sure. Meet me at the players' entrance."

"What time?"

"Shit! Let's see . . . we start at four. Meet me at three fifteen."

"One more thing. Can I move in for a few days?"

"What? Not with Don anymore?"

"I can't go back with him. Not after last night."

"Okay, but you know my house is hectic. Guys come and guys go."

"How about I let you fuck me once a day in lieu of rent?"

"That goes without saying," Jesus chuckled. "You know you can't resist my cock."

"You're so full of shit!"

"Don't yell," Jesus pleaded. "My head's killing me."

Okay. See you at three fifteen. Bye."

"I said, 'Don't yell.'"

Gregg and Harry headed for their room, discussing how to spend the day. Just as they entered, Alvaro put his phone away.

"Talking to Jesus?" Gregg asked, turning down the TV volume.

"Yeah. Gonna meet later at the Azteca. He's doing a camp for orphans at four o'clock."

"He's not a pedophile, is he?" Harry asked, opening his laptop. "Seems he spends a lot of time with boys."

Alvaro smiled. "Oh, he likes boys alright—adult boys."

"We had breakfast with Don. He said something about

194

climbing the Temple of the Sun today."

"Good! That'll get him out of my hair. When he leaves, I'll get my things and high tail it out of here."

"Hope all goes well with you staying with Jesus," Gregg said.

"Wait about thirty minutes," Harry said, "and I'll knock on his door to see if he's gone, but first, I have to shave and shower. Why don't you watch TV, until we know he's gone?"

Harry returned to his room and announced, "Don is gone. The desk clerk saw him get in a taxi about ten minutes ago."

"Good," Alvaro said, smiling. "I'll get my things and let you guys relax. Here's my cell number. Keep in touch. Let's have a drink sometime and thanks for everything."

"Stay sober!" Harry said as Alvaro left.

Harry asked Gregg, "What are we going to say when Don asks if we've seen Alvaro?"

"Why would he ask?"

"Because he'll see Alvaro's things are gone, dummy. He will assume we saw the kid."

Gregg shrugged. "We'll tell the truth—or most of it. We won't tell him Alvaro spent the night or hid out here while we had breakfast. Let's just say we saw him with his things."

"Hey guys. Waiting for a dinner of tube steak?" Don asked as he walked toward Harry and Gregg, lounging beside the pool. "You must have been here all day—your dicks are sun-burned."

Harry and Gregg lifted ball caps from their eyes and squinted at Don. "Well, look who's back?"

"From all the glasses on that table, I'd say you two have emptied the Tequila cellar. Mind if I join you?"

"Nope," Harry answered. "Mind rubbing some sun block on my cock."

195

"First, let me get a drink and get naked, then I'll be back with the lotion. We can oil each other's cock."

Don went to the bar, and after a few minutes, he returned with a Margarita.

"Have fun at the pyramids?" Gregg asked.

"Fuckin A! I climbed behind a good-looking guy wearing short shorts. He had a butt to fight over. Every once in a while, I got a look up his shorts—all the way to his crotch. No underwear. But, damn it, I never got a full view of his cock or balls—just glimpses."

"Was he Mexican?" Harry asked.

"I don't think so. He looked more like a *gringo*. Maybe mixed."

"Why didn't you invite him for a drink?" Harry asked.

"I didn't want to have to fight you guys off," Don chuckled, walking toward his room.

Minutes later, Don returned, naked, carrying his drink. He spread his towel on a lounge, laid down, and rubbed sun block on his arms and chest. "Gregg, wanna oil my cock?"

"Ring the waiter bell," Harry said. "Maybe the he'll oil it for you."

Don chuckled, "But your more my type."

Don lowered his lounge backrest then closed his eyes. A few seconds of silence ensued. He fluffed his balls then cleared his throat. "See Alvaro today?"

"Yeah," Harry said, "he got his things."

"Was Jesus with him?" Don asked.

"I don't think so," Gregg answered. "I mean I didn't see him. I think he was alone."

"Did he say anything about Jesus or me?" Don asked.

"No," Gregg said. "Nothing."

"And Jesus?" Don asked.

"Nope."

"Come on," Don said. "What did he say about Jesus?"

"Don, I won't lie," Gregg said. "Alvaro is meeting Jesus at the Azteca—today—for an orphan's soccer camp."

196

"Yeah, seen some posters about that," Don said, then gulped his Margarita. "You guys want another drink?"

"Sure! Make it three," Harry said.

Chapter 15

Monday's heat and humidity intensified Mexico City's smog while the sun scorched everything unshaded at the hotel pool.

Ice melted so fast Margaritas were diluted within minutes. Don wrapped several paper napkins around his glass to absorb condensation and provide a bit of insulation against the hot, humid air.

"Gregg, are you ready for another round?" Don asked with slurred speech.

"Why not? I'm already drunk. One more won't hurt."

"Me too," Harry said.

Don rang the waiter bell then rubbed sun block on his sweaty chest.

"Hey, Gregg, my cock needs more lotion," Don chortled and flicked condensation from his glass onto Gregg's abdomen.

"Sure you don't want the waiter to do that?" Gregg asked.

Minutes later, the waiter arrived. Eyeing the empty glasses, he said, "Don't tell me. You want another round."

"You guessed it," Don said. "And some lunch. What's good?"

"Just got some Argentinean steaks. Care for one?"

"Sounds good," Don said. "Make it medium rare. A rib eye if you have one."

"We do, and they're well marbled. Anyone else ordering?"

"Nope," Harry said.

"Me neither," Gregg said.

"I'll get right on it, Señor Don," the waiter said.

"Don't forget our Margaritas," Don yelled as the waiter left.

Harry and Gregg turned onto their abdomen, seeking heat relief for their bellies.

Don rubbed sun block on his abdomen and continued sunning, face up.

The waiter returned with cold glasses of Margaritas.

Don rubbed the cold, wet bottom of his glass over his chest. "Damn. It's hot. I don't know about you guys, but I'm going in."

A short time later, the waiter returned with Don's lunch and placed a steak knife on the table. Don accidently bumped the waiter's hand, knocking the knife to the deck, almost hitting Don's foot.

"Sorry!" the waiter said.

"No problem." Don stared at the knife. "Glad it didn't stab my foot, but what the hell is that thing?"

"A steak knife," the waiter said.

"Looks like a Bowie Knife to me." Don noted the waiter's confused looking face. "What? You never heard of the Alamo and Jim Bowie?"

"No, sir."

"Are you Mexican?" Don asked without waiting for an answer. "If you are, you should be ashamed of yourself." Don sipped his Margarita then said, "Jim Bowie grew up as an American frontiers man who moved to Mexico in the 1800s. He became a Mexican citizen and married a daughter of a Mexican governor. When the Mexican-American war, the so-called Texas Revolution, broke out, Jim fought alongside the Americans at the Alamo."

Don turned the knife in his hand and examined its backside. "Bowie died there, but before that, he used a knife like this to kill a lot of bad guys. That earned him the reputation of a tough dude. Even got a knife named after him—the Bowie Knife." Holding up the knife, Don looked at the waiter. "What you have here, Sir, is a Bowie Knife."

"Thank you for the lesson, *Señor*," the waiter said, sounding perturbed at being lectured. "Enjoy your steak."

Don sliced his rib eye then examined its degree of doneness. The blade flashed in the sunlight like a mirror, reflecting light into Gregg's eyes.

"Hey, you trying to blind me," Gregg yelled. "What is that thing?"

"A Bowie Knife." Don said, waving the knife over his head. He took a swig of his Margarita. "It's used to gut pigs, warring Mexicans, and cut steaks."

"Who you calling a pig?" resounded from the far end of the garden as Richard and James stepped into view.

"Hey guys. Where ya been?" Don yelled.

"Sightseeing," James said, taking off his shirt. "We visited some churches and went to the archeology museum. Man, do they have some cool stuff." Staring at Don's steak, James asked, "How's the steak?"

"Best I've had in Mexico. Cuts like butter."

Don finished his steak and then the group began their afternoon job—getting drunk. After several drinks, the gang of five felt no hurt. Four of them splashed around in the pool, engaging in sophomoric pranks and horseplay. One thing led to another, and the guys began playing hump-the-host. It appeared everyone wanted to top, but no one wanted to bottom. Each attempt resulted in the kind of laughter heard only in a girls' grammar school.

Lust and alcohol's obliteration of inhibitions had Richard and Gregg more interested in sex than horseplay. Gregg French kissed Richard, while each stroked the other's cock.

James, watching from his longue, yelled, "Gregg, I'm coming for yer ass."

James joined the fray as Harry rubbed his crotch against Richard's ass.

Not to be out done, Don joined the orgy by trying to suck Gregg and Richard's cock, underwater. James interrupted kissing Richard and slurred an invitation, "Why don't we all go to my room. We have a plastic sheet. We'll oil—everything!"

"Sounds hot," Don said.

The waiter returned to collect the lunch plates, but

seeing an orgy in progress, he must have decided dishes could wait and left.

Everyone dried off and staggered to James' and Richard's room where James searched in a drawer. Seconds later, he pulled out a painter's plastic drop cloth.

"You brought that from America?" Don asked.

"Yep, Richard and I use 'em for sex," James said, flashing a devilish grin. "Take them everywhere."

James and Richard covered the bed with the plastic sheet then smoothed out its wrinkles. James tossed a bottle of baby oil to Richard and said, "Do it."

Richard poured half the oil onto the middle of the plastic then belly-crawled into the puddle.

"Okay, guys," James said. "Get on."

As each man got on the plastic sheet, Richard doused them with oil, beginning with cocks. The guys seemed delighted to slide over each other's body. Soon, the room filled with drunken giggles and the fragrance associated with babies.

Lying on their bellies between Harry and James, whose cocks pointed at the ceiling, Don and Richard gave the two guys a blow job.

Gregg lay on his back between Don and Richard and slapped his feet against their butts while they sucked cock.

After a few foot-slaps, Gregg pushed a big toe into Don's and Richard's hole.

Don must have thought he felt a cock, because he slurred, "Yeah! Fuck me."

Richard must have thought the same thing and pulled at his butt cheeks to allow the presumed cock access.

Gregg laughed and wiggled his toes.

Seconds later, Don realized something other than a cock had attacked his ass. "Use yer cock," he said, "you muthafucka!"

Gregg withdrew the toe and focused his attention and the other toe's action on Richard's ass. Richard responded by moving his rear back and forth.

202

A leg cramp caused Gregg to surrender Richard's ass. Gregg managed to lick the back of Don's cock, half pressed against the bed. At first, Gregg didn't like the taste of baby oil, but his distaste waned, and he sucked Don's cock with the skill of a plumber's plunger on the upstroke.

Don mumbled to Gregg, "Pull my balls."

Gregg complied, pulling and squeezing Don's nuts as much as possible given his oily hand. Don moaned his delight. Gregg's other hand searched under Richard's pelvis then stroked his cock. Gregg asked, "Richard, are you about to cum?"

"Getting close."

"You know where I want it," Gregg said.

Richard mumbled, "Then you'd better get under me."

Gregg stopped sucking Don's cock then wiggled, chest up, under Richard's jack-knifed hips. The oil made it easy for Gregg to slide under Richard. Once Gregg's chest reached Richard's cock, Gregg stroked it.

James called to Richard, "Let's try to come together."

"I'll try," Richard mumbled with a mouthful of James' cock.

Despite his intoxication, Gregg gauged James' approaching climax and adjusted his stroking of Richard's cock.

Gregg maneuvered his left hand under James' butt and inserted a finger. At first, James tightened then relaxed his sphincter. The digit found James' prostate and massaged it. Sphincter tightening suggested a climax would soon happen so Gregg quickened his stroking of Richard's cock and fingering James' ass. Within seconds, James shot his load while Richard's load flooded Gregg's chest.

Gregg moaned. "Ahhh. Hot. Hot." He then slid from under Richard and went to the left side of the bed where Don continued to suck Harry's cock. Gregg rolled on a condom and pushed his throbber inside Don. Baby oil and Don's zeal to be fucked made for easy entry.

Don mumbled, "Yeah, fuck me!"

Gregg pounded Don's butt with all the energy he could Muster, but a climax eluded him. He yelled, "Don. Tighten up."

"Fuck it!" Don yelled. "Just fuck it!"

Gregg thrust as fast as he could, but he couldn't get off. "Damn it.

I'll have to jerk off."

"Don't," Don yelled. "Fuck me!"

"I can't get off fucking you."

"Well fuck me anyway!"

Gregg ignored Don's order and jerked off on Don's back.

"Damn it!" Don yelled. "You should have fucked me. Who taught you how to fuck?"

"Same person who taught you how to get fucked," Gregg retorted, "Alvaro."

"You son-of-a-bitch," Don yelled and glared at Gregg.

Gregg fell onto the bed, laughing. "Your ass fucks like Alvaro's. I don't know what Jesus sees in his or your ass."

"You fucker!" Don yelled and lunged at Gregg. "I'm gonna kill you!"

Harry caught Don in a slippery neck lock, pulling him against the bed. Richard and James jumped on Don, restraining him as they yelled, "Calm down!"

Oiled bodies made it difficult for the men to restrain Don as he yelled, "That son-of-a-bitch can't talk like that about the man I love."

"You're crazy," Gregg yelled, "Alvaro doesn't love you. If he did, he'd be with you, but he isn't—he's with Jesus and his little boys."

Don had a sudden burst of rage. *You bastard!* He struggled to free himself, but the men reapplied pressure.

"Calm . . . down," Harry yelled.

Don stopped struggling, sank into the mattress, and sobbed. He managed to say, "Leave Alvaro out of this."

Harry released his hold on Don's arm then stroked his

forehead.

"The party's over, guys," Richard said.

"Yeah," Harry said, "I can't take any more of this shit."

"Everybody out," Richard said.

Harry and Gregg grabbed their towels and slip-slid-ed, on oily feet, toward the door.

"Sorry about the raucous," Gregg said.

"See you guys tomorrow," Harry said.

Glistening like contestants at a bodybuilders compete-tion, Don followed Harry out then slouched into the solitude of a shadowed pool chair.

The next morning, Don stumbled from his room to his poolside table. He rang the waiter bell then slumped into his chair. Staring at a colorful bird drinking from the side of the pool, he listened to the monotonous gurgling of water flowing from the pool's jets.

Approaching Don's table, the waiter asked, "You rang, *señor*?"

"You're goddamn right I rang! Bring me a drink. A Margarita—a double one!"

"Maybe a single?"

"Damn it, man. I said a *double*."

Don waited, for what seemed a month, for his drink. Tired of waiting, he rose to return to his room just as the waiter delivered a tall, salt-rimmed glass and sat it in front of him.

"Took long enough," Don said, glaring at the waiter then sitting down.

Don took a gulp then placed the glass on the table. He stared at its contents like a gypsy trying to see the future then began to cry. He mumbled, "How can anyone doubt Alvaro loves me, or that I love him." Tears trundled down his cheeks. A few fell into his drink. He dragged a fingertip over the salted rim then licked it. *What the hell is happening to me? To Alvaro?*

Don gulped the Margarita. After downing the last drop,

he placed his head on his folded arms, resting on the table. He seemed to slip into unconsciousness but moments later he sat upright. "Shit! Alvaro's with that damn Jesus—that son-of-a-bitch. Somebody has to teach him a lesson. Yeah . . . a lesson."

Don staggered into the hotel's dining room where he searched drawers, and then shelves. "Where are they?" he mumbled as he hoisted and examined some unknown contraption then continued his quest. His rummaging attracted the attention of the desk clerk. He entered the dining room and watched Don for a moment. "*Señor*, you know you shouldn't be here—naked. May I help you."

Yeah. I'm looking for a knife—a Bowie Knife."

"May I ask why?"

"To cut something!"

"Would a small knife help?"

"No damn it! I need a *big* knife. Where is it?"

"Why do you need big knife?"

"None of yer damn business! You gonna get me a knife or not?"

"All right, *señor*. Calm down."

The clerk went to the kitchen then returned with a Bowie Knife. "Don't come naked in front rooms of the hotel again, and please return the knife when you finish. I don't have to pay for it."

"I will—all nice and shiny!"

"Thank you," the clerk said then left.

Don clutched the knife as he walked through the reception area. He grabbed a free newspaper then rolled it around the knife.

He staggered to his room where he adjusted the shower-water temperature. Feeling his Margaritas, Don slid down the shower wall and let the water run over his head. After a few minutes, he dressed, staggered to the sidewalk, and hailed a taxi.

"Where to, *señor*?" the cabbie asked.

The Azteca. Players' entrance."

Don clutched his newspaper-wrapped knife as the driver's erratic driving jostled him about. "Turn on the air conditioning," Don yelled, rolling up his window. "I can't take this polluted air."

"Sorry, *señor*. AC no work."

"Shit!" Don rolled down his window.

Thirty minutes later, the driver pulled to the curb. "The arena, *señor*."

Don placed his newspaper on the seat, opened his billfold, glanced at the meter, then gave the driver 200 *pesos*. "Keep the change."

Don had headed for the players' gate when he heard the taxi driver yell. "*Señor*, you left your paper."

Shit! Can't leave that.

Don retrieved the newspaper, thanked the driver, and then headed for the players' entrance. His hands shook as he stood beside the rusting gate. He began pacing the graveled path outside the gate. Every five minutes, he looked down the tunnel leading to the players' dressing room, hoping to see Jesus.

Don's pacing attracted the attention of a security guard. "Who you wait for?"

"Jesus Gonzales."

"He won't be here for some time."

Don waved off the guard. "I'll wait."

"Okay," the guard said and walked away, crunching pea gravel under foot as he disappeared down the arched passageway.

Don slumped against an exterior arena wall where he could watch the gate. He felt happy the guard hadn't inquired about his newspaper.

The arena held only ten percent of its capacity that day, but the intermittent roar of the crowd sounded like a throng. Besides observers, Don knew the crowd contained TV crews, print-media representatives, orphans from several institutions, and numerous players from several soccer teams.

Hundreds of volunteers were there to assist, hoping the orphans would have a memorable day. To do so, volunteer teams rotated turns at energizing the crowd with chants and team cheers.

Every few minutes, the players' gate opened, and small groups of people exited the arena. Each occurrence caused Don's heart to race in anticipation that Alvaro and Jesus might be among them.

Don had waited thirty minutes, but he recognized no one except the guard to whom he had spoken earlier.

"What time is the demonstration over?" Don asked the guard.

The guard looked at his watch. "An hour."

"Another hour, eh?" Don pointed across the street. "Think I'll have a drink at the Rooster Bar. See ya in an hour."

The Rooster Bar had little bluster and no substance. The painted facade of green, white, and red stripes gave way to a dark and drab blue interior. Clear plastic table covers made no attempt to hide the holes and tattered hems of the red and white checkered tablecloths beneath.

Grit, from road dust, covered the ubiquitous white plastic chairs and could be seen vibrating when the bar's cheap sound system blasted deep bass notes.

Ignoring the bar's negative attributes, Don brushed clean a seat at a curbside table then sat down where he could see the players' gate across the street. He placed his newspaper-wrapped knife on the chair beside him.

A short, rotund waiter, wearing a long, black apron approached. "You want something to eat or drink, *señor?*"

"*Una* Margarita *doble, por favor.*"

Don wiped sweat from his brow as the waiter returned with a quart size champagne glass filled with a frothy Margarita. Don took a sip then smacked his lips. *Damn. They make a good drink here.*

As the day's heat reached its zenith, the refreshing effect of Don's drink waned. He yelled for the waiter.

Throwing a towel over his shoulder, the waiter left the bar's cool interior and strolled to Don's table.

"Bring me the tallest, largest glass you have and fill it with a Margarita just like this one."

Minutes later, the waiter returned with a larger bowl-shaped champagne glass that held five pints.

"Oh, my god!" Don exclaimed, with disbelief. "How the fuck am I going to drink that?"

"You want a straw?" the waiter asked.

"Yeah, a big one."

The waiter returned with a long, flexible plastic straw. "Enjoy, your drink, *señor*."

Don sucked his Margarita through the straw until he could lift the container and not spill his drink. After drinking half his second Margarita, he felt less anxious.

An empty, sputtering, and rusting hulk of a school bus pulled to the curb near Don's chair. The engine idled like it would die any moment. Foul exhaust billowed from its broken tailpipe, adding to the already polluted air.

Don coughed then muttered, "Son-of-a-bitching bus should be taken off the road." *Why the hell did he park here? He's blocking my view.* He yelled to the driver. "Get the hell away from here!" Between coughs, Don waved at the driver and yelled, "Move it!"

The driver cupped his ear and shrugged as if to ask, 'What?'

The engine back fired causing Don to yell, "Get the hell out of here! Move it."

The driver shrugged then unrolled a newspaper, revealing a large tamale, which he ate as he sat behind the steering wheel, engine running.

Enraged, Don yelled, "Get the fuck outta here! Eat somewhere else."

The driver ignored Don's middle finger salute.

Don's anger control napped. He hurled his glass at the bus. A trail of liquid followed its trajectory. The glass struck the bus just below the driver's window.

Glaring, the driver shook his fist. His red face glowed beneath his scraggy beard as he exited the bus. Toddling, he yelled profanities in Spanish as his giggling pear shaped body waddled toward Don.

Intoxicated, Don stood on shaky legs ready to meet the on-coming threat.

The waiter rushed to prevent an altercation. After a heated discussion with the waiter, the driver seemed to calm down and headed toward his bus.

Don breathed a sigh of relief and sat down. *Maybe the damn bus will leave now.*

Suddenly, the bus driver turned and ran toward Don. He stood prepared to fight.

The driver, a man of fifty, weighing close to three-hundred pounds, threw a right hook and walloped Don's left temple.

Don struck the driver's jaw, knocking him to the side-walk. Don attempted to straddle and pummel the driver, but he pushed Don to the ground, sat on his chest, and then pounded his face. Blood flowed from Don's nose now deviated to the left. He felt his nose then yelled, "You bastard, you broke it!"

The driver must have thought Don hurled more insults at him, so he pummeled Don harder. Don tried in vain to block the blows.

A cut opened over Don's left eyebrow, and blood flowed into his eye and down his cheek. He grasped a table leg for leverage, raised his feet to the height of the driver's head then wrapped his legs around the driver's neck, slamming him to the ground. His head struck the sidewalk with a thud. "Die you son-of-a-bitch," Don yelled then sprang to his feet, ready to stomp the downed driver, but he grabbed Don's foot and pulled him to the ground while yelling derogatory Spanish epithets.

So far, the waiter had avoided the scuffle, no doubt

fearing being injured, but as the driver mounted another attack, the waiter intervened. Each combatant struggled to get at the other, but the waiter pushed them apart.

During the fight, another waiter had called police.

Two patrol cars, sirens blaring, arrived and disgorged four officers, wearing black uniforms, black helmets, black sunglasses, and black bulletproof vests, they looked like aliens.

The peace-keeping waiter held the fighters at bay, until the policemen could hold them in check.

The officer with the most gold stripes on his sleeve questioned the bus driver.

A second waiter spoke to another officer in Spanish, then pointed at Don.

"You sons-a-bitches better speak in English!" Don yelled.

The policeman restraining Don pointed his nightstick at Don's head and gestured he should be quiet.

"Can't you see I'm bleeding? My nose is broken." Don yelled, "I need a doctor!"

The restraining officer jerked Don's arm and yelled, "*Silencio!*"

The driver and waiter continued to speak to the officer in charge. He took notes and often glared at Don who continued to yell insults. After ten minutes of taking notes, the officer closed his notebook and walked toward Don.

"*Señor*, you go to jail," the officer said.

"You speak English?" Don asked.

"A little."

"You bastard. Can't you see I need medical attention?"

"I see you need jail."

Don watched the bus driver sign a paper then head for his bus.

The officer holding Don, jerked his arm and pushed him toward a patrol car.

"You can't let that son-of-a-bitch go," Don yelled. "He started this shit."

"Shut up and get in the car," the officer said, clenching his teeth and staring Don in the eye.

Two officers clamped handcuffs on Don and yanked him toward the open door of the patrol car.

Don let his legs go limp, yelling, "You can't do this to me. I'm an American citizen. Oh shit!" Don said as if having an epiphany. *I hope they don't do fingerprints or search Interpol. Shit! I'm in trouble. Oh God. That waiter is gonna find the knife. What if he tells police? Shit!*

A policeman pushed Don's head down as another forced him onto the back seat of the patrol car.

"*El Centro,*" the lead officer yelled to the driver. "Book and print him."

Don settled onto the seat as the driver of the bus, parked in front of the patrol car, gunned his engine, creating a black cloud of foul exhaust that engulfed Don's patrol car.

Coughing, Don yelled, "How do you people put up with this shit?"

The bus moved away from the curb, its engine sputtering. When its cloud of pollution cleared, Don had a view of the players' entrance. He scanned the face of each member of a group of people leaving the arena. *Where the hell is Jesus? Shit! I can't do anything about him now.*

The officer driving Don's car said something to him in Spanish then pulled into traffic.

"Why don't you people learn to speak English?"

Don watched the players' entrance fade into the distance as Alvaro and Jesus exited the player's gate. Jesus placed his arm around Alvaro's shoulder. Alvaro mimicked the move.

Don muttered, "Sons-of-bitches!"

The Rooster waiter shook his head as he swept up the broken glass left by Don's assault on the bus. "That bastard didn't pay for his drinks, and he left his trash for me to clean up." The waiter picked up Don's newspaper. S*trange. It's heavy.* The waiter unfolded the paper, revealing the knife. Its

212

size startled him, and he dropped it, nicking his foot. "Ow!" His painful yell caused another waiter to come running. "What happened?"

Looking down at the knife, the injured waiter said, "This damn thing is sharp. At first, I didn't feel a thing, but now it hurts, and I'm bleeding." Staring the other waiter in the eye, the injured man asked, "Why would a *gringo* wrap a knife in a newspaper?"

"He was watching the players' gate," the second waiter said. "Maybe he wanted to stab a player."

The waiter limped to the *baño* to wash blood from his foot. Along the way, he asked the manager for a Band-Aid.

"Why do you need a Band-Aid?" the manager asked.

The waiter pointed to his foot and told the boss about the knife.

"Knife?" the manager asked. "Bring it to me."

The waiter cared for his cut then gave the knife to his boss.

The manager stared at it with amazement. "The owner of this is up to no good. Notify police. This is a weapon."

The waiter called to a passing patrolman then showed him the knife. The officer examined it and the newspaper and decided to take both to Police Central.

The policeman registered the knife as evidence then showed it to Carlos Xanthus, the officer in charge of Don's arrest records.

"*Por Dios*," Carlos exclaimed, his eyes darting over the reflective surface of the knife. "This is not a kitchen knife—this is a weapon. What the hell did that *gringo* intend to do with it?"

"Shall I lock it up?" the policeman asked.

"No, I want to confront our prisoner with it—see what he says."

The jail's camera did not work, so the usual prisoner photographs were not taken. Following Don's registration and fingerprinting, he walked, under duress, to a cell.

Cloaked in shadows, Don's new, graffiti-covered home had nothing to recommend it. Illuminated by a twenty-five-watt bulb, the hallway's rusting ceiling-light dangled from a frayed, electrical cord just outside Don's cell. He would share the ten foot by ten-foot space with three prisoners. Two gringo-looking men sat on their bare bedsprings staring at the new comer.

"Hi," Don said, nodding.

His mates said nothing but did nod.

A third man, appearing to have a Mexican-Mayan heritage, lay on his bed, smoking a self-rolled cigarette while watching a fly crawl across the ceiling. It and the smoker were soon shrouded in an acrid cloud of cheap tobacco smoke that grew larger, puff-by-puff. It soon claimed the cell that reeked of urine.

Gently squeezing his nose shut, Don stared at excrement in an unflushed toilet stuffed with what were once white socks.

"An angry *gringo* did that," the Mexican prisoner said, pointing to the toilet.

Don looked around. *Only thing missing in this third-rate movie set is a black rat.*

The prisoners' sole luxury consisted of one roll of toilet paper per man.

"What the fuck is this?" Don asked, holding up his roll. "This fucker has all of sixteen single ply squares.

"That's everybody allotment," a gringo mumbled. "It's to prevent a death by plugging yer own or yer cellmate's throat."

Don sat down on the edge of the empty metal bedframe below the smoker. Don stared at the bare concrete visible through the floor's worn grey paint. He breathed through his mouth because his nasal passages were obstructed by swelling secondary to his broken nose.

"I can't stand this nose shit," Don said to his disinterested cellmates. "My nose is broken and the bastards won't let me see a doctor. I gotta take matters in my own hands."

"Uh huh," a prisoner said. "Good luck getting help."

Don touched his aching nose. "Shit! I can feel the bones move. Sounds like pinching Rice Krispies. Gotta straighten it myself if I want to breathe again."

Don leaned back and steadied his head against the cool stone wall.

He placed the first and second fingertips of each hand along each side of his nose. The painful crunch of the broken bones caused him to suck air. He closed his eyes and took a deep breath. "Okay," he said, "gotta do it." He clenched his jaw, mustered his nerve, and then pushed both sides of the nasal bones toward each other. "Yauuu . . .!" Don yelled as if someone had hit him in the face with a baseball bat.

The dozing *gringo* cellmates sprang upright. "What the fuck?" they asked.

The Mexican prisoner had no discernable reaction.

Don's nose bled. He wanted to pinch its middle to stop the bleeding but he feared he might dislodge the bones he had just repositioned, so he pinched only the tip. The bleeding continued, dripping on his shirt. "Shit!" He ripped off a piece of his shirttail and made two small wads. Gritting his teeth, and shuddering with pain, he pushed a wad of fabric into each nasal opening. "Jesus!" He panted with pain for a few seconds. *Thank God that's over.*

He held his left palm beneath his nose. *Bleeding has stopped.*

Don's yelling had caused two guards to come running, pistols drawn. Seeing fresh blood on Don's face and shirt, they apparently presumed a cellmate had struck him.

One guard remained outside the cell while the other entered. Waving his revolver in the faces of the prisoners and demanded to know who had struck Don, the inside guard asked, "*Quién?* Who?" Twisting the arm of a prisoner, the guard shouted, "*Quién?*"

The guards appeared ready to drag each prisoner away to extract a confession, but Don intervened. The guards had

215

difficulty understanding he had caused the bleeding when he straightened his fractured nose. The guards, finding nothing amiss, retreated to their station.

Officer Carlos, a dapper man, always wore a uniform with sharp creases and an expensive cologne. He stood outside Don's cell and cleared his throat. "*Señor* Don, I need to speak to you. How is your nose?"

"Just peachy," Don quipped, sounding like he had a head cold.

"Step to the door."

Don forced himself to the door where Carlos held out a newspaper then unrolled it. He peeled back the last page, revealing a knife. He grasped its handle and held the blade at Don's eye level. The blade glinted as Carlos moved it under the hall's dim light.

Don's cell mates gasped at the sight of the blade.

"Why did you carry this, *Señor* Don?"

"I don't know anything about it," Don murmured, looking away. "It's not mine."

"*Señor* Don, you must look at this knife. I insist."

Don glanced at the knife. "Don't know nothing about it."

"*Señor*, we have checked the knife for fingerprints. It has yours."

"Check again. They're my twin's—not mine."

"No, *Señor*. They are yours. Why did you carry this kni—?"

"Do you have aspirins?" Don asked. "I have a head-ache."

"Tell me why you carried this, and I will give you *aspirina*."

"Okay," Don mumbled. "Get 'em."

Carlos walked to the far edge of the cell and yelled toward the guard station, "*Dos aspirinas*."

Using his thumb and forefinger, Carlos sharpened the

creases of his shirt as he waited at Don's cell.

Soon, a guard arrived. "*Dos aspirinas, Señor* Carlos," the guard said, handing the officer a small package then leaving.

"Here are your *aspirinas*," Carlos said, holding them toward Don.

Without being asked, Don walked to the cell door, extended a hand between the bars, and turned his palm up, so Carlos could drop the pills in his outstretched hand.

"How do you know to put your palm up? Have you ever been in prison?"

"Seen it in the movies," Don said taking the pills from his palm. He grimaced as he swallowed them without water.

Carlos called the guard back. "Check Interpol for this man's prints."

"Now," Carlos said, brandishing the blade in Don's face. "Why did you have this knife, *Señor*?"

"Okay. Okay. I'll tell you. I wanted to kill dogs—stray dogs."

"*Señor* Don. We have no stray dogs in *el centro*."

"That's because I killed them all. I intended to start in the country where there are lots of strays but that crazy bus driver attacked me."

"*Señor*, I don't believe you," Carlos sniped. "I will leave you for a few days to think about the question. Then, I'll bring your food. You tell the truth, and you eat."

"Thanks, but I don't think I care for Chef Montezuma's cooking. I'll forgo your award-winning cuisine—thank you."

"We'll see," Carlos said, walking away. "We'll see. Enjoy your vacation."

A minute seemed to take an hour to pass. Don felt like three days had elapsed since Carlos' visit.

Don paced like a caged tiger. He had grown hungry and thirsty, waiting for Carlos to return with food and water.

While waiting, Don saw three men pass out from a lack

217

of both. *They don't care if we rot in this God forsaken hell hole.*

Each noontime, the sun sent a few rays of sunlight through a high, narrow window at the end of Don's dark corridor. The light helped Don track time. *Is this the day we get food and water?*

Don's cell block reeked of desperate silence except for the drip, drip, drip of a leaky faucet near the guard's station. Having reached his breaking point, he yelled, "Where the fuck is our food? Get us some water, damn it!"

Don's cellmates joined in the raucous and yelled in unison, "We want water! We want water!"

Soon other prisoners joined the uprising.

"*Silencio!*" a guard yelled, walking toward Don's cell while dragging his nightstick over cell bars. "*Silencio!*"

Carlos joined the guard under the dim light outside Don's cell. "What's going on?" Carlos asked.

"We need water," Don said. "We haven't had any in months. We'll die in this heat."

"*Caballeros,*" Carlos said, "You have been here two days. Anyway, someone is here to see *Señor* Don."

A tall man, dressed in a pinstriped black suit and shiny black shoes, stepped forward then removed his Panama straw hat. The dim light revealed a pale, grim-faced man with a jagged scar on his left cheek. Staring at Don, the man fidgeted with his hat and polished the tops of his shoes against the back of his pant legs.

"Don Johns?" the man asked. "I'm Richard Lyons. I'm the consul from the American Embassy. Here's my card."

Don sniffed the card. "Hmmm. Lavender cologne."

"What?" Consul Lyons asked.

"Your cologne is lavender based. I like it. I'll keep the card."

"Thank you," the consul said, smiling. "Officer Carlos contacted the embassy after receiving a notice from Interpol that your fingerprints, found on an impounded knife, matched those of a fugitive American citizen. I'm here to tell you authorities in

Philadelphia are attempting to extradite you. Our embassy can provide some assistance, if you wish to appeal." The consul reached inside his coat and pulled out a folded white paper. "This contains the names of several English-speaking Mexican attorneys. Take it. Choose one and call them. You must, however, make your own financial arrangements regarding the attorney's fees. Our office cannot provide any assistance in such matters."

Don clutched the page as though he feared it might be stolen. "What if I don't have any money?"

"You should contact an attorney anyway," the consul said, fingering the brim of his hat. "Some attorneys might be willing to schedule periodic payments. I've made arrangements for the guards to assist you in placing up to ten local calls. I suggest you use them wisely. Oh, yes, because of your particular problem, I cannot provide any more assistance. I must remain neutral, outside the information I have already provided, except for emergency health issues. If you need medical care, the guards will let you to call the embassy. You have my card but do *not* call unless you have a medical emergency."

"Who is us?" the consul inquired.

"These Americans,*"* Don said, pointing to his cellmates sitting on the edge of their bare bedframes.

"I'll try, but I can't interfere with the policies of the jail. You and I must work within the Mexican legal system."

The consul asked Officer Carlos, "Could you please see that these Americans get food and water today?"

"*Si, Señor* Consul. They are scheduled to be fed today."

"Well, Don," the consul said, grinning, "seems this is your lucky day."

"Tell me, Consul, what are my chances of being extradited?"

"In cases like yours, I'd say there is a ninety percent chance."

"Whatta ya mean in cases like mine?"

"You're wanted for aiding and abetting the escape of a

219

prisoner.

Mexicans don't like policemen committing such crimes. They believe that failing to extradite a prisoner, *like you*, would reflect badly on their own police. There is little doubt that you will *not* remain in Mexico."

"What happens to the local charges? By the way, what are the local charges? No one has told me anything."

The consul breathed on his round wire-framed glasses, wiped them with a handkerchief then removed a legal looking document from inside his coat. "The charges are: disturbing the peace assault, resisting arrest, and concealing a deadly weapon." The consul looked up. "Nasty charges. Oh, one other thing. Flight to avoid arrest."

"If I'm extradited, what happens with the local charges?"

"I can only guess, but I believe you would first stand trial in Mexico and serve any penalty handed down by Mexican courts before being returned to America. These are matters you need to discuss with your attorney.

"If I were to stand trial and sentenced to do time, what would the prison be like?"

Winking, out of sight of Officer Carlos, the consul said, "The other prison would be much nicer."

Winking back, Don thought, *Shit! Worse than this hell hole.* "That's nice to know," he quipped. "So far I haven't had a shower. When do we get to shower?"

The consul turned to Officer Carlos. "When may Mister Johns and the other Americans shower?"

"Prisoners are scheduled to shower tomorrow," Carlos said.

"Again, Mister Johns, you're in luck." The consul smiled. "Well, if there's nothing more, I have to be on my way. Good luck."

Hopelessness filled the pit of Don's stomach as he watched the consul disappear into distant shadows. *What's going to happen to me now?*

Chapter 16

Two metal food carts clattered over the prison's crack-ed concrete floor then stop for a moment in front of each cell. Don sniffed the air. "No doubt about it, I smell chilies." He hoped his nose lied, because his stomach hated chilies.

A dented and rusted steel cart, pushed by a stooped woman of advanced age, arrived at Don's cell. Her smile-less, wrinkled face appeared grim. She wore a grey, grease spotted apron and had long unkempt greyish hair, which she kept throwing over her shoulder.

The prisoners rushed their cell door, anticipating God only knew what on metal plates accompanied by a plastic spoon. The sound "plop" indicated gruel had been dropped on-to the plates. The server passed each plate through a rectangular opening in the cell door—followed by a twelve-ounce plastic bottle of warm water.

Don examined the greyish colored mound on his plate. It contained boiled ground meat and red chili sauce, accompa-nied by two corn tortillas and a dead fly. He flicked the fly from the sauce then used a piece of a tortilla to separate the chilies from the meat. A teaspoonful of chilies could sicken him and cause vomiting. He scooped a few lumps of beef on a piece of soggy tortilla. *This stuff has got to be Mexico's culinary re-venge on gringos?*

The little chili sauce remaining on the meat caused Don's tongue to burn and him wanting gallons of water. He stuck out his tongue and rubbed it with a finger to see if he could extinguish the flames. After six gulps of water, he had emptied his water bottle.

For the second time, Don spoke to his cellmates. "Is this the standard fare in this hell hole?"

Downing their gruel, the Americans nodded.

"Thanks for those encouraging reviews," Don mum-bled, placing his half-empty plate on the floor. "We've got to get out of here. We can't stay in a hell hole like this."

One of the Americans looked up from his plate. "Where's your sawblade, Houdini? Without it, ya ain't goin' nowhere."

"Oh, yes I am!"

A guard yelled, "Lights out in fifteen minutes!"

Don clutched his abdomen. He moaned and feigned gagging as he heard the guard start the evening headcount. When the guard neared his cell, Don moaned louder, gripped his abdomen, and squirmed on the bedsprings.

The guard shined his flashlight on Don's grimacing face. "What?" the guard asked.

"*Muy infirmo,*" Don whined. "Very sick."

"Too bad," the guard said, walking way.

Don sat up, feigning vomiting. He gagged so hard his retching echoed throughout the cell block.

A distant prisoner yelled, "For God's sake, get him a doctor."

A prisoner in the adjacent cell yelled, "Yeah. We don't want him throwing up all over our little paradise."

Don clutched his abdomen and feigned more gagging.

The guard moped to Don's cell then shined the paltry beam of his flashlight on Don's face. He had retained a mouthful of saliva, and between faked retches, let it roll onto his chin.

"Help me. *Ayuda me.*" Don whispered, in a quivering voice.

The guard strolled toward his station. Don heard him dial a rotary phone, mutter something in Spanish, and then hang up. He returned to Don's cell, drew his pistol, and unlocked the cell door. Using the gun like an extension of his arm, he poked Don in the ribs to get him out of the cell.

Bent over, Don gripped his abdomen and stumbled ahead of the guard who repeatedly poked his gun in Don's back as they headed toward the guard station. Once inside, Don slumped onto a chair, clutched his belly, and feigned gagging. The guard dialed a few numbers and then handed the sticky handset to Don. Between gags, Don asked, "Who'd you call?"

"You speak to consul," the guard said.

"Consul, is that you?" Don asked.

"Yesssss. Who is this?"

"This is Don—Don Johns—the prisoner. I'm sick. It's appendicitis."

Sounding annoyed, the consul asked, "Mister Johns, why do you think you have appendicitis?"

Gagging, Don said, "First of all, I still have mine. Secondly, I'm having a lot of pain in the appendix area, it hurts when I push on it, and I'm vomiting."

"Give the phone to the guard. I'll have him arrange a medical evaluation."

Don handed the phone to the guard who listened as if he didn't appreciate being bothered. Don understood only a portion of the terse Spanish conversation leaking from the handset.

The guard hung up then placed another call, spoke for a minute, and then hung up. He thumbed through some papers, extracted one, then wrote on it. He sat down in a dilapidated swivel chair and pointed his pistol at Don. After a few minutes, the phone rang. The guard grabbed the handset and listened. He nodded and said *si* so many times Don thought the guard might be hypnotized. After Don had feigned two retches during the call, the guard handed the phone to Don. He listened to a man speak in broken English. "We take you doctor's *officina privata*. It's not far, only few blocks."

Don hung up, feeling relieved knowing that he would get off site. *This is my chance to bolt this hell hole.* He continued to feign painful abdominal cramps.

When the guard turned his back, Don stuck his finger down his throat and induced vomiting. The vomit, containing tinges of red chili sauce, splashed on the stone floor.

Don pointed to the vomit and yelled, "Look. *Sangre*. I'm vomiting blood."

The guard slapped Don. "No vomit on my floor."

The guard stepped outside the station to escape the smell of vomit while waiting for the transport guard.

Good acting, Don! The sight of that stuff almost made me sick.

The transport guard appeared to have just gotten out of bed as he waddled into the guard's station. The back of his rumpled shirttail hung out of the back of his baggy trousers, which sagged low on his ample hips. His grease-spotted and unknotted necktie dangled from his neck. His hat sat so far back on his head it could have fallen off at any moment.

The guard motioned for Don to stand and turn around so he could be handcuffed.

Don stood and feigned a vomiting attack and clutched his abdomen. The guards backed away to avoid being a target.

After a brief discussion in Spanish, the guards apparently decided Don would not be handcuffed. The transport guard grabbed Don's left wrist, twisted it behind his back, then pushed him along the hall—pistol muzzle against his spine.

Don feigned another gagging attack and slumped against the wall, right hand clutching his abdomen. The guard released Don's wrist, moved back a few feet, and pointed his gun at Don's head. Pretending to have recovered, Don stood and resumed his trek along the hall.

After several turns down dark, dank smelly passageways, the men reached a loading dock. A vintage paddy wagon and its driver waited. He dropped his cigarette on the dock and then got behind the steering wheel.

The transport guard opened the van's rear door and waved his gun toward a worn metal bench on the right side of the cargo area. Don sat in the middle of the bench. His guard, pistol drawn, sat down on the bench opposite him.

Don smiled on seeing the side windows of the vehicle had bars instead of glass. He felt relieved knowing the windowless openings allowed ventilation.

Screeching tires marked the van's departure from the

224

prison's courtyard and filled the air with the smell of burning rubber.

Don's guard spoke to the driver through a perforated, plastic window that separated the cab from the cargo area. The guard's unholstered gun rested on his thigh. The driver and guard appeared to discuss a curvaceous, bikini clad woman's photograph secured by a rubber band to the driver's frayed sun visor. Don presumed, from the tenor of the discussion, the driver knew the female beauty.

Don cleared his throat to get his guard's attention and permission to remove his shoe so he could scratch his foot.

The guard nodded approval, ignoring the fact that the shoe could be a weapon. The guard returned to his conversation with the driver about the bikini-clad woman.

For emergencies, Don always carried US currency in his socks. Blocking the view of his stash, he peeled off a $1,000 note then secreted the remaining money in his sock. He made exaggerated scratching motions on his foot then replaced his sock and shoe.

The guard merely glanced at Don's scratching.

Don coughed to get his guard's attention. Having done so, he glanced back and forth between the driver and guard, trying to a certain if he could interact with the guard without the driver suspecting mischief.

Several times, Don indicated he wanted the guard to open the van's rear door. The guard smiled and shook his head as if he thought Don had gone mad. After several attempts to get the guard to comply, Don showed the guard the $1,000 bill, the equivalent of three month's salary. The guard grabbed at the bill, but Don held it between the bars of the side window open--ing, threatening to let it be blown away. He then moved the bill into the guard's view and motioned for him to open the rear door. The guard shrugged and pointed toward the driver.

At that point, Don knew he had the guard's interest. Don mimed striking the guard and his falling off the bench. Using faulty Spanish, Don said the guard should mimic his

225

actions and fall off his bench as if Don had struck him. While the guard lay on the floor, he and Don would exchange the key and money. Don would then open the door and make his getaway.

The guard nodded his agreement and stuck out his hand. "*Dinero*."

"*Momento*," Don said, patting the air to calm the guard. "When la porta is opened."

The theatrics of escape began with Don yelling and flailing his arms. He faked striking the guard who fell off his bench then passed the key to Don. He sprang for the door, unlocked and pushed it open, then dropped the $1,000 US note on the van floor.

Don jumped from the van, rolling into a ball when he struck the ground as he had been taught at the police academy. He forced his bruised and aching body upright and looked around. The dark street appeared to be empty. *Hope no one saw me. Better get off the street.*

Hearing and seeing part of the commotion, the driver slammed on the brakes, and the van screeched to halt.

Don watched the driver and the guard bolt from the vehicle then run down a dark alley, which had been selected by the bribed guard so Don would not be found and implicate the guard in the escape.

Limping, Don ran down a narrow street and disappeared into the night. He scanned the area, wondering where he should go. He ran from darkened doorway to darkened doorway, thinking how lucky he had been when police were unable to photograph him. That meant officials could not distribute wanted posters with his recent photo. The only photo available to police had been filed with Interpol years earlier when he first joined the police force. He had a beard then.

Now, where do I go? I need to get my money at the hotel. After that, what? Come on Don, you're a policeman—okay, ex-policeman. Think man! Think! Where would police look for me? What about an obvious unobvious place?

He reasoned he should lay low at the hotel. To his knowledge, no official in the states suspected him of being gay. They wouldn't think to look for him in a gay hotel, and local police had no reason to suspect he might be gay. *Yeah. I'll stay at the hotel—let this whole thing blow over—like hiding from the blind.*

Don arrived at the Angel Hotel's empty dining room just in time to get breakfast.

"*Buenos dias, Señor* Don," the waiter said. "Haven't seen you in a few days."

"Been partying hard," Don said. "I'd like some coffee with toast and eggs—scrambled—and a Mimosa, please."

"Coming right up."

"Another thing," Don asked, squirming on his sore butt. "Are my *gringo* friends still here?"

"*Si, señor*. Two are at the pool. I just took them Mimosas."

Don finished breakfast, picked up his Mimosa, and walked toward the pool.

"Well, look what the dogs dragged in," Richard said, looking at Don while squinting from the sun.

"Where've you been?" James asked. "We were getting worried."

"Oh, had a little run-in with the law," Don said. "Public intoxication, but I made my escape."

"You were in jail?" James asked, putting down a book.

"Something like that," Don muttered, easing himself down on a chair.

James stared at Don's arm. "How the hell did you get those bruises?"

"Let's just say I fell off a truck."

"Fell off a truck huh?" James mumbled. "Sure you weren 't pushed, or were you fighting off good looking jail guys who wanted to fuck you?"

Richard chuckled, "Were there *any* good-looking jail-birds waiting to get fucked?".

"Far from it, my friends . . . The damnedest, most foul place you never want to see. Take my advice—stay outta Mexican jails."

James patted a chair. "Sit over here and tell us all about it."

Don's butt's ached too much from his tumble to stay seated.

"Thanks," he said, "I think I'll stand for a while. As for jail, I went in. I got out." He sipped his Mimosa. "Anything exciting happen during my absence?"

Richard smiled. "Two Italians. That's what happened."

"And did they happen," James said. "For twenty-four hours we fucked, sucked, and choked here. Antonio somebody had the biggest 'hose' outside a Milano fire-house. Milano—that's where he's from. I don't know which hurts the most—my throat or my ass. Sex with that man was . . . Wow!"

"And what were *you* doing all this time, Richard?" Don asked.

"I played with mighty mouse—the other Italian, Giuseppe. He's Roman, and shorter than most Italians I've known, but hung like a Lipizzaner stallion. My jaw still aches from trying to satisfy that man's need for blow jobs. I've sucked so much cock I can't get my lips around anything thicker than a soda straw now."

"Poor baby," Don said. "What about Harry and Gregg?"

"They're in the same boat," James said. "They had their way with the Italians after Richard and I had at them."

"I'm surprised the Italians had anything left after you two guys abused them. Where are Harry and Gregg, now?"

"Sleeping," James said. "They entertained the Italians until four a.m. so they're sleeping in. The Italians were sup-posed to leave before breakfast. They had an early flight. I'm guessing they're on their way home, since we haven't seen them."

"Guys, your tans are crazy dark," Don said. "Been spending a lot of time out here?"

"Every day—except for Italian day," James said, smiling and shading his eyes from the sun.

"Well, James," Don said. "Your cock could vie for a black man's. It's getting quite dark."

Pulling up a chair to try to sit down, Don asked, "Heard anything from Alvaro?"

Don's sore butt just touched the chair's bottom when he decided to stand.

"Alvaro called yesterday, "Richard said. "Wanted us to join him for a drink. We're going to see him tomorrow. Want us to tell him you're back?"

"Nah. Maybe I'll give him a call, if he hasn't gotten a new phone."

"I don't think he has," James said. "They cost *pesos*, and he said he wasn't working."

"Then how the fuck is he going to buy drinks for you guys?"

"Damn if I know," James said, "but I don't turn down free drinks—no matter who's buying."

"It's gotta be Jesus' money," Don said. "He's buying Alvaro's drinks, his ass, and maybe his soul." Don stared at the deck for a moment, took a sip of his Mimosa, and then muttered, "What the fuck is to become of us?"

"Probably nothing," James said. "I got the impression he considered your relationship over."

"He might be upset, but I know he love me." Don shifted his ass on the thin chair cushion. "I know he does.

"If you come with us, you can see," James said.

"You know . . . I think I will, but don't tell him."

"Don, you know we don't lie," Richard said. "If he asks, we'll tell him. If he doesn't, then we won't."

"Sounds fair."

229

Chapter 17

James, Don, and Richard stood at the curb, trying to hail a taxi. Surprisingly, a late model Mercedes-Benz cab stopped.

"Hot damn," James said. "We've got a *real* ride this time."

The men took seats in the rear of the spacious taxi.

"You speak English?" Don asked the driver.

"*Si*. I speak English."

Richard handed the driver a slip of paper. "Take us to this address."

"This is the first Mercedes taxi I've seen in Mexico," James said. "Driver, do you own this car or drive it for someone else?"

"Oh no, *señor,* I am owner." The driver smiled, revealing a gleaming gold tooth. "I won the Mexican Lottery and buy this taxi. Now, I have no problem getting society-passengers and long fares. I pay taxi logo tax, but the other money is mine."

"We'll have to get your phone number," Don said, "In case we need a cab again."

"*Bueno*. Here is my card."

The ride continued with the passengers commenting about the working air conditioner and the cab's comfort.

After weaving in and out of heavy traffic, the taxi stopped in front of the Vaca Morada.

"Guys, this is the Purple Cow," James said, pointing to a sign displaying a plump purple cow.

"Shit!" Don exclaimed. "I've read about this place.

It's a hangout for soccer teams. Has quite a reputation for hard partying."

"Well," James said, "this is where Alvaro wanted to meet. Let's go in."

The men stepped into the cool, dark space filled with

Loud salsa music and hundreds of symbols of Mexican pride. The walls were plastered with signed photographs of Mexico's Famous soccer players. Everywhere James looked, he saw the red, white, and green colors of the Mexican flag. Thousands of Mexican themed banners obscured the ceiling. The place looked like a Himalayan Buddhist shrine awash in prayer flags. Hanging between the banners were long strings of red chili peppers.

Alvaro sat alone at a table in the far corner, facing the entrance. "Hey, guys—back here."

The group walked to his table.

"Nice to see you guys," Alvaro said. "Glad you could come, Don."

Alvaro offered his hand, but Don pulled Alvaro from his chair and gave him a bear hug. "Nice to see you," Don said, smiling. *God, how I've missed you.* "What've you been up to?" *Not fucking around I hope.*

"Nutin' much. Just layin' low," Alvaro said, giving James then Richard a kiss on the cheek. "Have a seat," Alvaro said, gesturing toward chairs opposite his bench.

Don looked at Alvaro and smiled. "I hope you've stayed out of trouble."

"Well, no trouble with police or jail time," Alvaro said, sitting down on his bench. "What are you guys drinking?"

The men looked at each other, nodded, and then James said, "Margaritas."

"Margaritas it is," Alvaro said, waving for a waiter.

Two half-empty beer bottles sat in front of Alvaro. Don stopped wondering to whom the second one belonged when Jesus arrived and picked it up.

"*Buenos tardes*," Jesus said, waving his arm like a matador. His short shorts fitted like a leotard around his upper hips, but the leg openings were large and loose.

James and Richard shook Jesus' hand.

Don remained seated with his hands on the table.

"How are you, Don?" Jesus asked, and then sipped his

beer.

"Just great," Don said, staring at Jesus' crotch. "I see you're wearing your 'work' clothes."

Jesus pulled at the legs of his shorts. "Glad you like them."

Alvaro slid along his bench to make room for Jesus to sit beside him. He gave Alvaro a lingering kiss on the cheek.

Clearing his throat, Jesus asked, "Did Alvaro tell you guys that I am going to receive The Belisario Dominguez Medal of Honour from the Mexican government for winning so many games?"

"Congratulations," James said, smiling. "We hadn't heard. Sounds like quite an honor."

"It's a great honor, not only for me but for my team and my family." Jesus kissed Alvaro on the lips. "I owe a lot of the honor to Alvaro who inspired me."

"Inspiration shit!" Don said, slamming his fist on the table. "Your inspiration is Alvaro's ass. I bet you rush home every day just to fuck it. That's your inspiration—ass—just ass. Alvaro's ass."

James and Richard said, "Don! Calm down! Please. Don't make a scene."

Alvaro reached across the table, grabbed Don's hands, and held them. "Calm down!"

"Yeah, Don, let's have a respectable social time," James said. "Here comes our drinks. Let's enjoy them."

The waiter held the check aloft. "Who gets this?"

Jesus grabbed it, examined it, and then handed some *pesos* to the waiter.

"Oh no, mister victory guy," Don said, "I'm paying for my drink."

Don slammed a 200 *peso* note on the table.

The Americans drank Margaritas as fast as the Purple Cow waiters could deliver them. After several rounds, the men were drunk—not falling down drunk, just loosened morals

233

drunk.

Jesus engaged in overt sexual innuendos with Alvaro as did Don.

Pawing various parts of Jesus' body, James said, "Richard and I have always thought you had endless sex appeal, and we have no qualms telling you we like your legs, pecs, and especially your cock."

Jesus smiled at the flattery. He sat across from James who had removed one of his flip-flops then walked his toes up Jesus' shin, into his shorts, and then onto his crotch. James' foot so stimulated Jesus that he, under cover of the tablecloth, unbuttoned his shorts then pushed them to his knees. He smiled as if his cock had been released from prison. This gave James' foot total access to Jesus' crotch.

Several times, Alvaro pushed James' foot away, but Jesus continued to accept it.

"Stop that," Alvaro said, staring first at James and then Jesus.

"You can play with it later," Jesus said to Alvaro.

Jesus repositioned James' foot on his growing erection and held it there.

"But that's mine," Alvaro said, frowning at Jesus.

"True," Jesus said, "but it's on loan for a while."

Jesus kissed Alvaro and ran his hand over the kid's chest.

Alvaro kissed back but then pulled away. "Shit! This isn't a gay bar. We're gonna get kicked outta here."

"Relax," James said. "The bartender can't see us, and those guys at the bar are too drunk to mind."

Don appeared angry. "God damn it, Alvaro. I don't know what's going on, but can't you leave that whore alone?"

"Who are you calling a whore," Jesus yelled, pushing Alvaro away.

"Oh, God," James said, rolling his eyes. "Not again."

"If the soccer shoe fits—wear it," Don said, peeling a handful of wet napkins off his sweating glass then throwing them on the table.

"What the hell is that supposed to mean?" Jesus asked, pulling his shorts up.

"You wear whore shoes because you're a whore," Don said.

Jesus lunged across the table, trying to grab Don's throat. Alvaro grabbed Jesus' waist and pulled him backward. James grabbed Don by the shoulders and pushed him down on his seat.

"For god's sake," James said, squeezing Don's shoulder. "No more fighting. I think you should go back to the hotel and sober up! Fighting will land us all in jail."

Don suddenly calmed down then threw some pesos on the table. "I'm outta here. Going home."

Don staggered out of the bar to wait for a cab.

James said, "That's the most reasonable thing I've ever seen Don do."

"He almost seemed scared," Alvaro said.

"Who the shit cares," Jesus said. "I'm glad he's gone."

Don sat at his hotel bar having a Margarita.

Finishing his drink, he heard familiar voices behind him. He turned to see Richard and James in the lobby.

"What are you doing here?" Don called. "I left you only minutes ago."

"Jesus and Alvaro decided to go off by themselves," Richard said, "so we decided to come back here. Why are you drinking here? It's too hot to drink inside."

"When I got here, nobody else was around, and I didn't wanna sit alone at the pool. Here, I can talk to the bartender."

"We're going to get naked and take a dip," James said. "Care to join us?"

"Okay," Don said. "Bartender, another Margarita—to go."

Minutes later, Don, Richard, and James made their way to the pool, towels over their shoulders. Don and James stretched out on a lounge. Richard dived into the pool and swam about. James rang the waiter bell then placed a book over his face and waited for his drink.

"You rang, *Señores*?" the waiter asked.

Without looking up, James took three quick sniffs. "That's a cologne I haven't smelled before." He sniffed the air two more times then moved the book from his face to see who wore the fragrance. "You're new," James said, staring into the face of an angel.

The handsome eighteenish-looking man of nice proportions, stood inches away, smiling like innocence personified.

James sat up to absorb the vision. The waiter wore black trousers and a tight-fitting shirt. Its vertical black and white stripes and his upswept styled hair gave him the appearance of being a six-foot-tall football referee. James' gaze came to rest on the waiter's bulging crotch.

"And who might you be?" Don asked.

"I'm Ramon—the new waiter."

"Well, whoever hired you knew what he was doing."

"The owner is my new friend," Ramon said then grinned.

"When you say friend, do you mean friend-friend or lover?" Don asked.

"Maybe a little of both," Ramon said, blushing.

Richard noted the new waiter and swam to the edge of the pool and close to James' lounge.

"You must be new," Richard said, with an inquisitive tone to his voice.

"*Si, Señor.* I started today. My name is Ramon."

"You like to swim, Ramon?" Richard asked.

"*Si. Mucho.*"

"Well, why don't you get naked and join me—for a swim?"

"I'm not supposed to be social with guests, *señor*."

"I'm sure your boss meant only during working hours."

"Maybe," Ramon said. "I see you don't wear swimsuits.

You like swimming naked?"

"You bet, and you'll love it too."

"Maybe," Ramon said, his face as red as a stoplight.

"Do you ever swim naked?" James asked.

"No," Ramon said then paused. "A few times—in the river—when I was a boy."

"Well it's more fun in a pool," Don said, splashing water. "You have to try it sometime."

"We could show you how it's done," James said.

"*Señor*, you are joking with me. No learning is necessary to be naked."

"Well," Richard said, "check with your boss. See if he'd mind if you joined us, after hours, for a drink and a dip. But for now, we need Margaritas."

"*Si*. I'll get them."

"Now that's a breath of fresh air," Richard said, wiping water from his smiling face.

"He's cute," James said, "but we don't want to get the kid fired on his first day. Go easy on him."

Ramon made several deliveries of Margaritas. With each round of drinks, the gringos became more embolden toward him.

"Ramon," Don asked, "do you know that you're working in a gay hotel?"

"*Si, señor*. I may be gay too."

"Do you mean you *are* gay or that you are unsure?" Don asked.

"I'm sure, *señor*."

"You're sure you're gay?" Don asked.

"*Si*. I'm gay. I'm sure."

"Ramon, would you please bring another round of Margaritas?" James asked.

After Ramon left, Don whispered loud enough for his friends to hear him. "Guys, we're on the right track. Ramon is gay. He said so."

Ramon returned with a tray of Margaritas and placed it

237

on Don's table. "Who is signing for these?"

"Put them on my bill," Don said and walked to the shallow end of the pool. "Ramon, show us your cock and I'll add a two-hundred-*peso* tip."

"S*eñores*. I'm shy, and I am working."

"Two hundred pesos is a lot of money," James said.

"Do you earn two hundred pesos working here?" Don asked.

"No, *señor*. Two-hundred pesos is *mucho dinero* for a waiter."

"Your boss is out for the day. Right?" Don said. "Who's gonna know—except us, your friends—that you showed us your cock."

"Uh . . . I don't know, *señor*."

"That's okay," Don said. "I'll keep my money."

"Okay," Ramon said, "I'll show you."

Ramon stood tall, took a deep breath, and unbuckled his belt. His hands shook, and his face turned red as he released the top button of his slacks, unzipped his fly, and then revealed his tightie-whities. He tucked the front of his shirttail under his chin, pushed his underwear down a few inches, and then lifted his cock over the waistband. A cloud of white talcum powder accompanied the reveal. For a moment, the cloud obscured his cock.

"What the hell?" Don asked, coughing.

"*Talco*. It keeps me dry."

After the talcum cloud dissipated, the guys stared at Ramon's baby snake.

"Wow," Don exclaimed. "Any balls under there?"

Ramon pulled his balls over his briefs then held them for everyone to see.

"That's worth two hundred pesos," Don said, smiling. "Where do I sign?"

Ramon replaced his equipment then handed the bill and a pen to Don.

Don held the bill to his nose and sniffed it.

"What are you doing?" James asked.

"The hand that touched this check touched his cock. I'm enjoying his crotch by proxy."

Ramon chuckled, collected the empty glasses, and headed for the bar. Moments later, he returned to the pool. He smiled, waved a two hundred *peso* note over his head, and then pointed at Don. "Thank you, *señor*."

The afternoon gave way to evening. The pool and courtyard lights came on just as Harry and Gregg strolled toward the pool, towels around their waists.

"Look who's up and about," Don said. "It's the prodigal sons. Don't tell me you guys have been sleeping all this time."

Harry pulled his towel from his waist then sat down on a chair.

"We just showered," Gregg said. "Harry and I fucked the Italians until the wee hours of the morning. I needed time to recover."

"Ditto for me," Harry added. "I won't be able to fuck for a week."

"Sorry I missed the fun," Don said. "I'll have to hang out here more often."

"I'm glad the Italians are gone," Harry said. "Don't get me wrong. They were hot, but I would have fucked myself to death if they had stayed longer."

"And that's the worse way to go?" James chuckled.

"Guys," Richard said, drying his hair. "You missed the inaugural run of the new waiter."

"What are you talking about?" Gregg asked.

"There's a cute, new waiter working here," James said. "His name is Ramon. Don gave him two hundred *pesos* to see his cock. For an eighteen-year-old, he's got a nice set of balls and a big dick, even when soft."

"I thought Don was an ass man," Gregg said. "What did the waiter's butt look like?"

"We haven't seen it—yet," Don said, entering the pool.

239

"Well then, when?" Gregg asked, like an impatient John waiting for a hooker to strip.

"Tonight—we hope," Don said. "Richard and James are trying to get him in the pool for a swim after his shift. They're going to teach him how to skinny dip."

"What do you mean teach?" Harry asked. "If he can swim, he doesn't need naked lessons."

"Guess we'd better stick around," Gregg said, "if we want to see the kid's butt."

Gregg dropped the towel from his waist and headed for the pool.

"Are you ready for a drink?" Don asked Harry. "If you are, ring the bell and you'll get a chance to meet the young man."

"Yeah, I could use a drink," Harry said, ringing the bell.

Ramon walked to the pool. He looked surprised to see the additional guests. "You are all *amigos*?"

"Yep," James replied, waving a wet hand. "We're friends."

Harry extended his hand. "Hello, Ramon. I'm Harry, a hotel guest. Would you mind turning around?"

Puzzled, Ramon wrinkled his brow but did as requested.

"Anyone ever tell you that you have a nice butt?" Harry asked.

"No," Ramon said, blushing as he picked up his tray.

"Did you ask your boss about joining us for skinny dipping?" Don asked.

"What is skinny dipping?"

"You know—naked—swimming," Don said. "No swimsuit."

"My manager said okay—swim after work."

"I'm sure your naked butt will love this water," James said, cupping a handful then letting it trickle into the pool.

"Maybe," Ramon said, blushing.

240

"Do you have a boyfriend?" James asked.

"No, *Señor*. I'm too young for a boyfriend."

"If you had a boyfriend, how old would he be?" Don asked.

"I like older guys," Ramon said, holding his tray behind his butt and shifting his weight.

"How about boys between twenty and twenty-five?" Don asked.

"Maybe a little older."

"Thirty to fifty?"

"Fifty is too old. Maybe thirty," Ramon said.

"Well, I'm in my thirties," Don said. "We'd make a nice couple."

Ramon shook his head. "I'm not ready for a boyfriend."

"How about sex? Have you had sex with a thirty-year-old man?"

"*Si*! Several times, s*eñor*. My boss."

"Was it fun?"

"*Mucho*—most of it, but I have much to learn."

Pulling himself from the pool to sit on the coping, Don asked, "Where did you learn to speak English?"

"Some from TV, some from school, and some from friends."

"Well, I'm a great teacher" Don said. "I could teach you English *and* lots of fun things."

"Don, don't get selfish," James yelled. "Ramon, we could all teach you fun stuff. Have you ever had sex with more than one guy?"

Ramon blushed. "No, *señor*, but seems like fun."

"Join us after work, here in the pool," Harry said, splashing water, "and I guarantee you'll have a good time."

"I like having a good time, and I like *hombres* who are a little older than me."

Harry swam to the edge of the pool and extended his hand to Ramon.

"It's a deal," Harry said, shaking Ramon's cold hand.

"Sorry my hand is wet, but we'll have fun after work."

"Okay. I need a good teacher."

"What time do you finish work?" James asked.

"*A las once.* Huh, sorry. I mean eleven o'clock."

Chapter 18

Almost palpable, anxiety hung over the *gringos* waiting poolside.

Harry watched the outdoor clock as if expecting it to explode instead of chiming eleven o'clock. Anyone happening on the scene might have thought the Americans waited for a rock star instead of an eighteen-year-old Mexican waiter.

Harry held his breath as the clock in the lobby chimed eleven times. Minutes later, Ramon walked onto the pool's coping—fully dressed. A resounding "Ugh" filled the night air.

"You're not supposed to be dressed," Don said.

"I'm a little shy," Ramon said.

"Use the pool *baño* and get undressed," Harry said.

"Okay . . . " Ramon sulked toward the restroom.

The men repositioned their chairs so everyone had an unobstructed view of the restroom door. Minutes later, Ramon stuck his head out and smiled. Ten hungry eyes were ready to devour him.

"Come out," Don yelled.

Ramon extended his bare left foot and then his left arm. After a few seconds, he stepped from behind the door still wearing his "tightie whities."

"For God's sake, take your underwear off!" Harry yelled.

Ramon inched toward the men. "Do I have to? I'm shy."

Sensing Ramon's uneasiness, Harry said, "Guys. Give him a break. He's got to do it because he wants to. This isn't the rape of Lucretia."

"Thank you, *Señor* Harry," Ramon said.

"Ramon," Don said. "You're off duty. How'd you like a Margarita? I'm buying."

"*Si*. I'd like one." Ramon smiled then dived into the pool.

Harry whispered to Gregg, "I bet Don is going to get

243

the kid drunk and fuck him."

"I heard that," Don said. "It's not true—maybe we'll all fuck him."

Don rang the waiter bell and the night clerk came out.

"I know," the clerk said, "a round of Margaritas."

"Six," Don said. "Ramon is having one."

"Ramon?" the clerk asked. "I didn't know he was a slut."

"Careful with your language," Don said. "He's just having a little fun."

"I doubt he'll have much fun."

"Keep your opinions to yourself," Don said, "just bring our drinks—*clerk.*"

Not wanting Ramon to feel lonely, the men dived into the pool. For a brief period, everyone played dunk your partner. Soon the games turned to let's-steal-Ramon's-underwear.

Ramon tried to protect his modest, but he lost. His briefs were thrown from man-to-man while he tried to recapture them. His trials lasted five minutes, and then he tired of the game. "Okay, *amigos*," he said and swam to the pool's steps. "I surrender. I'm not playing anymore."

Harry watched Ramon's bubble butt propel his lean, muscular frame up the steps and out of the pool. He grabbed Don's towel, dried off with his back to the pool, and then wrapped the towel around his waist.

"Thank you, Ramon," Harry said.

Ramon turned and asked, "For what?"

"For showing us your butt. You have a nice one, and I'm glad you chose my towel to dry it."

Appearing upset, Ramon said, "I think you're making fun of me."

"No. Really," Don said. "We were just admiring one of God's wonderful creations."

"You speak of God, but I don't think you're religious."

"We're Sorry if we offended you," Gregg said. "We just happen to be a group of guys who like to look at butts.

Nice butts. Some people like blue eyes, some guys like big chests, and some guys—like us—appreciate nice butts."

"You think I have nice butt?"

"Absolutely," Harry said. "You have a *wonderful* butt. You shouldn't be afraid, or ashamed, to share it—in the right places—with the right people, and this is one of the right places, and we're the right people. Aficionados like us should be allowed to admire it."

Cocking his head to one side and staring into Ramon's eyes, Harry said, "I caught you looking at ours earlier—weren't you?"

"A little," Ramon said, blushing.

"Well, what do you think?" Don asked. "Do we have nice butts?"

"Uhhhh, *si, señor*. You have a good butt. It looks like it is made of muscle. Is it hard?"

"Thanks for the compliment," Don said then smiled. "It's pretty hard. Would you like to feel it? See how hard it is?"

"It's okay if I feel?" Ramon asked.

"Of course, if I can touch yours," Don said and winked at Harry.

"Okay, you can touch it," Ramon said.

Don exited the pool. For a moment, he stood in front of Ramon, staring him in the eyes, then smiled and turned, presenting his butt for inspection. Everyone watched Don tense his glutes as Ramon pointed his index finger at the flexed butt. The finger moved closer and closer and then made contact. For a second, Ramon's finger remained motionless then he pushed it into Don's flesh.

"You have a muscle butt, *Señor* Don."

"Thank you. Touch it with your whole hand if you want."

Ramon paused for a moment and then placed a palm on each of Don's butt cheeks. He flexed and tightened both as hard as he could.

Ramon laughed.

"What's so funny?" Don asked.

"It gets small when it gets hard."

"Hear that guys?" Don said. "Ramon says I have a small butt."

"Don't fool yourself," Harry yelled. "The kid needs glasses."

Smiling, Ramon left his hands on Don's butt. He seemed to enjoy the firmness of Don's flexed glutes.

Don relaxed then alternated contracting his glutes faster and faster until they danced the samba.

"That's funny," Ramon chuckled, watching his hands being jostled about.

Don faced Ramon. "Glad I could entertain you."

Staring into his eyes, Don moved closer. Ramon reached around Don's waist and placed his hands on Don's butt.

"Seems we have a shared interest," Don said.

"What?" Ramon asked.

"We like butts." Don pulled Ramon close then put his hands under the kid's towel and squeezed his glutes. "Tighten them."

Ramon tightened his butt and giggled.

"What's so funny?"

"When you touch my butt, yours goes soft."

Harry yelled, "Don, your ass is like your cock. You can't keep either hard."

Staring into Ramon's eyes, Don flashed a middle finger at Harry. "Shut up."

Don brought his lips close to Ramon's and paused.

Ramon lunged upward, kissing Don hard. Each guy grasped the other's butt with death grips, pulling themselves closer.

Moving to the edge of the pool, Gregg nudged Harry. "Looks like the party has started. Gotta get in on this."

"You bet," Harry said.

Harry and Gregg left the water and walked behind

246

Ramon. Harry loosened Ramon's towel and let it to fall to the deck. Harry tried to insinuate his hand between Don's and Ramon's rock-hard cocks but could not. Don pushed at Harry's hand, but the interloper refused to go away. Moments later, Don replaced Harry's hand with his own and squeezed Ramon's cock. He moaned his approval.

Harry moved behind Ramon and rubbed his wet crotch against Ramon's butt. He jumped and said, "Cold," but made no further protests. Harry wiggled his fingers between the waiter's butt cheeks then massaged his hole. Ramon moaned and wiggled his butt in appreciation.

Don stopped kissing Ramon and knelt to take the young, throbbing cock in his mouth. First, he tongued it then swallowed it. Ramon dropped his head backward and let his hands fall to his side. Moments later, he placed them on Don's head to guide his talented mouth.

"That's good," Ramon said, "but I want to fuck you."

"Hey guys," Don called out. "Why don't we go to my room? I have condoms."

"Sure," Harry said.

The trio walked to Don's room with everyone holding or touching a part of Ramon's body

So far, Richard and James had been spectators.

As the group passed, James said, "Now there's a party."

"Three's a party. Five's a crowd," Richard said and faced James. "You have any interests in the kid?"

James smiled. "You know I don't like little boys. I'm content to stay and play with you."

The clerk walked into the area carrying six Margaritas. "Where is everyone?"

"Partying," James said. "There's a fuck fest in Don's room."

"What do I do with these drinks?" the clerk asked, holding out his tray.

"Put 'em on the table," Richard said. "We'll drink

them."

Don awoke at 6:00 a.m.

Ramon slept beside him, hugging a pillow. His bare butt peeked from under the sheet tucked between his knees.

Don admired the butt for a moment, yawned, and then scanned the room. "The guys must have gone home.

Don pulled on his pants and a t-shirt. Barefooted, he made his way to the dining room.

"Coffee," Don said to a waiter and took a sunny window seat. Salsa music played in the background. Despite a headache, Don mentally replayed the previous evening. He pondered the strange resemblances between Alvaro and Ramon and wondered if those similarities had caused him to put the make on the new waiter?

A waiter placed a cup of coffee in front of Don. Anything to eat, sir?"

"Yeah, toast and scrambled eggs, uhhh, *pan tostado y huevos revultos.*"

"That's okay, *señor.* Your Spanish is good, but I understand English."

"One more thing," Don said, touching the waiter's arm. "Please turn that music down? I have a hell of a headache."

Don sipped his coffee and stared into space. Moments later, James and Richard walked to his table.

"How's it going, old man?" James asked.

"God, I do feel like an old man this morning." Don used his foot to push a chair out for James to sit down. "I've gotta stop drinking—and sex." Don shook his head. "Damn, I never thought I'd say that."

The waiter placed Don's breakfast on the table. "Thanks," Don said.

"Yeah. I'm beginning to wonder about our livers," James said. "I calculate each of us is drinking a quart of Tequila a day."

"Wonderful stuff ain't it." Don said then smiled.

248

"Thank God for the Mexicans. Look what they gave us."

"You mean little Ramon?" Richard asked.

"Yeah. Nice kid isn't he?" Don asked. "I see a lot of Alvaro in him. Something about him makes me want to take care of him—protect him."

"Yeah, after you've fucked him," James said.

"Watch it," Don said, putting his cup down. "Ramon freely joined our group. He knew what to expect. He willingly participated. No one—let me repeat, *no one*—raped the kid or made him do anything he didn't wanna do."

"Think you might have pushed him in the direction you wanted him to go?" Richard asked.

"*Guided* is the word," Don said. "He's legal. We *guided* him."

"What time did he leave?" James asked.

"Leave?" Don asked, looking shocked. "He hasn't. He's asleep in my bed."

"Sure you didn't tie him to it," Richard asked, "so he wouldn't run away?"

"Funny," Don said sneering, anger tinting the word.

"Let's be honest," James said. "You have an obsessive attitude toward young guys who cross your path— or should I say your bed."

Don winked. "Call it what you want. I call it attentive love." *But what business of yours is it?*

The waiter placed a cup of coffee in front of James and Richard then refilled Don's cup.

"Bring us what he's having," Richard said to the waiter, pointing to Don's breakfast. "What are you planning today, Don?"

Don picked up the morning paper. "I'm waiting until Ramon wakes up. See if there's anything we might do together." Don took a bite of toast. "James, would ya pass the jelly?"

"Think you should give the kid a rest?" James asked as he passed the jam.

249

"What's with you this morning? Don asked, turning his hands to the heavens and shrugging. "Are you jealous?" *Stay away from Ramon.*

"Relax," James said. "We don't want you getting involved in a situation that you know isn't going anywhere."

"Who says it has to go anywhere?"

"You, Don—that's who," Richard said. "You'll smoother the kid like you did Alvaro. You can't own people so don't try it with Ramon."

"Give me a fucking break!" Don said, slapping the table. "Alvaro will be back. You wait and see. He's having trouble admitting it, but he loves me—and I love him. We'll work things out. I know it."

"So you'll use Ramon as fill until Alvaro returns?" James asked, nodding toward Don's room. "Isn't that usury?"

"Look who's talking about using people," Don said, raising his voice. "I've seen how you use people—both of you."

The manager approached the table. "Gentlemen, please keep your voices down. You're disturbing other diners."

"Okay, okay. I'm about finished anyway," Don said. "Get me a coffee to go will you?"

"Don, I'm sorry for the way I spoke," Richard said, extending his hand. "Friends?"

"Friends," Don said, shaking Richard's hand.

Don opened the door to his room. Bright, morning sunlight filled the space, illuminating Ramon's bubble butt peeking from under the sheet. Don admired the scene as Ramon stirred.

Don chided himself for having left the door open. He made a mental bet the first thing Ramon would do would be cover his butt.

Ramon stretched his arms, yawned, and then pulled the sheet over his butt.

"Wished you hadn't done that," Don said.

"Done what?"

250

"Cover your butt. That's the part I like most. On second thought, that's not true. I like all your parts *and* your butt."

"What time it is?" Ramon asked, rubbing his eyes.

Don checked his watch. "Almost nine thirty."

"I've never stayed out so late. What time did amigos leave?"

"About four—except for you, my friend."

"Uff! My aunt will be angry . . . me out all night. I need to go home."

"Why go home? Anything special?"

"No, but I must let her know I'm okay."

"You don't have to leave to report in. Call her on my phone."

"*Señor,* my aunt has no phone. I must see her."

"How far away does she live?"

"On bus, one and half hours."

"Ninety minutes. That's a long ride just to check in.

Tell you what. We'll take a taxi. You check in, and then we'll come back and spend the afternoon doing fun things. How does that sound?"

"But *señor*, I don't have money for a taxi."

"I didn't mean you would pay. I will. You'll be my guest, and this afternoon, we'll do anything you want. By the way, I brought you a coffee."

Taking the coffee cup, Ramon said, "Thank you, s*eñor*. I mostly drink Coca Cola, but what you say sounds like fun."

Ramon's face suggested he didn't like the taste of coffee. He put the cup down and said, "May I please take shower and then we leave. Okay?"

Chapter 19

Don called his favorite cabdriver. In a matter of minutes, the Mercedes taxi arrived.

Ramon admired the car, dragging his fingers over the door's smooth, polished surface. "I have never ridden in a Mercedes, and I've never been in car with air conditioning."

"Better than a bus, eh?" Don asked.

"Yes, the bus has only God's air."

"Better tell the driver the address."

Speaking in Spanish with hundreds of hand gestures, Ramon gave the driver the address.

As the taxi headed south, Don noted the neighborhoods shifted more and more toward the poverty end of Mexico's economy. After twenty miles, paved roads gave way to dirt roads that became bumpy and dusty.

"I'm glad we have air conditioning," Don said. "Can you imagine how bad it would be to ride through this dust with the windows down?"

"I know, *señor*. I ride bus *mucho*."

"Ramon, please call me Don and drop the *señor* stuff, okay?"

"*Si*, if you want."

The taxi stopped in front of a small house, half hidden behind a uncompleted concrete block wall. Coconut palms, dust, children, and feral dogs filled Ramon's neighborhood. From around or through broken gates, several children peeked at the fancy, dust laden taxi.

"Come in and meet my *tia*—my aunt," Ramon said.

"Okay," Don said. "Driver, please wait for us. We won't be long."

Ramon pushed a squeaky, dilapidated iron gate open, while supporting one of the rusty hinges missing its pin.

"Careful," Ramon said. "Don't let it fall on you."

The dusty courtyard contained numerous clay pots covered with hand painted flowers and faces. Each pot con-

253

tained a flowering plant. A red nylon hammock hung between the front wall of the house and a concrete column supporting the porch roof.

"Come in," Ramon said, holding the hammock out of the way.

"*Tia* Teresa," he called as he entered the front room.

The small space contained three plastic chairs, a white plastic dining table, and a wooden stand that held a blaring TV tuned to a *novella.*

What a way to live, Don thought.

A short, rotund barefooted woman with long black hair entered the room. Her wizened face smiled when she saw Ramon, but she appeared surprised to see Don.

Speaking in Spanish, Ramon introduced Don to *tia* Teresa. "This is my friend Don."

Teresa wiped her course dry hands on her bright red skirt then shook Don's hand. Her smile revealed several empty dental spaces as she greeted Don. *"Mucho gusto. Quiere aqua?"*

"She is happy to meet you," Ramon said. "She wants to know if you would like a glass of water?"

Don thought, *Should I?* "I don't think I should drink local water."

"No worry," Ramon said. "We drink bottled water."

"Then I'll have some," Don said, feeling relieved. "My throat is dry from all the dust." *God, I hope the glass is clean.*

From the front porch, someone yelled, "Ramon!"

"That sounds like Rodriguez," Ramon said. "We play the game you call soccer."

"You play soccer?" Don asked.

"*Si*! I'm captain of neighborhood team. We win many games."

Before he could stop himself, Don said, "I know Jesus Gonzales." *Why the fuck did I say that?*

"You know Jesus Gonzales?" Ramon asked.

254

"I'm sorry to say, I do."

"You introduce me. Please! I want to meet him more than anything in world. He is hero to the neighborhood."

"I'll think about it, but he's a busy man."

Rodriguez joined the group in tia's back room. He and Ramon exchanged a club-type handshake and shoulder bumps.

"You like my 'stach, man?" Rodriguez asked, running is finger over his almost visible mustache.

"Tortured," Ramon replied. "It'll be good when it's older."

Turning to Don, Ramon said, "Rodriguez and I learn English watching TV music channel. He likes rap. The mustache honors his favorite rapper."

"You want to play some ball?" Rodriguez asked Ramon.

"*No, hoy,*" Ramon answered, "but my friend, Don, say hello to Don, he knows Jesus Gonzales."

"For real, man? You know Jesus?" Rodriguez asked, astonishment filling his face and voice.

"Kinda," Don said.

"Don will introduce me," Ramon said, shaking with excitement.

Not understanding English, Aunt Teresa looked on in puzzlement as everyone smiled.

"We'll see," Don said, "but we should go. We have a cab waiting."

Ramon kissed his aunt and said something in Spanish. She shook Don's hand and said, "*Vaya con dios.*"

Rodriguez shook Don's hand then said goodbye to all.

"How should we spend the day?" Don asked Ramon as the taxi retraced its way downtown.

"I'd like to go to a big dance club in Zona Rosa. I visited only two in the past."

"How about we paint the town red?"

Ramon looked puzzled. "I don't want to work. I want

255

have fun."

Don laughed. "That's an American expression. It means have a good time."

"*Bueno*. I like to have a time good."

Don opened the sliding Plexiglas partition mounted on the driver's seat back. "Zona Rosa, *Señor*—the Wayward Bar."

"*Si*. Wayward."

Don closed the partition and stared out the window. "There must be fifteen bars in the Zona Rosa. We won't be able to have a drink in each of them and still walk. How 'bout we visit five of the largest? We should drink beer, not Margaritas if we want to go all night."

"Okay." Ramon said then smiled. "I want to dance to-night."

Walking into the Wayward bar, Don said, "This is one quiet place."

"It's too early for a crowd."

The men had a beer and watched a TV on which a recorded soccer game flickered.

"Since you've never been here," Don said, "look around, check out the place."

"*Si*. I'll check it out."

A few minutes later, Ramon returned. "This is a fancy nice place. I want to come back when it's crowded. It's a good place to dance."

"Let's go to the Surprise Bar," Don said. "It's at the end of this block. Won't be much of a crowd, but we need to check it out."

As they walked toward the Surprise Bar, Don took Ramon's hand, but he jerked it away and stared at Don.

"Don't worry," Don said. "Guys hold hands in the Zona Rosa all the time. You don't have to worry about being gay here."

Ramon let Don hold his hand. Both men smiled.

Salsa music filled the Surprise Bar. The guys selected one of many modern Italian barstools made of leather and chrome. They waited for the bartender—a dapper man with a classic Aztecan nose and high cheek bones. He wore earphones and appeared to be doing a free form dance as he washed a glass. Minutes later, he looked up but took his time getting to his only customers.

Don thought, *Is he slow because he's evaluating the relationship between me and Ramon? Does he think I'm a sugar daddy?*

"*Hola,*" the bartender said, drying his hands. He asked Ramon for ID. Ramon presented it, and the bartender asked, "What'll you have?"

"Two Sols," Don said.

Don looked around the space. "This place feels like a funeral home at midnight. I can't believe the TV isn't on. I've never been in a Mexican bar that didn't have one blaring." Don took a few swigs of beer. "Let's get out of here."

"Where will we go?" Ramon asked.

"The Revenge. It's a block and a half away."

Don grabbed Ramon's hand as they left for the next watering hole. Along the way, they passed the Leather Pup. A rainbow flag hung over its entrance.

"What is this place?" Ramon asked, starring at various leather and chrome objects in the window.

"It's a leather bar, but it's closed now. I don't think you'd like the place. It can get very scary."

"Why? What happens there?"

"People do bad things to nice people in there," Don said, increasing his pace.

"What things?"

"Whips, chains, tying people up, using sex toys. That kinda thing."

"I'd like to visit sometime."

"Maybe, but not now."

At the Revenge, the men sat at a sidewalk table. The inside area bustled with cleaning activities.

Two parked cars shared audio systems designed to

blast quarry rock. The owners had opened their trunks to blast salsa music from thirty-six-inch woofers.

"That's awful?' Don said, pointing at two cars a hundred feet away.

"Mexicans like music loud," Ramon said, squirming on his chair in time to the music's tempo.

Don waved his hand in a dismissive manner. A waiter mistook the wave for a request for service and approached asking for Don's order.

"Sorry. We've already ordered," Don said, "and I see our waiter coming now."

Their cold beer mugs sweated from the high humidity. Each man drank half their ale in two gulps to maximum its cooling effect.

"Damn, it's hot today," Don said, wiping sweat. "What say we go to the hotel and take a dip? We can have Margaritas and wait there until the dance clubs open. Maybe we can have dinner before we set out for the night."

Ramon grinned. "You want me to swim naked."

"Well, that's not a bad thing?"

"Maybe."

"Whatta you think?"

"Okay. We swim."

Don phoned his taxi driver. Minutes later he arrived in his dust-free Mercedes.

"Hotel Angel, s*eñor*," Don said, "and thanks for having the air conditioner on."

"Leave your clothes in my room," Don said, leading the way through the hotel.

Inside, his room, Don began to undress. Ramon leaned against the back of the closed door and watched Don strip.

Don turned, and for a moment, he glared at Ramon. "Well? Undress, damn it."

"I like watch you get naked. For me, like Christmas."

"Thanks for the flattery, but you can watch and un-

258

dress at the same time."

Don pushed his underwear down. When they reached his knees, Ramon grabbed Don's balls.

"Oh, you're a ball lover are you?"

"*Si*, you have *testiculos grande*. I like."

"First time I ever heard that, but hey, it's been so long since I've seen yours I can't remember what they look like."

Don tugged at Ramon's shirt.

"Okay, I undress."

Ramon feigned a strip dance and hummed a Mexican tune. As the dance proceeded, he called on all his skills to tease Don with peeks of his ass and crotch. With only tighty-whities protecting his modesty, Ramon turned his back and pushed them down. They fell to the floor. Ramon kicked them out of the way then resumed dancing. Keeping his back to Don, he shook his booty like a rent boy.

Don felt deprived watching the impromptu butt dance. "Okay," he said. "You can stop that butt stuff. Turn around and refresh my memory."

Ramon turned to reveal his viper and apples.

"Nice." Don chuckled, "but I miss the talcum."

Ramon moved toward Don who met him in the middle of the room.

They French kissed. As Ramon grew excited, Don match-ed his arousal.

"We have to stop or we can't go to the pool with any modesty," Ramon said.

Don grabbed two towels and said, "Here." He wrapped one around his waist, and suggested Ramon do the same. "Just until your boner's gone," Don said, "unless you want to display your wares to whoever might be at the pool."

"There were no people at pool," Ramon said, eyeing Don's crotch. "I like you hard. Don't wear the towel."

"How can I say no to such a beautiful face?" Without waiting for Ramon's reply, Don said, "Okay. We'll go— boner and all."

259

With towels over their shoulders, the guys headed for the pool. Much to their surprise, there were two strangers—bears—in the pool. One had a body hidden by hair.

Ramon paused then pushed Don ahead.

One bear nudged the other and said, "Now that's a welcoming committee."

Don waved to the strangers. "Welcome. When did you guys arrive?"

"Today," the larger man said, staring at Ramon. "We read about this place being clothing optional, but we never guessed management would surprise us by sending naked guys with erections as a welcoming committee."

Ramon blushed and dived in the pool. Don followed but swam toward the bears.

"Where're you guys from?" Don asked.

"Baltimore," the larger man answered. "I'm George and this is my partner Harry. People call him Harry because he's hairy. They call me George because . . . I'm George

Everyone chuckled.

"Nice to meet you," Don said, extending his hand.

Ramon kept his distance and waved. "Hi," he called out. "I'm Ramon."

"Don't mind him," Don said to the new comers. "He's shy, but you'll be seeing a lot of him because he's the evening waiter."

"Does he work naked?" Harry asked, grinning.

"Sorry to say he doesn't," Don replied.

"Too bad." George winked at Don. "I noticed ya have a nice set of low hangers. You wear a ball stretcher?"

"Occasionally, but I've always had long nuts.

"Mind if I feel?" George asked.

"Sure." Don said, spreading his legs. "Knock yourself out. They like attention."

George's meaty hand manipulated Don's balls for a moment then pulled them hard.

"So, you're a ball *aficionado*," Don said.

"I know how to make 'em feel good," George said. He dropped below the surface and mouthed Don's nuts, tongued each for a moment, and then tightened his lips around them and tugged.

"Wow," Don said as George came up for air. "They liked that."

"Me too. You've got quite a mouthful."

"They're glad to have met your mouth. They'll have to date sometime."

"Just say when."

Harry asked Don, "Are you and Ramon partners?"

"We're friends getting to be better friends."

"Join us," Harry called, waving to Ramon. "We won't kill you, but we might eat ya."

Ramon swam closer to Don.

Sensing Ramon's discomfort, Don pulled the kid close and held him in a face-to-face embrace.

"Can't let him get too far away," Don said. "He's still learning about gay life. Every kid needs a mentor. Like old Socrates in ancient Greece."

"Can't blame you," Harry said. "Somebody might steal him."

"You're one of the hairiest guys I've ever seen," Don said. "Ever shave it?"

"Not often, but I've had a few people shave me—if they're real hot."

"There's a couple of guys staying here who would like to get you *totally* naked," Don said, "if you get what I mean."

"I do. We'll see."

"How do we get a Margarita out here?" George asked. "If Ramon is in the pool, who brings the drinks?

"I work night shift," Ramon said, "but tonight am off."

"You guys want Margaritas?" Don asked.

Harry and George looked at each other. "That'd be great."

Don exited the pool. He knew every eye watched his

261

butt as he walked to his table and rang the waiter bell.

"So that's how it's done," George said.

The waiter arrived, smiling. "Let's see. Margaritas for Don and Ramon. What about you new guys?"

"Same for us," George said.

Minutes later, drinks were delivered. As the waiter left, Ramon left the pool to take a sip from his drink. "Anyone want their drink in the pool?" he asked.

George yelled, "Ramon, stay right where you are, young man. I like looking at your butt. How'd you like a mouth job on your balls?"

Ramon blushed. After a second of thought, he must have decided to immerse himself in the role of entertainer. He shook his ass and humped his crotch like bad lap dancer. He worked his way to the pool's steps, which he descended until the water reached his crotch.

Don thought, *I wished he wouldn't do that.*

George swam toward the grinning kid until his mouth reached Ramon's balls. "Those look good enough to eat." In a flash, they disappeared into George's mouth. Ramon moaned, and stroked his cock while George worked his magic on the captured nuts.

"Hope you don't mind, Don," Harry said.

"Nope. Kid has a mind of his own, and it looks like he's enjoying George's handiwork, or should I say his tongue?"

Don felt a pang of jealousy watching Ramon lose himself in the pleasure of George's mouth.

Harry moved to Don's side and attempted to grab his nuts.

Don brushed his hand away and called to Ramon. "Okay. Break it up, kid. We have drinks to kill."

Ramon looked at Don. He glared back. Ramon pushed George's head from his crotch and said, "Time for rest."

Ramon left the pool and took a chair at Don's table.

Seconds later, Don left the pool and sat down beside him. "Forget about those guys. Let's just enjoy our drinks."

George swam back to Harry and whispered something. He then yelled, "Thanks for desert, Ramon.

Chapter 20

Hours later, the searing sun had retreated, leaving the pool in hot shadows.

Don raised his head from the lounge and peered at Ramon. "How about we get some dinner, before we head to the clubs?"

"Sounds good. We didn't have lunch."

"I've never eaten there, but I understand the Tango Club, a fancy dance palace, has a restaurant serving great Argentinean steaks."

"Steak is good," Ramon said, licking his lips.

"Before the night is over, you're going to need lots of protein. Let's get dressed and get out of here."

Don's favorite taxi delivered him and Ramon to the popular Tango Club where a line of men outside waited to enter.

"God, that music is loud," Don said. "Sounds like the speakers are out here. God only knows what they sound like inside."

"It's good for dancing," Ramon said, wiggling his hips and clicking his fingers.

Don and Ramon joined the line, standing on a small bridge over a manmade stream. It flowed along the club's perimeter and glowed a bluish-green color from underwater lights.

A doorman checked guests' ID. Getting the okay, the guys entered the pulsating walls then pushed their way up a narrow flight of stairs. Passing descending partiers, Don and Ramon step onto the roof terrace covered with slippery tiles. A full moon provided most of the lighting for the crowded, vibrating space.

"This is half the size of a football field," Don said, "and look at the white sofas. Never seen a club with so much seating." Don pointed toward the far end of the terrace. "Let's head for that bar with the blue lights—it's less crowded."

The sound system's sub-bass notes pushed the guys forward, compressing their chests almost to the point of interfering with breathing

"This isn't music," Don yelled, "it's torturing noise."

At the bar, Don grabbed a paper napkin, rolled pieces into two wads, and then pushed one into each ear. "An hour of this shit will destroy your hearing." He held the torn napkin toward Ramon. "Make yourself some ear protection."

Ramon laughed. "No. I like music loud."

Don yelled to the bartender, "*Dos* Soles, *por favor*!" He handed over two beers, and Don gave him *pesos*. "Keep the change."

Don yelled to Ramon. "Let's move on. There're too many pushy people here."

The guys leaned against a broad column at the edge of the terrace. The location provided an expansive view of the dance floor, fewer elbow jabs, and protection from getting crushed toes.

Don, the oldest guy in noise hell, surveyed the crowd and noticed an attractive young lady staring at Ramon. Don nudged him. "I hear this place attracts a lot of straight, gay-friendly people." He nodded to his right. "I think that gal in the red dress is interested in you. She keeps smiling your way."

"That's okay," Ramon said. "I like dance with girls."

"I think she wants more than a dance. Ever fuck a girl?"

"Once. It's not bad."

"Keep smiling at her and you'll give her the wrong impression."

"Should I ask her for a dance?"

"What if she asked you to fuck her?"

"I'd tell her I'm gay." Ramon shook his hips. "I want only to dance."

"We could dance if you want. Which would you prefer? Eating or dancing?"

266

"Dancing." Ramon pulled Don through the gyrating crowd then stopped under a flashy disco ball.

Subsonic bass notes blasted Don's ears and compressed his chest, causing him to move farther away from the speakers. He marveled at Ramon's sexy, lithe, and muscular body's wiggling. Overhead lights exaggerated the depth of his pecs and the shape of his bubble butt as each butt cheek contracted, in snyc with the beat of the music.

"How did you get such a great ass?" Don yelled in Ramon's ear.

"Bicycle and soccer."

"Keep at it. I like the results." *Love to fuck it.*

Don and Ramon got caught up in the music's forever beat. Don began to sweat. He noticed several men had removed their shirts, so he removed his and tucked it behind the waistband of his pants.

Ramon stared at and then placed his hands on Don's sweaty pecs. Don flexed them, causing Ramon to smile and tighten his grip.

Don pulled Ramon's sweaty shirt over his head, revealing Ramon's muscular chest. Don waved the shirt overhead and in time with the beat of the throaty bass notes then tucked it in his rear waistband.

Ramon squeezed Don's pecs and smiled. Don gripped Ramon's waist then lifted him until his pecs were at mouth level. He stared at them for a second then sucked and nibbled the right nipple. Don wanted to elicit the same pleasure George had delivered at the pool.

Ramon moaned then said, "If you are hungry, we should eat."

Lowering Ramon, Don said, "I like chest steak."

"Let's try *rez* . . . uh, cow steak," Ramon chuckled.

The two men headed for the first-floor restaurant. Fifty feet ahead, Don spotted Alvaro talking to three guys at the head of the stairs. Each wore tight, short white shirts that revealed their six-packs. Alvaro wore the beige pants Don had purchased for him when they were in Tijuana.

Those pants make his butt look better than any he has ever worn.

"I want you to meet someone," Don said, pulling Ramon along.

Halfway to the stairs, Don and Alvaro's eyes met. Alvaro left his friends and walked toward Don.

"Surprised to see you here," Alvaro said, extending his hand.

"How're you doing?" Don asked, hugging Alvaro and then kissing him of the forehead.

"I'm fine."

Don gestured toward Ramon. "This is Ramon. He's the new waiter at the Angel."

"*Mucho gusto,*" Ramon said. "A friend of Don's is an *amigo de mio.*"

"Not sure I'm much of a friend," Alvaro said, winking at Ramon and shaking his hand. "How long have you known Don?"

Don interrupted and squeezed Ramon's shoulder. "A long time."

"A few days," Ramon said.

Alvaro furrowed his brow. "Which is it, Don—hours or days?"

"It's been a long, few days," Don said, feeling his face warm from blushing.

Alvaro burst out laughing.

"What's so funny?" Don asked.

"That's the first time I've seen you blush—at a lie."

"I didn't blush. It's the red lights out here."

"Yeah, red lights and maybe some of that funny smoke your breathing."

Staring into Alvaro's eyes, Don asked. "Working yet?"

"A few odd jobs, and—no—I'm not sellin' me bod."

"Living off Jesus?"

"I stay there. Nothing more."

268

Ramon tugged Don's arm. "We get steak now?"

"Don, would you like to dance?" Alvaro asked.

"You want to dance with me?" Don asked.

"Yeah, why not? Put your shirt on and I'll dance with you."

"Why do I have to put my shirt on?"

"So no one thinks there is anything between us," Alvaro said and winked.

"Don't tell me you're worried about Jesus?"

"Just cautious."

"Well, I'm not putting my shirt on. Dance with someone else."

Alvaro turned to Ramon, "How'd you like to dance?"

Ramon's eyes sparkled. "I like to dance with everybody."

"Then let's go." Alvaro pulled Ramon to the center of the dance floor.

Don thought, *He's trying to make me jealous.*

Alvaro pulled Ramon close then ground crotches. He dropped his hands to Ramon's butt, gripped it, and then shook it.

Ramon put his arms around Alvaro's neck and smiled.

Don though, *It's not going to work, Alvaro. He likes older guys.*

Don took a seat at a table near the edge of the terrace and waited. A waiter inquired about drinks, and Don ordered two Margaritas.

The waiter hurried back with the drinks. Don sipped his and watched his friends dance.

After dancing, Alvaro and Ramon pushed their way to Don's table.

"Didn't think you'd be coming back," Don said, staring at Alvaro, "otherwise, I would have ordered you a drink."

Don handed Ramon a Margarita.

"Oh that's okay," Alvaro said, picking up Don's drink.

269

"I'll have this one."

Alvaro clanked his glass on Ramon's. "*Salud.*"

Don thought, *He knows he's provoked me by taking my drink.*

Don yelled to a waiter, "*Una* Margarita!"

Alvaro slapped Ramon's rear. "When we were dancing, I couldn't help notice you have a hard butt."

"I play soccer and ride bicycle. It's good for my muscles. You play soccer, no?"

"I've played some," Alvaro said, "but I mostly watch my friend, Jesus Gonzales, play. I prefer watching him than playing myself."

Excited, Ramon asked, "You know Jesus?"

"He's a friend of Don and me. Well, a friend of mine. He knows Don—but not well."

"I like meet him," Ramon said, bouncing about.

"You going to be here around one thirty?" Alvaro asked.

Ramon looked at Don. "We stay until one thirty?"

"Anything you want," Don said then faked a smile. *Hope Jesus doesn't show up.*

"Wow! *Marvilloso!*" Ramon shouted. "I'll meet Jesus!"

"Quiet down," Don said, patting the air. "People are staring. Sit down."

Ramon and Alvaro sat down beside each other, facing Don.

Ramon took Alvaro's hands in his and smiled. "You will introduce me to Jesus, *si?*"

"Of course. He'd like to meet you," Alvaro said, staring at Don.

"I can't wait to meet him."

"I'm goin' outside," Alvaro said. "I need a cigarette."

"We're having dinner here," Don said, putting on his shirt. "See you later, Alvaro."

Chapter 21

The dining room's decor consisted of dim, pink lighting from twenty chandeliers dripping with sparkling crystals. The tufted arm chairs were covered in dark-pink velvet upholstery. The tables were draped with pale-pink tablecloths, which hung to the floor and topped with crystal vases containing pink and white artificial flowers. Pink up-lights illuminated pink tulle-draped walls.

"Look at this place," Ramon said as he and Don took seats at a corner table.

"Yeah, someone had a sale on pink," Don said, looking around. "I bet the toilet seats are pink too."

The waiter handed Don and Ramon menus bound in pink leather.

"Fancy," Don said to the waiter while examining both sides of the binder. "Do you have one in English?"

"Si, señor," the man said then left.

"No worry," Ramon said. "I'll translate for you."

"I know the Spanish word for steak, and that's what I want."

"Me too," Ramon said and waved for the waiter.

The waiter took their order for rib eye steaks. "Care to see our wine list?"

Don looked at Ramon and raised an eyebrow. "You drink wine?"

"Maybe. I don't know *mucho* about wine."

"Well, I'll teach you," Don said. "Waiter, a bottle of Mexican Merlot."

Ramon fidgeted in his chair and rapped his fingers on the table.

"Calm down," Don said. "I know you're anxious to meet Jesus, but calm down or you'll shred your pants."

"I'm sorry for nerves, but I'm anxious to meet him. He is big hero in Mexico."

"Let me warn you. He'll try to rape you."

271

"He's gay?" Ramon asked, looking astonished. "I heard he might be, but is he?"

"Very! He's the kind of guy who'd fuck you a few times and then leave you at the side of the road."

"Fucking is okay but leaving someone alone on road is bad."

"I didn't mean road literally. I meant he would stop seeing you as soon as another cute guy came along."

"Excuse me," the waiter said, holding a wine bottle toward Don.

Don examined its label. After scanning the label, he nodded approval. A loud "pop" filled the room as the bottle ceded its cork. Don sniffed it then indicated the waiter should pour some wine for tasting. Don examined the wine in his glass then swirled it. "It's tough to judge a wine's color against all this pink." He nosed the glass and inhaled. He took a mouthful then "chewed" it. "Fine," he said. "Please, fill our glasses and hold our steaks."

Ramon stared at his glass. "I've never had a glass like this."

"It's lead crystal. Hold it by the stem. Take some wine in your mouth and chew it. Note its taste."

Ramon swallowed a mouthful. "*Bueno.*"

"I'm glad you like it but, next time, hold it in your mouth a little longer. Learn to taste the various flavors. Enjoy it before you gulp it down."

Don queried Ramon about subjects he discussed at home.

Aunt Teresa's garden produced most of Ramon's fresh foods, and a vine produced enough grapes to make a sweet wine. During this time, they consumed their bottle of wine.

Don waived to the waiter. "Another bottle, please."

Minutes later, the waiter brought another bottle and their steaks.

"I didn't want our steaks now," Don said, "but . . .

okay. Leave them." Don sipped the new wine. "Damn. This taste better than the first bottle."

"*Si*!" Ramon said, swallowing half a glass of the new wine. "It's *muy bueno*."

After a few bites of steak, the conversation returned to American baseball. In no time, the second bottle of wine had been consumed.

We still have half our steak." Don said, shaking the empty bottle. "We need wine to wash it down."

Ramon nodded his agreement.

"Waiter—another bottle," Don yelled.

Don inquired as to how Ramon realized he might be gay and how he came out.

"With friends. We start jerking off—in front of each other. Then jerk each other. One boy handled me in a way I liked, so we had private visits. Later, we give each other mouth sex."

Don learned it took the intervention of an older boy to initiate Ramon into being fucked and to fuck.

"First time I did it, it hurt," Ramon said, wincing at the memory. "It hurt bad, but I couldn't get up. He was big and held me down. It didn't feel good until he ready to shoot."

"Sounds like you were raped. How long did it take for you to try again?"

Ramon thought a minute then sipped his wine. "Two weeks. But with a different boy. He started with finger then cock. He started slow. It felt good—*muy bueno*. Since then, I like fucking."

"I noticed," Don said, smiling. "You rode my steed quite well."

"*Si* . . . you have nice *caballo*. I mean horse." Ramon had a light slur to his speech and an impish glint in his eye. "I'd like to ride again."

Nice to know I can entertain the younger set.

All the discussion about sex excited Don. His cock strained against his fly. He rearranged his napkin to cover the

273

bulge growing below the table's edge.

Don leaned forward and whispered, "If we keep talking like this, and my cock keeps growing, we might have to go to those bushes out back, so I can fuck you."

Ramon smiled then rubbed his bare toes along Don's leg. Don reached under the table, grabbed the foot and squeezed it.

Ramon smiled and cut a piece of steak. Using his fingers, he held the meat toward Don who accepted the food then sucked Ramon's fingers as they were teased from his mouth.

"You like my meat?" Ramon asked.

"You betcha, and I want more. I want all your meat—down to the bone."

"But you'd chew it, no?"

"I promise I won't—I'll swallow it whole."

Uninhibited, Ramon rubbed his foot against Don's leg. He then almost disappeared under the table as he extended his foot into Don's crotch. Don grabbed the foot and rubbed it against his "throbber" held hostage by a zipper.

"I think we should have another bottle," Don said, his speech slurring. "Waiter—*por favor*. We need another bottle."

The waiter nodded then left.

Intoxicated, Don became reckless. After Ramon's foot had caressed Don's crotch for a while, Don wanted to raise his crotch-pleasure a notch. He unzipped his fly, giving his cock unfettered freedom—save for his napkin.

"Put your foot in my lap," Don said, speech slurred.

Ramon slid down in his chair and extended his leg. "*Por Dios*, you took it out!"

"Just for you."

Don scooted down a few inches so Ramon did not have to extend his leg any farther.

"You make me happy," Ramon said as the waiter place an opened bottle of wine on the table.

"Glad to be of service," the waiter said.

Ramon looked at the waiter. "No. My friend. He makes

me happy."

"Sorry, *Señor,"* the waiter said then walked away. "Enjoy your wine."

Ramon stared at Don a few seconds then twisted his signet ring from his finger. For a moment, he dangled it then let it fall to the floor. "Ut oh. I dropped my ring." He raised the tablecloth and peered under the table. "I don't see it." He crawled under the table to search for the ring. He found it within seconds but took time to swallow Don's cock.

Don asked, "Find your ring?"

"Not yet."

Don enjoyed the interlude for a few seconds then pushed Ramon's mouth from his cock. "Find the ring yet?"

"*Si*, I have it." Ramon crawled from under the table.

Don used his tented napkin to dry his cock. "Better drink up, Ramon."

Ramon sipped his wine then went giant-eyed as he peered over Don's head.

Someone tapped Don on the shoulder.

"Who the hell?" Don asked, turning around. "Son-of-a-bitch. Jesus. What the hell are you doing here?"

"Alvaro said you have a friend I should meet."

"I have a friend, but *I* don't want him meeting you. *He* wants to meet you—I don't." *I don't care if I never see you again.*

"Is this your friend, Don?" Jesus asked, extending his hand toward Ramon.

"He's *my* friend and keep your hands off."

"*Señor* Jesus, I am a longtime admirer. Me and my *amigos* watch all your games. I play the same position as you, on my team."

"Your English is quite good," Jesus said. "Who is your team?"

"I play for the Eagles. We are regional champions this season."

"Glad your team did so well," Jesus said, slapping

275

Ramon on the back.

At that moment, Alvaro approached Don and said, "I see Ramon has met Jesus."

Don nodded toward Jesus and slurred, "Yeah, golden boy has another admirer, but for the love of Mary, I don't understand what people see in him."

"You don't recognize excellence," Jesus said then smiled. "You can't play football and you can't fuck—not with what I've seen of that little thing of yours."

Don sneered. "Ramon, ignore this son-of-a-bitch. He's as conceited as a male peacock in heat—plus full of shit. He doesn't know his ass from Shinola." Holding up his little finger, Don slurred, "His cock is smaller than this."

"*Señor* Jesus, how do you exercise your legs?" Ramon asked. "They are so big. Have they helped you win games?"

"You're very observant," Jesus said, holding Ramon's hand against his pants-covered, flexed thigh. "I do lots of leg exercises plus running, and yes, they've helped me beyond words. Would you like to see them?"

Ramon's eyes grew to the size of a hub cap. "*Si.*"

"My pleasure." Jesus sat down in a chair beside Ramon then rolled his pant leg above his knee.

Ramon extended his index finger to test the firmness of the leg, smiled, and then looked at Jesus for a second before squeezing the thigh.

"You like legs?" Jesus asked, patting Ramon's thigh.

Ramon squeezed Jesus' thigh again. "I've never touch ed such a hard muscle."

"Jesus," Alvaro said, "why don't we go back to our table; let Don and Ramon enjoy their wine?"

"Yeah, Jesus, why don't you toddle over to your table," Don said. "You've sucked enough air out of the room." Don turned to Ramon and snarled, "Remember why your here, son."

Don's harsh words shocked Ramon. "What do you mean why am I here?"

"You're here because I brought you; I buy your drinks; I buy your food; I paid the taxi; I paid the cover charge."

"You know I don't have *mucho dinero*. You bring me here—I didn't ask."

"You asked me to bring you to a dance club, so I did. You owe me something."

"Something *si*—so I say *gracias*, but you don't purchase me."

"Show a little gratitude."

"*Señor* Don, I'm sorry I didn't show gratitude. *Por favor*, forgive me."

"No *problema*. Drink your wine."

Jesus moved behind Ramon and placed a hand on each of his shoulders. "Guys, enjoy your wine. Nice meeting you, Ramon. Maybe you can visit me at the arena sometime."

"*Si*! I like that."

"*Hasta lluego!*" Jesus said, turning to leave.

Jesus and Alvaro returned to their banquette and sat side-by-side, scanning menus. Alvaro put his menu down and cleared his throat. "Why did you taunt Don like that?"

Without looking up, Jesus said, "Somebody has to bring that bastard down a notch or two."

"Maybe so but does it have to be you—and here?"

"Here's as good a place as any."

"Damn it, Jesus. This is a club. We're supposed to laugh, dance, and have fun here—not argue or fight."

"Okay," Don said, putting down his menu. "I'm very sorry if I offended you."

As Jesus spoke, he gripped Alvaro's thigh.

"Stop playing with my leg," Alvaro sneered, "and why are you so uptight?"

"It's you. You get me wound up. Everyone saw how you played Ramon while the two of you danced."

"You saw us?" Alvaro asked then sat motionless for a moment. He faced Jesus. "To me, Ramon seemed like one of

277

those orphans you say you care for. He needed someone . . . to dance with."

"So?"

Alvaro stared Jesus in the eye. "Are you sure you aren't sexually interested in Ramon, unlike one of those orphans you say you have so much heartfelt charity for?"

"Shit," Jesus said, striking the table. "I spend time with orphans, because I have to. Team owners demand the players educate and train the orphans. It's all for publicity. The owners and the press get more from our appearances than the kids, and I'm tired of the PR shit. That's not to say I don't care about the kids, I do, but most of the effort is for selfish PR."

"Then why do it?"

"It's an obligation. As for the orphans, I do *not* want to have sex with those kids! My fun is with legal guys. I have no interest in going to jail or getting kicked off the team."

"What about me? You still interested in me?"

Jesus patted Alvaro's hand. "You know I'm interested in you. Why do you think I let you stay at the house? Why do I take you places? Don't I treat you well?"

"With worldly things, you're very generous, but do you have any feelings for me?"

"Of course, I have feelings for you." Jesus pushed his menu across the table.

Alvaro felt anger grow in his belly. "Do you think the way you treated Ramon indicated your feelings for me?"

"When you asked to stay at my place, I told you guys would be coming and going. I have access to lots of hot guys—you included—but don't expect me to be monogamous. It's not in me. But look at you. All that small talk around that hotel pool made me believe that even though you liked Don, you played around—a lot."

"So? I did it more for spite than whoring, but I guess I expected too much from you."

Looking around the dining room, Jesus asked, "Where is that waiter? I want a drink."

278

"Haven't seen him in a while," Alvaro said, scanning the room. "I'll find him. What do you want?"

"A Margarita."

Jesus sat alone reading the menu. He peered over it and noted Don staring at him. Jesus muttered, "Why the hell is he staring at me?" Jesus went back to reading the menu.

Moments later, Alvaro returned with two Margaritas.

Jesus glanced toward Don's table and hoisted his drink in a toast. Don just stared.

"Wonder why Don is staring so hard?" Alvaro asked.

"Who knows."

Jesus and Alvaro ordered dinner and a bottle of wine. Jesus tried to direct conversation away from his sexual partners and his relationship with Alvaro. He delved into Alvaro's interest in painting and his murals. Because Jesus knew numerous artists, he agreed to introduce Alvaro to the best painters in Mexico City.

Alvaro's interest became focused. "Why didn't you tell me you knew artists?"

"You never asked."

"Are many of them gay?"

"Some," Jesus said. "Some are straight, and some are straight but gay friendly."

"I don't know anything about Mexican artists—except Diego Rivera—and he's dead. He did murals like me."

"There are gallery openings all the time. I'll find where the best artists are showing and we'll go. You'll meet some nice painters . . . sculptors. Openings are always fun—strange characters but lots of nice artists."

"I miss my art . . . Having nothing to do is depressing. Who knows, I might start painting again."

"Tell you what. I'll buy some art supplies for you, and you whip up some canvases. I'll show them around—share them with a few artists I know—see what they say. If they like them, they might hook you up with a gallery. Who knows, you might become Mexico's Picasso."

279

"Wow. I haven't felt this excited since I got my first check for a Philly mural." *Shit! I shouldn't have said that. What if he mentions murals to his friends, and they check on me. Shit!*

"If my friends like your work, and you get a gallery connection, I'll buy a painting." Jesus sipped his wine. "That kind of publicity could generate publicity. It could help your career a lot."

Alvaro laughed. "I can see the picture now—front page: 'Soccer hero, Jesus Gonzales, invests in art by rising star Alvaro.' That would be better than one of those endorsements you do for shoes."

"Careful what you say about my sponsors, but I hadn't thought of it that way. Why not? I like the idea of using one name for your career—like Picasso—he used only one name."

"This calls for a celebration," Alvaro exclaimed. "Will you buy me something special?"

"What do you want?"

"Champagne?" Alvaro said, bouncing in his chair.

"That's the least I can do for Mexico's Picasso. Let's ask if this place has any."

"*Señor*," the waiter said, "French champagne cost too much for the owner to keep in stock. He felt it wouldn't sell, so we sell sparkling wine instead."

"Then bring us a bottle," Jesus said.

The evening grew festive, and Jesus ordered a second and a third bottle of sparkling wine.

Alvaro felt he would burst from joy and excitement. "I want to tell Don about my new career. He'll be happy to hear I won't have to work the streets."

"Go ahead. Maybe good news will keep him off my back."

Alvaro called the waiter and asked for two more champagne glasses.

"What are you going to do with those?" Jesus asked.

"I want to have a celebration drink with Don and

280

Ramon."

"Do you have to?"

"Ahhh, come on, Jesus. Don't be a party pooper."

Alvaro took the glasses to Don's table. Jesus followed, carrying a bottle of sparkling wine.

Alvaro placed an empty glass in front of Ramon and Don.

Don looked up. "What's this shit for?"

Alvaro smiled. "I thought you and Ramon would help me celebrate my new career."

"What career?" Don asked, looking perplexed.

"I'm goin' to start painting again. Jesus is going to get me a gallery connection—something to keep me off the streets. I'd like to think I could support myself with my art. Be happy for me."

"Son-of-a-bitch," Don shouted as Jesus started to fill the glasses. "Do you realize where your so called new career could lead? Think kid, think! Do you want to wind up in the states?"

"What's wrong with Alvaro being in the states?" Jesus asked.

"Ask him," Don said, staring into the eyes of his ex-American protégé. "What about *me*, kid? You'd better think long and hard about what art publicity could do to your career. *Our* careers."

Appearing perplexed by the conversation, Jesus said, "Shit! If Alvaro's art is any good, and with the right connections—like me—he could earn a damn good living—live like a king."

"Or a bird in a cage," Don slurred.

"I don't know what the hell is going on," Jesus ranted, almost dropping the champagne bottle. "Alvaro had good news to share, and you rain on his parade."

"Shut up, bastard!" Don yelled. "What we're talking about is way bigger than a ball kicker like you."

"Fuck you, Don!" Alvaro yelled. "Come on, Jesus,

281

let's go back to our table."

Chapter 22

Don stared at the glass of celebratory wine sitting in front of him. He started to drink it but hurled it toward Jesus' table.

The sound of breaking glass attracted the attention of everyone in the restaurant. The room buzzed with disbelief as fingers wagged at every table.

Shocked by Don's behavior, Ramon said, "That glass could hurt someone. Maybe we should leave."

"Stay where you are," Don snarled. "We ain't goin' no place."

The manager rushed to Jesus' table and inquired about the broken glass.

"One of your drunken guests threw it," Jesus shouted.

"That is unacceptable, *señor*." Waving to a waiter, the manager asked Jesus, "Please, point out the person who threw it?"

"He did it," Jesus shouted, pointing to Don who turned his back to Jesus and Alvaro. "The gringo sitting at that table—with that young Mexican. The *gringo* threw it."

Ramon tapped Don's hand while staring over Don's shoulder. "Don. I think we in trouble. An angry looking *hombre* is coming here."

The manager stopped beside Don. "*Señor*, I hear you threw a glass. It just missed Jesus and shattered on the floor. You heard it, no? Did you throw the glass, *señor*?"

"*Señor* manager, I did not throw the glass. I simply tried to return some unwanted champagne, and the glass slipped from my hand."

"I heard that," Jesus yelled. "You're lying. You threw the damn glass. Ask anyone in the restaurant. They saw what happened."

The earlier beckoned waiter arrived, and the manager said, "Get security—now."

The manager addressed Don. "*Señor*, I must ask you to

leave. Please go quietly. We do not want a scene."

Ramon started to get up, but Don pushed him down in his seat. "We're going no place." Don picked up his wine glass. "We have wine to finish."

Two three-hundred-pound security guards, dressed in funeral black, arrived. The taller of the men addressed Don in English. "*Señor*, it's time to go. Please, leave or we'll have to remove you—forcibly."

Don ignored the invitation.

Without warning, the men grabbed Don by his arms and pulled him to his feet, knocking his wine glass from his hand.

A hush fell over the dining room as all eyes watched the drama unfold.

Ramon pleaded, "Don, please. I don't want trouble *para me* or you."

Don struggled against the guard's vice-like grips. "Okay. I'll leave but let go of my arms. I don't need your assistance to walk out of this dump."

Few of the guests spoke English, but those who did gasped so loudly at Don's insult they drowned out the music from the dance area.

Ramon grabbed Don's arm and led him to the exit. "Let's go outside. You need air."

The men passed Jesus' table where Don suddenly lungled at Jesus. A scuffle ensued. In defending himself, Jesus knocked over his table. Dishes, utensils, and glasses flew across the room. A half-empty bottle of wine and an ice bucket rolled under a nearby table, spilling their contents over the floor. An additional security guard ran into the dining room. He assisted the guards and Alvaro in pulling Don off Jesus, pinned to the floor.

The guards dragged Don to the exit where they tossed him out like a bag of garbage.

Following close behind came Alvaro and Ramon. Jesus stood in the doorway watching.

Alvaro gripped Ramon's arm and said, "I know what you're goin' through. Trust me. He cannot afford any more trouble. I'll help you get him in that cab. Take him to the hotel."

The manager yelled from the doorway, "Don't come back. If you do, security will have you removed and the police called."

Don awoke to see Ramon standing at the side of the bed with a morning cup of coffee in one hand and two aspirin in the other.

"Where am I?" Don asked, throwing the sheets back. "God. I'm naked."

"You're in the Angel hotel," Ramon said. "We got here early this morning. You had too much to drink."

"Thanks for the aspirin," Don said then gulped them down. "I don't remember last night. Did you undress me?"

"*Si, Señor*. Your billfold on table. I took *dinero* to pay the cab. The rest is in your billfold."

"You didn't take advantage of me—did you?"

"What you mean advantage?"

"Fuck me or something."

"Oh, *Señor*, I fucked you all night—many times." Ramon laughed then said, "You didn't want me to stop."

"Shit!" Don said, rubbing his head. "I don't remember having that kind of fun."

"*Señor*, I no fuck you. I make joke. We only sleep."

"Maybe you could fuck me after I'm over this headache." Don looked at the bedside clock. "Damn, it's eleven thirty. Let's get some coffee, maybe lunch."

Don pulled on shorts and a t-shirt, then he and Ramon headed for the dining room.

They had just started to eat when Alvaro walked in.

"What the hell you doing here?" Don asked.

"I need to talk to you about last night." Alvaro nodded toward the lobby. "Ramon, would you mind if Don and I talked alone for a few minutes?"

"No *problema*." Ramon took his coffee to the garden.

Alvaro sighed then said, "Don, I need something to do here—some kinda work. Talking soccer and sex all day and drinking all night is depressing. I can't get a regular job because I don't speak Spanish, and I don't have a work permit." He took a sip of Don's coffee. "I can't get a work permit, but I can paint. Jesus is going to buy supplies and give me space to work. If people like my art, maybe I could sell a piece or two. If I did, I'd be able to support myself . . . be self-sufficient again."

Alvaro began to pace.

Don said nothing. *What the fuck does he want for me? Prison?*

"Aren't you going to say anything?" Alvaro asked, staring at Don.

"Sit down."

Alvaro took a seat and continued. "If I'm going to be successful, I need publicity. That's the only way I can sell anything. I need customers—buyers—and Jesus can help with that."

Don looked around to make sure no one could hear him. "You know publicity could get you noticed by the wrong people. You could wind up in jail. God only knows how long."

"That's a possibility. That's why I'm growing a beard. Somebody once told me I'd look good in a beard, so I'm gonna grow one. I'm not going to let anyone photograph me again without it. Hopefully, it'll keep me unrecognized."

"That's all good and dandy for you, but what about me?

"Don . . . I hate to say this, but I'm at a point where I have to worry about me. I need to do what *I* need to do. I have to plan a life for *me*. You need to do the same."

Don pushed his chair back. "What are you saying? You want rid of me? Is that it?"

"Don, you're special to me and always will be, but you are the one who has to decide the kind of life *you* want but get sober then we'll see how I fit in. If you're afraid my publicity might get you in trouble, then you'll have to set limits on our meetings." Alvaro stood, ready to leave. "One more thing. You have got to control your drinking. You've lost control too many times because of booze. You almost killed Jesus—several times. So far he hasn't called police, but yer drinking is going to land you in jail. If that happens, you're off to the States. Your discovery could lead to my discovery, and I'd get sent back. Be careful for both of us."

"Is this goodbye?" Don asked, sadness tingeing his voice.

"Absolutely not. I'll see you around, but not when you're drinking. Maybe *you* should find work. You'd have less time to drink. One other thing. Ramon is a good kid. Be kind to him."

Alvaro and Jesus visited the largest art store in Mexico City. As they strolled along the aisles, several customers recognized Jesus, engaged him in conversation, and asked for his autograph.

Dressed in the paint-smeared clothing of a starving artist, two gay students eyed Jesus. He knew they had looked him over. He had overheard them mention his legs and their discussion about whether or not to approach him.

Jesus ambled along the aisle, where the students shopped, pretending to look for something.

"*Perdon, Señor* Jesus. Kiki and I are students . . . at the School of Beau Arts. We're majoring in painting and minoring in portraits. We would like to paint your portrait. In your uniform."

"*Caballeros*, I'd be honored," Jesus said, extending his hand to Kiki while noting the students' physical attributes. "And what is your friend's name?"

"Sorry, *Señor,*" Kiki said. "This is Dab. He got his nickname from his painting technique."

"I would love to be your model," Jesus said to Kiki.

"Maybe you guys could come by my house sometime. I could do a sitting. I can't give you much time, but if a couple of hours would work, I would be happy to help."

"Oh thank you," Dab said while clapping.

"We would be honored," Kiki said, "We would get high marks for such a portrait."

"Here's my number." Jesus handed Kiki a card. "Call when you're ready and bring cameras. You should take some photos for reference while finishing the portrait."

Alvaro joined the trio. "Hello."

"Alvaro," Jesus said. "This is Kiki and Dab. They're art students. I've agreed to sit for them so they can paint my portrait for a school project." Pointing to Alvaro, Jesus said, "This is Alvaro, an American friend who is also a painter."

"Nice to meet you," Alvaro said and extended his hand.

"What's your art preference?" Kiki asked.

"Realism—slightly abstracted," Alvaro said. "We probably have common interests."

Alvaro looked at Jesus. "We need to get out of here, but I look forward to seeing your friends again."

Each person bid the other goodbye.

Alvaro asked, "Are those new conquests—new meat? Do you really think they'll complete your portrait?"

"If they don't, it won't be my fault. They have to decide how they spend their time. If they want to play around, who am I to stop them?"

Wearing only shorts, Alvaro sweated as he worked on a painting beside Jesus' pool. Jesus crept up behind him and hugged his waist.

"You didn't surprise me," Alvaro said, without missing a stroke. "I heard you coming."

"Damn," Jesus said then eyed the new painting. "It's looking good."

"Thanks. A couple more hours and it'll be finished."

Alvaro scanned Jesus' shorts. "Revealing aren't they? Let me guess. The students are coming."

"Lucky guess. Stick around this afternoon. I have a feeling there'll be some skinny dipping."

"Ha! I know there will," Alvaro said, stepping back to inspect his painting.

"I'm going to make Margaritas for our guests. Have one. It'll help you paint?"

"Sure there'll be enough, considering the students will have big thirsts."

"Don't worry about us running out."

"Then I'll have one. I'm thirsty."

Jesus had just returned with glasses and a pitcher of Margaritas when the doorbell rang.

"The students," Alvaro said, stepping back to evaluate his last paint stroke.

"Where the fuck did I put my jersey?" Jesus asked, scanning the area.

"Don't bother," Alvaro said. "The students won't mind if you're shirtless. Things will go faster if you're half-naked."

"Think they'll be interested in these pecs?" Jesus asked as he bounced them while heading for the door.

Opening the ornate wooden door, Jesus saw Kiki's and Dab's mouth gape as they stared at his chest.

"Welcome." Jesus said and pointed toward the pool. "Let's go outside."

At the pool, Jesus nodded toward Alvaro. "You guys remember Alvaro?"

"Yes. Hello, Alvaro," the students said.

"Hi, guys. Welcome."

The students scanned the expansive pool, lavishly out-fitted patio, and sumptuously landscaped grounds.

"I like your work," Kiki said as he and Dab examined Alvaro's painting.

"Thanks," Alvaro said, smiling. "Do you guys mind if I continue painting while you work with Jesus?"

"Not at all," Dab said. "Don't let us bother you."

"Guys," Jesus said, "would you like to work outside or inside?"

"The light is good out here," Kiki said. "Let's work here."

The students set up a tripod with a camera as well as easels with blank canvases.

"Let's get started," Kiki said.

Jesus attempted every pose requested. After thirty minutes of posing, painting, and photographing from all angles everyone sweated.

"Anyone care for a Margarita?" Jesus asked. "Might cool us off."

Almost shaking with excitement, the students yelled, "Yeah."

Jesus poured a round for everyone and then returned to posing for another photo shoot.

Alvaro cleaned his brush. "That's enough for me," he said, glancing at Dab's work. "I can see you are going to be a great artist."

"Guys, we've been at this for an hour," Jesus said. "It's time for my afternoon swim. Who wants to join me?"

Kiki and Dab looked at each other. "Yeah. *Por qué no*?"

"I agree. Why not," Jesus said, shedding his shorts. Naked, he dived into the pool.

"It's okay guys. You don't need swim suits," Alvaro said. He too stripped and dived in.

Dab mumbled, "I hadn't expected this, but . . ."

The students stripped to their underwear.

"You don't want to wear wet underwear home do you?" Jesus yelled. "It's just us guys. The water is great. You'll like it."

The students glanced at each other, dropped their underwear, and then dived in.

Jesus whispered to Alvaro, "From the way they dived

in, they didn't want us to see their cocks."

Alvaro snickered then whispered, "Maybe my younger eyes gave me an advantage. I got a good look. Neither has anything to be ashamed of."

The students laughed and splashed about as if they hadn't been sized up.

Jesus thought, *These guys have butts cheeks that will nicely fit my hand. Which guy should I hit on first?*

Jesus grabbed a floating ball and tossed it to Kiki. Alvaro and Dab tried to snatch it. All their activities resulted in a game of water polo intended to bring the men's bodies in contact. Jesus took every opportunity to get his crotch against the students' butts.

Jesus thought, *Kiki is going out of his way to get his butt against my or Alvaro's crotch and Dab is interested my rear.*

The lackluster game lasted several minutes. Jesus said, "Everyone, drink your Margaritas or the melting ice will ruin them."

Jesus hoped the drinks would reduce the students' inhibitions regarding sex.

Repeated cycles of water polo and drinking led to less and less polo and more body contact. It didn't take long before Jesus grabbed each student's crotch.

Kiki and Dab stopped bobbing and stared at each other as if trying to decide whether they were intimidated by the other's presence.

Alvaro approached the students from the rear and rubbed their butts. Kiki looked at Alvaro and smiled.

Jesus grabbed Dab's butt, turned him, and then pulled him close. Jesus kissed him on the lips. Dab returned the kiss as he groped Jesus. Jesus pulled away and then cock-teased Dab's ass.

Not to be outdone, Alvaro turned his attention to Kiki.

Jesus smiled as he watched Alvaro.

Alvaro gripped Kiki's butt cheeks then fingered the beckoning ass. After a few slow twists, a second finger joined

291

the first finger.

Kiki welcomed the attention so much that Jesus and Alvaro knew Kiki had experience.

Alvaro cock teased Kiki's waiting ass. He seemed to like being a bottom.

Alvaro accepted the invitation and pushed inside. He guided Kiki to the shallow end of the pool where Kiki cradled his head on his folded arms, which he rested on the coping. Alvaro rode Kiki's ass while the student sucked air and moaned his approval.

Chapter 23

Deep in the heart of Mexico City, Alvaro rushed around the Di Monaco Gallery of Art. The gallery had the distinction of hosting the city's wealthiest people at opening night exhibitions of new and established artists.

Alvaro had devoted a year to creating the paintings that would constitute his introduction to Mexico's art world. One that would determine whether or not his work warranted the sacrifices he had made to prepare for this night.

Exhausted, he finished last minute adjustments for his first, one-man show. He worried that the caterer had not arrived, and the liquor store had not delivered the wines and champagne.

Elleña Di Monaco, a woman of aristocratic bearing and worried gallery owner, darted about the gallery checking on the most minute detail involved in displaying Alvaro's paintings. A woman of about seventy-five, she tried to cam-ouflage her age with too much makeup. It appeared to have been applied with an artist's trowel. To hide her wrinkled throat, she wore a tight four-inch-wide necklace.

Alvaro presumed the necklace's large glittering stones were genuine diamonds nestled among South Pacific pearls.

She climbed to the upper rung of a five-foot ladder and made sure the art hung vertically then adjusted a spotlight on two of the paintings.

"Lighting is so important in selling art," she said, lifting her blue sequent-covered Yves St. Laurent gown, while descending the ladder. She took several steps back from the wall of paintings, tilted her head, squinted, and then adjusted the alignment of the bottom of two ornate frames. "Looks fine to me. What do you think, Alvaro?"

"Elleña, you've done a beautiful job." He squeezed her hand and stared into her grey-blue eyes. "I don't know how I can ever repay you."

"Don't thank me—just make me a little richer. Sell all

these paintings tonight. I need to pay for the food and wine—if it ever arrives." She shook her head and tousled her too darkly dyed hair. "I need the money to buy more diamonds."

"Hasn't Jesus spoken to you about money?"

"No. What about it?" Elleña asked, rearranging the already arranged floral display on the table awaiting *canapés*.

"If we don't sell enough paintings to cover your costs, he'll pay for the spread—the food and wine."

"Great!" Elleña straightened a flower and squinted at its position. "I like that kind of insurance."

A clunky sound from the doorway caused her to look up. "Ah, I see Marco has arrived. He's our photographer. Come, I'll introduce you."

Elleña kissed Marco on each cheek. "Marco, this is Alvaro. The man of the hour. He's Mexico's newest Picasso."

Elleña looked at Alvaro and smiled. "Don't worry about Marco; he's straight but gay friendly—although I wonder at times."

"Thanks for coming tonight," Alvaro said. "I've heard a lot about your work."

Marco smiled. "My pleasure. By the way, I was happy to hear Jesus Gonzales will be here. I've photographed him several times. His PR people let everyone in Mexico City know he'd be here." Marco backslapped Alvaro. "Jesus' attendance will attract many photographers, meaning extra publicity for you, my friend."

"Have no fear, *caballeros,*" Elleña said. "Jesus and I have invited the city's most important people. There will be so much diamond bling Marco will have to put filters on his lens."

Marco smiled at Alvaro. "She means Mexico's *nouveau riche*."

"The operative word is *riche*, Elleña said, "and they spend money." She pointed Marco toward a door at the back of the room. "Store your equipment in there."

Elleña put her hand on Alvaro's shoulder. "I invited the directors and curators of the city's most important art museums, critics from the major newspapers, and eleven art professors."

"Wow. I hope I live up to your expectations." *God, help me.* "I'm nervous as hell, but there's one thing I've been meaning to ask. How do you know Jesus?"

"He didn't tell you?" Elleña asked, staring at the door. "Where are those caterers? Well, we went to the same school—years apart—way out in the suburbs. We were both interested in promoting the school's future and met while serving on a school committee. Over time, we got to know each other and became friends—that is before he discovered himself and men. Never the less, we've remained friends. We've had a few dates to attend publicity parties. You know, fund raisers."

"So you liked to date younger men?"

"What older woman doesn't?"

Seeing her reflection in the glass covering a painting, Elleña ran her hand over her starched hair then brushed at the thick layer of red rouge on her left cheek. "Years ago, he came to an opening at a gallery where I worked as an art associate, meaning I was a salesperson. At the time, he already had a reputation as a good soccer player. He surprised me by buying a painting. He has continued to be a supporter of mine and has helped me sell a lot of paintings over the years."

"I hope he and his friends aren't disappointed in my work," Alvaro said, rubbing his shaky hands together. "All this is very stressful for a guy like me." *God, help me get through this.*

"Relax. The select few I invited to preview your work were ecstatic about it. I'm sure others will be too. My friend Pedro, in Monterrey, has a gallery. He's interested in doing a show for you in eight weeks."

"Oh my God," Alvaro gasped. "Monterrey too?"

"Yes. And I'm working on other venues as well. I guess I'm becoming your agent."

"I don't know how I can ever thank. Look." Alvaro pointed toward the twenty-foot-wide front window. "The liquor truck is here."

"Thank God," Elleña sighed, rearranging the rearranged flowers again. "We need to get the wines on ice right away. They must be cold by opening time."

"Thank God, the caterer's truck has arrived too," Alvaro said, exhaling a sigh of relief. "If the crowd doesn't like my art, they can at least eat and drink."

Elleña directed the caterer to a small kitchen where the cold foods would be stored. She helped one of the servers prepare tables for hot foods while Alvaro assisted a waiter stuff champagne and wine bottles in wine coolers filled with ice.

Elleña called out. "The wines will chill faster if they're in ice water instead of sitting on top of that ice."

Marco stood out of the way, observing the activities.

Elleña called to him. "Before the crowd arrives, would you take a few shots of Alvaro and his paintings."

"Good idea," Marco said. "Maybe I could shoot you two together."

Marco took about twenty photographs of Alvaro and Elleña. Peering through his viewfinder, Marco said, "That painting's wide swatches of blue and red is a great background for photographs."

As the photo shoot neared completion, the musicians arrived.

"Glad you're here. Set up in that corner," Elleña said, directing the musicians to a raised platform.

"Alvaro," she said, "all this picture taking reminds me. Have you seen the invitation I sent to our guest?"

"No. Is there one here?"

"Yes, and I need to put some out for anyone wanting to take one for a friend. Wait here. I'll be right back."

Elleña returned, waving a colorful flyer printed on stiff stock. "Take a look at this. Keep a copy for your *dossier*."

"My what?"

"Your d*ossier*. It's like a professional scrap book. Don't worry, we'll discuss it later."

296

The thirty-five by fifty-five-foot long gallery took on the air of a society party. The wait staff wore white tie and tails and white gloves. The finger foods rested on silver trays, and the wines were served in crystal stemware. The string quartet, composed of musicians from the symphony, would play light classical music to set the mood.

"I can't believe all this is happening to me—for me," Alvaro said, watching and listening to the musicians warming up. "I feel so underdressed in these jeans."

"You look fine," Elleña said, patting the air to indicate Alvaro should calm down, "besides, your about-to-be adoring public expects you to dress informally. Even a little sloppy would not be bad. Many people believe an artist should dress that way. I know millionaire artists who dress more bizarrely than you, my dear, so Relax. Enjoy yourself."

"This is all so new."

"Take it all in," Elleña said. "Remember it well. You only get one first opening and a one-man show rolled into one event. Now, make sure your art is just as you want it, and I'll check on the food."

Elleña and the caterer went from table to table, examining the layout of the food. "Looks like everything is ready," she said to the event manager, "except for a knife to cut that big cheese wheel. Will you get one from the kitchen?"

"Alvaro, when our guests arrive, you and I will stand at the door. I want to introduce you to each guest—even if I don't know them. Shake every hand, look everyone in the eye, and make sure you thank each one, by name, for coming.

"How will I know their names?" Alvaro asked, holding up his shaking, sweaty hands for Elleña's viewing.

"Stay calm and follow my lead. Listen for the names. You'll be okay."

"Boy, am I glad you've done this before. I wouldn't know what to do."

"My darling, relax. One other thing, when someone buys a painting, let them know you would be happy to inscribe a personal message on its back and sign it, if they want."

"It doesn't have to be in Spanish does it?"

"Oh no. Most, if not all, our guests write and speak English. They're well educated. When a painting is sold, we hand the buyer a red sticker and say, 'Would you like to place this sticker on the title card of *your* painting? It will inform guests that the painting has been purchased by a person of exceptional taste.' That makes buyers feel special."

"God, I have lots to learn about selling," Alvaro said, rubbing his palms together.

"Marco," Elleña said. "I want you to roam around, take lots of candid shots. Photograph interesting looking people, festive groups, high fashion ladies, and celebrities mixing with celebrities. Make sure you get lots of shots of Jesus, Alvaro, and others in front of his art." Elleña scanned the space. "I'm counting on your photographs to help me sell Alvaro's work not for just a week but throughout the year."

"Don't worry," Marco said. "I'll shoot anything that moves, speaks, or laughs."

Looking at Alvaro and then her diamond watch, Elleña said, "Even though the opening is scheduled for 9:00 p.m., don't expect anyone until 9:45 p.m. or 10:00 p.m." She cleaned her watch crystal with a handkerchief. "Being socially late began in Spain but the concept spread to Mexico. Let's relax and have some champagne while waiting for our guests."

Alvaro followed Elleña to her office where he and she lounged on a copy of Salvador Dali's Red Lips Sofa. Trying to make herself comfortable, she adjusted her tight gown and asked, "How did you and Jesus meet?"

Alvaro sat motionless thinking, *Where is this headed?* "Through the desk clerk at a hotel where I stayed." Alvaro fingered his glass. "Jesus' cousin managed the reception desk. He introduced us."

"Jesus has a very large family," Elleña said then sipped her champagne. "I don't know all of them, but they're very nice people. When did you learn about his . . . *lifestyle?*"

298

Searching for the right words, Alvaro took a sip of champagne. "First rumors and then his cousin, the clerk."

"Jesus is a wonderful man. He's always helping people. His public doesn't know it, but he supports several charities—orphanages, free health clinics, unwed mothers, and one convent that I know of. Believe me, his interests in orphanages is for all the right reasons. Oh, don't get me wrong. He has certain interests in some men, and the relationships haven't always been good ones, but why am I telling you?" Elleña stared Alvaro in the eye. You're a nice young man, and I think you have a great future, but I don't want you to get hurt."

Alvaro blushed. "Thanks for your interest and concern, but I've already been hurt, but . . . I'm over it. We've worked things out—we're friends. Jesus has been very good to me. He provided me a place to live, helped me with what I needed for painting, and introduced me to lots of people—important people—people like you. I don't know how to thank him—or you."

"I'm happy for you—" Elleña said, interrupting herself. "I think I hear guests. "Come. I know most of these people, and I want to introduce you to your public."

After the first guest arrived, it took only minutes for the gallery to fill. Alvaro took a deep breath and dived into the social aspect of selling art.

Elleña introduced him to a distinguished looking woman, Señora Montalba. A tall woman of regal bearing, she walked with the grace of a ballerina and wore her hair in a tight bun at the back of her head. Despite her rumored age of ninety-two, she had black-as-ink hair. She spoke beautiful British English as only a highborn Mexican of Spanish descent, educated in England, could. She dripped of jewelry that contained a fortune in diamonds, giving her the appearance of Queen Elizabeth's cousin.

"Señor Alvaro," Señora Montalba said. "I would be delighted if you would give me a personal tour of your art."

Elleña overheard the request and nodded her approval

for Alvaro to ignore other guests for a few minutes.

Señora Montalba took Alvaro's arm and led him toward his largest painting. "That is breathtaking. Its inspiration could only have come from Mexico."

"You guessed it," Alvaro said. "You know a lot about art."

"Young man, I've lived around art all my life. My husband served as Mexico's ambassador to the United States. We lived in Washington DC where I loved visiting galleries and meeting many artists who lived in or around the city. During that time, I developed an interest in abstract paintings. As a matter of fact, I decided to attend this opening because of the featured painting on the gallery invitation.

"How nice of you to say that," Alvaro said and patted her hand gripping his forearm.

She smiled and threw her head back. "My darling, nice has nothing to do with it. I liked the painting."

"Before we begin the tour, may I get you a glass of champagne?"

"How thoughtful of you." She smiled, and then stifled a giggle. "Yes, some bubbly—to keep our strength up as we tour."

Alvaro handed his new friend a glass of champagne and took one for himself. *This woman is a hoot.*

Señora Montalba clutched his arm as they strolled and examined paintings. After fifteen minutes of touring, the *Señora* said she wanted to rest. "I should sit with those people," she said, pointing to a well-dressed group of huddled guests.

Alvaro escorted her to the group. One gentleman rose and offered his chair. "Countess, please sit here."

Wow! She's royalty, Alvaro thought, holding the chair for his elderly guest.

Elleña interrupted the conversation. "Excuse me, Countess, but I must introduce Alvaro to a dear friend. Come Alvaro."

The countess nodded.

300

As Alvaro left, the countess called out, "Alvaro. I want to purchase the painting featured on the invitation. Would you place a red sticker on the title card for me?"

Smiling, Alvaro said, "My pleasure, Countess."

Elleña whispered to Alvaro, "I'm so glad you had a chance to speak to her. Her title is real—something left over from old Spain, but she rarely uses it. I've often thought she should change her title to cougar." Elleña stifled a giggle. "The old gal often travels with a bevy of young men, but they were not with her this evening. That's why she latched on to you so quickly."

Shocked by Elleña's revelation, Alvaro said, "You're not sayin' that kind old lady has boy toys are you?"

"The countess has a reputation for keeping at least one piece of eye-candy in her employ at all times. Rumor has it the men are forbidden to wear clothes in her home." Elleña looked at Alvaro and smiled. "Don't worry. She only hires men in their mid-thirties.

"Gosh! Alvaro said. "That's a wild tale. You're not joking are you?"

"I've never seen her men naked, but I can understand why she would want them so. They are very handsome." Elleña nodded to a gentleman who had lifted a glass toward her. "One can tell her men's bodies are wrought by the hands of Greek gods, but come, let's stand by the door. We have to meet and greet." Elleña shook hands with a guest then continued. "The countess is one of my most valued clients. When she buys your art, you know you have an inside track to the city's wealthiest art lovers."

Greeting more guests at the entrance, Elleña nudged Alvaro. "So far, you have met 187 guests."

"Really? How do you know?"

Elleña extended her hand, revealing a click-counter. "I keep count. See, 187."

Alvaro chuckled. "More stuff to learn about selling art."

301

Alvaro went about schmoozing with his guests and discussing his art.

Elleña waved for Alvaro to join her. "A *comisario* wants you to inscribe a note on a painting he purchased."

"I sold another one?"

"Surprised are you? Well, I'm happy to tell you that, so far, you've sold seven."

"Oh my God," Alvaro said, shocked. "You gotta be kidding. I can't believe it. Jesus is going to be so surprised, and you'll cover your costs."

"Oh. I'll do better than that. Jesus just called to say he's on his way. We should save some champagne for him."

"I'm so happy he's coming," Alvaro said, feeling very proud.

"I'm anxious to tell him how many paintings I've sold." Alvaro kissed Elleña on the cheek. "Thank you for everything."

"Come, talk to the *comisario* and sign his painting. I have to make sure the servers set out more food and champagne."

Alvaro busied himself with small talk with the *comisario* and his wife while they decided on the verbiage to be written on the back of their painting. "Okay. We're ready," the *comisario* said. Alvaro wrote and then signed the dictated inscription. He held it for the new owners to admire while Marco snapped a photo of the three holding the painting.

Just as the camera clicked, a roar erupted from the guests as they clapped. Jesus had arrived. He strutted like a matador, and given the tight fit of his shiny suit and bulging crotch, he looked like one. He stopped to shake gentlemen's hands and kiss ladies.

"Where is Mexico's Picasso?" he called, thrusting his hands toward the heavens.

Alvaro rushed forward. He and Jesus engaged in a long embrace like long lost lovers.

"Congratulations, my friend," Jesus said, pulling back. "How does it feel to be so adored?"

302

"This is too much." Alvaro smiled from sideburn to sideburn. "I don't know whether to pinch myself or scream. I'm afraid this is all a dream, and I'll wake up to find it all gone."

"This is no dream, my friend. *You* have arrived, and these people are your adoring public." Jesus grabbed Alvaro's hand, and raised it overhead. "*Damas y caballeros.* This is Mexico's new Picasso. For those of you who have not yet purchased one of his paintings, I will arrange for your tires to be slashed."

A hush fell over the crowd. Jesus smiled then broke into laughter. The guests began to chuckle, then clap, and then roared with laughter.

"Come, show me your paintings," Jesus asked. "I didn't peek while you were painting them."

Several guests tried to get Jesus to sign autographs, but he pushed them aside saying, "This is a night for our new Picasso." He whispered to Alvaro, "Pretend I'm not here."

Alvaro felt elated that Mexico's most famous soccer star would spend time promoting his art. The consideration overwhelmed Alvaro who had not expected so much public attention.

Marco approached the two men. "*Caballeros*, I would like to get some shots of the two of you in front of the paintings. Alvaro, why don't you select them?"

Music and wine flowed nonstop. Alvaro needed a break from the stuffy gallery and its hot lights. Jesus and he stepped outside where he took a deep breath and paced an oval path, often staring at the moon.

"I can't believe this is happening for me. I've sold paintings for money—real money—well pesos. I can't believe it."

"I knew you had it in you," Jesus said and slapped Alvaro on the back. "I'm proud and happy I could help."

"I hope Elleña won't mind my being out here for a few minutes. I've never felt comfortable in crowds, and this

303

one is beginning to get to me."

"Don't worry. She'll understand, but we shouldn't be out here too long."

Feeling anxious, Alvaro continued to pace. The cool, evening breeze didn't seem to refresh or quiet him.

"Have you noticed all those fancy cars?" Alvaro asked, nodding toward some Rolls Royces.

"Impressive, aren't they? They represent the big money in Mexico City. You've done well, kid."

Alvaro counted six Rolls Royces, five Bentleys and thirty-seven of the largest cars Mercedes-Benz made. Farther down the street, he noticed a yellow Mercedes-Benz taxi. "God. Is that Don's taxi?"

"Let's go in," Jesus said. "I don't want a confrontation."

Alvaro turned to enter the gallery when he heard his name called from down the street.

"That sounds like Don," Alvaro said.

Alvaro turned to see who had called then watched as Don teetered from the shadows. He waved and staggered toward the men.

Alvaro sighed, dropped his shoulders and raised his palms to the sky. "Now what?"

From fifty feet away, Don extended his hand in greet--ing.

Alvaro stood motionless. "What are you doing here, Don?"

"Didn't wanna miss your opening. Had to see the big new star . . . *the* celebrity."

"Don, are you drunk?"

"Nope! Just celebrating your success, and how is your mister soccer player?"

Jesus said nothing.

Alvaro shook his head. "Don . . . look at yourself. You can't come in dressed in shorts and a t-shirt. It's not acceptable. Not here. Besides, you're drunk."

"I don't want to embarrass you or Mister Jesus, so I'll

304

wait out here—until you have time for an old friend—to have a drink together." Don almost fell, but grabbed Alvaro's arm to steady himself. "Maybe I could have a glass of that expensive champagne."

"That's not possible," Jesus said. "Look at the way You're dressed. Shorts and flip flops don't cut it here."

"Well, you guys go on in," Don said to Jesus. "I'll wait here until Alvaro has time for his old friend."

"Whatever," Alvaro said, "but I gotta get inside. I gotta make nice to all kinds of people. My pocket and my f uture depend on it."

Alvaro peeled Don's fingers from his arm then he and Jesus returned to the festivities.

"I hope Don doesn't do anything stupid," Alvaro muttered.

Jesus shook his head. "Me too."

Alvaro wandered among the guest, stopping to shake hands or listen to someone talk about one of Jesus' special games.

Alvaro took Jesus arm. "Let's pretend to look at my paintings, so we can get away from these people."

"Lead the way." Jesus looked at one painting for a long time. "Alvaro, I like this one, but I don't like the title. If I buy it, would it be okay if I changed—no, if you changed its name?"

Alvaro grinned. "As we say in America, 'The customer is always right.' I'll name it anything you want. But you don't have to buy it. Not after all you have done for me."

Elleña overheard the conversation and handed Alvaro a red sticker. "You know what to do."

Alvaro looked Jesus in the eye. "Would you like to put this sticker on the title card to show everyone that it has been purchased by a discriminating art collector?"

"Elleña has taught you well." Jesus said and kissed Alvaro on the cheek.

Suddenly, a loud thud filled the front of the gallery.

Alvaro turned toward the sound and saw what looked like a vagrant using both hands to support himself on the gallery's largest window. The man glared into the gallery. His head bobbed like that of a drunken soldier.

Alvaro and Jesus exclaimed, "Don!"

Don pushed himself away from the window. Holding onto its frame and then the wall, he stumbled toward the doorway where he stopped for a moment then staggered inside. Guests moved aside as if he had leprosy. Reeking of alcohol and wearing one flip-flop, he wobbled toward Alvaro.

"Ain't you going to offer an old friend a drink?" Don asked.

Startled, the musicians stopped playing.

The wait staff scanned the space looking for Elleña as if seeking instructions as to what, if anything, they should do.

Jesus stepped forward and raised his hand as if to say stop. "Don. You're not welcome here. Please leave. Don't ruin Alvaro's night."

Staggering about, Don slurred, "I can't. I sent the taxi away. I mean no harm. Just wanted to help the young man celebrate his success." Don put out his hand. "Alvaro, please, some champagne?"

Alvaro steadied Don. "Okay, but let's go outside. I'll help you out."

A waiter handed Alvaro a glass of champagne.

Outside, he gave it to Don who steadied himself by hold-ing onto Alvaro's arm.

While guests must have wondered who the intruder might be, Alvaro moved Don away from the windows.

"Please, resume playing," Alvaro heard Elleña instruct the musicians.

Jesus stood by Alvaro side, perhaps fearing he might have to stop a fight.

Exasperated, Alvaro asked Don, "Why did you do such a stupid thing? Don't you know that showing up here could endanger my future—your future?"

306

Taking a gulp of champagne, Don said, "I just wanted to wish you well and see how you were doing."

Alvaro shook Don's shoulder. "You don't understand anything, do you? You can't comprehend what's happening here. How could you? You're drunk. I told you I didn't wanna see you when you're drunk." Alvaro walked toward the gallery. "I'm going inside and see if I can quiet our guests. Finish your drink and leave the glass by the door. *Outside*! Please, don't break it. It's expensive."

Don staggered toward his taxi, spilling some of his champagne.

Alvaro returned to the gallery where Jesus helped calm the group and cajoled his friends to buy Alvaro's paintings.

"Alvaro, I need something to nibble on."

"Let's get some of Elleña's expensive chow."

Alvaro walked toward the table with the *canapés*.

Jesus jested, "When I said nibble, I didn't have *canapés* in mind."

"You can do that later, but now, let's get some chow."

Elleña approached the men. "May I speak to you in my office?"

"I'm so sorry about what happened," Alvaro said, entering the office then slumping into a chair.

"Jesus, how do you and Alvaro know that drunk?"

"I met him through Alvaro," Jesus said. "His name is Don something or the other. He's only an acquaintance. Definitely *not* a friend."

"Alvaro, what kind of relationship do you have with that man?"

"Don is a man who befriended me back in the states. He's a good man—just drinks too much."

"Nothing like this has ever happened here," Elleña said. "I'm not sure what to tell our guests, but I have to come up with a story—a good one—especially for the press. If I

307

don't, they'll cast this incident as something it isn't."

Jesus rubbed his forehead and stared at the floor. "I think I have an idea . . . I know how to squelch any bad PR that might come from this mess."

"What are you thinking?" Elleña asked.

"I'll bribe them. I'll promise each reporter an exclusive interview and a free ticket to a home game with midfield seats."

"Hell, I'd take that to be quiet," Alvaro said.

"Let's hope it works," Elleña said, waving her hands above her head.

The trio returned to the gallery. Alvaro watched Jesus move from reporter to reporter whispering his offer. Anxious, Alvaro and Elleña watched each journalist nod their acceptance of the bribe. After speaking to the last reporter, Jesus returned to the worriers. He wore a smile that reassured everyone all would be okay.

Elleña returned to schmoozing her guests while Alvaro headed for the *hors d oeuvres* table. He cut several chunks of cheese, selected some *canapés*, and loaded caviar onto a cracker smeared with cream cheese. He and Jesus discussed Alvaro's success.

Suddenly, the guests uttered a loud "Uhh!"

Alvaro turned to see Don staggering toward the *hors d oeuvres* table. Alvaro and Jesus stood shoulder-to-shoulder to block Don's access to the food.

"Got any food for a hungry admirer?" Don asked, trying to reach the *canapés.*

Alvaro pushed Don's hand away. "Please don't do this. You're embarrassing me."

"Come on, Alvaro," Don pleaded, motioning for him and Jesus to step aside. "Just a little food, for a hungry friend."

Don managed to get the cheese knife. "I'm gonna cut myself a chunk of that cheese."

Jesus tried to knock the knife from Don's hand but failed. Don waved it in the air. Several guests gasped, for fear they might be attacked.

"All I want is a piece of that damn cheese," Don said, eyes glaring. "God knows you have enough."

"Give me the knife," Alvaro begged. "You should not be here. You're not welcome, and you can't have any of the cheese. Get out!"

Elleña approached Don and stared him in the eye. "Sir, you are invited to leave. *Immediately!* The police have been called. If you are not gone when they arrive, I will have you arrested and file charges of trespassing and petty theft. Now, *leave* my gallery!"

"Poopy pu, poopy pu," Don slurred, in a sing-song way. "All I want is a piece of that damn cheese."

"We told you, you can't have any," Alvaro said. "Now get outta here!"

Alvaro tried to shake the knife from Don's hand.

"Son-of-a-bitch," Don yelled. "I'm going to have a piece of that cheese. The *hoi polloi* won't miss it."

Alvaro and Jesus struggled with Don. They tried to shake the knife from his grip while attempting to get him out the door.

En mass, the guests moved aside like the parting of the Red Sea.

They watched in disbelief as Alvaro and Jesus half-dragged Don toward the door.

The sound of a distant siren grew louder.

"Don," Alvaro pleaded, "The police are coming. For God's sake give me the knife and get outta here. You don't want the police arresting you. Remember Philadelphia."

Don stopped struggling, stood erect, and stared at Alvaro.

Alvaro loosened his grip on Don's arm. "Don, please leave."

"Who the fuck cares!" Don yelled. "You don't. You'd sell me out for a ballplayer and some pesos—after all I've done for you. Well, take yer ball player and take your pesos, you god

309

damn son-of-a-bitch!"

The word bitch had no sooner left Don's lips, when he yelled and thrust the twelve-inch knife at Alvaro. Jesus pushed Alvaro aside and grabbed Don's wrist. He tried to shake the knife from his hand.

Alvaro yelled, "Don! No!"

Don and Jesus struggled, knocking one guest to the floor and overturning several chairs.

At one point, Don managed to get free of Jesus' grip. He glared at Jesus, raised the knife, and then lunged at him. Jesus moved about like a prize fighter avoiding punches. As the slashing knife passed Jesus' chest, he grabbed Don's wrist, twisted it hard, and hooked his foot around Don's leg like a soccer player stealing a midfield ball. Don fell to the floor dragging Jesus with him. Both men emitted a loud "*UH*" as they hit the floor, their arms and legs intertwined. Eight limbs squirmed, jerked, shook, and then stilled.

Both men stared at a pool of blood that rapidly spread beneath them. Staring into each other's eyes, Don and Jesus pushed themselves apart. Jesus, then Don, pushed himself up from the floor with blood covered hands.

Señora Montalba clutched her chest then fell backwards, unconscious. Two elderly gentlemen, standing behind her, caught her, eased her to the floor, and called for a doctor.

Jesus rose to his knees and watched Don struggled to get to his feet. Both men's pants and shirts were covered with blood. Those guests at the front of the cowering crowd gasped as Don looked toward his abdomen. The knife, buried to the hilt, protruded from his lower chest. He started to raise both hands toward the handle as though he would extract the blade, but his hands fell to his side, and he crumbled to the floor where he lay on his left side.

Alvaro heard a gurgling sound from the chest wound as Don gasped for air—eyes filled with death's fear. Shrouded in a palpable sense of impending doom, Don's face blanched and his jaw sagged. Frothy blood flowed from his mouth. He

310

coughed and gasped.

Guests, and Alvaro, frozen with fright, stood motionless, staring at the mayhem. Someone yelled, "Call an ambulance. Do something!"

Alvaro regained his inner strength and knelt beside Don. Jesus, then Alvaro, put a hand on the dying man's shoulder. Alvaro and Don stared eye-to-eye—one man dying and one wishing too.

Jesus teared up. "What have I done? What have I done?"

Alvaro, crying, caressed Don's face and forehead. Alvaro mumbled, "Don . . . Don."

The hardened soccer player cried. Between great sobs, he prayed "God, forgive me . . . forgive me." He looked at Alvaro then Don and wailed, "Don, I'm sorry . . . sorry." Jesus rocked back and forth, sobbing and saying, "God, forgive me."

Elleña had moved behind a table for protection. She, removed its tablecloth to cover Don. Only his head remained in view. She and others made the sign of the cross while a few guests wept and others rushed toward the exit.

Patrol car sirens grew louder and louder and then stopped outside.

Waving pistols, four policemen ran in as if ready to arrest or shoot someone. They walked to the center of the room where Don lay motionless in a pool of blood being wicked into his covering tablecloth.

Like a cogged machine wheel, Don turned his head until he faced the ceiling. A hint of a smile crept across his lips, as his eyes seemed to search for something. Then his and Alvaro's eyes met. Alvaro wiped his tears and squeezed Don's shoulder. Don exhaled a long slow breath and closed his eyes.

One guest, a doctor, made his way to Don's side, felt his carotid pulse, and then shook his head.

Chapter 24

Sunday morning, Alvaro woke with a start then shook Jesus' shoulder.

"What?" Jesus asked as if dazed.

"Don had a lot of cash that he brought from the states. I've got to find it before someone else does."

Sitting up, Jesus asked, "Where do you think it is?"

"It must be hidden in his room at the Angel. We have to look for it."

Alvaro got out of bed and started to dress.

Jesus looked at the bedside clock. "Alvaro . . . It's 6:00 a.m."

"I know. I want to get there before the maids clean. I'm hoping the police haven't discovered where Don lived and sealed his damn room."

"Okay. I'll go with you."

Smiling, Alvaro and Jesus walked to the hotel desk.

"Morning, Alvaro. Jesus," the desk clerk said. "You guys are up early."

"Yeah," Alvaro said. "We wanted to get here before Don left for the day. You haven't seen him have you?"

"Not yet. Guess he's still asleep," the clerk said. "Want me to call him?"

Shit, Alvaro thought. *I can't just ask for the key.* "Yes. Would you please?"

The clerk phoned Don's room. "He's not answering.

Guess he hasn't gotten in yet. You know how he likes to party."

"We sure do," Alvaro said. He stared at the floor for a moment. "When Jesus and I were here last, I left my phone in Don's room. Would you mind letting me have his key so we can look for it?"

The clerk stared at the rack of keys. "I guess . . . that would be okay. Sure. You guys are friends."

"Thanks," Alvaro said, accepting the key.

Entering Don's room, Jesus said, "I worried the guy wouldn't give us the key."

"Me too, but we need to be quick if we don't want to arouse suspicion."

The guys first looked in the toilet water box, but they found no money. They searched the closet and all drawers. With nothing more to search, Alvaro examined one of Don's shoes. The shoe had a pair of socks stuffed inside. After the socks were removed, Alvaro said, "Oh my God!"

Alvaro held up a large roll of bills. "It's here!"

Jesus and Alvaro searched the remaining shoes. Each shoe contained rolls of American notes.

"There must be half a million dollars here," Alvaro said. "How are we going to get it out of here?"

"Stuff it inside our shirts, pants' pockets and socks."

Alvaro led the way to the lobby. He tried to be nonchalant as he placed the room key on the desk and waved his cell phone. "Found it. Tell Don we said hello when he returns."

Sitting at Jesus's kitchen table, Alvaro counted the last of Don's money. "That's $470, 300. 00. Too bad he won't get to enjoy it."

"Yeah . . . too bad," Jesus said. "I didn't like him, but I hate he's dead. What are you going to do with the cash?"

"After all you have done for me, I'd like for you to have half. You did help me find it."

"Tempting," Jesus said, "but I couldn't do that—given I abetted his death. No, you keep it. You've earned it for putting up with his shit."

Alvaro nodded several times then threw the cash into the air. "Wow. I'm rich. Mexican rich."

The next morning, Alvaro awoke, rubbed his eyes,

stretched his arms, and discovered the California King size bed empty. *Where is Jesus?* Alvaro pulled on a pair of shorts then made his way to the flower bedecked terrace where Jesus sat at a table reading, *El Universal*, the morning paper.

"Why are you up so early?" Alvaro asked.

"Couldn't sleep anymore."

"I didn't sleep very well either. What are you reading? Any news?"

"You bet," Jesus said, folding the newspaper to page two. "Our story is all over the paper. Take a look."

Alvaro sat down in a chair beside Jesus and stared into space. "I can't believe he's dead. We had so much going for us. I just wish he hadn't been so damn jealous. His drinking didn't help, but I did love him in my own way. He gave up a lot for me. It's hard to believe he's gone."

"Shit. How do you think I feel? Well . . . read this."

Alvaro looked at a ten by twelve inch black and white picture of Don's body lying on the gallery floor. The photograph attribution named Marco. "That's painful to see but you know I don't read Spanish well enough to know what the article says. Interpret for me."

Jesus fluffed the page. "'Mexican soccer star, Jesus Gonzales, is hero in life and death struggle at society art gallery.' Farther down the article says,

> . . . Drunken, knife-wielding escaped criminal, wanted for crimes in America and Mexico, died in a struggle with Jesus Gonzales who stepped in to protect Mexico's Picasso, known as Alvaro, at an opening reception for the artist at Elleña Di Monaco's Gallery of Art Saturday evening. The drunken man attempted to steal food being served to gallery guests. When confronted, the man grabbed a chef's knife and struck at the artist, leading to the struggle . . .

Jesus pointed to the bottom of the column. "Here's the good part."

> . . . The prosecutor said he will not press charges
> or present a trial request. More than a hundred
> of the Federal District's leading citizens witnessed
> the protective act that led to an unfortunate out-
> come. *Señor* Gonzales, Alvaro, and the gallery
> owner are free to live their lives without further
> government action.'"

Smiling, Jesus pointed farther down the right-hand column. "What do you think about that?"

"Oh my God. That's an ad for my upcoming show in Monterrey. Elleña moves fast. I'd better start more paintings."

Jesus smiled. "Don't think I'm going to let you go by yourself. I've arranged to stay with you in Monterrey."

The End

Brad Barham has written two other gay themed novels: *A Façade of Muscle* and *Men Who Loved*